THE STAINED GLASS JUNGLE

THE
STAINED GLASS
JUNGLE

BY

Gregory Wilson

DOUBLEDAY & COMPANY, INC.
GARDEN CITY, NEW YORK

All of the characters in this book are fictitious, and any resemblance to actual persons, living or dead, is purely coincidental.

This Book
Is
for My Wife:
Sweetheart, Friend,
and
Fellow Soldier

THE STAINED GLASS JUNGLE

I

The Red Button

JACK stood before the mirror between the elevator doors for a moment after the elevator had gone down, combing his hair and trying to smooth out the rumples in his dark tie and dark suit. He reached for his handkerchief to rub up his shoes, but his handkerchief was missing, too, like his Homburg. The pain in his feet was so great he could scarcely stand, but he got the tie right at last. It was going to be tough enough facing Wes as it was, without looking like a wreck.

Searching his pockets once more for the handkerchief, he found his socks again, wadded into balls; he found the canceled ticket stub: "New York to Middleton," which at least proved where he had been. He pulled out the red button again and studied it for the tenth time —a square of glossy red plastic with a raveled fragment of torn red material attached as if it had been ripped from a jacket or coat. . . . Cheap . . . glossy . . . vulgar. He had never seen Thelma wearing anything of that precise shade, but it could not have been anyone's but hers. He glanced at his watch. It was past four A.M.

The walk down the long corridor was pure torture; his legs felt almost too sore to move. He slid his key noiselessly into the hotel-room lock, but Wes was wide awake and glaring at him through a haze of stale cigar smoke from the easy chair in the corner. He had flung his shiny black coat on the bed and was sitting with his huge, gnarled hands hooked in the armholes of his vest.

"Where in thunderation have you been?"

Jack hobbled over to close the window and draw the drapes, although the June night was unseasonably warm. Then he gingerly removed his shoes, took the shredded socks out of his coat pocket, and stretched out on the bed.

"New York, I think."

"Don't you *know?*"

"I honestly do not know."

Wes glanced at the drapes, scratched his shaggy white head, and lowered his voice to a rumble.

"At least a dozen Methodist preachers have knocked on our door today wanting to know where you were. I told them you were away cooking up something big. So what happened to you? And where's your hat? I never thought I'd see you without that everlasting Homburg."

Jack wanted to get into a hot tub to soak the aching soreness out of his legs, but the effort seemed enormous.

"Wes, I've had some sort of blackout. I started off for the church this morning . . . *yesterday* morning—Monday—with a list of delegates to see. I parked half a block from Belfair. I stepped off the curb near the church. I came to myself on a train from New York when they called Middleton. I got off. Now you know as much as I do."

There was no point in telling Wes about the button. Even if it were hers, all that was of the past. Besides, he did not even know where it had come from. He had found it in his pocket while searching for cab fare to the hotel.

"Could you have been hit by a car?"

"There weren't any on the streets. Just a cab in front of the church, letting somebody out, I think."

Wes sat down on the edge of the bed, the rugged creases in his face suddenly deeper.

"Then it *was* you Dirkwell saw."

"Where? When?"

"Dirkwell said he thought he saw you getting into a cab Monday morning in front of the church. As he came around the corner, he saw you talking to a woman; then you both got in the cab and it pulled away before he could be sure."

Jack raised himself on one elbow.

"Did he recognize the woman?"

"Too far away. She was wearing a black dress of some sort of shiny material and carried a white purse."

Jack sank back and closed his eyes against the bright light and the stale smoke. Thelma *never* wore black. Then who . . . ? Wes's gravelly rumble broke in.

"Boy, listen to me. We're in a tough fight. Our little corner of Methodism has been run by a machine for almost thirty years now. Year after year the men with real courage and integrity have all transferred to other conferences. You're the first young preacher to join us in fifteen years with courage and brains enough to stick and fight. You're all we've got! It just never occurred to me to mention this before, but they pressured one of those men into transferring by digging up—"

Jack opened his eyes.

"I'm *not* having an affair with a woman!" This was true. He had not seen Thelma for over a month. He would never see her again, and she knew it.

Wes expelled a vast sigh.

"Sorry, boy! I apologize for asking. But we all know that's one thing *no* minister can get mixed up in, even without a political fracas on his hands. And Belovèd hasn't ruled this conference for thirty years because he was too squeamish to use dirt—or just the suspicion of dirt."

Belovèd . . . Jack could see Dr. Worthington's round, pink, lamblike face and baby-blue eyes. Had any man's voice and dress and manner ever been more misleading? His roly-poly figure in its rumpled suit, his cherubic smile, his ridiculous habit of calling everyone "belovèd"—everything about the man made one take him for a small-church preacher as everyday and placid as a bowl of Jell-o.

Jack realized that Wes kept staring at him. He was looking at him exactly as Coach Nelson had looked at Jack after he had been knocked unconscious for a minute in that scrimmage against the Foxull High School varsity.

"Son, do you think you're in shape to go on with all this? I mean—" Wes hesitated.

"My name," said Jack irritably, raising himself on one elbow again, "is Jack Winters Lee; I'm twenty-seven, single, got my B.A. in '53, my B.D. in '56, and for the past four years I've been minister of the Wentworth Methodist Church. This is Tuesday morning, June 7, 1960, and we are in room 604 of the Middleton Hotel, where we'll be staying through next Sunday afternoon to attend annual conference at Belfair Methodist Church."

"Okay, okay!" said Wes. "I apologize."

"And you," Jack went on, "are Wesley Alford Phillips; you claim to be only sixty-four; you're supposed to be a Methodist preacher but you use tobacco and are forever talking church politics. You've been fighting an unbeatable machine so long that everybody agrees you're nuts, and how I ever got teamed up with you trying to reform a Methodist annual conference I will never understand."

"That ain't a bad obituary," said Wes, his craggy features relaxing and his ice-blue eyes thoughtful. "Be sure you put all that in when you preach my funeral. You remember you promised to preach my funeral."

He gave Jack a resounding slap on the thigh and stood up. Jack clutched his leg in agony, and the old man looked shocked.

"What's the matter with you, anyway? And what happened to your *feet?* They look like hamburger!"

"I can't explain that either. My legs haven't been this sore since I ran the mile in high school ten years ago. I must have run barefooted on some gravel—or in my sock feet rather. My socks are torn all to shreds."

While Jack soaked his feet they went over and over the problem but came out nowhere. Dirkwell had seen Jack get into the cab about eight-thirty Monday morning. He had come to on the train at three-thirty Tuesday morning, about an hour ago. The nineteen hours between remained a blank.

Wes handed Jack another towel; the water was quite pink.

"Well, boy, if you win this fight—or even give the machine a tough battle—you could be headed for big things in the church. I'd hate to see you reach the top and *then* crack up. It's been done. If pastor Jack W. Lee of the Wentworth Methodist Church blanks out, it's interesting. But if twenty years from now Bishop J. Winters Lee blanks out, it would make headlines."

Jack spread a big towel across the bottom of the bed in case the cuts bled during the night.

"Patricia always insisted," he said, as Wes snapped off the lights, "that I had another self in me she couldn't understand or catch hold of. That's one reason we never married—I mean, haven't married."

"Patricia Worthington," said Wes sourly, "doesn't know everything, even if her papa *is* the slickest politician who ever ruled a Methodist conference."

"I always laughed at her about it," said Jack. "I've spent my whole life analyzing my own motives and being sure I knew the right thing to do and was doing it for the right reasons. But now it begins to seem that I've overlooked something. If we weren't right on the eve of this political battle, I could hunt up a psychoanalyst and try to unscramble myself. But half the preachers in this conference already think I'm off my rocker to tackle Belovèd."

Wes unlaced a high-topped shoe.

"What *can* you do, boy?"

"Dig. I've got to use every scrap of spare time this week to dredge up my past life. I have a feeling that whatever happened to me is connected with . . ." Jack hesitated. ". . . with a lot of stuff I've never enjoyed remembering very much. And that must be why my memory has gone blank about it."

Wes yanked open the drapes and raised the window.

"I'll let you sleep till ten. Then, if you're able, we oughta try to catch some of the early delegates and begin lining up some votes. We didn't lose too much ground today. Nobody of importance comes in on Monday anyway."

But while Wes snored, Jack lay wide-eyed in the gloom, too taut and exhausted for sleep. It was ironic, in a way, that he had spent all these years telling Patricia that she knew all of him there was to know and that he had no "other self." Because now, in these impossible circumstances, he was being forced to dig frantically, desperately into the past for some clue to that other self's existence. For although he did not know what had happened during those hours in New York today, he did know from a strange, blind, sweating terror that was only now beginning to subside, that he had passed through an immense danger. He knew that this unknown self was threatening to destroy him.

II

The Seventh Trip

THE PAST . . .

The past held so much pain that Jack wondered whether he could actually bear to call it to mind. . . . Things like that ghastly seventh trip to see Thelma. That afternoon in New York before he saw her should certainly have warned him that his other self existed and that its possibilities were horrifying, and now the pain of that event seemed to intensify the numbing pain in his feet and legs as he lay in the gloom remembering. . . .

It had happened on the first Monday in November, 1959.

But it had to happen sooner or later.

A certain number of people from Wentworth went to New York on the 6:21; the train had a limited number of coaches. Jack had worked it all out in advance a hundred times. A voice would say:

"Reverend Lee! This *is* a pleasant surprise!"

He would turn, rise, smile, and play it by feel, depending on the situation. If it were the Armstrongs, he would tell jokes and Sara would giggle and Carl would promise to "remember that one for Rotary!" For Miss Abernathy he would be very ministerial about relaxing on Monday after the burdens of the Lord's day. For Steinfelt . . . well, Steinfelt was one of those people who think the worst even of their pastor. Jack would perhaps talk about church finances, whereupon Steinfelt would flee. . . .

Jack was prepared for those who might enjoy unmasking him. And, strangely, he had always suspected that every congregation would enjoy unmasking the minister, though they might not be aware of their desire. He had sensed this even before Thelma.

But it was not anybody suspicious or giddy or venomous.

It was Miss Mollie.

He pushed open the door of the coach and was staring straight down into her eyes.

And Miss Mollie had no need to feel vengefully inferior to her pastor, or to wince at his sermons, for when he first appeared in the community—young, eager, brash, utterly unable by gifts or experience to measure up to the congregation's rosy hopes—she took all of him into a heart of love, lifted all his youthful follies in her prayers, and adopted him as her child in Christ. It was she who taught him out of the wisdom of her years the deeper meanings of Scripture; it was she who shamed his aggressive materialism by the calm confidence with which she gave out of her poverty year after year "God's tenth" to the church. It was she whose tactful and disinterested advice saved him from repeated blunders and whose lifelong devotion to her Master disarmed all his pride and stubbornness.

"I've been calling the parsonage," she said, moving her worn black valise so he could take the train seat opposite her. The gentle, lined face, framed by its silver hair, was distraught. "Did someone give you my message?"

"N-no . . ." said Jack. "I . . . I was just going in to the city to do some shopping." This was partly true. He *had* thought about buying some shirts at Macy's, and the thought of lying to Miss Mollie was unendurable.

That trapped him. Hopelessly.

Miss Mollie had just had a call from New York that her only sister, an elderly maiden lady named Louise, was at the point of death. Jack knew that if he refused to accompany her at a time like this and to minister in whatever way he could, he would never be able to live with himself again. The degradation and loss of self-respect he had suffered since his affair with Thelma had been devastating, as had the falsifying of all his relations to his congregation. But to reject Miss Mollie now—and with some cheap and complicated lie—was out of the question.

Her clear, beautiful eyes were radiant as he assured her he would come and would stay as long as she needed him. Then she gave a rueful smile and nervously smoothed a pleat in her one good black dress.

"I'm afraid I've been rather good at telling other people how to bear their troubles. But now . . ." Her voice trailed off.

"Do they—" Jack blurted, then stopped.

"No. There's no hope. The young woman who called said it was a matter of hours."

Jack was aware that something had risen almost into consciousness —something he had hastily pushed back—because he was wondering how long he could restrain himself once they had reached New York. His impatience on these trips was sometimes so unbearable that he actually wanted to rush through the entire train to the first coach just to be that much nearer. Now he would have to control his mind and imagination for hours beyond the trip . . . even for the whole day! And already he felt almost physically ill with yearning.

Always on these Monday trips he took his seat with a delicious sickness in his stomach, like the stage fright that indicated a brilliant sermon to come—sharpening every sense, deepening his voice, enlarging all his talents. It mounted with the swaying of the train, the flying away of the rotating landscapes beyond the sound-proofed windows, the clickety-clickety-clickety of the wheels, the vanishing of the intimate beauty of the countryside and the slow dawn of the city with more towns, more buildings, more factories, more tracks, more bridges, more power lines, more people, more noise, till it reached a kind of sustained climax as they roared under the viaducts and through the thundering tunnels. It pounded in his whole body, like the throbbing of a fever, as he plunged through the swarming crowds, shoving, skipping, half-running, trotting a few steps in the street or the gutter. And it suddenly modulated, as a mighty symphony modulates to the woodwinds and strings, when he strolled carelessly into the lobby of Thelma's apartment building and stepped into the elevator.

It crashed to a shattering, pulse-pounding roar as she opened her door to him, and it surged and pounded and broke and surged again with the awesome fury of a wild ocean as the door closed softly behind him.

When it was all over, it left like an ebbing tide, revealing no glistening beauty of silver sand but a dead grayness and calm through which he gazed in dawning uneasiness at endless, ugly images of discovery, exposure, and the total destruction of his name and career.

And he had actually imagined this sort of affair to be a state of continual bliss! But for him, at any rate, it was always preceded by agonizing moral struggles, was carried out in a fever of excitement, and followed by racking anxiety. When he did win some minor victory over his cravings, it brought him no peace, only more struggle. Once he went all the way to New York, forced himself to return home without calling her; then yielded, caught the next train in, arrived at four in the morning, and found that Thelma was down with the flu. He took the train back to Wentworth feeling abjectly ridiculous and furious with himself for the waste of his time and money, and, in that state, spent the next two days trying to help Mrs. Neill through the tragedy of her husband's death in a hunting accident.

They had very poor communication since he had forbidden Thelma to write or phone him. He could only rarely find some way to call her, and he never put even the briefest message to her in writing if he could avoid it. He battled his passion for her endlessly, won occasional small, temporary victories, and once managed not to go in to New York for an entire month. But that month he butchered his sermons, found his mind muddied and inattentive in counseling, and went through the motions of his pastoral routine like a sleepwalker. His love had little foundation except enjoyment of her body; and when that was denied him, he felt frenzied with anger and frustration; and when it had been fulfilled, he made the most transparent excuses to flee Thelma's empty mind and deadly conversation. But even as he fled, he knew that a week later—or a day later!—he would be frantic for her again, and she would find some way to make him pay for his flight.

Miss Mollie was saying something about the church, but Jack only half-heard. The images produced by her words kept getting entangled in other images. They still had a long way to go, plus an unknown period of waiting when they arrived. Jack tried to focus his imagination on Wentworth, to picture the tall spire of his church rising against a background of neat little homes encircled by snow-mantled hills . . . a sleepy little village where the commuter trains paused briefly . . . a lovely little church supported by a clique of moneyed people, the Stantons and the Richardsons.

He tried to re-create yesterday morning's worship service, but the scent of flowers banked about the pulpit kept giving way to the scent of Thelma's dusting powder . . . cheap, heady, and vulgar, like everything else about her. He tried to remember the anthem, which had been especially good yesterday, but the voices of the choir and Miss Mollie's gentle voice kept yielding to Thelma's nasal monotone.

He recited to himself all the things people had said to him at the door of the church following the service: "Wonderful!" "You really told 'em that time, Reverend!" "I don't know *when* I've heard such an original sermon." "If only I could get George to come; he simply doesn't know what he's missing!" "A real masterpiece . . ." That seemed to help a little, but the trouble was that the way some of the Wentworth matrons gazed up at him reminded him of Thelma's puffy-lidded, brown eyes with their look of humorless, uncritical adoration. He tried desperately to recall his sermon, but all he could remember was that agonizing battle to look calm and self-assured while a fearful weight was squeezing all the life and resonance out of his voice, was recurrently threatening his mind with a terrifying blankness, was making him long with an unutterable longing for the moment he could at last close the parsonage door, drag himself to the bed, and lie with his face to the wall.

And all for what? *That* was the most bewildering, insoluble, hysterically unbelievable part of it: All for a slovenly girl with owlish brown eyes and a sulky mouth and a mind as literal and humorless as a want-ad!

Jack stared at Miss Mollie fiercely. He *could* not let go this way! He made himself pay attention, made himself answer, made himself think about his work; and the rotating landscapes flew away and the train inched agonizingly toward New York.

Once those spellbound faces on Sunday morning had been the great reward of his ministry. Now the Sunday sermon was an ordeal that drained the last drop of his courage, and he would never be able to communicate to another human being what self-mastery it took to raise his eyes from the Bible and look down into those hundreds of unsuspecting faces. For suppose some Sunday they were suddenly gleeful, knowing, shining like augers as they drilled through his own gaze and into the obscene and naked shames inside him, into the killing burden that seemed heavier each week? For his guilt and shame had become almost a physical presence now, crushing his spirits, numbing his mind, exhausting his body. He felt like a man treading a darkening path that could lead only to tragedy, burdened by a weight he no longer had strength to bear, but absolutely unable to shake off the burden or to turn back toward safety and light.

He began dreading those eyes each week from the moment he left Thelma's apartment on Monday night. They rose up before him in the street, on the subway, on the train returning to Wentworth, rows and rows of eyes in semicircles—the polite, attentive eyes of the men; the admiring eyes of the women; the shining, friendly eyes of the children. Tuesday mornings it took every ounce of his will power to make himself walk through the parsonage door out into the sunlight and down to the post office, especially to meet the first pair of eyes that day—which was always the test. Wednesday-night prayer meetings were a special little horror, with the faithful few staring straight at him from so near. By Saturday he had persuaded himself that he would never see Thelma again and hence had no need to fear anyone's eyes next morning, for he preached a God of mercy and forgiveness. But he knew from experience, without quite admitting it and so destroying this pathetic stratagem, that his repentance was temporary and would scarcely last through the youth program Sunday night. Ah, the carefree joys of sin!

But suppose he finally found those eyes unbearable?

Suppose some Sunday he yielded to the recurring impulse—stronger every week—to confess? For he was somehow convinced that confession would at least make him one man again, would end this nightmare existence of trying to seem one person before an entire community while wondering if anyone knew his other self. It was the hypocrisy, the dishonesty, the never-ending little lies that appalled him most—the knowledge that he did not deserve all their adoration. And somehow he kept imagining that if he were honest enough to confess everything

—to crucify himself publicly—he would both keep and deserve their unending adoration. He would be at peace again with himself and the world. He would be free from this madhouse of mirrors; for in Wentworth nobody's smile ever seemed quite natural, no gesture the right size, nobody his true and simple self.

This impulse was sometimes so strong that he had to restrain himself almost by force from jumping up from his pulpit chair in the midst of the anthem, tearing off his black pulpit robe, trampling it under his feet, and screaming out the truth at the top of his lungs. With curses! With obscenities! With a volcano of lewdness that would blast out of existence the mountain of all his past labors, cover with ashes the furthest horizons of his future hopes. He would scream it so loud that—

Jack's heart gave a sickening lunge.

He sat up straighter.

The whole coach was as still as death.

Miss Mollie's grave, beautiful eyes were fixed on him in astonishment. The man in the seat ahead of her had half-turned and was staring at Jack. A horrifying possibility came to him: he had shouted out something unspeakable that had paralyzed every mind, every tongue, in the entire coach. But just at that moment the buzzing confusion of voices resumed, and Jack sagged against the seat.

"Reverend Lee, what is it? Are you ill?"

"Wh . . . what was I just saying?"

"You were telling about how God speaks to some people through the things that happen in their lives, like illness or trouble. But are you certain you're all right?"

Jack had choked his breakfast down too fast that morning. On recent Monday mornings he had sometimes found it almost impossible to eat. Now the pounding in his pulses, the swaying of the train, the clickety-clickety in his nerves, the rending division of will and imagination, telescoped on him like a blow in the pit of his stomach. He rose, swaying and waving off their outstretched hands. In the men's room he vomited in the lavatory, washed his mouth out several times with cold water, dashed water over his face, and stood before the little mirror to comb his hair. His face looked ashen, his eyes bloodshot, his lips puffy and bloodless. He straightened his dark tie and adjusted the handkerchief in the breast pocket of his impeccably tailored dark suit.

Then the loudspeaker was announcing New York; he unlocked the door and pulled it open and stepped out to meet all the eyes again.

Ah, the gay life!
Ah, the carefree joys of sin!

The cab ride through the brash clamor of the city seemed to help him a little. The crush of cars and people and lights and noises was so violent it seemed to drown out the clamor inside him, to release it, to express its violence and discord. Then suddenly an apartment door had hissed shut behind them and the nearly soundless hum of an elevator plunged them into total isolation from the vast and teeming life outside.

Miss Louise's flat consisted of a living-room-bedroom combination with what appeared to be a kitchenette and bath further back. From somewhere in the stuffy silence he could hear the slow, stately tick of a clock.

Miss Mollie was motioning him over to a high, four-poster bed with intricately carved black walnut headboard and a faded rose canopy. The smell of furniture polish and lilac mingled with the smell of medicine and disinfectant.

The bed was too high for Miss Mollie to rest her elbows on it; she knelt and pressed her clasped hands and forehead against the coverlet. The nurse withdrew a few steps, bowing her head. Jack gazed down at the contents of the bed, recalling things Miss Mollie had told him: Miss Louise had given up teaching because of ill health at the age of . . . forty? She had invested a little inheritance once and the venture had proved the difference between genteel poverty and lifelong need. She was very old now, and the wheelchair by the window facing an eyeless brick wall had been her world for all the days of her life after that.

The almost invisible pile of brittle bones scarcely broke the flat lines of the sheet. The inevitable tube and needle were taped to a purplish bruise on her forearm. The skeletal head lay propped on damp pillows, the stringy neck arched back, the sunken eyes already threatening to roll back but still staying focused somehow in a fishy stare at the canopy. Once her free hand made a feeble, clawlike gesture toward the tube in her nostril but fell back strengthless. The sunken cheeks and sucked-in lips showed that her teeth had been removed but were being kept handy for prompt replacement before the jaws began to rigidify. Someone had tied a pert blue ribbon about Miss Louise's damp, tousled hair, and her upper lip was covered with an almost masculine growth of fine white hair. Even the tick of the clock sounded loud against the faint whisper of her breathing.

Jack read from his Testament and Psalms:

"The Lord is my shepherd, I shall not want . . ."

Then he knelt by Miss Mollie and took one of her trembling hands in his own:

"Eternal and everliving God, Thou who inhabitest eternity, in Whose sight a thousand years are but as yesterday when it is past and as a watch in the night, grant us, we pray Thee, strength for whatever this hour may bring. Though Miss Louise may now be beyond our voices and her mind withdrawn beyond our minds, we thank Thee that as she withdraws from us, she comes nearer Thee, that as the sounds of this earthly mansion fade upon her ear, the triumph-strain of Heaven swells and magnifies from the doorway of her mansion there, her house which hath foundations whose builder and maker is God."

Though it had been fashionable in seminary to make light of the traditional symbols of the afterlife, in the actual presence of approaching death Jack had found no substitutes for the phrases which dying men and women had heard in distant childhood fall naturally and simply from the lips of their fathers and mothers.

The morning and afternoon were torture. Jack had done his duty as far as he could understand it, and now waited with Miss Mollie for the end. The nurse, a large, expressionless woman of middle age, checked on her patient as methodically as the tick of the ancient clock by the highboy, and between times sat dozing in Miss Louise's wheelchair. Jack passed the time trying to imagine what happened to an intelligent, sensitive woman who spent forty years in a wheelchair before a window that opened on nothing—not even on a single bough whose green trumpeted the coming spring and whose bareness signaled another winter. Forty years without love or children or even a career . . . just a slow, deliberate clock that ticked away your youth, your dreams, and finally your ability to feel that you even cared any longer about that enormous waste and mystery . . .

At lunch Jack tried to get Miss Mollie to eat, for he knew she had come off without breakfast, but she could not and only sat while he and the nurse tried with their small talk to distract her from that unceasing whisper from the walnut bed.

Jack still remembered with shame his one real faltering, his one brief abandonment of Miss Mollie that day. For after lunch he had become terrified by the possibility that Thelma might decide he was not coming and might go out for the afternoon. And this had brought on that idiotic business of the dime in the pay phone.

He knew he could not possibly make the call from Miss Louise's phone; he excused himself "to get a breath of air for a few minutes," raced down the hall to the elevator, waited an eternity for it to come, and on the way down reflected that he would never forgive himself if Miss Mollie found herself alone with only the nurse when her sister died. He found a phone booth at the corner, yanked the door shut, and fumbled for a dime. He had no change. He absently stuck his finger in the coin return box and found that it contained a dime. He snatched it out, started to put it in the slot, hesitated, stuck it in, got the dial tone, then hesitated again. Finally he dialed the operator. The coin jangled back into the return box.

"Operator—" What could he say?

"Yes, sir?"

"I—this isn't my dime. It was in the telephone—I mean, in the little box where you return the money."

"Yes, sir?"

"Well, what am I supposed to *do* with it?"

"I don't believe I understand you, sir."

"Do I return it to the phone company? Whose is it?"

"If you found it in the coin return box, sir, I presume it was returned to a previous caller."

"But there's nobody here! Should I return it to the company?"

The cool voice sounded intrigued.

"Why not leave it where you found it, sir? Perhaps the owner will come back for it."

"But the real owner might not even remember it! Somebody else will get it, and that wouldn't be right. I would be letting him take what belonged to someone else!"

The voice thawed unexpectedly.

"Pardon me, sir, but are you a clergyman?"

Jack was dismayed. He was positive he had long ago got rid of any trace of that sickening ministerial tone he had affected in college.

"No! I mean, yes . . . yes. But that's got nothing to do with it. It's a question of right and wrong."

There was a short silence.

"Will you hold on a moment, please."

Jack drummed on the wall with his fingers. Finally another voice took over, curt and humorless.

"Sir, the company would be most happy for you to use the coin in placing your call. We can consider it a legitimate expenditure for public relations to assist the clergy in this way."

"Thank you. That's very kind of you."

He hung up and stood for a moment with the dime in his hand. The smallest decisions were becoming more and more difficult since his involvement with Thelma. Sometimes his mind seemed to be trying to stop dead, to blank out. With an effort he got his thoughts in order: It was absurd on the face of it to accept a clergy rebate for a call like this. But a ten-cent piece had no moral significance whatever in comparison with his present situation: he was betraying his calling and the faith of a whole church and community; he was so burdened by shame that nothing could increase it; and though it might be a sin to use the dime, it would be a greater sin to delay longer and risk letting Miss Mollie go through her sister's death alone and unsupported.

He put the coin in the slot and dialed Thelma's number.

Back in Miss Louise's apartment at last, he found the afternoon dragging by with unbelievable slowness, made worse now by his having heard Thelma's voice. He had been so unnerved by the experience on the train that morning that he had been keeping his thoughts rigidly under control, but now Miss Mollie had dozed off in the prim, high-backed old rocker, her white head bowed over her open Bible. The nurse sat in the wheelchair dozing in the stuffy heat. Jack knew from experience that dying people often hang by a single thread for hours, days, or even weeks. He wondered what Miss Louise had looked like in youth. The thin, almost transparent profile stood out now from the depths of the pillows like a beak-nosed, crescent-mouthed bird of prey, and the sunken eyes remained fixed on the faded rosette in the center of the canopy. The eye sockets seemed more prominent, but perhaps that was from the dull glare of the afternoon sun on the brick wall.

Behind its glass face with the tarnished gold patterns and chipped black numerals, the clock made its sudden buzzing before it struck. Four o'clock. Something kept rising from the back of his mind and he kept pushing it away; and finally, to escape it, he let his thoughts begin to wander again. . . .

Last Monday had been a sunny afternoon, too, and Thelma's marvelous skin had had that unbearable, creamy glow in the warm light that filtered through the flimsy paper shade at her window. She still blushed sometimes, unexpectedly, and a faint pearly mist would mantle her forehead and her plump cheeks, while the solemn brown eyes went dreamy-lidded and the normally sulky lips curled upward in a relaxed, ineffably peaceful smile. Her complexion had been the first thing he had noticed about her that day so long ago. It was milk-white, almost translucent, against the frame of her dark auburn hair. . . .

Jack sat on the quaint, old-fashioned sofa and looked at his watch for the hundredth time and for the hundredth time refused to let himself even begin thinking of some excuse to leave Miss Mollie now. Yet he was in a state of such disunity, he felt he could not hang on another minute without something happening that would be unspeakable. His sense of being trapped in a self-acting suit of armor, a sense he had almost never been without since the day he entered the ministry, was becoming unendurable. The armor forced one into all sorts of unnatural poses and gestures, made the smallest natural or spontaneous movement impossible. And sometimes it seemed to race along with a terrifying momentum of its own, carrying inside it a gasping, exhausted, helpless and will-less creature absurdly unlike the heroic and purposeful man of iron to whom the world gave way. Jack had once seen a news item about a minister who had blown out his brains sitting before a study desk crammed with lewd magazines and photographs: he had neither been able to get out of the armor nor to live up to its iron poses.

Jack had resolved at the outset that if he ever found himself in such contradictions, he would leave the ministry at once. But now, gazing across the high walnut bed at Miss Mollie's silvered hair and gentle features, he knew why the man at the desk had chosen death instead. He drew a deep, shuddering breath and gripped the worn carving on the arm of the sofa. The nurse breathed in regular, placid, monotonous rhythm. The grandfather clock ticked on. The afternoon sunlight seemed frozen upon the blind brick wall.

The ministry was so different from what he had expected. He had thought it would be just standing before a congregation and proclaiming the word of God each Sunday morning. He had never realized it meant running an organization, putting on financial campaigns, selling people on the programs and policies of a gigantic bureaucracy, being a sort of public-relations man at the Rotary and the P.T.A., and getting involved with the Community Chest and the Boy Scouts and all sorts of things that dissipated one's energy and purpose in a dozen directions.

In his student pastorates in college and seminary he had always felt he did rather well with sick-calling and funerals and bereavement. But he had not quite realized that the full-time pastorate involved this recurrent, inescapable confrontation by death in its ugliest, most depressing forms. The sucked-in cheeks and the whispered breathing had been shattering that first time, when old Mrs. Cottrell lingered four months with cancer. Yet, perhaps, for that very reason, he had been of real help to the old gentleman and the Cottrell boys. He had felt the full horror of it even as they had. Now he sometimes wondered whether he was helping people or not. For the gradual hardening had begun, the ability to feel enough to be sincerely concerned, but not enough to be exhausted and demoralized by your job. What was the next stage? To feel nothing? To be forced to pretend one's concern?

Suddenly the thing Jack had been fighting back all day could be resisted no longer. He felt his eyes swing toward the bed and rivet upon the hideous pile of bones as if magnetized, and a sibilant whisper emerged of its own accord from between his clenched teeth:

"Damn you, why won't you *die!?*"

Even now, remembering the sound of his own words at that moment, Jack still felt a thrill of horror. It was as if a veil had been drawn aside and he had suddenly been face to face with a part of himself he had never known existed—wild, arrogant, hate-filled!

He jumped to his feet and walked heavily past the nurse, wanting to wake her, not wanting to be alone another instant with himself. He splashed some water over his face in the bathroom, went into the kitchen, and gulped down a cup of hot coffee from the pot on the stove.

At six Miss Mollie woke, and the nurse fixed dinner. But before they could sit down to eat, it happened.

The silence.

They stared at each other across the kitchen table, waiting for the snorting rattle and the beginning again of the whisper, but the clock ticked and the coffeepot burbled and the whisper did not commence. Miss Mollie sank suddenly into her chair, and Jack sat down beside her while the nurse picked up her stethoscope from the table and vanished. After a moment Jack followed her.

The bones were silent. The eyes stared back fixedly at some point impossibly far behind the skeletal head, from which the perky blue ribbon had now been removed. The nurse swabbed the eyeballs, pressed the lids down till they stuck, fitted the false teeth into place, and crossed the transparent blue claws over the sunken chest. When Miss Mollie came in at last, her step was firm but she shivered once as though the suffocatingly hot apartment had struck a chilling frost into her soul. She knelt in silence while Jack again opened his Testament:

"I am the resurrection and the life. He that believeth on me, though he were dead, yet shall he live. . . ."

Jack made some calls for Miss Mollie, helped her with a few decisions; and finally a nephew arrived, then two nieces. She decided to remain overnight with them, which simplified everything. At the door he turned, and she suddenly gripped his hand hard in both of hers.

"You've been my strength—"

Her voice faltered; her eyes brimmed over. Jack squeezed her hand and nodded, thinking how impossible it would be for him ever to give back to this wonderful woman a fraction of all she had given him. The ministry, he had discovered, had its own special rewards, peculiar to itself—a handclasp, four simple words—but of such shining coin was forged the suit of armor so easy to put on, so difficult ever to be free from again.

III

The Cause of All the Ruckus

WES WOKE Jack at ten that morning and presented him breakfast in bed. They stopped by a clothing store where Jack bought a new Homburg and were at the church by eleven, though Jack's soreness and the condition of his feet made walking pure torture. Wes had collected the names of some of the younger men who would be joining the conference in time to vote and who had come early to attend to the red tape. Dan Starr knew several of them from his home state and got a partial commitment from one, but Jack discovered that most of them were incredibly green about the possibility of power politics within the church. Their disbelieving questions kept making Jack feel like some sour and aged cynic determined to corrupt the youth of the ministry and to undermine their faith in their superiors. He kept reminding himself that he had been quite as naïve when he finished school four years ago.

The young Stengland couple were perhaps the worst: Cecil was a terribly intellectual young man who had majored in Augustinian theology, but apparently had very little knowledge of the church in the twentieth century. Dorcas was a former Congregationalist and had extremely hazy ideas about any form of church government more complex than simple rule by the local congregation. Jack, Dirkwell, and Cecil Stengland tried various comparisons on her; for example, that Methodism covered the whole USA, with each conference resembling a separate state having a bishop as its governor; under him was his cabinet, made up of superintendents, each in charge of a district, etc.

"This particular conference we're in," Jack explained, "has almost five hundred ministers. Our bishop is in charge of it, plus one other conference, and these two conferences make up his area."

"But," said Dorcas, her large brown eyes earnest but troubled, "one minute you Methodists use conference to mean one thing, and the next minute it means something else."

"I've told you a dozen times," said Cecil, "that it usually means a geographical division! But when all the ministers in that space—and one layman from each church—get together once a year, *then* the word conference means an annual get-together. We live *in* this conference, but you are now *at* this conference."

They were standing on the lawn. Dorcas turned to survey the gleaming new portico of Belfair Methodist Church and the little groups of ministers moving in and out already, though conference did not officially begin till the next morning, Wednesday.

"You mean that *all* the ministers and *all* the laymen come to Belfair every year? Whatever for?"

"Not to *Belfair* every year!" exclaimed Cecil. "This church was only finished three months ago! They meet at some church—any church—big enough to hold them. Oh, why didn't I marry a Methodist like Mother told me to!"

"Mrs. Stengland," said Jack, half-suspecting that Dorcas was enjoying finding herself the center of so much denominational concern, "we meet annually so the cabinet can assign each minister to a church, and that assignment is called his 'appointment.' We also hear committee reports, allocate money, and pass resolutions on everything from juvenile delinquency to intercessory prayer. This goes on for five days, and between business sessions we catch up on a year's gossip and spread rumors about who'll be going to First Church when the bishop winds it all up by reading the appointments Sunday afternoon."

Even the two men seemed impressed by this heroic oversimplification, so Jack went on:

"After annual conference is over we'll all go off to our home districts. My district has forty-seven ministers, some of whom serve two or three churches at once, which is called a 'circuit.'"

"My!" said Dorcas. "Don't they get all confused?"

"Terribly," said Dirkwell. "But Jack wouldn't know about that. He's never been on a circuit. Yet!"

"My superintendent," Jack went on, ignoring the "yet," "is named Dr. Fred Worthington. He's the little roly-poly man you've seen bouncing around all over the conference like a loose tennis ball. He's the one everybody calls 'Belovèd.'"

"But not to his face," said Dirkwell.

"What an outlandish name!" exclaimed Dorcas.

"It's a Scriptural salutation," said Jack. "Somebody hung it on him years ago because he addresses everyone that way—men, women, and children."

"Worthington . . . Fred Worthington," said Dorcas, placing the tip of one finger against a dimpled cheek. "Why, Cecil, that must be the one who sent the bun-warmer!" She opened her smart red purse, rummaged about while the men gazed in with interest, and finally handed Jack a small white card. "We got such a lovely bun-warmer with our wedding presents, and we couldn't *imagine* who it came from!"

Jack studied the round, familiar script: "Hearty congratulations and all best wishes!" Then the neat black type: "Frederick John Worthington." He saw Dirkwell's freckled face break up in his slow, crooked grin.

"That's funny," said Stengland, "I knew I'd heard the name somewhere. But I've never even met the man! It just hadn't occurred to me that one of the superintendents might send *us* something." He glanced up at Jack, his scholarly face slightly alarmed. "And is *this* the same one you've been telling us about, the one who runs the whole conference and the cabinet and practically tells the bishop whom to appoint?"

"The same," said Jack.

"But he's only a superintendent, and the bishop can appoint and remove his superintendents whenever he wants to!"

"It's not that simple," said Jack. "Bishops are rarely assigned to their home areas—too many personal ties. Our bishop came here as a stranger, and he simply inherited most of his cabinet. But Dr. Worthington had swung a bloc of votes to him that got him elected to the episcopacy. So, Belovèd was the first superintendent the bishop chose himself; the bishop admires him and turns to him constantly."

"Do you mean to say," asked Stengland, "that this is the only source of all the power you insist this man has?"

"Not exactly," said Jack. "He also mails out quite a few bun-warmers."

"It's a dream!" said Dorcas, dimpling. "It has the cleverest little thingamajig on top that keeps the buns from getting damp or soggy. And I think you're both exaggerating about what an awful monster this poor Dr. Worthington is!"

"He's no monster!" said Jack. "He describes himself as 'a Christian gentleman who gets things done,' and half the time I think he's right. At least he believes it himself."

Stengland frowned.

"Then what in Heaven's name is the cause of all the ruckus?"

"The ruckus," said Jack, "is because Belovèd now has the bishop in his vest pocket; he controls practically all the programs, policies, and appointments; he hand-picks the delegates to be sent to general and jurisdictional conference every four years; and this year he expects those delegates to help elect him a bishop himself! But what he doesn't know is that this whole conference is fed up with him and his machine, and that's why some of us are going around asking you new men to vote for a different slate. Not a slate of our own men, you understand, but of the best men in the conference. We want to split his delegation, keep him from getting elected, and get our present bishop transferred to another area. Then we can begin all over in this conference with a restoration of Methodist forms of government." This was a drastic oversimplification of a complicated problem, but it was the best Jack could do.

"How many is this 'we'?" asked Stengland.

"At least fifteen. Maybe nineteen. As of this moment."

"Out of nearly *five hundred* votes?!"

"The machine only controls about a hundred odd. We keep telling everybody they run things by default."

"What happens if you lose?" asked Stengland.

Jack glanced briefly at the glittering maze of suburban homes beyond the church.

"Oh," he said, "let's just say you may never end up as pastor of Belfair Methodist in Suburbia."

There was a sudden silence.

For the first time Dorcas looked completely serious.

"How many of these conferences are there in the Methodist Church —I mean, in the whole thing?" she asked Jack.

"About a hundred. It covers the whole USA."

"Are they all like this one?"

"Heaven forbid!" said Jack. Then he sobered. "I doubt that anyone really knows. It's an inside sort of thing, and even within your home conference you're never sure how much of this sort of thing goes on, and how much is gossip or disappointed ambition. Who could know all the conferences—or even a dozen of them—at first hand?"

"Cecil," said Dorcas, "you said you'd never heard of anything like this back home." She looked at Jack. "Couldn't we transfer back to Cecil's home conference?"

"That's been a very popular solution."

"No," said Stengland. "I want to talk to Dr. Whitley. I entered the ministry after hearing him preach when I was in college. I wanted to be in the same conference with him. If William Pierce Whitley says stay, we'll stay. Incidentally, is Dr. Whitley on your side?"

Jack smiled. There was nothing to do now but leave a friendly impression, and stop wasting any more time.

"If William Pierce Whitley ever joined us, it would turn this conference upside down. No, Dr. Whitley never concerns himself in conference politics of any sort."

"Well," said Stengland, thrusting out his hand, "I don't know whether you're right or wrong, but you've sure got a lot of guts. Fifteen votes against five hundred!"

When they had gone, Jack passed one hand over his face.

"Dirk, my feet are killing me. I've got to sit down a while. You be checking out the other names." He sighed. "Lost—one golden hour! Why didn't the kid tell us at the start he was a disciple of Whitley? Well, at least he won't have to transfer; Whitley will just tell him that a Christian gentleman never dabbles in politics. And, oh, that Dorcas!"

They both burst out laughing.

"Jack," said Dirkwell, "you warned us this would be a tough fight; but, gosh, who'd have ever thought of sending Dorcas that bun-warmer! If he had thrown in a half dozen rolls, I actually think he'd have won them both."

"Old Belovèd," said Jack, "thinks of everything."

Jack made his way to the church basement, bought a cup of coffee, and found an empty chair in a corner of the bookroom which was being set up by people from the publishing house. He untied his shoelaces and propped his feet in another chair, and was studying his list of prospects when a young man in a crew cut and sports coat approached him.

"Aren't you Jack Lee? I'm Ted Smathers, coming in on trial this year. I've been trying to locate an old gentleman named Elwood, but they tell me he's not well and won't be in till late Thursday, or Friday."

The boy was going on about his seminary work but Jack only half heard. There went another vote. Jack looked down his list of names, found "Pastor Elwood," and scribbled "too late" beside it. By then the whole thing would have been decided one way or another. A year ago, at the 1959 conference, Pastor Elwood had sought Jack out and questioned him at great length about Foxull, where the old man had been pastor for many years, and about Jack's parents. Jack had answered smoothly, promptly, accurately, with all sorts of detailed information on current happenings in Foxull. He winced as he remembered how Pastor Elwood's clear, direct eyes rested on him with such pride as he said:

"I don't think I ever knew a child who loved his mother as you did yours, Jack. Not in all my ministry!"

Well, all that was of the past now, except that now it might be necessary to dig it all up again.

Ted Smathers finally seemed to be getting around to the point.

"My district superintendent told me to get hold of Frank Longworth or Brother Elwood or to talk to you. He tells me I'll probably be going to the Foxull appointment and said you originally came from there. I thought maybe you could brief me on what the church is like. It's my first work, and I'll have to admit I'm sorta nervous about it." The boy sat on the very edge of his chair and kept fiddling with his clip-on bow tie. He wore white buckskin shoes.

"It's just a typical small town," said Jack. "One clothing store, one gas station, one movie house, one church and one cemetery. You preach twice a Sunday; prayer meeting is Wednesday night at seven; and from there on you just do what seems expected. And there's a mill —Harlowe's Mill."

"Does the town have a doctor or a nurse? Frances—that's my wife— is expecting our first in November."

"Yes, there's Dr. Bannister; his daughter is a registered nurse and also his receptionist. Christine and the doc will take care of you folks splendidly."

"Swell! Do you have some people there?"

"Yes. You'll meet my parents, Mr. and Mrs. Bruce Lee. They live . . . alone. In a big white house. I'm an only child."

"I see. Well, I suppose I'll be seeing you in Foxull—I mean, at Christmas and Easter holidays and things."

"In the pastorate," said Jack, "Christmas and Easter aren't exactly holidays the way they are in seminary."

"Oh, gee—that's right, isn't it!" Which got them over that question. What next? "Do you happen to know the lay delegate from the Foxull church—a Mr. Fred Hummaker?"

"Mr. Hummaker will probably be in tomorrow," said Jack. "Registration desk can give you his hotel."

"Oh, say," said the boy, getting up at last, and noticing Jack's list, "aren't you the one who . . . I mean, the one who's kicking up the fracas?" He hesitated. "You've sure got guts."

"That's what they all tell me," said Jack. "But they won't *vote* with me."

Ted Smathers laughed nervously, and was gone at last.

"And you're the one," Jack muttered to himself, "whose daddy holds the Middleton district in line for Belovèd, and you needn't have looked for your name on my list."

Jack propped his feet up again and reached for his coffee. He had been so tense during Smathers' questioning he had forgotten it completely. If he could not bear to tell a stranger that Foxull had a mill and a store, how could he possibly dig up everything else? And tomorrow he would have to start dodging Fred Hummaker again, as he dodged him every year at conference. He could already hear the high, twangy voice telling Smathers:

"Do I know Foxull? Sonny boy, you're looking at the biggest Foxullian of them all. I've been everything in Foxull from barber to mayor. You say you're our new pastor? Well, I'm a goggle-eyed tree toad! Just wait till I tell the folks back home. . . . Do I know Jackie Lee? I gave him his first haircut! Jackie hasn't been home for quite a spell now, but he'll be back. You can get the boy out of Foxull, I always say, but you'll never get Foxull out of the boy."

Jack covered his face with one hand. He had thought he could bury it all, but that had proved impossible from the day of his first annual conference four years ago. Steve McCullen, one of the older ministers who was helping Jack with his insurance forms, and who had preached a revival in Foxull years before, had asked him unexpectedly:

"Jack, how's your mother?"

And Jack had heard himself snap just as unexpectedly:

"Frankly, I've no idea."

He never forgot the expression of shock and curiosity on McCullen's face. Prior to that time he had been throwing Christine Bannister's letters in the trash. After that he realized that, even though he might refuse to receive any information about his parents, it would be wise to keep up at least an appearance of contact with Foxull. And so he began reading the letters with care, underlining important items like births and deaths, and he even fixed up a manila folder for them and filed it—not without a sardonic smile—under the H's as "Home-&-Family." On the first of each month he wrote Christine some sort of answer—enough to maintain the flow of her long, newsy letters, but not enough to reveal anything about himself, for he knew she passed everything on to his parents. A couple of three-month silences soon got the ground rules through her head that he did not wish any paragraphs about them, and since that time Miss Christine Bannister, R.N., had enabled him to answer most questions about Foxull as though he had just got back from a visit yesterday. But he had not set foot in the village for ten years and would never set foot in it again as long as he lived.

IV

The Way

JACK uncovered his eyes and glanced down at his hand. It was trembling, and his face was sweating. This would never do. He went back to the little snack stand which had been set up in one corner of the basement by the youth group of Belfair Church and got another cup of coffee. Then he returned to his chair, took the red button out of his pocket, and studied the torn fragment on the back. One simply could not be in this sort of political battle and be running about with nineteen hours missing from one's memory.

He was convinced that whatever had happened in New York was related somehow to Foxull. One could not bottle up that much of the past and not have trouble someday. He wondered if Ted Smathers had sensed his nervousness under all that questioning. . . . But where did one begin in reconstructing an entire world of experiences so long avoided and repressed? Of course, there was always that fight with Jess Guthrie on the Foxull schoolground, when they told Jack afterwards that he had picked up a rock. They even showed him the rock, an appalling object that might easily have killed Jess if Coach Nelson—as they all claimed—had not run up just in time to wrench it out of Jack's hand. But if he had picked up a rock, especially one that heavy, why could he never remember it afterwards?

Jack sat leaning back against the wall, watching the men from the publishing house unpacking their books. Through one of the high, narrow windows over their heads he could see a feathery green bough hanging motionless in the sunlight against the June sky.

Foxull had lots of elms too. . . . Their first leaves had just begun to fall that Sunday when Pastor and Mrs. Elwood came to lunch with the Bruce Lees after church, and the birches had blazed white among their leafy glory against a chill gray autumn sky. That day, at least, was a day still beautiful to remember and Pastor Elwood always pleasant to call into mind. . . .

The minister had looked much smaller in the living room of the Lee home than he had in the pulpit of the Foxull church, where in Jack's childhood he had always seemed of towering height, and Jack was a little disappointed that he did not speak in the same sonorous voice. His thick dark hair was slightly tousled when he took off his hat, and Jack noticed that he wore high-topped shoes whose gleaming polish could not quite conceal the cracks across the insteps. He did not speak of high and lofty subjects but only talked of little things with Jack's father, who sat opposite him, not smoking or removing his coat and tie. Occasionally the pastor's alert, kindly eyes wandered to Jack's face, and his square, clean-cut features relaxed in a smile. Once he spoke briefly, and almost in his sermon voice, of the dance at the high school gym, but Jack's father did not seem to notice the remark.

Jack knew that his parents had danced when they were in high school, and once he waked late at night, and heard music from the living room. Peering in through a crack, he saw them dancing by the radio. His mother's apron lay on the sofa; her feet made bewilderingly swift and intricate patterns on the linoleum, and her smile was saucy, and proud.

"Mil," said his father, puffing, "you can still dance rings around 'em all! And you're still the prettiest girl on the floor!"

The music had stopped and Jack withdrew. Tomorrow was a school day, and his father was inflexible about bedtime hours. Jack lay in the darkness, realizing that his mother did look as young as some of the high school girls, especially dancing that way—so slim and straight, with her feet flying and that funny smile. Christine's mother always said that Millie was the prettiest girl the town ever saw.

"The Blalocks had been in Foxull a week before we knew there were five other children," Mrs. Bannister said once. "All we could look at was your mother!"

Jack could see his mother as she sat at the table that Sunday, her lovely oval face framed by her pale gold hair, the fingertips of one exquisite hand resting on the good tablecloth they were using. Jack was very much aware of the dining room suite that day; it was a rich, dark mahogany and his parents had joked a great deal about having made the last payment on it that past month. "Now that it's all paid for at last," Bruce Lee had said, "we'll have to have Pastor Elwood come and consecrate it." Jack could remember studying Pastor Elwood's stern features and deciding that this was surely how the Old Testament prophets had looked: fearless, uncompromising, friendly in a way yet like iron underneath. Their words rang out as his did every Sunday like the hard, pure notes of a silver trumpet. Kings trembled at their "Thou art the man!" and the rich and mighty came to their door with fabulous gifts to beg for mercy and blessing. People loved them, but treated them with the greatest respect, the way Jack's father did, wearing his yellow shoes that were too tight but not daring to untie them and let the laces trail the way he always did after church.

The prospect of facing Pastor Elwood alone began to oppress Jack. He could scarcely eat and had great difficulty keeping his mind on what the grownups were saying. Finally, when the men had pushed back their chairs, his mother brought up the subject.

"Pastor," she said, standing in the doorway to the kitchen and tying her apron, "our Jackie is only ten, but he's quite mature for his years—religiously, I mean—and he has something he's been wanting to talk over with you."

"Well, Jack," said Pastor Elwood, "suppose you show me those pet rabbits you've been bragging about, and we can catch a breath of air while we talk."

It seemed odd that the pastor should think of anything like the rabbits at such a moment, and outside Jack was overcome by a dreadful shyness and pulled nervously at the sleeves of his sweater. In his room last night, with his mother sitting on the side of his bed, he had rehearsed his statement several times, but now the words seemed small and pale under the huge gray sky, hardly significant enough to use on such a momentous occasion:

"I'll just tell him," he had said, " 'Pastor Elwood, I want to give my heart to Jesus Christ and live for him.' "

When they had finished admiring the rabbits, they turned back to the house and the pastor sat down on the back steps, took out a small penknife, and began whittling a twig. This activity seemed to make the silence not at all unnatural, and Jack had almost nerved himself to begin when he heard the sound of footsteps, and Christine Bannister came racing around the corner of the back porch. She was a thin, tanned stick of a nine-year-old whose pigtails bounced as she ran and whose gray-green eyes went wide as she jolted to a stop at sight of the minister. She had on play clothes now instead of the new dress she had worn to Sunday school and church. She always came over on Sunday after lunch to see what Jack was doing. She could outrun any boy in Foxull and she never cried or tattled like other girls.

"Christine!" Jack heard his mother calling. Christine whirled, raced up the back steps, and slammed into the house.

Beyond the rabbit hutches and the back fence the birches gleamed white against the blue-gray hills, the black smokestacks of Harlowe's Mill stood silent against the leaden sky, and now and then a car glittered briefly on the ribbon of highway as someone took a Sunday drive through the hills. And suddenly the words began to come.

Pastor Elwood listened gravely, not smiling the way Jack's mother had once or twice—a smile that was more with the eyes than with the mouth. He asked questions now and then, not really religious questions one might have expected, but questions about home and school and Jack's birthday and his Sunday school teacher. Finally there was silence again. Pastor Elwood had put away his penknife and now he reached inside his coat and brought out a small New Testament, its grainy leather cover worn smooth, its gold edges tarnished from long handling.

"Jack," he said in a voice unexpectedly firm and clear, almost like the thrilling voice he used in the pulpit, "it's true that you're a little young. But I'm not sure I've ever met a youngster who was as spiritually mature as you at such an early age. You seem to have had some genuine experiences of the presence and power of God. Indeed, I wish some of our good church members had things to report as vivid and as real. You speak of feeling as if God were actually there when you see the light from the windows falling on the cross in church, and of knowing somebody is behind the stars and the sky at night. That's all fine, and perhaps you're a little of a mystic, son. But being a Christian is *more* that that."

He opened the Testament and began reading:

"Jesus saith unto him, I am the way, the truth, and the life: no man cometh unto the Father, but by me. If ye had known me, ye should have known my Father also: and from henceforth ye know him, and have seen him."

He held the Testament so that Jack could see it too, and indicated the two words "by me" with his forefinger.

"It's by *him* we become Christians, son, and not by any other means —not even by the beauty of God in the stars or, as you say, when everything is very still on a summer morning and the flowers and trees sort of tremble as the daylight comes. By *him!*"

Jack nodded. This was how he had expected it to be. The man of
God would be hard, uncompromising. Jack felt the same delicious uneasiness he felt that day he had wandered to the very lip of the abandoned quarry near the river and had gazed down suddenly into the
chasm. He had wanted to jump—had felt an almost physical pull! And
now, too, he wanted to jump, throw himself away, be dragged in by
an overwhelming, terrifying Something that would be like dying only
not really dying at all.

"Jack," said the minister, "do you understand that to become a Christian means you *belong* to Christ—heart, mind, soul, and strength?
Everything. That you are *his* man?" Nobody had ever called Jack a
"man" before.

Again the delicious, terrifying pull—stronger now.

"Yes, sir."

"Do you truly want to live for him all your life—trusting everything
to his care? Your relationship to your mother and father, to your teachers and friends at school, everything and everyone?"

"Yes, sir." The pull grew stronger and swifter, like a current gathering
speed toward a foaming, thundering abyss.

"You understand that it will not be easy. It may mean a cross. Christ
demands all. Your time, your energy, your hopes and dreams—you must
lay them all on the altar."

The minister gazed searchingly into his eyes and Jack nodded, his
chest tight with an unendurable longing.

"Let's pray," said Pastor Elwood in a voice subtly changed and deepened by an awful finality.

They knelt on the smooth, pocked surface of the slab of rock where
the back steps ended, and the minister put his arm about Jack's
shoulders.

"Dear heavenly Father," he said in a voice unexpectedly gentle and
almost husky, "we thank Thee that Thou hast drawn Jack to Thyself
by the leadings of the Holy Spirit. He belongs to Thee, Father. He
holds nothing back. All that he has and is and will ever be are Thine
alone. If Jack has done anything wrong or wicked, he is truly sorry and
asks to be forgiven. He repents of his sins; he believes in Thy only
begotten Son. May the Holy Spirit descend upon him in power!" The
strong arm tightened about Jack's shoulders. "May this child be used of
Thee in a most marvelous way!"

Jack did not hear all of the prayer. He felt a strange nervelessness, as though something tight and hard inside him had dissolved, as though he might begin to cry, or laugh, or do both at the same time. It was a disturbing sensation, but wonderful, too. It was as if the current had carried you over the abyss, yet somehow preserved you; had drowned you, yet somehow had also brought you safely through into a place of inexpressible beauty, of clear still waters that buoyed you up . . . of leafy boughs that enclosed the universe in peace. . . .

Later, in the living room, Pastor Elwood had prayer with the whole family. Afterwards his mother kissed Jack hard, but his father only squeezed his shoulder and seemed almost as if he were sad, or were remembering something he had lost and could not find again.

Membership day that spring, on Palm Sunday, was exciting and dramatic, but nothing to compare with that experience at the back steps, with the scent of autumn in the air, the glory of the maples and birches, the sight of Pastor Elwood's swift muscular hands, the crisp, authoritative ring of his words—so positive and Biblical. Everything about that afternoon was memorable. Later, secretly, Jack even bought a small pearl-handled penknife exactly like Pastor Elwood's and sometimes he would pick up a stick and whittle, pursing his lips as the minister had.

Jack had done a great deal of whittling in the years that followed. He smiled as he remembered his childhood conviction that the very act of whittling, because Pastor Elwood did it, would somehow bring answers to the most impossible problems. For there had been problems. Like Grandfather Blalock . . .

Jack had seen Gramps at the Lee home only once or twice. The Blalocks lived apart from the rest of the little village, in a settlement near the mill. All the girls were married and all had children except Aunt Alicia, whose husband was a foreman in the mill. The two boys were also married, and Gramps lived with Ham Blalock and his wife in the old family place. They were clannish and violent, and Jack knew that the people of Foxull resented them as "outsiders" and feared their moody, unpredictable ways.

They were his mother's people, but somehow Jack never felt a part of them. The Blalock boys had been the backbone of Foxull's football team in their school days, and Jack had played one year with the scrubs himself, but he was too light to make the varsity at that time and afterwards had confined himself to track. The Blalock name had been the occasion of Jack's only fight during his school days. His mother had driven him to school one rainy morning and as she drove away, he heard one of the older boys say something, and several people sniggered and glanced at Jack. He dropped his books on the wet sidewalk.

"What did you say?"

"I said, 'She's a Blalock, ain't she?'" said the boy, smirking. He was a head taller than Jack and did not even take his big fists out of the pockets of his football jacket. "Better run in to teacher, Jackie. You'll get wet."

Jack slapped him so hard the boy's head flew back, and the crowd spread back in a half-circle, their faces gleeful.

"Watch out, Jess! I believe he's mad!" someone yelled.

Jess stepped out into the rain, his wide, freckled face more startled than angry, his thick lips smirking again.

Jack had never fought before, but a fury possessed him, and he did not seem to feel Jess's blows, even when they knocked him off his feet. He scrambled up, flailing wildly, half-blinded by the water and blood running into his eyes, frantic to erase that thick-lipped grin, to utterly destroy that bobbing, dancing face. The smirk began to give way to uneasiness, then to fear, and then the older boy's retreating foot slipped and Jack was on top of him, pounding wildly, blindly. Then someone was yanking him off bodily, and he heard the voices of Coach Nelson and the principal, shouting. The ring of faces staring at him was mute and shocked. Through the ringing in his ears, Jack heard the coach's voice as they shoved him inside the principal's office:

"Damn fool. Didn't Jess know better than to cross a Blalock? This boy mighta killed him with that rock."

Which was the first Jack knew about the rock. . . .

Jack slept in a small room just off the kitchen, where his father sometimes worked late on the books from the mill. One night he was awakened by loud voices. Leaning on one elbow and peering through a crack in the door, he saw Gramps and his father, who was sitting before the big ledgers spread on the kitchen table amid a clutter of papers.

"Stop yelling, Gramps, before you wake Mil and the boy. It's past one."

Over his father's shoulder Jack could see Gramps's heavy-jowled face, flushed and unshaven. He had thrown his dirty Mackinaw on the drainboard of the sink, where the snow was melting from it, but he still wore his galoshes, and they made a jingling sound. Gray-white hair showed above his yellowed sweatshirt at the base of his massive neck, sweat glistened in the roots of the tousled white hair at his temples and his fierce black brows were contorted now over his beady eyes.

"The boy! The boy! If you gave a damn about him, you'd do this and get him outa this town! Harlowe's lawyer says it's airtight." Harlowe was the owner of the mill. "Bruce, if you won't think of yourself, think of the kid."

Jack's father pushed back his chair and stood up stiffly. The seat of his trousers was shiny, and his shirttail was almost untucked and protruded from under his vest. He scratched the small of his back, put a lump of coal in the kitchen stove, and drank the last swallow of coffee from his cup, holding it in that odd way he had, by the side opposite the handle, because his forefinger had a bumpy crook in it from years of writing those small, neat figures in the ledgers.

"I've *been* thinking about him. I haven't slept three hours a night since you brought up this dirty deal—"

"It ain't a dirty deal!"

"They want me to juggle these books for 'em." Jack's father turned over one of the big pages and examined it, as if seeing it for the first time. "I've kept 'em sixteen years and I'd show 'em to the Lord in judgment—every decimal. They're asking me to help 'em steal from the government—"

"Steal? Who's stealing? The government's got billions! It's legal, and everybody's doing it."

"It's stealing to me."

Gramps's beady eyes glinted.

"And who the hell are you? A hired hand in a textile mill. Thirty-five years old, and right where you started. So you coulda been a big professor or scientific genius or something! Coulda! For sixteen years you been telling us what you coulda done with that scholarship. Coulda! How do you know? The smartest men in the country say this is all right. Who are you to say it's wrong?"

Gramps poured his coffee into his saucer, blew on it, and sucked it in noisily. Jack's father stared at the stove.

"A man can be mistaken about his ability, Gramps," he said slowly. "He can die still wondering if he was only average. . . . But even if he's uncertain about his real worth, he always knows when he's sold himself. Why are you selling yourself, Gramps? Is the mill gonna throw you some business if you can talk me into this? Let you saw 'em some logs?"

Gramps's yellow teeth gleamed and he shook his big head.

"It's no use a man trying to outfox you, Bruce Lee. I don't stand to *lose* nothing; but I'm just human enough to want to help my own daughter. Let bygones be bygones, I say. Jackie's my own flesh and blood and I hate to see you ruin his chances like you ruined yours. Mil's my own child. What kind of a father won't help his own?"

"You're lying, Gramps. You've always hated Jackie. But you hate Mil worse. I used to think it was just because she was the prettiest and had hurt your pride. But it's really because she's never been afraid of you, because you couldn't make her feel dirty and ashamed—not with all your beatings and yellings. You've never loved anything but money, Gramps. You don't care whether Mil and Jackie live or die."

Gramps studied his massive fist, his face clouded.

"Ma said once Mil was like a young birch," he said; "the harder you bend her down and rub her nose in the dirt, the straighter and prettier she stands up again. Mil was her pet. . . . I'm glad Ma never lived . . ." The hoarse voice trailed off; and the little eyes were nakedly hate-filled. "She's mean!" With an obvious effort the old man controlled himself. "But I didn't come here to argue, Bruce. She's my daughter. I'm tired of this town looking down its nose at the Blalocks. Call it pride, if you want to, but I'm asking you to make something of yourself. And even if I didn't like Jackie, he's a Blalock. You can tell it a mile away! Bruce, if you turn Harlowe down on this, your kid'll be damn *glad* to get a job logging! But I was just kidding about how do you know you coulda made good. Hell, Harlowe knows he couldn't buy half your brains for twice the money. Why, the boys in Fred Hummaker's was telling me last week—"

Jack's father suddenly banged his fist on the metal top of the table. His voice was harsh.

"I know! The boys were telling you how they call out six-digit figures and I multiply them in my head!"

Gramps's sweaty face showed bewilderment, and Jack tried to see the expression on his father's face, now turned away. Jack had often sat in the barber shop on Saturday afternoons, feeling enormously self-conscious and proud, while his father lounged back in the shoeshine chair, his cigar stuck out at an angle, thumbs hooked in his vest. Scarcely had the last syllable of the problem died away before his father, not even bothering to remove the cigar, rapped out the answer. Sometimes a visitor, not one of the regular gang, would take pencil and paper and laboriously work the thing through amid winks and sniggers, while Jack's father gazed down in pity. But now, mysteriously, Jack's father was no longer disdainful. His voice was low.

"My son's not going to be a clown, Gramps. A man with a gift from God needs to live among people he can talk to, and share things with, and learn something from. When a man's got nobody to talk to about what he knows, the waste and lonesomeness of life run him crazy. He . . . does things he'd never do in his right mind. And he winds up doing tricks in the middle of Main Street just to prove to himself he has something different, something *big*, even if he'll never get a chance to use it." His father's voice had sunk to a whisper, and he slumped wearily into his chair, apparently speaking half to himself. "But my boy's not gonna taste that lonesomeness, or go back and forth from this house to the mill office all his life, like a lion cramped up in a cage. He's going to school—if me and Mil have to kill ourselves to do it. He's gonna sit down in a library that has a million books, and blossom! . . . not grow crazy and twisted under a stone."

Jack felt a sudden lump in his throat. He wanted to go off and make the most brilliant record any college had ever known. But Gramps's cunning eyes were dry and alert. He put the fingertips of his great, hairy hands on the edge of the table.

"Them's fine words, Bruce. But you're smarter than Jackie will ever be—"

"Jackie's a good student! He got A's in chemistry!"

"You got A's in everything, Bruce, and you never got out of here. You was always the biggest talker in town, and twenty years from now you'll still be talking big—and Jackie still won't be out. He'll be right there in the mill like you." A look of anguish seized Jack's father, who had turned away from Gramps as though he wanted to run. His eyes were bloodshot; he kept running his hand over the row of pencils in his vest pocket. "Bruce, if you buck Harlowe on this, I swear it might be the last straw. You're thirty-five, and that's old for job-hunting these days. And he'd blacklist you with every mill in the valley. Bruce, do this and I swear he'll make you comptroller! Jackie could go to

Harvard, or one of them places! Millie could finish fixing up this place like she's always wanted to. And you'd be somebody!"

Jack's father sat silent for a long time, and when he spoke at last, his voice was dreamlike.

"And then when they've bought your brains and your body and worked them so long it's too late to start again somewhere else, they come bidding for your soul. They wave the big club one last time, and send somebody that can twist the knife where it hurts, and this time you can't say no because they hold a voting majority of your years and opportunities." Jack felt a sudden uneasiness. His father had slumped lower in the chair, his eyes were lackluster, and his Adam's apple bobbed when he talked, head back, eyes staring at the stain in the wallpaper around the flue. Gramps had his grizzled features clenched tight to force back the smile. "They catch you when you've finally lost faith in yourself, and they give you a chance to prove you are somebody after all . . . and you realize that honesty is just meaningless and suicidal in a little man. . . . And you see that a big gesture won't make you look a hero but just a bigger fool. And if you won't give in, they'll make you morally responsible for your child getting his heart broken and his dreams made a standing joke like yours. . . . So at the end you see that doing wrong is really the only helpful and unselfish thing you can do."

The tired voice stopped. Jack felt sick and frightened, as though he had just seen something die. And he felt embarrassed and ashamed, for his father not only looked defeated, he looked funny: his chin had sunk into his chest, his arms hung limp with the fingertips almost touching the floor, his shirttail was untucked, and his slight frame looked broken and paunchy.

Gramps tiptoed over to the sink, his galoshes clinking in the stillness, and cautiously pulled on his big Mackinaw. His face was noncommittal but under their craggy black brows his eyes glowed. He came around and stood before Jack's father, buckling his thick plaid belt.

"You want *me* to tell 'em?"

Jack's father stood up awkwardly. Gramps towered over everyone, but now he seemed a giant; for Jack's father did not straighten completely. "No, I'll tell them myself." He dragged the coffeepot across the top of the stove, poured himself a cup, sloshed some cream and sugar into it, and stood with head bowed drinking from his spoon. His voice was mild and he seemed intent on the coffee. "Because I *still* won't do it."

The transformation in Gramps was terrifying. His thick face crimsoned to the roots of his bristly white hair; the deep-set eyes bulged from their pockets of fat; his heavy jowls knotted; and the hands adjusting the belt suddenly turned into tremendous fists, raised high over his head. Jack sat bolt upright in bed, trying to cry out a warning, but no sound came out—only a dry, squeaky thumping in his throat. Gramps had once killed a man with his fists. His lawyer had him plead self-defense and say he could not remember what happened, but everybody knew the jury was just afraid of Gramps and the Blalocks. Everybody said a Blalock would kill you if you crossed him.

Jack's father glanced up. His eyes were calm and his hand steady as he stirred the coffee and drank another sip.

"Don't ever come in my house again, Gramps."

The old man stood for a moment, transfixed, a vein throbbing in his temple, his chest heaving. Then he lowered his arms, whirled, and slammed out of the room, and Jack heard his heavy feet across the back porch, as though he were going to shake the whole house down.

Jack's mother appeared in the hall doorway, in her robe.

"It's past two, dear."

Jack's father smiled and sank into his chair.

"Aren't you interested in what answer I gave Gramps?"

She came and stood behind his chair, her beautiful hands resting on his shoulders.

"I could have told you a week ago," she said.

Jack's father laughed and patted her hand and kissed it.

"If only we could be *sure* . . ." His face was somber.

"Of what?"

"That God *would* take care of Jackie!"

She began fixing the coffeepot for the morning.

"That's why I love you, Bruce Lee."

"Why?"

"Because we'd all trust God if we could be sure." She put the pot on the front of the stove. "Better come to bed."

But Jack's father lingered in the kitchen alone. He washed the coffee cups, and seemed to take forever doing it, almost as if he were prolonging the activity. Then he snapped off the light; but instead of going to bed, he sat down by the table and lit a cigar. In the flare of the match

Jack saw his features briefly. They were utterly peaceful, as though he were on some remote and unassailable height, yet the eyes held a kind of secret, jealous ecstasy, almost like a hot flame answering the flame of the match. His doctor had limited him to two cigars a day; he smoked one after lunch and one with the evening paper. But tonight he sat in the kitchen alone, in darkness, and smoked a third; and Jack watched the coal fade and glow and wondered why. He sensed vaguely that his father had discovered something rare and precious, like an exotic plant flowering high in a granite niche, its intimate and unexpected splendor sacred to the lonely climber. One could not pluck it, for its glory could never be separated from the cold wind and the tall sky and the doubts and dangers of the climb. Nor could one even describe it later on. One could only linger.

Finally the chair scraped; Jack heard the familiar squeak of his bedroom door; his father stood for a moment in the gloom, his face turned toward Jack's bed. Then he was gone.

Somehow, paradoxically, nothing in all the after years had ever stained the brightness of that hour. In the study hall of the Foxull High School was a picture of Sir Galahad, sword in hand, his snow-white armor gleaming, his fresh young face aglow with holy zeal. But to Jack the picture of his father that night, standing by that dripping faucet he always meant to fix, his shoulders bowed, his shirttail untucked, and the baggy seat of his trousers all shiny, had a grandeur that no Galahad could match.

V

Just as I Am

THE BRUCE LEE home in Foxull stood on a slight elevation on the western edge of town. From his bedroom window Jack could see the length of Main Street, the towers of the high school and the steeple of the church, and the stacks of Harlowe's Mill beyond the railway tracks. It was a large, rambling frame house which had been very run-down when his parents moved into it in 1932, at the depth of the depression, and they had lived in only three of the rooms at the beginning, keeping the others closed off to save fuel. But the house was almost paid for now, and over the years they had gradually reclaimed more and more of the structure, inside and out, and Bruce Lee had done such a spectacular job on his lawns and especially on his boxwood garden that each year the Foxull Garden Club held one of its meetings there.

The boxwoods were Bruce Lee's only hobby. When things went wrong at the mill, or when he had a problem on his mind, Jack's father would putter about among the neat, impeccable hedges and presently he would come into the house looking relaxed and at peace again. He had the hedges laid out in geometrical designs on the front, sides, and rear of the house, and it was the boxwoods, actually, that had led Dr. and Mrs. Bannister to buy next door to the Lees. The Bannisters had always lived on the opposite side of Foxull, near the Harlowes, which was always considered *the* section of Foxull. But Dr. Bannister liked the view from the western section, Mrs. Bannister was a gardening enthusiast, and one day they decided to build there so that she would have more room for her flowers and could enjoy Bruce Lee's formal garden next door.

Jack was fifteen in December, 1947, a few weeks before the argument between his father and Gramps about the mill books in January. One morning in April Pastor Elwood appeared at the Foxull High School chapel program with a visiting evangelist who made a stirring appeal for careers of "full-time Christian service." Pastor Elwood urged all the students to attend revival services that week at the Foxull Methodist Church. The evangelist came from the South, and after chapel, Walt Morgan, one of Jack's best friends, did an irreverent imitation of the visitor's southern accent and of his "altar call," which was also something strange to Foxull.

Walking home from school that afternoon with Walt, who was the son of Foxull's undertaker, and "Pole" Kowalski, Jack and the others discussed the future. Pole's father wanted him to be a lawyer; Walt pointed out that "all lawyers are crooks" and spoke of studying medicine "to fix people up before it don't do any good." To this he added a detailed description of a body his father had embalmed the night before.

"Jack, what are you gonna be—a bookkeeper like your old man?" asked Pole.

Pole's father took such pride in working in the mill that Jack hesitated.

"I . . . don't know yet."

The decision seemed very long ago and far away now, as Jack sat in the bookroom in the basement of Belfair Church in Middleton. Between him and that spring of 1948 lay all the vast worlds of college and seminary and four years in the pastorate. A group of young men came down the basement stairs just then and passed by Jack's chair. They had come to conference early to face the Board of Ministerial Training, which was meeting just off the bookroom, and one of them was worrying aloud in a high-pitched nasal voice: "They might ask me if I believe in the Virgin Birth! Or if Moses really wrote the Pentateuch!" To which an unruffled baritone responded: "Relax. They never have but one question: 'Do you solemnly promise not to use tobacco?'"

Jack watched them chatting and laughing at the snack counter and wondered how many of them had a little church like Foxull Methodist somewhere in the background, and a faithful shepherd who had spoken to them one day just as Pastor Elwood had spoken to Jack in January of 1948 before the revival that spring. . . .

He and Jack had been walking down the sidewalk toward the parsonage gate when he said it:

"Jackie, you're fifteen now and have another year of high school, but you're spiritually mature far beyond your years. Has it ever occurred to you that God might be calling you to the ministry?"

Jack remembered glancing up to see whether he were joking, but the strong, square face was grave. Jack turned to look at the parsonage, then at the church with its tall plain steeple white against the naked elms and the overcast sky. In his mind's eye he saw a succession of Foxull ministers—solemn or humorous, mild-mannered or stern, but all different from ordinary people. Jack tried to imagine himself standing in the pulpit as one of these separate men, utterly righteous and pure, and instantly the vision was overlaid by grotesque images of adolescent sin.

"No, sir . . . I'd never thought of such a thing." Jack pushed the white gate shut between them. "That's crazy!"

But all that winter and spring he had thought about it, and his sins seemed more frightening yet more irresistible. Some Sundays he pretended to have a headache to avoid church. Often he fell into day-dreams during the services.

Sitting between his parents in the tall, severe sanctuary, Jack would see himself as a missionary in remote jungles, surrounded by eager black folk who gazed on him with awe and reverence. Or he directed a mission project in a city slum, where each day the needy and helpless received food and clothing and spiritual blessing from his hand. Newspapers published his doings around the world, and each night he wrote his mother of his victories for the Kingdom of God. Sometimes, gazing out the window at school, Jack would imagine the drab, grimy buildings of Main Street hung with banners. The famed evangelist had come home. People crowded about his car, tried to touch his hand, and remarked, "How humble he is!" and "He hasn't changed a bit!" And always, before a packed church that night he insisted that the credit for his exploits belonged to Pastor Elwood—and to his mother.

She never missed church or prayer meeting. Each night she read a chapter from her white leather Testament. Throughout Jack's childhood she used to hear his prayers at night, placing one of her lovely hands on his shoulder in a way she had and lightly running the fingers of the other through his hair. Her hands were small with slender tapering fingers and tiny dimples, yet on the keyboard of the old upright piano in the living room they flashed with dazzling dexterity and power.

The family attended the revival faithfully that spring, and each night Jack felt an impulse to go down to the altar and tell Pastor Elwood he had decided to enter the ministry, but always he would imagine the faces of his schoolmates next day, leering suggestively while they made obscene gestures and roared with laughter. Some days he could scarcely eat; some nights he felt that if he could not decide the thing he would faint or die. During the sermons, bits of Scripture kept floating through his mind: "Whosoever shall be ashamed of me . . . of him shall the Son of man be ashamed when he comes . . ." "I am the way . . ." "Lovest thou me?" "Go ye into all the world and preach . . ." Walt was going to follow Christine's father and be a doctor; Pole was going to follow Lincoln and be a lawyer. Why should Jack not follow Christ and be a minister?

On the final night the evangelist was unable to speak. He had shouted and gesticulated in shirtsleeves the previous night, an unseasonably warm one for April, till his collar wilted and his shirt clung wetly to his big shoulders and his voice became a rasp. So now he sat on the rostrum listening to Pastor Elwood, nodding vigorously, and whispering an occasional, "Yesss, yesss!"

Jack had somehow been able to resist the evangelist's overwhelming appeals, but when he saw Pastor Elwood's kind, square features and heard his familiar voice, he knew there was no way out—whatever his sins, whatever the ridicule he might face, whatever unknown and terrifying events might follow.

But when he stood up for the closing hymn, his legs would scarcely support him. His father stood between him and the aisle, he could not think what he would say to get past him, and suddenly this seemed a perfectly sound reason not to go down at all. He wanted to ask his mother to go with him, but he was fifteen and already taller than she was, and everyone would laugh. In sudden terror he realized that they had begun the final verse of the hymn:

> *Just as I am!—Thou wilt receive*
> *Wilt welcome, pardon, cleanse, relieve;*
> *Because thy promise I believe,*
> *O Lamb of God, I come! I come!*

He pushed toward the aisle, clumsily stepping on his father's feet and feeling that this was absurd and humiliating at such a moment. His "excuse me" came out as a kind of squeak in the sudden appalling silence that had fallen. The aisle seemed miles long. He wanted to turn and run in the opposite direction, but just then Miss Irene struck a chord on the piano, and the congregation began again on the first verse: "Just as I am, without one plea, But that thy blood was shed for me . . ." The music seemed to restore his courage, to give him strength to carry out his decision; it almost seemed to lift and carry him down the long aisle like a big breaker of sound cresting toward the altar. He fixed his eyes on Pastor Elwood's face.

The pastor's strong hands were gripping his own; in the stillness he heard his own voice, thin but clear:

"I want to be a minister like you."

Pastor Elwood did not speak. He simply stood gripping Jack's hand, his eyes bright. The evangelist threw back his head, and flung wide his arms with a hoarse whisper.

"Praise the Lord! Ohhhh, praise the Lord!"

Jack remembered both the ministers praying; he recalled the congregation and how all their faces blurred together, with everyone standing while the evangelist spoke for what seemed ages in an impassioned whisper.

But mostly Jack remembered his mother as she came down the aisle with his father to stand beside him—her graceful, willowy walk, the way her small feet were so swift and certain. She carried her head high, and the overhead lights made a soft halo of her pale gold hair, and her eyes never left his face. He had feared she might be hurt that he had not shared so important a decision with her, but her face glowed with a kind of serenity and pride and happiness all mingled. She kissed his cheek hard, and he was startled to feel tears on her own. Then his father was shaking his hand very soberly, and the congregation began to file past.

Surprisingly, they were all very serious—even his schoolmates. Pole was not there because he was a Catholic, but Walt seemed almost abashed, and the adults spoke to him as if he had overnight become an adult too. They all shook his father's hand first, then his, and several of the women kissed him, which was unexpected and embarrassing. A number of them kissed his mother too, and for some reason, when they did, several of them were crying.

In the weeks that followed, Pastor Elwood counseled Jack about the choice of a college, and about plans for seminary afterwards. The future seemed plain and assured—till Gramps Blalock came back.

For the old man did return to the Lee home. He suffered a stroke in June that left him totally paralyzed and unable to speak; the Blalock clan all found excuses not to take him into their homes, though Aunt Alicia had a big empty house and time on her hands, and Jed's wife had been a practical nurse. But Jack's mother would not hear of putting Gramps in a nursing home, and in the end she gave up her job at the mill and cared for her father herself, night and day, month after month, through the exhausting heat of that summer, and through the beauty of the autumn she never got out to see, and into the dead of a terrible winter.

A number of times Jack overheard his father argue about her decision.

"Why *you*, Millie? Every one of the Blalocks has more reason to love him and take care of him than you!"

Usually her answer was, "He's my father." Once she said, "It's not a burden, Bruce. It's an opportunity."

"For what?"

"To make it all up to him. To atone."

"I *have* atoned!" said Bruce Lee in a voice Jack had never heard before.

Jack found Gramps enormously heavy at the beginning. It disturbed him to think of his mother's lifting the old man when she bathed him and changed his bed. Sometimes Pastor Elwood helped during one of his calls; sometimes Christine stayed home from school and helped, or just sat with Gramps or read to him while Jack's mother caught a few hours' sleep. Jack's father would not permit him to miss school, and he could only help his mother after school hours. But toward the end Gramps began to lose weight; the massive plates of muscle on his shoulders and chest seemed to wither; the thick jowls became pale and flabby; the huge stomach appeared only as a hollow in the sheets.

Christine was quick and strong, and though a year younger than Jack, she was much more calm and helpful in a sickroom; for she had learned a great deal by accompanying her father on his rounds. His mother found her good humor and her pranks a welcome diversion. Once, on a mild autumn afternoon when she was sewing on the front porch, Chris snatched up her bobbin.

"Christine Bannister, give me that this instant!"

"Catch me and I will!" Chris was on the girls' track squad at the high school. She stuck out her tongue, her gray-green eyes shining, her tan cheeks puckered with mischief, and raced off across the lawn. Jack watched in astonishment as his mother chased her in a big circle across the grass, their feet flying through the gold and scarlet leaves, their bodies flashing in and out among the slanting bars of the afternoon sun.

"Catch her, Mrs. Lee!" screamed Alex, Christine's younger brother, an awkward boy who wearied of her feats at track.

Finally Jack's mother chased her down, pushed her into the small mountain of leaves Alex had been raking, and recovered the bobbin.

"Gosh, she's like lightning!" Christine gasped, as Jack pulled her out, her thick brown hair full of dust and leaves. "Who'da thought your mother could outrun *me!*"

But such moments were rare, and toward the end Jack's mother grew shockingly weary. Sometimes she seemed unable to decide very simple things; she dropped things in the kitchen; during the winter she could never keep warm. The Blalocks made brief, infrequent calls on Gramps, always making the same apologies for not coming more often, and the silent man on the bed blinked and stared into space.

His silence was oppressive. Christine filled it with reading, or with cheery small talk, but Jack knew that the old man had things he wanted to say, and sometimes the sight of his eyes, almost bulging from their hollow sockets in the effort to communicate, was more than Jack could bear. He kept remembering the strange things Gramps and his father had said in their argument over the mill books.

"He wants something," his mother said one night, putting her book down. She turned the lamp further from Gramps's face, glancing at his eyes for confirmation. "No, it's not the light." She reached for one of his pulp Westerns, but the sunken eyes only became more hopeless. "What could it possibly be?"

Her lovely face was not angry or impatient the way other people's were when they could not interpret Gramps, but only distressed at not being able to meet his needs. Suddenly Jack remembered the way her brothers and sisters looked at Gramps now, as if impatient for him to die, and thought how different his mother's face must look to the man on the bed.

"Mother—" Jack glanced down into the hollow face with its burning eyes and the mouth all dragged down at the corner by the stroke. For an instant he was afraid of Gramps again, as if he might magically rise up and tower over them all and shake the huge fists that had killed the man from Otha City, the fists that had terrorized his wife and children so many years. But the fleshless fingers on the coverlet did not stir. Jack heard himself say suddenly:

"He wants to say he's sorry."

The old man's eyelids blinked rapidly, the way they did to indicate a "yes," and he kept blinking them while the tears trickled down. A terrible sound came from the twisted mouth, harsh and unmusical, the only sound Gramps made during his entire illness, like the grinding of hinges long locked in rust as a door swung open. Jack's mother fell on the sick man, sobbing, her head pillowed on his bony shoulder, one hand clenched in his damp white hair.

The next day there was a subtle difference in Gramps, a kind of yielding, as if the purpose for which he had clung to life during the last terrible month was now fulfilled. Six days later, on the tenth of February, while Jack and Chris were sitting at the foot of his bed talking, Gramps died.

The Blalock children bought a giant cross of white carnations with red roses across it that spelled out "F A T H E R," and during Pastor Elwood's message the huge brawny men moaned and blubbered like boys. The Blalock women screamed, all except Jack's mother, who sat with her hands clenched in her lap staring straight ahead and blinking now and then. She was very pale, and sometimes Jack thought he felt her trembling. At the cemetery Aunt Alicia screamed, "Daddy! Ohhhhhhhhh, Daddy! Noooooo, no, nooooooooo!" and fainted in the snow as the casket was being lowered into the ground. Mr. Morgan and Walt, who often helped his father with the big funerals, floundered in the frozen slush as they tried to get her back into her chair.

That night Jack sat by the big iron stove in the living room with his father, listening to the rattle and splash as his mother did the dishes.

"Why did they all cry except Mother?"

"To let everyone know how much they loved their father."

"Then why didn't Mother cry?"

"Because she *did* love him. Which is something some of us will never fathom in this life. . . . You and I will just have to love her even when we can't understand her."

"Aunt Alicia cried louder than anybody."

Jack's father bit the end off of a new cigar and spat it into the coal scuttle.

"She had a bigger crowd to convince."

The death of Gramps had cracked open for Jack glimpses of an abyss he had never known existed. For his mother fell ill soon after the funeral, and Jack found himself obsessed by the vision of her suddenly becoming inert and speechless, like Gramps, to lie for months—for years!—unable to lift her lovely hands, to tell him what all this meant and what to do and how to feel. Dr. Bannister assured them that she was suffering mainly from exhaustion and must have complete rest. Jack's father, still refusing to let him miss a day of school, hired a woman to stay with her during the daytime, and gradually she began to improve.

But the family income had been cut sharply when Gramps came

and Jack's mother left the mill; Dr. Bannister had charged them absurdly low fees, but now there was the practical nurse to pay, and the bills at the drugstore, and even a question about Jack's scholarship aid next fall, for his report card was now sprinkled with C's and even one D. And to see his father sign the card in dead silence—without demanding any explanation—was frightening.

Then, just two weeks before Jack's graduation, the letter came concerning the chemistry scholarship. Jack had made his best marks in that subject the year before; and Mr. Nettleton, the science teacher, had had him take a competitive examination that spring. His paper was among the first three, and the letter informed him that a four-year college scholarship from Dynaplast Chemicals, Inc., was available. The arrival of the letter, coupled with recent periods of temptation and despair, seemed almost an omen that Jack had never been meant for the ministry in the first place, even though he had already had his letters of recommendation mailed in. He had got one from Pastor Elwood, and from Mr. Harlowe, Sr., at Harlowe's Mill, from Mayor Fred Hummaker at the barber shop, and from Miss Martin, his English teacher at Foxull High School.

He decided he should inform Pastor Elwood of his changing prospects. But when he sat down in the pastor's study, a curious thing happened, a thing that always seemed to happen to Jack in Pastor Elwood's presence.

The sight of the bronze cross on the desk, the portrait of Christ with his crown of thorns, even the titles of the books in orderly rows on the shelves and the sight of the pastor's worn but well-polished black shoes—all gave Jack a sudden sense of stability and hope. And, above all, the pastor's kind, squarish features and unwavering eyes seemed to say that illness, death, and all the quirks of circumstance were only part of the wholeness of life, that he had faced them all in a thousand homes in a dozen communities, and that all could be met and mastered.

"So I can't see any solution," Jack concluded, "but to give up the idea of the ministry for a while, and—"

Pastor Elwood held up one strong, small hand.

"Jackie, do you believe that you can find real peace and security through having this corporation pay your way through school and then provide you with a fine job and a big salary if you will serve *them?*"

"I . . . I don't guess so, sir."

"Do you believe you can serve God *and* Mammon?"

"Oh, no, sir!"

"Then it's clear that you are confronted with a choice, aren't you? Either take this exciting offer and commit your life to money and things, or turn your back on the world and the kind of success it promises and seek real peace and security through obedience to God. It is true that God's security may involve suffering and danger, but unless you bear the cross, you cannot wear the crown. It's that simple."

"But, sir, Mother's sick, and Dad's in debt, and he doesn't even know how we can pay the bills at the drugstore. All he's ever wanted all his life was for me to go to college! This way I can. How could he get me through now, with things as they are? And how would he take care of Mother?"

"Jackie, listen to me!" The minister's voice was hard and demanding, the way Jack had wanted his father's voice to be about the low marks. "I don't think I've ever known a youngster who put his parents up on a pedestal—and his minister, too!—in the way you do yours. It's beautiful, but it's disturbing. We should never put mere human beings above our love for Christ, no matter how much we love them. The questions you have asked are the oldest in the world: What shall we eat? What shall we drink? Wherewithal shall we be clothed? My dear boy, the Christian life is a venture of faith! I confess I have no idea how you can possibly finance four years of college and then three years of seminary—or even the first year of it all! Or how your father can meet his bills. Or whether your mother will ever be strong enough to work again. But I know one thing: I know the Bible."

He opened it in that careful, reverent way he had:

"But seek ye first the kingdom of God and his righteousness; and *all these things* shall be added unto you." He pushed the open Bible across the desk toward Jack. "Son, do you believe a minister of Jesus Christ can listen to any other adviser except Jesus Christ?"

"No, sir."

"Are you a follower of the Lamb?"

"Yes, sir."

"Then follow him!"

Jack walked the two blocks from the pastor's study to the drugstore with head high. When Mr. Walton rang up the cost of his mother's prescription, Jack said:

"I thought it was six-sixty."

The druggist pushed the half dollar and the dime back toward him. "That's your professional discount. You're going off this fall to study for the ministry, aren't you?"

Jack picked up the silver. The word "professional" made him feel he should appear grave and dignified, but the smile burst through.

"Yes, sir," he said. "Thank you very much. Yes, I am!"

He kept his fingers clenched till he was half a block from home, then opened them stiffly and wonderingly.

Sixty cents . . . not a very big sign.

But from God.

He broke into a run, vaulted the boxwood hedge, and slammed through the door, whistling.

VI

Hell Hath No Fury

JACK went to bed early Tuesday night, but found himself unable to sleep. The Middleton Hotel was in the downtown section of the city, and from his window he could see the distant lights of the suburban development surrounding Belfair Methodist Church. During the day he and Wes had held a number of strategy sessions with Adams, Perriman, Dirkwell, Starr, and the rest of the rebels, trying to formulate meaningful plans in this near hopeless struggle to unhorse Dr. Worthington. Delegates would not arrive in force until tomorrow morning, Wednesday, when the conference formally opened. The rush of events then would leave little time for reflection, and meantime Jack still had the strain and mystery of those missing nineteen hours to account for.

He rolled over facing the wall. He knew that whatever had happened in New York during those nineteen hours went back much further than his affair with Thelma. It all went back—everything in his present life always went back somehow—to a gray Friday afternoon in late September of 1950, when he was seventeen.

If only Pastor Elwood had been there everything might have been different. But Pastor Elwood had left Foxull in '49, the same year Jack went off to college, and Jack had had no one to turn to.

Jack had been planning to return to college on Monday to begin his sophomore year. Upperclassmen were not due till Wednesday, but he had promised to help Christine Bannister register with the freshmen. After Gramps's death in February of '47, Jack's mother had been confined to bed for several months.

When Jack had left to begin his freshman year, she had gone back to Harlowe's Mill, only to collapse in the heat of the following summer; and she had been in bed again since August. Jack's father had been enormously proud of Jack's first year's work; and in spite of his wife's illness and the family debts and the fact that they were drawing heavily on their savings, Bruce Lee was quite a different person that summer. Then, on the first of September, when Mr. Harlowe made his son comptroller of the mill, Jack's father turned suddenly silent and withdrawn. He would go out to work among the boxwoods; but Jack would see him simply standing there, staring, and once he left his garden tools out overnight in the rain, a thing he had never done before.

Mrs. Catlett came by that Friday afternoon, just back from one of her periodic shopping sprees in New York. Jack's mother always enjoyed her short, gossipy visits. Her husband had been killed in the war in the Pacific only six months after their marriage. She never remarried, lived in a boarding house across town, and spent her pension on clothes.

Christine had made herself a low hurdle from some wooden slats, and Jack had been practicing broad jumps on the lawn beside her. Coming into the kitchen for a glass of water, he caught a glimpse of Mrs. Catlett through the door of his mother's room. She was staring out the window, and her voice was husky as she talked while letting cigarette smoke drift out of her mouth in a way she had:

"Look at that child! She doesn't jump—she just floats over that damn thing! I tell you, Mil, a chiropractor couldn't get me in that position today."

Jack heard his mother's laugh for the first time in weeks.

"Oh, Viv! You *are* good for me!"

Mrs. Catlett tapped the floor with her sandal. She was very tall, and wore her hair piled high in bright gold ringlets in addition. Her black eyes flashed under their penciled brows as she turned to grind out her cigarette.

"Christine Bannister, the original 4-H girl. All good clean suntan and freckles. A million-dollar figure and a father with money to burn, and what's she taking to college this fall? Her spiked shoes and her 'lucky sweatshirt'! 'But why should I go to New York?' she asked me. 'When I can get everything I need right here?' " Mrs. Catlett flicked an ash off her sleeve with a brilliant red nail. She invariably wore long-sleeved blouses with high ruffled necks and sometimes a four-strand pearl choker. "Foxull! One bar; one movie; one clothing store—ladies' wear on the right, men's on the left!"

"Oh, Viv, she's only sixteen!"

"And never been kissed." Mrs. Catlett jumped up. "Gotta go."

From the lawn, Jack and Chris watched her walk away. She did not slump as many tall women did but had an almost contemptuous elegance of carriage.

Christine flopped down in a split, hands on hips, and began bending and twisting her torso.

"They say it's a crime what she spends on clothes."

"Mother says it's a crime people don't visit the sick the way she does instead of sitting around gossiping!"

Jack angrily jogged away to practice his jumps. Once his mother had sent him for Mrs. Catlett. When she finally appeared in her door, he knew she had been drinking, and his mother never sent for her again without telephoning first. She had run over someone in her big convertible and had her license revoked, which was why she walked everywhere. Jack liked her because she was kind to his mother, but sometimes she roused vague and upsetting sensations.

"Won't this kid be a knockout in the pulpit!" she would say, standing close to Jack, and once she drew a little circle in the hairs on his forearm with her bright fingernail and said, "Just between you and I, Mil, a lot of women are gonna begin to think about their souls when he starts preaching!" She had a rather large mouth with big white teeth, but the canines were too long, and sometimes this gave her smile a cruel, wolfish expression. "He's the spitting image of Bruce our last year at Foxull High, don't you think, Mil?" she said. "Brings back the old days!"

Usually Mrs. Bannister sent them something over for supper when Jack's mother was ill, but Dr. Bannister had taken her with him to a medical convention and they were not expected back till after midnight. At five-thirty Chris came over to fix some sandwiches, having changed from her warm-up suit to a dress, and a few minutes later Jack's father came in. He glanced at Christine's preparations.

"Your mother seems to be dozing," he said. "I'll just get a meal downtown and be back later."

"Well, I like that!" said Christine, her gray-green eyes flashing as she brandished the butcher knife at him.

Jack and Christine never felt any need to talk; often they walked all the way home from school together without exchanging a word, and sometimes they broke the silence with the same thought at the same instant, which always seemed immensely curious and delightful. Chris had forgotten to button the top button of her dress; and when she leaned over the table, stretching out her slim brown arm for the butter knife, Jack caught a sudden glimpse of a startling whiteness, not tan at all. She glanced up, colored faintly, buttoned the dress, and went on slapping thick smears of mayonnaise on the bread. Jack hastily began to search the cabinet for something.

As they were finishing up the sandwiches, it occurred to him that he was seventeen and had never kissed a girl! Even for a minister this did not seem quite right. What would Mrs. Catlett say about *him*, after her amusement at Chris? One had to begin somewhere . . . on somebody. . . . Chris had turned away and was doing something at the sink. Why not now?

In the movies the man usually approached the girl from the rear, spoke her name in a low voice, and she turned and melted into his arms. Jack stood up, scrubbing his lips vigorously with the end of a dish towel and almost knocking over his glass of milk. But suppose his voice came out thin or cracked, as it had so often lately—especially that horrible time he had preached for Pastor Elwood and had intended to open with a deep and reassuring tone, using the words, "The Lord is my light and my salvation; whom shall I fear?"

Jack studied Christine's straight, slim shoulders and wondered if he should simply step up and kiss the place between the top of her dress and the tangled ends of her brown hair, not saying anything at all. . . . No. That might be too startling. He took a step forward, clearing his throat and humming a snatch of the Foxull "Alma Mater" to get control of his voice. Chris glanced sideways, but went on with her business. Jack advanced another step.

"Christine—" The tone came out low and meaningful, just the way it sounded in the movies.

She turned with unexpected swiftness, the empty milk glass in her left hand almost striking his chest. Her eyes were wide. In the movies the man always gazed at the girl's lips for a long moment, until she lowered her eyes and leaned meltingly toward him. Jack looked down. Christine's mouth had a long, thick mustache of milk on the upper lip, very white against her tan face. Her mouth was slightly ajar, and instead of leaning toward him she seemed to stiffen and lean back.

"You sick?" she asked. "Your voice sounds crazy!"

Jack hesitated. In the movies any resistance was met by sweeping the girl into your arms and crushing her to you, but what about the glass? And could you really kiss anyone with that much milk on her mouth? Christine was continuing to gaze at him in puzzled alarm, and now she suddenly ran the tip of her pink tongue slowly and evenly along the line of milk from one corner of her mouth to the other. That eliminated the milk problem—or ninety percent of it. Jack took a deep breath. But then she threw her mouth wide open—so wide he saw a small filling in one of her bottom jaw teeth—stuffed the rest of her sandwich in, and munched thoughtfully, her brown cheeks bulging, her gray-green eyes studying his face.

"You look just like a patient Dad lost last winter," she mumbled, giving her head little backward tosses to keep a scrap of lettuce from falling out. "Pasty complexion . . . coarse tremor . . . What's the matter with you?"

"I was . . . just wondering," Jack blurted, "if . . . you'd fix me one of those too."

"Sure!"

As he watched her, he reflected that Chris was the only girl who never laughed at any of the awkward and foolish things he did. She swallowed noisily, pushed the back of her hand across her lips; and suddenly, watching the slim, intent face and downcast eyes, Jack felt a painful unfamiliar tenderness, protective and possessive at the same time. The starched green dress with little white daisies at the neck and cuffs, the hint of her breasts, the swift, efficient hands—all seemed to imprison a tremulous mystery, like spring imprisoned in a slender bough against a clear, clean sky.

Chris had not even laughed about the coat of arms. Jack had done an essay in high school English on heraldry, and Miss Martin had asked him to repeat it for the entire student body in chapel. At the close he added a description of the family coat of arms which Grandmother Lee had given him—a ceramic plaque with a lion rampant on a field of blue and above this a white banner: "Truth and Fidelity!" All the students seemed to find this very funny; the teachers were all too expressionless, especially Miss Martin. The boys called him "Sir Jack" for some time after, and he later discovered that Grandmother Lee had bought the plaque in a curio shop at Otha City.

Christine sliced the edges off the sandwich, came around the table, and held it out to him smiling.

"There! Is that what you wanted?"

Jack stood up, not smiling, and as he stretched out his hand the tips of his fingers touched the inside of her wrist, and he left them there. He bent down and put his lips to hers, not actually kissing them but simply touching them with his own, for that way seemed to express something he felt—fragile and protective. When he withdrew, the gray-green eyes were larger and seemed much darker. They stared into his for a long moment with no certain expression, and their darkness seemed part of a larger darkness that suddenly enfolded them both, like the predawn darkness of a night in spring—hushed, breathless, without any sound yet latent with the voices of myriads of hidden, nesting birds about to rise and fill the dawn with music.

The sound of his mother's voice dissolved the stillness. Christine looked down at his fingers, still resting on her wrist.

"I'll see what your mother wants," she said. Her voice had a strange uncertainty he had never heard before; and when she put the sandwich down on the cabinet and raised her hand to the little starched white daisies at the neck of her dress, her fingers seemed to tremble.

They never alluded to the incident afterwards and he never kissed her again.

When his mother had eaten a few bites, she pushed the tray aside. Jack wished that Pastor Elwood were still in Foxull. The new minister, Reverend Longworth, called regularly, but somehow the mere presence of Pastor Elwood had an effect on Jack he had never experienced with any other minister.

Jack and Christine sat with his mother, not looking at each other. He took from the bureau the little wooden church he had made as a bank for the family tithe when he was nine. The sides were crooked and the gaudy colors always made it look out of place in his mother's room with its light, lovely wallpaper, spotless ivory trim, and snowy curtains. Throughout their worst difficulties she insisted on setting aside "God's tenth" every month. Jack removed the bottom and counted the bills and the silver into piles. Inside, painted in a wavering, childish hand were the words, "I love you. Jackie."

Once he had asked his mother whether one could be a Christian and still do things that were wrong "after he believes God has forgiven everything."

"None of us is perfect—"

"You are!"

"Oh, Jackie!" A look of pain crossed the lovely, oval face. Finally she said, "None of us is perfect, but when God forgives us he makes us able to pay our old self's debts without whimpering. And when we meet them, we know they are our own deserving." She lifted her head high, in a way she had, and the lovely hands, which had suddenly clenched his arm so hard, relaxed, and the slim shoulders were straight and unyielding.

At a little before eight Jack noticed that his mother's eyes were half-open and glittered strangely, and her forehead felt scorching. When he tried to hold a glass of water to her dry lips, the eyes stared vacantly through him. Chris was pale under her tan, and her bottom lip trembled, though normally she was never upset in a sickroom.

"You'd better get your father," she said shakily.

Just then his mother's labored breathing turned to a hideous, rattling snore. Jack's eyes locked with Christine's.

It was the sound Gramps had made just before—

Jack snatched up his coat as he ran down the hall and out into the damp, rainy night. He had often tried to think what would happen if his mother died, but the actual possibility now had a completely different feeling, a feeling that made the world about him seem to leap into his eyes and ears and mouth and skin as though for the first time all the doors of his senses had been flung wide. Everything had an almost painful vividness—the pearly rings of mist about the lonely street lights, the unexpected wideness of Main Street empty of automobiles except for Doc Walton's at the drugstore, the hollow darkness beyond the railway crossing, even the cracks in the sidewalk under his pounding feet and the particles of mist that hung in the cold air as it swept past his face.

A few shop fronts were still lighted. Jack rapped on the locked door of the drugstore, where Mr. Walton was checking out at the cash register. His lungs ached and his heart pounded, but he seemed to see the whole interior of the drugstore with fantastically detailed awareness— even to the point of imagining he could read the fine print on the myriads of bottles and cartons. He saw Mr. Walton's mild pink face turned toward the door just as he had seen it a thousand times before —yet never really seen it at all!

"It's after eight, Jackie." Mr. Walton opened the door only a few inches. "Is anything the matter?"

No, he had not seen Jack's father. He said the same things he always said, as if this night were not utterly different from all others! Jack suddenly felt a fierce jealousy, an inability to communicate his unspeakably intimate terror to this bland, businesslike little man. He shook his head, whirled, and raced across the street to the filling station.

It leaped at him too—in its entirety, as if he were on all sides of it at once!—the four loafers sitting on the curb, their quiet voices and laughter mingled as they chewed tobacco and spat at the oil spots on the concrete; the poster still taped to the window about the senior play four months ago. As Jack turned away he seemed to have lost touch with time as well as space and seemed to see all the nights in all the seasons the loafers had sat under this shelter and talked.

Inside the movie the manager dozed in a back seat with his head against the wall, while down front three small children's heads were framed in the glare of the screen, and a blare of music reverberated discordantly in the emptiness. At the "Blue Belz" Café, where his father sometimes ate, Ma Belz sat alone with her pudgy forearms on the counter, her eternal cigarette stub in the center of her mouth, toothpick in the corner. Jack's father disliked her prying, busybody ways and Jack knew he could not possibly share any part of this with her.

In the pool hall the chairs alongside the wall were empty. Jack turned away, but the whole room stayed in his vision as if stamped there: the white shirtsleeve of the player thrust out straight and down under the arc of smoky light; the man by the wall rubbing his cue tip with chalk. . . . Jack raced down the alley toward the railway station. Sometimes his father passed the time with the railway agent till the 8:40 had gone through. The only other train was the southbound at 9:09 every morning.

Mr. Denton turned from his desk in the grimy bay window that faced the tracks. He had been talking to Mr. Fred Hummaker, the barber, who was standing by the worn counter with his jaunty little hat cocked over one eye. Mr. Denton pushed back his green eyeshade with the dirty adhesive patch on it while listening to Jack. No, Jack's father had not been in tonight. He and Mr. Hummaker exchanged a glance. Was anything wrong? But again Jack felt that jealous inability to share this awful thing that was happening to his mother.

He stumbled down the platform, gasping, and stood at the crossing trying to think. From the station he could hear Mr. Hummaker's twangy voice and his laugh; he passed a lot of time at the station swapping stories with Mr. Denton and Jack's father. The lights in the drugstore went out, and he saw Mr. Walton's car drive slowly away under the pearly street lamps, leaving Main Street empty. Then he saw two of the loafers amble across the street from the filling station and disappear down the alley opposite. The terror he had been holding back suddenly engulfed him. They were all doing the same things they always did— and his mother would simply die because he could not speak!

The tavern was the only other place still open. It was directly below him, on the same side of the tracks as the station, but his father never went there. The blare of the nickelodeon and a sound of men's voices laughing floated up the embankment. Chuckie, the clean-up boy, opened the side door and threw out a scattering of something from his dust pan, and Jack caught sight of the pay phone on the wall. He would call home and ask Chris if his father had come back. But he had come off without any money—not even a dime! He turned away, the problem of the dime suddenly seeming monstrous, insoluble, and on the other side of the tracks in the hollow he saw the big, shapeless outline of the rooming house where Mrs. Catlett stayed.

He could borrow her phone!

Jack leaped down the embankment, his terror now out of control. He could see Christine and his father as the phone rang, his father kneeling by the silent, motionless form on the bed, his face buried in his hands. His mother's face was a waxy white in its frame of pale gold hair, and with that strange new sharpness of sense Jack saw every detail of the scene down to the tiny blue veins in her eyelids, the individual stitches in the lacework of the snowy curtains, the gleam of the polished floor, even the childish inscription inside the little toy church which they had placed in her exquisite hands, now lifeless and unfeeling.

In the dim light behind the shade of Mrs. Catlett's window he stumbled across the porch, yanked open the rickety screen door, and stood in the dark hall sobbing for breath as he knocked.

"Is that you, Chuckie?" Her voice sounded thick and uneven above the faint strains of her radio. "Christ Almighty, how long does it take to get a drink in this town?"

A key rattled and the door opened part way. In the dimness he saw Mrs. Catlett's golden head and black eyes, and at first her mouth seemed to be missing, but then he realized that she had on no lipstick. She had one bare arm thrust out toward him, and when she swayed slightly her shoulder appeared in the opening with a red satin robe draped about it.

"Mrs. Catlett, I've got to use the phone—"

Jack's eyes went past her, and in the dingy mirror of her dressing table he saw the inside of the room.

And his father.

He was lighting a cigarette, and the cigarette was completely strange because his father had smoked only two cigars a day now for years—

"Dad!" He lunged into the opening of the door, which Mrs. Catlett seemed to be trying to close against him: "Mother's *dying!*"

The words hung in the stillness, for a terrible silence rose up and surrounded the three of them, enclosing the tinny blare of the cracked plastic radio on the night table, and holding suspended in a kind of crystal prison the sound of Jack's labored breathing.

Jack's father was staring at him with an expression of utter disbelief, which Jack at first associated with his remark about his mother. His father's face seemed to say that this simply was not happening. He was staring across the sputtering flame, which burned and burned and seemingly burned forever without noticeably advancing down the match stem.

Jack's eyes wonderingly took in the rest of his father. He was wearing his vest, with the rows of pens and pencils in the pocket, but his shirt was unbuttoned, and his tie hung loose.

Jack turned toward Mrs. Catlett, sure that she would have the explanation. Again he received the impression that something was dreadfully wrong with his own face, that he was something loathsome or incredible suddenly thrust upon them. Mrs. Catlett's red satin robe had slipped from her shoulders to the floor and she kept making little teetering, bending motions as if she wanted to reach for it but was afraid she would fall. She had on nothing but a white slip. Her eyes seemed more intensely black and more enormous than usual, her wide mouth—looking bloodless and strange without lipstick—was pulled down sharply at the corners as though she had tasted something nauseous and bitter. One of the brilliant gold ringlets hung down over her flushed forehead, and as Jack's eyes moved to her neck and down her body, he felt an eerie sensation of looking at a make-believe creature, stuck together of things that did not match. The bright gold head and the hands and feet with their scarlet nails were Mrs. Catlett's but somehow they had got stuck onto the body of an old woman!

The firm, voluptuous young body he had unconsciously assumed to exist under her spectacular clothes was not there; and his eyes wandered in disbelief and revulsion down the deep lines and crevices of her neck, the flabby, pendulous breasts, the cruel, paunchy sag of her abdomen.

He whirled toward his father and his own voice finally broke the silence, ripping it to shreds in a horrid, cracked, womanish screech of pain:

"You're *here*—when Mother could be dead!"

The flaming match fell to the dusty carpet. His father turned away, both hands over his face, and the cigarette too fell from his fingers. His voice was low, almost inaudible, as though something had squeezed all the resonance out of it.

"Son . . . you don't understand—"

"I don't *want* to understand!" Jack screamed, snatching up his father's coat from the back of a chair and hurling it at him so that it struck his forearms and fell to the floor. "Well, are you just going to *stay* here?"

His father stooped and picked up the coat, not dusting it off but holding it to his chest as though in a stupor.

"Son, your mother seemed much better—"

But Jack leaned forward, as though his father were deaf, and screeched:

"*Are* you just going to *stay* here?"

As his father pushed open the door leading to the rear, Jack saw the litter of cold food on the kitchen table, and the two plates and two coffee cups. And with that same timeless and spaceless clairvoyance he had possessed before, he seemed to see his father stumbling down the back steps of the rooming house into the alley, climbing the railway embankment, circling the end of the depot, and slinking through the jumble of weed-grown lots and back streets toward home . . . as he must have done how many times before?

Jack turned toward the front door, but Mrs. Catlett leaned against it, swaying and simpering.

"Now, listen, Zhakie. Don't you look at Bruce that way. There ain't a finer man in town than Bruce Lee, but he's a *man*, and Mil ain't been a real wife to him for a year now, putting on that sick act and—"

Jack gazed at her, thunderstruck that this fantastic creature could presume—in such circumstances—to take his mother's name on her lips! He started to smash that big, loose-lipped slovenly mouth with his fist, but even in the act of clenching his hands he realized that a blow in the mouth would not hurt Mrs. Catlett *permanently*. He suddenly understood everything about Mrs. Catlett—her clothes, her sandals, her high-necked blouses, her strut, her smile, the reason she had drawn that little circle in the hairs on his forearm that day.

He deliberately ran his eyes over her from head to foot, then averted his gaze with unconcealed revulsion and said:

"You're not worthy to speak my mother's name! How could my father bring himself to *touch* you!" The words felt like a steel blade in his hands now, and he drove them into her all the way, speaking the last words in a tone quite mild and matter of fact. Something told him this would enormously lengthen the blade and deepen the wound: "You're ugly and old."

Nor did he intend to let her see his exultation as she suddenly stopped swaying, as if turned into stone. He saw the flushed face sag whitely, the big loose lips tremble for an instant like a hurt child about to blubber, and the huge black eyes turn into naked pools of searing anguish all the way down to their depths.

But his pleasure had no time to form.

He scarcely tasted it.

For the anguish vanished almost in the act of appearing, so swiftly that what followed seemed almost to come before.

First came the sobering.

For his brutality sobered her completely, and he was never able afterwards to persuade himself that it was all simply a product of her drunkenness. She stood stock still. Her upper lip writhed up and back from the long wolfish teeth; the black eyes bulged from their sockets; the wide shoulders hunched. For an interminable moment she stared at him without speaking, and the tinny music of the radio sprinkled across the faint haze of cigarette smoke in the dim light of the bed lamp. A nameless dread began to make Jack tremble. He wanted to

flee, but the black eyes held a loathsome magnetism that recalled something he had read once about a bird hypnotized by a poisonous reptile.

Mrs. Catlett took three steps forward—slow, straight, firm. Her long
bare white arm slowly snaked up into the air as if she were waving to
someone, and for one wild instant Jack imagined he heard someone
else's voice—a man's—as the grinning lips wrinkled down and the eyes
narrowed into two brimming black slots of evil. The voice came in a
guttural hiss, terrifyingly intense, as if the words were being ground
out between coarse flat stones. She spat them at him, literally, and a
tiny fleck of saliva skewed from her writhing lips, and the words struck
him along with the smell of liquor as she thrust herself at him.

"Damn you, Viv Catlett's not *that* hard to look at!"

Her voice rose to a scream:

"*Look—at—me!*"

Her circling hand finally found the pull cord of the ceiling light,
snapping it apart in one frenzied yank, and the whole room burst upon
Jack in a piercing blaze of brightness, instantaneous and unforgettable,
burned into his consciousness with needles of fire so that he saw it in
his dreams, had it rise before him on the streets, shrank from it even in
the pulpit where it came back complete in every detail with stark,
photographic cruelty: the girdle trampled into a heap beside the bathroom door; the hotel towel tacked across the bottom of the window
where the shade was torn; the dressing table with its forest of jars and
bottles and boxes, its spilled powder and tarnished mirror; the closet
jammed with all the spectacular dresses—each familiar yet unfamiliar in
this shabby room; the coffee cup on the frayed carpet by the bed with
limp brown cigarettes drowned in its dregs; the dingy wallpaper hung
with souvenir plaques of birchwood with vulgar mottoes burned on
them . . .

"No . . ." he said feebly, "I've got to get home—"

The big hands shot out, imprisoning his wrists. Jack twisted his face
away and struggled to get free; but her grip was terrifying, and her
hands were as strong as a man's.

"Look at me!" she shrilled, tugging on his wrists and thrusting herself at him. Her voice shifted to a hiss again, contemptuous and knowing: "Who do you think you're fooling with that preacher act? Ain't
you never seen a woman before? No, *you're* too good! You just preach
about it and then run home and lock yourself in the bathroom, ain't
that what you're doing? Ain'tcha? Ain'tcha? *Ain'tcha?!*"

She jerked his wrists with each repetition, and Jack felt his face burn scarlet and heard the clenched hissing of her laughter, malicious and suggestive.

"*Reverend* Lee! You're no different than anyone else!"

She twisted herself sideways, trying to get into his line of vision as he pulled and jerked wildly.

"Haven't you never wondered how a man as smart as your dad could ever have married someone as stupid as Mil Blalock? When *I* was the one he really wanted—and *still* wants? Huh? *Huh?*" She kept thrusting her face into his, the words on her nauseous breath making him think he would faint. He had never seen a face so contorted with rage and hatred: she was like a madwoman, like someone with a fire inside that flamed out in her brittle gold ringlets as they bounced and shook, blazed in her molten eyes, burned through the iron fingers imprisoning his wrists. And as she spat out more words, their meaning splashed over him like white-hot metal, searing his mind and body, as if puddles of it sank blazing through his throat and chest and stomach.

"Haven't you never wondered why your dad passed up a scholarship and a chance to be somebody? Why he married a Blalock and let himself get trapped in this one-horse town for life?" She wrenched at him with terrifying strength. "It's because Doc Bannister told her she was pregnant!"

"No . . . No!" He gazed into her eyes, certain they would correct what he had heard, but saw only two triumphant and glittering pools of fathomless black malice.

"Yes . . . yes!" she mimicked. "Everybody in Foxull knows all about it. Your little girl friend next door knows all about it—ask her sometime. Ask Mil to show you her wedding pictures. You don't even know where they got married, do you! Old man Blalock marched them down to Cabbagehead Larsen's at two in the morning, and they had a J.P. wedding in the kitchen because Cabbagehead's brother was sleeping off a drunk on the front-room sofa. That's the *only* way a Blalock could ever have married Bruce Lee—got herself two months pregnant and then blabbed to her old man for Bruce to make an honest woman of her. And that shotgun sure made Millie honest! She's been putting on airs ever since."

They lurched and staggered as Jack struggled frantically, beside himself that he could not break free from this hideous old woman. He tossed his head from side to side and heard his own gasping cry, half pain and half hysteria. The tawdry room was suffocating him with its smell of liquor and dusting powder, stale food and smoky air, of vague odors he could not identify. Everywhere he looked it blazed at him: the damp towel hung over the keyhole; the chenille bedspread and its faded peacock dragging the floor; the two pillows at the headboard, rumpled and dented; the woolly puffs of dust that skidded and drifted further under the bed, rolling over the piece of cleansing tissue smeared with Mrs. Catlett's wide red mouth.

But most unbearable of all was the woman herself, with her stringy neck and her wolfish teeth and her bloodless lips grinning like the Greek mask on the sleazy curtains at the movie as her words kept slashing him:

"*Reverend* Lee—claiming people ain't worthy to speak Mil Blalock's name! Well, me and Herman got married in the daylight, and because we wanted to; and it wasn't done by no barefooted justice of the peace in no bathrobe neither! Viv Catlett's still a better woman any day in the week than all your Blalock trash—laying around the house all day pretending to be sick. Blalocks are strong as mules. Mil's old man killed Blackie Detlow just with his bare fists! And he shoulda got life for it, but you know what? He said he couldn't *remember* killing Blackie! That's a Blalock for you. Mil's lost her man, that's all, and thinks she'll get him back with that sympathy pitch!

"What do you expect a grown, red-blooded man to do with a wife that's no wife at all? And seeing his promotion go to somebody as dumb as that Harlowe kid after all these years! Can't you let him forget even for one hour that he's stuck in this one-horse burg? And you having the gall to look at your own dad like he was dirt! Don't you know they never wanted you? You're what kept him from ever being what he wanted to be in this world—and coulda been. You're what jailed him for life in a two-bit job with a woman he never loved in the first place. You're what—"

Suddenly the voice stopped. Jack was standing mute and helpless, eyes closed, face averted and cast down, his arms and body so limp he was scarcely able to stand. Now he felt her bruising hands let go, and in the sudden silence he opened his eyes and saw that she had stooped down and was peering up into his face. And it was then that she gave him the most unforgivable wound of all:

She *pitied* him.

It was written large all over her face—in her staring black eyes, in her penciled black brows, in the way she held her bottom lip in her teeth as if wanting to bite back things she had said. It was in her whole expression—a kind of awe, a dawning of an almost motherly compassion.

"Aw, gee, kid, don't take it so hard . . ."

Jack stood inert for a moment, rubbing his wrists, his eyes on the floor, then turned and walked unsteadily toward the kitchen door. He did not want to look into any other face or to have any other person look into his. He did not seem able to make his feet work properly, and his legs kept giving way, but he blundered through the kitchen and out into the longed-for darkness of the back steps and the rainy night.

VII

Departure

THE AMAZING thing, Jack decided, staring up at the ceiling of the hotel room, was not that he was here at annual conference in 1960 leading a handful of reformers against Dr. Frederick John Worthington's political machine. The amazing thing was that he had ever returned to the ministry at all. For if he had been certain of anything when he returned to college to begin his sophomore year in the fall of 1950 it was that he would never stand in a pulpit again. And he had stayed certain throughout that winter, and up to the spring of 1951.

And then had come that vespers sermon at Norton's Chapel.

Dr. Burnett had forced him into it, of course. As head of the Department of Religion he had employed Jack occasionally to monitor exams. Jack had caught Dottie Caldwell cheating, but Burnett had refused to take action about it, and they had had a very emotional argument in the professor's office the day after the examination. It seemed that poor old Dr. Caldwell was "one of our most venerated faculty members," and "an old-fashioned man of honor," and so forth.

"If the Department of Religion," Jack said hotly, "has no interest in the moral standards of a church-related college, there surely must be ministers in this conference who do! The ministerial league will certainly be concerned about this, and so will the student council."

Jack knew that Dr. Burnett's liberal ideas kept him under constant surveillance by some of the more conservative members of the conference, but the professor seemed quite undisturbed as he stared at Jack, his long, horse face thoughtful.

"Are you a ministerial student, Jack?"

"Why . . . why, of course, sir!" There was nothing to do but lie.

"Jack . . ." Dr. Burnett hesitated, then seemed to plunge: "I was deeply impressed by your freshman year on this campus. But when you returned to us this fall, you . . . you scarcely seemed to be the same person. I understand that you have not attended a single meeting of the league this year; you spend Sundays in your room studying; you are scarcely civil to your brethren in the league; you never seem to be available to help with campus religious activities; and now you want to have this poor girl expelled for cheating, even though she is only six weeks short of graduation and her father is near retirement and would almost certainly be—be destroyed by such an event! Does that actually seem Christian in your judgment?"

Jack knew he should stop at once, but he could almost hear Dottie's high-pitched giggle, see her pouting red lips as she regaled her male admirers with how she put it over on poor old Burro in Religion 411.

"Dr. Burnett," he said, "Dottie Caldwell is little better than an amateur prostitute, as everybody knows, and—"

Burnett slapped his hand down on a stack of papers.

"I do not intend to hear dormitory gossip in this office! I have already spoken to Dottie. You may air all this before the league and the student council—and the conference—if you insist. Then, of course, the damage will be done." He whirled about in his swivel chair, and took a paper from his file cabinet. "Is it my understanding then that you are still a bona fide ministerial student and wish me to submit your name as usual for your ministerial scholarship?"

"Yes, sir."

The big, thick-veined hand scribbled on the paper, then held it suspended over the out basket on his desk. The normally humorous, kindly eyes were quite expressionless.

"A student deputation is to conduct vespers at Norton's Chapel Sunday evening at five. Dennis Waffler will be in charge. I should like you to bring the message." Waffler was one of the ministerial students who affected a black suit and sepulchral tone. He and his little circle were a constant embarrassment to the rest of the ministerial students on the campus. Jack knew that without the scholarship and the various discounts that accompanied it, he was through.

"I—I'll—do the best I can."

Burnett released the paper and turned away.

As Jack closed the door of Dr. Burnett's office and walked back to the dormitory, he reflected bitterly that he was long overdue for an unmasking. . . . The decision to return to college had been absurd on the face of it—had been made the morning after that terrible scene in Mrs. Catlett's room the preceding September. He had been in no condition to decide anything. . . .

Jack had not gone home that night when he left Mrs. Catlett's. He had walked the railway track for hours, stumbling along in the rain and darkness, falling several times. He had slept in a culvert under the tracks, or at least dozed intermittently, his sodden clothes making him ache all over, and had waked at dawn coughing.

He knew that he must decide what to do, but his mind seemed dazed and fumbling. Last night's intense awareness of sensory impressions was gone now, and gone too, he realized with befuddled surprise, was his terror that his mother might die; he could not even seem to feel shocked at his own unconcern. As the daylight increased, he lay on the damp sand of the culvert and finally came to a decision:

The ministry was out.

Forever.

He could not imagine ever standing in a pulpit again, facing the probing eyes, the knowing smiles, and prattling about virtue and honor and the Christian home and faith in God and whatever else he had once believed in. For these things had all been burned to ashes last night in the hissing fire of that dreadful voice, crushed to pulp in that pair of unbelievably violent hands.

But he could never go back to Foxull, and he had no place to flee to except college, and he could not continue there without the scholarship and the various discounts of a ministerial student. So he would pretend to be continuing in the ministry, and later he could pay back the scholarship and the rest of it somehow, when he had settled on some new occupation. . . .

He tried to work out the details as he stumbled back down the tracks toward home, coughing and rubbing his chest and arms to warm them.

He hid in the edge of the woods overlooking the village till he saw the plume of steam and heard the sound of the eight o'clock whistle at the mill. Glancing at his watch, he realized that it was his high school graduation present from his parents, pulled it off, and tossed it over his shoulder into the woods. His mother rarely woke till nine; his father would not dare ask for the morning off to look for Jack, for he had been on shaky ground at the office since his most recent run-in with young Harlowe. Jack could slip in and out again and be on the 9:09 before his mother woke.

As he scrambled down the hillside through the underbrush, every street and tree and building of the village beneath him brought new pain: the steeple of the church, where he had preached for Pastor Elwood . . . the towers of the high school where he had spoken in chapel about the Lee family's coat of arms . . . the schoolyard where Jess Guthrie had said something about Jack's mother and Jack had tried to kill him with a big rock, or so they all said later . . . Fred Hummaker's barber shop . . . and the depot where Fred and Louie Denton had exchanged glances last night when Jack came seeking his father. They knew where his father was. The whole town knew! Nothing ever stayed secret in Foxull!

Half a block from home, Jack saw Oley Larsen coming toward him with his peculiar, lunging stride. The longish head jerked up and the familiar idiot's grin flashed on, and as they met, Oley tried to seize his arm, the earnest brown eyes under their shock of lank brown hair reflecting some kind of inner excitement. But all Jack could think of was a horrid little scene, like a cartoon in a vulgar magazine: "Cabbagehead Larsen," Foxull's justice of the peace, standing in the kitchen in his bathrobe, peering at his book with nearsighted little eyes, and Oley, the Larsen's idiot child, peeping through the sleazy curtains at Jack's mother and father, while Gramps lounged in the shadows with his shotgun. Jack wrenched himself away so violently that he stumbled backward and fell, and Oley stared down at him in bewilderment, but with the same senseless grin, while Jack scrambled to his feet, incoherent with rage and humiliation.

Somehow that grotesque little encounter remained burned illogically into Jack's memory as his real farewell to Foxull: himself sprawled at the feet of the village idiot, whose persistent, meaningless grin blazed down at him as an ineffaceable symbol of the whole town's amusement and contempt.

The door of his mother's room was closed. His father always shut it while fixing breakfast. Jack turned away quickly to still the overwhelming surge of pain and loneliness. On the table, stuck through with one of his father's yellow pencils, was a note: "Son: Don't do anything foolish. I will talk to you at noon." Jack straightened, keeping his hands behind him. He would not give him the satisfaction of knowing whether it had been read.

The clock on his bureau showed eight thirty-five. He packed swiftly and noiselessly, washed up with cold water because the hot-water pipe made a strumming noise, put on his best suit, and turned to survey the room.

On the mantel before the mirror stood the coat of arms, its crimson letters screaming, "Truth and Fidelity!"

With a hoarse cry, Jack snatched it up in both hands and lifted it high, and as he did so he caught sight of himself in the mirror—a thin, pimply-faced boy in a ready-made suit with sleeves too short and shoulders too tight, the shirt obviously ironed by hand, the cheap necktie badly knotted. Behind the puffy, swollen face with its red-rimmed eyes and scratches, he saw the reflection of the village through the window: two blocks of grubby stores and shops, one filling station, a depot, a grade crossing, a rooming house . . .

Jack smashed the crest into the mirror with all his might, as if in one blow he would destroy the hateful creature before him and the whole village that had spawned it. He reeled back, gasping, letting the fragments of the base fall from his hands, and snatched up his grips.

His mother stood in the door.

Her face was pale; she was clutching the lapels of her white robe, and she was swaying slightly.

"Jackie! What was that terrible noise?" Her eyes traveled wonderingly to the shattered mirror and then to the floor. "What's happened to your face? And your hands? And why are you packed—this isn't Monday, is it?"

The flood tide of the past almost swept him away—the momentum of all the times he had been lonely or frightened and had fled to her arms and had sought solace in the familiar voice that was now rending him to pieces. He opened his mouth to say several contradictory things, but the conflict in him was so violent, the things stuck in his throat. And her questions kept tumbling out.

"Your bed—it hasn't been slept in! And what happened to the crest?" She stared down at the fragment of white banner reading, "Truth an——" Her eyes jumped from his bleeding hands to his face. "Did someone hurt you?"

A wild impulse to laugh twisted Jack's mouth, as his eyes locked with hers, and suddenly he beheld her instant and total comprehension, and the leaping anguish in her face struck him through. He must go!

He twisted sideways, holding one grip before him and one behind, and pushed past her in the narrow doorway. She stumbled backward against the cabinet in the kitchen, and laid one hand on his arm.

"Jackie, you're hurt! Can't I at least—"

He snatched his elbow away and screamed:

"Just don't *touch* me, *please!*"

She jerked as if he had struck her, and then slowly pushed herself up and away from the cabinet till she stood quite still and straight. Her eyes were large and much too bright, but they did not waver as they looked into his. She withdrew her hand, folding it over the other at her waist, with fingers trembling, and she lifted her chin slightly and threw back her shoulders. Her voice was low and firm and it carried a dreadful finality, as though she were summing up the life they had shared up to this instant, then laying it down forever.

"Goodbye, my son."

Jack fled.

He fled because he knew that if he had looked at his mother another instant she would have won him back forever.

Chris found him at the station. The sky was bright, and the air was clear and clean after the rain.

"Jackie! What on earth are you doing here?"

She had on the same print dress with the daisies, but it was rumpled, and her eyes were bloodshot.

"I'm going to college," he answered, resting one foot on the larger grip and grinding a cinder into the leather. The grips had once belonged to his father.

"But, where were you last night? I stayed with your father till past three this morning. He was half-crazy! Daddy didn't come in till after two; he said if he'd been another thirty minutes, your mother might have died!"

"I understand she's still with us," said Jack mildly.

"*Jackie!*" Christine leaned closer, staring. "Are you drunk? Do you know what you just said?"

"She's a Blalock, ain't she? I guarantee she won't die before her time."

Christine placed her fingertips over her parted lips.

"I'm going for your father this minute!"

"I shouldn't if I were you. I think he and I understand each other —at long last."

"But he thinks you've run away or got killed or something! He said if I found you to tell you to go back to college. He said it a hundred times!"

"But I *am* going back."

"Why today? You promised you'd go with me on Monday and help me register. Your father had the sheriff out looking for you. He even had Mr. Larsen out—"

"Shut up!" Jack shouted. "Shut up!" He raised his clenched fists, trembling. Had she brought up the J.P.'s name deliberately, to see what he might say? But no . . . no . . . she was plainly thunderstruck by his reaction. Jack lowered his arms and suddenly remembered his mother's remarks about making it all up to Gramps. Let them both make it up to Jack! Let them atone to him! Let them pay and pay and— "Listen. You run across to the office and tell him I'm going back to college, and I may go on through if I feel like it. Depends on how things shape up this semester." Let him sweat about that. "But tell him it's going to take a lot more money than he figured. He'll understand. Tell him to send me a hundred dollars right now in cash. I'm a little short." Jack knew that his father would probably have to ask old Harlowe for an advance—which would be splendid—good for his soul. Chris did not budge. "Hurry! My train will be here in ten minutes."

"But aren't you even going to tell him goodbye? And how can you leave your mother at a time like this? She needs you!"

Jack shook her till the tangled brown hair bounced and the gray-green eyes went wide with fear.

"*Tell him what I said!*"

Just as the train was pulling in, she brought the money. Four twenties and two tens—a nice little first installment on their atonement.

Jack stuffed it in his pocket without speaking, picked up his bags, and walked away. He heard her voice behind him:

"Jackie—?"

As he heaved his grips into the end of the coach and stepped up, he lifted his eyes to the faded sign perched on the tar paper shingles of the depot roof:

Foxull.

The flagman waved a gloved hand. The whistle shattered the air. The sign began to slip away. Jack heard running footsteps behind them on the cinders. He squared his shoulders, pushed open the door of the forward coach, and heard the cry again—shriller, more childish, verging on tears:

"Jackie—?"

But he did not look back.

VIII

Shadows on a Glass

Jack systematically avoided Christine at college, where she registered as a freshman at the beginning of his sophomore year, in the fall of 1950. He knew that she did not gossip, but she was a living symbol of Foxull, and he was always tense in her presence. Indeed, he avoided all girls on the campus. That fearful encounter with Mrs. Catlett had stirred all sorts of violent and repugnant emotions in him. Even his most casual contacts with the coeds in his classes and labs now seemed muddied and confused by a tangle of ugly, shameful images and desires. And still more upsetting were the couples he encountered everywhere on the campus—sitting on the lawns, parked in their cars at night.

His mother wrote him almost daily at the beginning. He held her letters upside down so as to avoid accidentally reading any of the words while he shook out the pages for checks or money orders. He did not go home for Christmas, and when two large parcels arrived from Foxull a few days later, he threw them into the incinerator behind the dormitory without opening them. He wrote checks on his father whenever he needed money, confident that Mr. Hardison at the Foxull bank would give his father a chance to cover them if necessary. Nor did he go home for spring holidays, although Christine had made a great to-do about his not going at Christmas time.

He would probably have given the whole thing up had it not been for those long letters from Pastor Elwood that spring, expressing such pride in reports of his progress. Pastor Elwood was no longer in Foxull but he still kept up with Jack.

His hatred of his parents Jack could understand, but he seemed possessed by a free-floating hatred for everyone else as well, especially for the professors whose words had overturned so many of the religious convictions of his childhood.

It was this which made him terrified of attempting to preach again when Dr. Burnett forced him into it that spring in 1951. For suppose he rose to speak, and those volcanic hatreds simply exploded? It was almost as if two selves were fighting for control of him—one loving, one hating; one angry with a righteous anger and wanting to uphold truth and right, the other angry with an animal ferocity and wanting to rend and slay.

He wrote out his sermon in full, then read it over half a dozen times. He went through agonies over what suit to wear, and what tie, and Dirkwell, who had also been his roommate the previous year, was much amused that Jack ended by buying a new suit just for the occasion. He gave a low whistle as Jack took it out of the box on Saturday afternoon. "Say, you and Dr. Forbes must use the same tailor!" Dr. Forbes was an Episcopal rector whose magnetism and wit made him a favorite chapel speaker. "And a black Homburg, too! I wish I had that kind of money to fling around. What did you tell me your dad does for a living?"

"Tricks," said Jack, retying the handsome new tie for the third time. "He does tricks in the middle of Main Street, not to mention the barber shop."

Dirkwell's wide, crooked smile vanished.

Norton's Chapel was only four blocks from the campus. Most of the local congregation were from its youth group, plus some middle-aged housewives and a few men. Several faculty members of the college turned up, and a fair sprinkling of the students—most of them girls. Jack recalled how Mrs. Catlett had always said women would come to hear him preach. The thought of Mrs. Catlett as he sat in the pulpit during the hymn was horribly unsettling, and he tried to fix his mind on the neat little sanctuary with its square, stained glass windows brightened by the rays of the late-afternoon sun.

Jack remembered plucking a thread from the sleeve of his new suit and being suddenly terrified that the tailor might have left a huge tag on it somewhere, or a horrid stain. He recalled Waffler's introducing him in that hollow, oily tone. He remembered Christine sitting on the very front row, dressed in one of those obscenely tight sweaters. She had tried to speak to him on the campus yesterday about Dottie Caldwell, but he had walked on. Dr. Burnett might compel Jack to prove himself a bona fide ministerial student by preaching again, but he could never compel him to save that pouting, posturing little cheat from being expelled. What she really needed was a public flogging! He remembered that Henderson girl, the one with the honey-colored hair, sitting very close to her escort in the shadows under the small balcony, looking pious and doubtless nudging the boy with her thigh.

But most of all he remembered his sudden desperation to throw Dr. Burnett's scholarship back in his face, to be through with this absurd masquerade of pretending to be a student for the ministry, to be done forever with these snobbish, country-club youngsters with their convertibles and their oversexed dress and their fraternities and sororities. They wanted to hear somebody preach?

Very well.

For once in their lives they would hear the truth!

He was already standing, unfolding his manuscript, when the hatred overcame him—or what began as hatred. He saw his own hand suddenly crumple the pages and fling them away.

"This house," he heard his voice ring out, "is the house of God!"

He must have then said something pretty specific to the Henderson girl, for she and her escort moved suddenly apart. He must have said all sorts of gauche, ill-mannered, spectacular things, for he could remember the disbelief and the grudging admiration on the faces of the college students present. During his freshman year, he had once introduced Dr. Forbes at chapel and had sat on the rostrum during the sermon. He was startled now to see that same curious unity grip the congregation in Norton's Chapel, that almost hypnotic oneness, riveting every eye on the speaker's face, stilling every movement.

Now, in the light of more mature judgment, Jack realized that the seeming unity of the congregation that night might have been woven of many strands: the clinical curiosity of Dr. Roberts as a psychologist, the fascination of well-bred college students at seeing someone skating so near the edges of bad taste, the joy of the ministerial league at having one of their number speak out so boldly, the pleasure of the local congregation in at last hearing a student speaker who was neither embarrassed nor inept. The unity must have been quite different, Jack now saw, from the thing Dr. Forbes had achieved with his learning, eloquence, and unerring good taste.

The whole performance must have been a little like that of the minister who was "agin adultery," and Jack still winced when some of his phrases and sentences came back to him. He distinctly remembered finding himself standing at the altar rail at one point, without knowing when he had left the pulpit, shouting: "Is anything I say not true? What does the word of God say? 'Not in rioting and drunkenness, not in chambering and wantonness, not in strife and envying. But put ye on the Lord Jesus Christ, and make no provision for the flesh, to fulfill the lusts thereof!'" Whole paragraphs and sentences occasionally came back, and sometimes mere words and phrases. "Whosoever looketh on a woman to lust after her hath committed adultery with her already in his heart!" "The man of God hates no one; he hates only sin; it gives him no pleasure to lay the cruel, chastening stripes on the quivering white flesh of sin!" "The Savior loves you, and I love you. My love embraces you, enfolds you, and will someday—pray God—win you to the Master."

He remembered glaring at Christine at one point and yelling, "What would you have the man of God say—that we can cheat and steal and lie and lust and no voice from the pulpit dare call it sin?" And Dirkwell, of course, always insisted afterwards that he had spat at them.

It must have been something different, to say the least, and what it actually looked like and sounded like, Jack would never know. He only knew that one thing remained crystal clear and unforgettable:

He was suddenly aware that for the first time in over seven months, for the first time since that encounter with Mrs. Catlett the previous September, he did not feel inept, ashamed, or timid before these sophisticated, beautifully groomed college people. He did not feel that bewildered awe before these terrifyingly learned professors. For suddenly they were no longer in command:

He was in command!

He was shocked to realize that he had been letting them call the tune! He had been trying vainly to live by *their* standards—social, intellectual, cultural. Yet all the while he had possessed in Scripture and in his divine call a standard infinitely superior to their own!

And they recognized this!

They accepted the relationship by the very act of coming to take their place at his feet. For, when he stepped into the pulpit and opened the Bible, he was more than his own individual self.

He was the voice of God.

His wrists seemed to be on fire and he kept rubbing them. Ordinary and mediocre indeed! How had he let himself fall into *their* grip? When it was *he* who had chosen Christ Himself as his master, he who knew truth, he who had *them* in *his* grip!

"The man of God is not ashamed! He is *not* restrained by the hands of evil!"

As the torrent of words swept him on, he could feel himself being carried safely and forever across a line, lifted out of a world of doubt and confusion, of moral complexities and conflicts of value, and swept into a world of crystal clarity, where all things stood out sharp and bold with razor edges and black and white outlines. You were for Christ or against Him; you were good or bad; you were honest or a cheat; you received peace or punishment. And the raging hatred, the uncontrollable anger that exploded in his words and gestures, the volcano inside him that he had dreaded and run from and been ashamed of he now recognized:

It was the wrath of God!

Studying the congregation, he saw that only one face seemed to have an individual expression of its own, apart from the total expression of the group: Christine's. Her eyes were somehow disbelieving, resistant; her hands were knotted in her lap; her face was pale and tense. Why was she refusing to surrender like the rest?

He paused to rest his voice, gasping and exhausted, and took out his handkerchief and swabbed his dripping face.

It was then that he noticed it.

The bond.

The strange fellowship that had sprung up between him and the congregation during his sermon. It was almost as if the harder he struck them, the more they wanted him to strike! For they were not hating him, they—for an instant the wild thought crossed his mind that they *loved* him, but this was so ridiculous he did not consider it further—they . . . they wanted *truth!*

People wanted truth, however hard, however crude or mannerless in expression. They did not want timid and flattering essays addressed to their egos. They hungered for someone who would give them the Word of Life!

He glanced at his watch and was shocked to see he had been speaking for almost forty minutes. Vespers talks were never more than twenty minutes.

"Forgive me," he said, and his voice was coming back a little. "I have not wanted to be harsh or unkind, but it was Christ Himself who said, 'If any man come to me, and *hate* not his father, and mother, yea, and his own life also, he cannot be my disciple.' "

Even before they came forward, even before Dr. Burnett came up, he knew that everything would be worked out—everything!

"Jack, I think perhaps we need to have a fuller understanding," said Burnett, his long face grave and troubled. "I confess I had not quite realized how deep some of these things went with you—I mean, as matters of Christian principle. I certainly cannot agree with everything you said just now, but no man could question your sincerity and dedication."

Waffler stood with one arm about Jack's shoulder, squeezing him as each new person came up and adding little asides: "Thank God for one ministerial student with the courage to call a spade a spade!" and, "You make us proud of our calling!" and, "Thank God we kept you on our prayer list."

Miss Crabtree smilingly brandished her little notebook and informed him she had been so carried out of herself she had forgotten to write down a single grammatical error!

"You made me ashamed of the English Department, you know! I never heard so many dangling participles in my life, but you said exactly what I've said in faculty meetings a dozen times."

People waited in line to shake his hand. True, many filed out after the benediction, but more stayed than had stayed at chapel last week to congratulate Dr. Forbes. Jack was upset to see Christine turn and push her way through the crowd surging down the aisle against her, almost fighting her way out. The coeds in particular shook his hand in a limp, wide-eyed way and said all sorts of absurd things. "I wish the whole faculty had been here," and, "That crack about these all-knowing psychology professors not knowing Christ, was long overdue on a church-school campus!"

How had he ever imagined he hated them, or dreaded their amusement? What difference did it make how he dressed? He knew his role in life now, and how it should be carried out. One of the local matrons, a Mrs. Pennington, informed him that Norton's Chapel would certainly ask for him as their next student pastor. The compliments were wonderful but unnecessary, actually. The flicker and crackle of the words about him added but a pleasant background to the vast warm bonfire in his heart. Of course, there were the expected criticisms—almost all from the college crowd. But Jack now accepted them with smiling unconcern. Slander and persecution seemed almost amusing: The petite blonde who smirked: "It's nice to know you *love* us, Reverend!" And Dr. Roberts of the psychology department, who offered a limp hand and murmured, "Fascinating! Wouldn't have missed it for the world!"

Presently the line before him had dwindled till only one person remained, a girl in a smart black suit, who stood before him, extending a gloved hand. She was wearing a hat—the only student in the congregation who wore one—and a single small rhinestone pin glittered in her lapel. He knew that she was one of the freshmen and he had noticed her about the campus now and then because of her small, chiseled features and her taste in clothes. They were sophisticated and attractive, yet not aggressively sexy like those of most coeds—and Christine.

"I'm Patricia Worthington," she said in a clipped, clear voice that somehow matched her cool, direct eyes and flawless grooming. "As a child of a Methodist parsonage, I can't recall *when* I've heard so many unexpected, colorful, and shocking things from one pulpit in one evening!" The tone was mildly amused, but he knew from her eyes that she too was on his side. "I'm sorry my father couldn't have heard you. He's forever complaining that our young ministers are afraid to let themselves go before a congregation."

"I'm afraid I may have overdone it."

"You did indeed! But I predict that if you can manage to get all that fire under a little better control—and shorten your sentences!— you'll be simply tremendous."

Watching her go, Jack asked Waffler:

"Who was that girl?"

"Why, I thought every ministerial student knew Patricia Worthington. Her father's quite a power in the conference. He turns up once or twice a year to speak in chapel. Don't you remember that fat little fellow last year with all the corny jokes? You know—the one who called Coach Harrigan 'belovèd'?"

But Jack could not recall him.

"By the way," he said, "when is the next meeting of the ministerial league?"

As Jack drew near the campus walking home, he passed the usual couples strolling in the dusk, but now they did not disturb him. Nothing disturbed him now, not even the ordinariness of his name, which he had lately begun signing "J. Winters Lee."

Christine called to him from the steps of the girl's dormitory. Her face and eyes looked different. He wondered if she had been crying. As he had expected, she argued at length about Dottie, but he remained firm.

"Oh, for Heaven's sake!" she burst out, "stop talking in that hollow tone; you sound just like Waffler. And where on earth did you get that awful black hat? It makes you look forty years old!"

"The congregation seemed not to mind my tone," he answered, still thinking she might at least compliment his sermon.

"They don't know the real you. Shouting about how you didn't care what they said in the philosophy department, a Christian always knew right from wrong! You know it's not that simple. You can't humiliate poor old Dr. Caldwell that way."

Philosophy, too! Ministerial students invariably sniped at the faculty in their sermons; Jack had been determined never to do this.

"I can because I must."

"Oh, Jackie, Jackie! What's become of you?"

Calling him "Jackie" as if he were still the boy next door!

"I've finally realized the kind of person God wants me to be. I've at last found myself."

"That's not true! I know you've been hurt, and you sorta drew back from everyone, and got all mixed up. But you've always been a real person—sincere and spontaneous. And honest and sweet. But now it's as if you've put on a big suit of armor against me and everyone." She laid one hand on his arm, smiling. "Be Jackie Lee from Foxull again, please. And stop talking in that crazy voice—we know you!"

Jack snatched his arm away.

"I see nothing funny about my family or my name or my call from God! And you needn't try to drag me back down because I'll never be that again. Never!"

"Jackie!" Her face was pale. "Nobody's laughing at you. Have you lost your sense of humor along with everything else?"

Jack controlled himself with an effort. The girl was utterly destroying the high mood of the evening.

"I'm sorry, Chris. But I do wish you could understand that I'm not putting on some sort of act." He turned his face toward the light from the dormitory lounge. "It's really me, Chris; don't you see it is?"

The gray-green eyes wandered over his face and tie and suit, studied the black Homburg in his hand.

"No. You've gone away. For a while I could still feel you were there— in little things you added as you went along, in expressions that would come over your face. But then this other self just took over. It was awful! Like watching someone die that you—" Her voice suddenly stopped and she averted her eyes. "Or like seeing him killed by someone hard and hateful. Why did you have to keep yelling how much you loved everybody? You looked so full of hatred and pain I could hardly bear to watch. Yelling 'Thus saith the Lord!' in every other breath, and then giving that awful smile that's not *your* smile at all."

"I am naturally distressed if my sermon offended you—"

But she jumped up, turning her face away.

"Oh, please! I can't stand any more!"

She fumbled at the door, sobbing, and disappeared.

As he passed the college chapel on his way to the dormitory, Jack met McElhaney, a classmate with whom he had had many involved discussions in the small hours of the night. They both turned to gaze at the chapel. Its entire front was a towering triangle of glass behind which an illumined statue of Christ in the narthex stood out clear and dazzling against the soaring gloom of the rafters behind. Jack saw them both reflected in one of the big sections—McElhaney short and shapeless in his rumpled suit, a crazy hat crushed over his forehead; Jack trim and flawlessly tailored, the Homburg making him look still taller.

"Well, Parson, you're a great walker. I tried to catch you last night. Who were you running away from?"

"I was not running *away* from anybody. I was running toward somebody."

"Of course, of course! The man of God and his Master! You have your pose; I have mine."

Often McElhaney's sharp thrusts had irritated Jack. Tonight he only found opposition entertaining.

"Tell me, Mac, do you think we ministers just put on the things we do and say like a suit of clothes, without honestly meaning or believing them?"

McElhaney puffed on his pipe, studying their reflections.

"Why single out preachers? What about us atheists? Look at me and this hat and pipe. All a pose! I sing in the choir back home; and I don't really enjoy smoking. But every man has to have some sort of pose; he'd be naked without one. What about professors? And doctors and judges and psychiatrists—are they incapable of self-deception? For the devil of it is, we believe our own poses. We'll even go out and die for them! So, who's in a position to criticize the clergy for hamming it up a little, too?

"Suppose," he went on slowly, "that what a man sincerely imagines to be his own deepest self turned out to be a pose. . . ." He jabbed at the reflections with his pipestem. "I don't mean the outer self that the world sees, the way we see those shadows. I mean the inner self— the man we see when we look inside our own hearts, with all his ideals and fears and dreams. The man we whittle at and work with all our lives, certain that it's our true self we're whittling out. But if so, who's the whittler? How can we be sure we aren't whittling something false?"

Jack pointed to the figure of Christ.

"We pick out a model."

"But why? How can a man be sure of his inmost motives? Who can be certain that he's running toward something because it's clear and clean and good, and not just running away from something else because it's faceless and formless and terrifying?"

"I'll take a clean-cut goal," said Jack. "I have only one life and a limited amount of energy."

"A businesslike decision! For, whatever else may seem uncertain, we can all agree that Christ is good and is worthy of disciples." He studied Jack's reflection. "Reverend Jack W. Lee certainly looks like a disciple. He sounds like a disciple. When he gazes into his own heart in the small hours, alone, he sees a disciple. But what about the gazer, is *he* a disciple, too?" He tamped some fresh tobacco into his pipe. "Life is strange, isn't it? Here we are, encased in shadow selves made up of clothes and faces and bodies that the world sees and imagines to be what we really are. And inside we behold other selves, and wonder if they are only shadows, too. Before us stands the Ideal, clean-cut and dazzling. Yet behind it, and all about us, framing the whole drama in a setting billions of light-years deep," he lit the pipe, flung his arms wide, and the flickering match-flame disappeared at the end of the arc as he gazed up into the night, "darkness."

Mac liked to ham it up a bit at times himself.

Jack glanced up, then down again briefly at the radiant Christ, and finally his eye settled on his own shadow—tall, clean-cut, commanding. Yes, the Homburg definitely gave him dignity. And how delightful that he would never again have to agonize over what hat to wear, or how to speak, or what to be!

"Nonsense!" he said, and strode away toward the dormitory, head high.

IX

Commencement

JACK glanced at the illuminated dial of his watch. Almost two A.M. Two A.M., Wednesday morning, June 8, 1960, with the first business session of annual conference scheduled for ten o'clock. He recited these facts to himself several times as a kind of reassurance that his mind was still functioning normally despite its inability to recall those nineteen hours in New York day before yesterday. Patricia had given him the watch one Christmas. . . . She and Aunt Katherine would probably be staying here at the Middleton with Dr. Worthington. . . .

He knew that he should try to sleep, but instead he lay listening to the sounds of the railway yards near the hotel and remembered how the light from the Christmas tree at the district parsonage had fallen across Patricia's pale gold hair as she sat on the floor and handed him up the little box wrapped in silver paper. She was wearing a simple, severe dress of green wool jersey; her cheeks were slightly flushed; her eyes were an intenser blue than usual; she looked stunningly lovely in her impeccable, understated way. He took the present from her hand and then sat down beside her and kissed her.

He was still certain that he loved her, even now, for the remembrance of her brought that same curious mixture of emotions he had felt the first time they met, in Norton's Chapel in April, 1951. He remembered being pleased then with her smart, tailored suit, and pleased too that she did *not* disturb him physically, the way Christine Bannister had that night, and the way Dottie Caldwell had when he caught her cheating. . . .

He had never before really let himself think through the implications of something so utterly unnatural on the face of it. But now he made himself think, made himself retrace his life up to the instant of that first meeting: He had had a sort of puppy love, he supposed, for Miss Martin, when she taught him English in Foxull. Then he had begun to feel something for Christine Bannister, probably just because she was the girl next door and he could relax with her and she never laughed at him. He had even kissed her that afternoon in the kitchen. . . . But after that encounter with Mrs. Catlett, he had never wanted to see another woman or have one touch him again as long as he lived.

But study and flight and evading Christine and every other girl on the campus and being full to bursting with hatred—none of it had worked. Only Pastor Elwood's occasional letters had kept him in school at all during those trying months, letters studded with familiar sentences that had guided him in the past. "Unless we bear the cross, we cannot wear the crown." Jack did not know what the cross would be then; it would certainly not be the Christian ministry; but somehow the sentences still conveyed their old sense of direction, their old faith and courage. Even though Pastor Elwood was no longer at Foxull, Jack still thought of him as his minister and always would. But nothing had really helped much. His mind and imagination had simply rotted. His dreams—by day or night—had been violent, sadistic, unspeakable. . . . And somewhere in the midst of this welter of absurdity and hatred and pain and lust and flight, he had preached that vespers sermon and had met Patricia and had believed all his problems solved.

For Patricia was someone to talk to, to take to social functions, to be seen with, to display as an irrefutable proof that he was like everyone else. Her father was a minister; he had served one stint as a district superintendent and was said to be slated again in the near future for another six-year term. Jack had met him when Dr. Worthington came up one weekend to take Patricia home. He was a little butterball of a man with China-doll eyes and a round bald head; his suit was slightly rumpled and his shoes a bit dusty, and all in all Jack was rather disappointed in him.

Patricia knew everything about the conference and the church at large, although Jack did not realize at the time how extraordinary some of her insight was for a girl of seventeen. They could talk for hours about these things, whereas he could never think of anything to say to other girls. She was quite beautiful in a cool, remote, severe sort of way with her pale gold hair and delicate features, her flawless taste, and her slim, elegant figure. And, best of all, she always knew the correct thing to do and say and somehow always managed to convey this to Jack. She never actually corrected him, but she smoothed and polished him just the same, and Jack realized that by the end of his senior year she had made him over into something quite different from a timid small-town boy.

Each year at commencement the president presented an award to the student who had contributed most to the religious life of the campus during the school year. Jack was named for the Spurrier Award in 1953, partly because of Patricia's unending store of ideas and suggestions, partly because he had made up for lack of intellectual brilliance by dogged concentration and hard work. He had been planning to give Patricia his fraternity pin the night before commencement, but though he knew she liked him and rarely dated anyone else, he froze with terror that night and could not go through with it. He had been excusing himself from seeking an understanding because he had three years of seminary ahead, and Patricia had another year of college. But on commencement morning he had worked up his nerve again, and was determined to settle things one way or another.

But he did not give her the pin.

Their goodbyes were almost formal, and even though he suspected that she was as miserable and upset as he, the whole thing had gotten so completely out of his control by then that he was scarcely able to make himself face her at all.

Commencement morning, in June 1953, was an experience Jack had rarely let himself think on in the seven years since. For he had known even at the time that he was being inconceivably relentless and vengeful. And he realized now that in 1953 he was still hard and green in the high calling of the ministry and insufferably self-righteous . . . and even still signing his name "J. Winters Lee." He had not then been made compassionate by his own disastrous follies. He had not then caught glimpses of his own parents in the lined faces and troubled voices of parishioners who sat across the desk from him in his study at Wentworth. Parishioners who told him—sometimes without being aware of it—stories of sacrifice and heroism and patient endurance, stories of unrequited love and benefits forgot by children of their own . . . stories that made him sick inside, that made the memories come flooding back despite all he could do.

It all began as he stood before the mirror in the dormitory, trying on his cap and gown.

It was then that he heard his father's laugh.

Jack would have known that grating guffaw anywhere and knew immediately what it meant: Christine! She had brought them down anyway—and after he had made it plain to her beyond all misunderstanding that he would *not* have them at his graduation!

Through a crack in the curtains he had drawn against the brilliant morning sunlight he gazed down on the lawn below and saw his father's shiny blue serge suit—a winter suit in June!—the hideous yellow shoes, the flaming, off-color tie, the vest with the rows of pencils and pens. His mother had her back to his window, and for an instant the partial glimpse of her melted something cold and hard inside him, nearly overwhelmed him, but he steeled himself against his sudden rush of emotion. The same tacky, hick-town dress and hat—with still another artificial flower stuck onto it! Christine was introducing them to someone—to *Patricia!* Patricia, cool, flawlessly groomed, her lime-green suit so impeccably tailored, grimacing at them in pretended pleasure and extending a white-gloved hand!

Christine had waited till today—the very last day he might have given Patricia his pin. He heard her voice:

"I think he's upstairs, although the seniors were due in chapel for a briefing session at nine—"

He did not wait for the rest. He flung the cap and gown on the bed, locked his door from the hall, raced down the back fire escape, and across the lawn to the library.

He stood on the library steps breathing hard, trying to think. The whole campus was a madhouse today—cars and visitors everywhere. They would go next to the chapel— His thoughts were interrupted by Carter Hastings, president of the student body, coming up the steps with an elderly couple—surely not his parents!

"Mother, Dad—this is Jack Lee. He's president of the ministerial league and one of the big men of the campus!"

Jack controlled his amazement as they chatted for a moment. The father looked for all the world like a day-laborer, and a foreigner at that! The mother was rather swarthy, too. Carter did not seem the least embarrassed by their taste in clothes, though he himself was this year's "Best Dressed Man" on the campus. He even seemed to be looking about for more people to present them to! His mother suddenly put her arm about Carter's waist.

"We're so proud we're bursting!" Her voice was quite American. "We've been looking forward to it for four years!"

"Well," said his father, staring through the glass doors at the reading room, "I'll say one thing: they sure got a lot of big books."

Carter only grinned, winked at Jack, and bent down and kissed the streak of white hair at his mother's temple. Then he was presenting them to someone else, and Jack edged away. He caught a taxi passing in the drive, and to his horror the cabbie turned and was taking him right past Christine and his parents. She was introducing them to Dean and Mrs. Harnwell, but none of the group glanced up. His father had one thumb hooked in the armhole of his vest, hat cocked on his head at a ridiculous angle, and was waving his cigar about as if he owned the college. Again that ghastly hee-haw! As the cab made the turn by the science hall, he glanced back and saw his father walking along, slapping some student on the shoulder as he went! His mother was straggling behind, for all the world like a countrywoman come to town. The sight of Christine's picture hat and flowered dress made Jack so furious, he banged his clenched fist into his palm.

He had the cabbie take him to Norton's Chapel, which he had been serving for the past two years as a student pastor, but he knew he could not stay here. Chris would soon realize what had happened, and would doubtless come straight to his church.

He thought he had arrived unseen, but Mrs. Pennington came from next door almost at once and there was nothing to do but open to her when she knocked. She had on her apron, and was in the midst of baking, but she simply had to come and tell him goodbye again. She repeated all the extravagant compliments people had paid him after his farewell sermon Sunday, waving her pudgy hands and leaning back in the easy chair, which was almost too small for her. He was the "most attentive student pastor" they had ever had; he made every person in the church feel important and worth while; the girls in the youth group thought he was "the handsomest thing" and were all "so jealous of Miss Worthington they could just die"; he was not afraid to be around the sick and dying, like so many student pastors, and was as calm at funerals as a man twice his age.

"I told Mrs. Norton on the phone this morning how I simply cried bucketfuls at your farewell sermon. They took her back last night, you know—"

"Back to the hospital?"

"Oh, dear, yes! But of course you wouldn't have heard. She seems healthy enough. . . ." Mrs. Norton, who had built the chapel in memory of her late husband, retired to a hospital bed at frequent intervals in terror that she had "a malignancy."

"I'll simply never forget your first sermon that evening you came out for vespers. The other students were always so timid, you know; but as Mr. Pennington said afterwards, when you stood up to preach you looked exactly like a stick of dynamite just waiting to go off. And then when you threw your notes away the very first thing—oh, dear me! It seems only yesterday, and here it's been over two years. Mr. Pennington was saying this morning how sad it would make him feel to look at the bulletin board and not see 'J. Winters Lee, Minister' any more. We were so in hopes you'd bring your parents out today! The other young ministers have always done it, you know, on commencement day."

Mrs. Pennington finally departed, after standing in the door for an additional ten minutes, and Jack watched her broad back vanish into the kitchen of her house. Her remark about Mrs. Norton had shown him the answer. He would call on Mrs. Norton at eleven, just as the commencement exercises were to begin. It was a flimsy out, but she was almost the sole financial stay of the church, and he might be able to make it believable. In fact, there would be something rather touching in a young minister's missing his graduation to be at the bedside of a sick parishioner. And how could one be sure Mrs. Norton was *not* sick?

Jack had scarcely locked the door again when he heard the taxi. He knew it was Christine, even before he heard the familiar patter of her

light, swift steps coming up the walk. He stood by the door not daring
to breathe, afraid to move for fear the keys in his pocket might jingle.
He could hear her breathing, hard and swift, on the other side of the
door. She knocked, rattled the knob, knocked again. Her voice was low.
His parents must be in the cab.

"Jackie, please don't do this to them. *Please!*"

The seconds dragged away. In another instant Mrs. Pennington was
sure to glance out her kitchen window. From the street he heard the
bell of an ice cream cart . . . the far-off shouts of children . . .

"Oh, that boy! Where on earth—?"

The footsteps retreated; the taxi hummed away into silence; Jack
sagged against the door.

He spent an hour sitting on a bench in a deserted amusement park
which had not yet opened for the summer. At ten-thirty he found a pay
phone and called Miss Pierce, the dean's secretary, to say he had been
detained by an emergency in his church and would not be able to attend
the exercises. Her voice broke in:

"Oh, how perfectly dreadful! Please hold on, we've been trying to
reach you—"

He hung up, pretending not to have heard; and at eleven he called
the hospital and was informed that Mrs. Norton was in room 412. He
had the taxi drop him at the florist's across from the hospital. Mrs.
Pennington normally was in charge of buying flowers for the sick, but
sometimes Jack got them himself and had the bill sent to her.

Miss Townsend, the day supervisor on the fourth floor, was startled
to see him. He explained about Mrs. Norton.

"Oh, you poor dear! For Heaven's sake, run, *run* to your graduation!
I'll call you a taxi. Mrs. Norton's healthy as a pig!" She picked up the
phone on her desk.

Jack hastily explained that this was no ordinary situation, that Mrs.
Norton was threatening to withdraw from the church. This was partly
true; she was always threatening to withdraw.

"Naturally, a person of Mrs. Norton's means can spell the difference
between an ongoing organization and no church at all. I felt I had to
come."

Miss Townsend sighed and replaced the phone.

"We'll never have another student minister like you, Reverend Lee.
Frankly, most of them are so terribly immature one feels silly calling
them 'Reverend.' And half of them moon around with some girl on

their minds; or they're afraid of any patient who's on the critical list. I was telling someone just tonight about that time they brought in that young Rittenhaus girl, remember?—the one with her face practically sheared off by the windshield. That's the only time I ever had *two* R.N.'s get sick on me in one emergency, and if you hadn't happened by just then to take care of the family, I don't know what would have happened. 'The worse they look,' I said, 'the calmer that young man is.'"

When Jack had gone she called after him:

"Switchboard says somebody's been calling for you!"

Christine. Suppose the operator had told her he called about Mrs. Norton? Well, it was past eleven now, so that was settled. But when he turned the corner of the hallway, Christine was waiting for him by Mrs. Norton's door. She was holding the picture hat in her hand with its two long ribbons almost trailing on the floor. She met him in the middle of the corridor.

"I have a taxi waiting downstairs."

Jack controlled his shock and anger.

"It happens that I have a very sick parishioner—"

Just then a nurse passed by, staring, and called out:

"Why, Reverend Lee, you've been holding out on us! She's *gorgeous!*"

Christine did not bother to lower her voice.

"I know all about Mrs. Norton and her malignancy! Aren't you ashamed of yourself, sulking and hiding like a child in a tantrum!"

Jack walked away to the sun porch, but she followed.

"Chistine, I'd have thought that by now you understood my feelings about these people. I cannot understand why you insisted on dragging them down here."

The slim brown hands clenched the brim of the hat.

"Because you haven't shared one minute of yourself with them for the past three years! You haven't been home once for Christmas or Easter or even summer vacations. You've never answered *one* of your mother's letters. You've made a good record, and today you'll get the Spurrier Medal. Your life is full; theirs is empty. Why shouldn't you let them bask in your glory for just one day—one hour?"

Jack suddenly felt shaken. He shrugged.

"Did she have to wear that awful dress?" He was admitting he had seen them, but he could never deceive Chris anyway. "And did you have to introduce them to Patricia in front of the whole dormitory! And him in that suit! Did he tell Pat his story about the bald-headed man?

Her father's quite bald, you know. Who else did you show them off to?" Jack felt his voice break. "And what did everyone *say?*"

"That awful dress," said Christine, swallowing hard and actually trembling, "helps pay for the clothes on your back. Are you even human at all? How can you accept sacrifices like that and then rush out and spend two hundred dollars joining a social fraternity? Do you know anything at all about your parents now? Did you know they've mortgaged the house—after working all their lives to be able to say it was theirs? They sold the car. The only pleasure your mother had left was those rides on Sunday afternoon. They sold her beautiful dining room suite—and for practically nothing! Oh, I want to cry every time I walk through that empty room. Your mother let her piano go, but she can't play it now anyway. But you wouldn't know that; you haven't seen her hands; you don't even let yourself think about what arthritis is doing to her, plus eight hours a day in that mill six days a week!

"Of course you don't want to see her, because then you'd see what you're doing to her! It's not just that your extravagance makes her keep working when she's sick. Dad says that by all the laws of medicine your mother should get well. But he says something is undermining her resistance to illness. Well, I know what it is: it's your hatred and unforgivingness!

"Your father even sold his boxwoods—the whole garden, front and back—to Mr. Harlowe. It took him twenty years to make those gardens. I was actually glad to leave after spring holidays; I couldn't stand looking out my window at those awful gashes in the ground."

"Chris, this is absolute nonsense!" Jack broke in. "They have two paychecks coming in every week. They had over two thousand dollars in savings the day I started my sophomore year!"

"Two thousand four hundred," said Chris, her voice suddenly muted. She did not look at him. "Your father sent it to that . . . that Catlett woman. She said she was going to California to set up a beauty shop. I didn't know what was in the box; she made me stay while she counted it."

Jack had always imagined he would perish of shame if anyone put these things into words in his presence, but the actual event, however terrible, was somehow less terrible than he had expected. Now at least he knew that Christine knew everything. And his mother. His father would have had to explain giving away all their savings. But everything had probably come out into the open when he left for school that morning anyway. Jack could not bring himself to raise his eyes. Finally Christine spoke again.

"But your father doesn't mind that it's taken everything. He's living his life over again in you. You've proved that *he* could have done it, too. He spent a whole hour with Dr. Wyzenski this morning, while your mother was lying down, and they literally had to tear Dr. Wyzenski away. He told me your father has the most original mathematical mind he's ever encountered and that it . . . it was a real tragedy he never got to go on." She paused. "Everyone likes them immensely. Patricia thought your mother was charming. And everyone has been telling them what a terrific job you've done in the ministerial league. Maybe your father does laugh a little louder than some people, but surely he can be forgiven for that today. And for telling a few jokes. I never thought I'd ever hear him tell one again." She put one hand timidly on his arm. "Please come with me, Jackie. Dirkwell is holding your cap and gown at the bleachers. Take the hyacinth to your mother—something she could show the neighbors; it's such a small town." Her voice was husky. "Jackie, isn't it time to forgive? Haven't they paid enough?"

Jack had put the hyacinth down on a table. He was standing by the window, staring at the floor, rubbing his wrists. He could literally feel the conflict of love and hatred, reason and unreason, clashing for control of his mind and will. If Christine had not dragged in his father and Mrs. Catlett, he felt sure love and reason would have won, which would have made him different, and then he and Patricia would never have had all those fearful arguments, and his entire life might have taken a different course. But Christine's words brought everything back as if it had been only last night. He could hear Fred Hummaker's loud laugh at the railway station, see Oley Larsen's idiot's grin, and the sea of smiling faces in the Foxull High School Chapel, and the smiling faces of the congregation in the Foxull Methodist Church. But worst of all, he could feel again that horrible woman yanking at his wrists, her hissing, suggestive laughter withering his soul to its roots. . . . He tried desperately to make himself think the sensible thing, say the sane and obvious thing that any adult in his right mind would have said.

It was no use.

"Nothing they can ever do," he heard himself say in a choked voice, "will be enough."

He picked up the plant and stared back at Christine. The tan face was set, the gray-green eyes held a kind of curiosity and almost a horror.

She slowly pushed back the thick brown hair from her cheek in a way she had, and her voice, which had been tremulous was low and clear:

"Jackie Lee, your mother is a sick woman, but the funny thing is, she says *you're* sick. 'He's in pain, Bruce,' she said just a few minutes ago. 'He's ill and not himself. I'll never forgive myself if we've made him miss his graduation.' But your dad just said, 'Let's go home, Mother. We knew what would happen when we came.'"

The gray-green eyes surveyed him slowly, his face, his handsome tailored suit, even his gleaming black shoes.

"And do you know what I think? I think you *are* sick. But it's pride that's made you so. I used to think you were full of contradictions and that someday you'd find your way through them and come out a real person again. But now I know you never will, because there *aren't* any contradictions. You're pure pride and malice all the way through. You despise your mother and father and . . . and everyone! Even the sick! You're actually happier here in this hospital where people are in pain or dying than you would be at your commencement! You're a complete egomaniac, that's what you are—from that silly black hat all the way down to your shoes. Nobody else could do what you've done today."

Now, lying in bed at the Middleton Hotel remembering it all, forcing himself to live it all over again after seven years of putting it out of mind, Jack did at last what he had wanted to do that morning so long ago:

He wept.

X

White Knight on a Gray Horse

JACK had gone to a doctor about his feet on Tuesday. They did not look quite "like hamburger," as Wes had expressed it when Jack first got back from New York, but they were badly cut and bruised. They had bothered him all day Tuesday, and the pain and swelling waked him at a little after five on Wednesday morning. He soaked them in hot water for a while, then went back to bed, and lay watching the daylight

brighten outside the hotel window and wondering what he could possibly have done in New York. He had obviously done a lot of running,
for his legs were still painfully sore. He must have done some of it in his
sock feet, for his socks were torn to shreds. But why had he saved the
shredded remains? And why hadn't he run with his shoes on?

The frustration and bewilderment of that memory-gap of nineteen
hours was unbearable. . . . Jack tried over and over to summon something out of the blankness that had descended when he stepped off the
curb in front of Belfair Church and had lifted again when the conductor on that train from New York had announced that the next stop was
Middleton. Finally, to distract himself from his own uneasiness and
frustration, he went back to piecing together his past life. That, at any
rate, stood out sharp and clear—particularly that first annual conference
four years ago. . . .

Jack had graduated from seminary in 1956. Patricia would normally
have completed her Master's in Christian Education the previous spring,
but she had taken extra work and received her degree on the same day
Jack received his Bachelor of Divinity. She already had a position in
view as director of Christian Education and part-time secretary to Steadman Loveless at St. John's, in Clifton, which was only twenty miles
from the district parsonage. She would live at home with her father
and Aunt Katherine and commute to work.

Annual conference in 1956 was held at Trinity, where Patricia joined
Jack on Saturday morning. He resisted the recurrent temptation to question her about his first appointment, for he disliked the way some of
the ministers picked up bits of conference gossip from the women. Dr.
Worthington had said little on Friday evening when most of the superintendents released "tentative" information. The round, pink face was
unreadable; the sweet, almost womanish voice said only:

"I'm doing my best for you, belovèd. But I know you understand
these things aren't easy."

Early word was often undependable anyway; no secret dream was
ever fully realized, and no fear irrevocably confirmed, till the bishop
read out the appointments in the final hour of conference Sunday afternoon. But Saturday night Patricia phoned Jack from her father's hotel
suite.

"Darling! Get out your '55 journal and look up Wentworth—in Dad's
district, of course!" And she hung up.

Jack picked up the thick, paper-bound volume for the preceding year, then hesitated. What could he look up except things like salary and statistics? It would seem an act of betrayal to his first congregation to snatch up the yearbook to see how much money they would pay him or how many members they boasted. For he was going to them not as an ambitious career man, but as the shepherd of their souls. Besides, nothing would be final till tomorrow. He laid the book back on the night table without opening it.

Dirkwell hailed him in front of Trinity Sunday afternoon.

"And what's *your* first appointment, big shot?"

"How should I know?"

Dirkwell's bony, freckled face reflected a curious mixture of amusement and surprise . . . and something else.

"Gosh, you're marrying the boss's daughter, aren't you?"

Jack frowned as he and Patricia found seats in the crowded sanctuary. He was getting a little tired of the phrase, "the boss's daughter." As soon as the hymn had been sung, Patricia took out her copy of last year's journal, and as the bishop's sonorous voice from the pulpit rolled through the list of districts, calling out the churches and the ministers appointed to serve them, she jotted down the changes in pencil.

"You know," whispered Jack, "it's amazing to think how God can use an organiza——"

"Shhh!" Patricia was scribbling frantically. "I knew they'd be cut. But not six hundred dollars!"

Jack sighed. Pat's habit of classifying churches by the pastor's salary was something they needed to discuss.

"Here comes our district!" she whispered.

Jack felt a tightness in his chest as the bishop's voice moved down the list. He was nearing the end. . . . Perhaps Pat had been mistaken. . . . How many W's were there?

"Wentworth: Jack W. Lee."

Patricia struck through a name and wrote in his own.

A rustling whisper seemed to move across the vast, crowded sanctuary for a moment, and Jack thought he saw several faces turned toward him. He scarcely heard the other districts. Then they were singing, "God Be with You Till We Meet Again," and on the steps outside people kept grabbing his hand, slapping his shoulder, waving to them as Patricia waited for her father to bring the car around.

"Congratulations!" "Why begin at the bottom?" "You'll handle it, Jack!" "Off to a fast start, eh, pal?"

Dirkwell's face bobbed into sight, his wide mouth forming a silent "Wow!" Dirk had been named to a country circuit somewhere. So had Dan Starr and that Prompton kid who had stood first in Jack's class in seminary. How good an appointment *was* Wentworth? Pat was holding his arm tightly, her small golden head high, her trim shoulders even straighter than usual, her eyes shining.

As her father's car pulled up, Jack started to thank him for his appointment, but Patricia suddenly burst into a stream of chatter, slammed the door, and they pulled away. Jack started toward the parking lot; he had checked out of his hotel that morning; his car was loaded and ready to go. It was certainly going to be nice being in Dr. Worthington's district, especially if he should happen to be near enough to the district parsonage to run over and see Pat at odd times. . . . Jack stopped. He did not even know where Wentworth was!

The crowd was thinning out, as delegates said their goodbyes and drove off. Jack turned back to the steps, feeling ridiculous to be asking where his own church was located.

"Jaaaack! Jaaaack Lee!"

A handsome, black-haired woman was coming down the steps toward him, followed by a man who was carrying a baby and shepherding three small children. Her voice was flat and penetrating. She was smiling broadly, showing beautiful white teeth. She held her gloved hand so high that Jack felt a little silly as he reached up for it.

"May I call you Jaaaack? I'm Emma Schell, and this is Kurt. And the children."

Jack had heard the man give a rather dull talk at a youth camp once, but he had never seen the woman before. She kept holding his hand in a very tight grip, still smiling. Suddenly he noticed that her dark eyes were utterly unsmiling.

"I'm afraid there's been some mistake," Jack began. "There's another Lee in the conference. I'm the one who's going to Wentworth."

"We know! We all know you and Paaaat."

The man finally came forward, shifting the baby to his other arm and shaking Jack's hand briefly. He was tall and heavy, with a balding blond head and pale eyes.

"And where are you folks going, Mrs. Schell?" asked Jack.

"You *really* don't know?" Still the fixed smile, the cold eyes. Jack made one last try at civility.

"I'm so new, I don't even know where Wentworth is!"

"How perfectly fantaaaastic!"

"Emma," the husband said, "it's hot, and the children are tired, and we have a long trip ahead of us."

"And you aaaactually don't know where *we* are?"

"I'm afraid I didn't listen to all the appointments as carefully as I should have—"

"Of course not! But then, you don't *have* to listen like the other ministers, do you? It's nice you and Paaaat will be so near each other. Such a happy chaaaance!"

Schell pulled out a handkerchief and mopped his face.

"Emma, can't you see Jack has never heard of us? What are you accomplishing by all this?"

"Sorry, darling. I simply had to see it to believe it. I think you were right: he's a sweet, dear boy. Well, Jaaaack, please accept our congratulations on your church."

"Thank you. I was sorta surprised myself. But that's Methodism!"

The dawning warmth vanished.

"Whatever it is, Jaaaack, it's *not* Methodism!" She turned away; then glanced back from the bottom step. "Do remember us when you come into your father-in-law's kingdom!"

Schell extended his hand, his face red but his smile of friendship obviously sincere.

"We're at Atwood, Jack. Not everything we might have hoped for, but it's all right." He smiled again and repeated, "It's all right."

Jack found Dirkwell in the empty bookroom at the soft-drink machine. Dirkwell hoisted his bottle in mock salute.

"Dirk, who are Kurt and Emma Schell?"

"Oh, Emma's rather ambitious. I understand she figured Kurt was slated for Wentworth."

"I'm sorry if they were disappointed. Just what kind of church is Wentworth?"

"Don't you even *know*?" Dirkwell looked genuinely astonished. "It's a nice little station; nothing sensational, but a lovely parsonage and a good salary. It's about what a fairly ordinary preacher would expect who had fifteen years' hard work in the conference and a wife and four kids."

"I'm *sorry* they were disappointed!" What was he supposed to say? Then he added, watching Dirkwell: "But we have to have faith that the bishop will send us where we're needed. After all, that's Methodism, isn't it?"

Dirk put his empty bottle in the rack.

"Well, I gotta run. Edwina's—"

Jack stepped in front of him.

"Dirk, you and I were freshman roommates in college. We went through seminary together. We've known each other for seven years. If there's something wrong with my appointment, I'm asking you to tell me what it is."

Dirkwell sank into a chair, obviously unhappy.

"Jack, has it actually not occurred to you to wonder," he said slowly, "how a beginner fresh out of seminary who's never held anything bigger than a couple of student-pastorates could land a church originally slated for a man with fifteen years' service? Weren't you even surprised?" Jack felt his face redden. "Edwina and I sorta expected I'd begin my career on a three-point circuit nine miles from nowhere and minus most of the conveniences you'll be enjoying in your bachelor parsonage. But didn't you even notice where the rest of your old school chums were sent—Dan Starr and Prompton and the others? In all honesty, you're not *that* much better than we are."

"I . . . I don't even know where Wentworth *is*," said Jack lamely. "Pat did say last night I'd be going there, but it didn't seem right to look it up in the yearbook as if the salary and membership were the important things."

Dirk stared at him open-mouthed. Finally he said:

"I used to think Dan Starr was the highest idealist of us all, but you make Dan look like Machiavelli. Not a preacher in Methodism would believe what you just said if he heard it with his own ears." Then he grinned his slow, crooked grin. "But I do!"

"Stop giving me that little-lost-lamb stuff! That's exactly the way Kurt Schell looked at me!"

"Nice guy. This was a blow to his standing in the conference, but he's smart enough to keep smiling. Belovèd dislikes seeing people unhappy. I'm glad Kurt got to meet you."

Things were finally beginning to fit into place.

"So he'll know I'm too green and harmless to have had any part in stealing his church, is that it? I don't really deserve it, but I'm marrying the D.S.'s daughter, is that it?" Jack sprang up.

"Jack, sit down, will you?" Something in the weary finality of his tone made Jack obey. "Now, do you really imagine all this came about just because Pat's father is a district superintendent?"

"You say so!"

"I said nothing of the kind. You met this girl way back there in college, the night you preached the vespers sermon at Norton's Chapel, right? You went through two more years of college with her after that, right? You've been with her for three years in seminary, and last month you finally got engaged, right? And you *still* have no idea who her father is?"

"I know he's a district superintendent. What else is there to know about the man?" Jack recalled the plump little figure, the bald head, and the round open face. Not a mysterious personality by any known standard.

"Jack," Dirk hesitated, then went on, "I know you're in love, but I can't let you flit about in your present state of innocence. Because an awful lot of preachers and their wives are going to be watching your every move and not only expecting, but hoping, to see you make one grand mess of your first church."

"Let's have it," said Jack, wincing.

"I assumed all along, when you began seeing so much of Pat, that *you* were now learning a lot of inside stuff about this conference, and I'm sorry to be the one to tell you this, but that lamb-faced, wide-eyed little man with the sugary voice who's going to be your father-in-law someday—Heaven forbid!—"

"Well, this is a new slant!"

"That friendly little tub of corny jokes and pious phrases named Belovèd is, in actual fact, as brutal, ruthless, and all-powerful a machine boss as ever sat in Tammany Hall. He's not just one more superintendent in the bishop's cabinet. He runs the cabinet and the whole conference and practically tells the bishop what to do." Dirkwell hesitated, apparently realizing he might have gone too far. "Surely you've heard such things. The boys talked about them enough in college and seminary."

Jack realized that they *had* argued about politics and machines, although possibly his relationship to Patricia might have caused some of the boys to go easy on specifics. . . . But those furious, good-humored verbal free-for-alls had been like everything else in college—lots of fun, but not exactly real. It was simply impossible to imagine that the ideas he had bandied about so lightheartedly might actually relate to Patricia and her father and to Jack's own personal integrity.

"Dirk, have you lost your mind? Dr. Worthington is a Christian gentleman, a minister of the Gospel, and one of the kindest and most thoughtful men I've ever known. He's no more a politician than I am."

They were both standing now. Dirk's face was flushed.

"I know. I know. 'A Christian gentleman who gets things done.' Did he also tell you about only wanting to be remembered as 'The Little Man's Friend at Court'? Jack, the man is more than he appears on the surface. *He* runs the whole show, singlehanded! *He is the boss.* Well, I shouldn't say 'singlehanded.' There's always Steadman Loveless."

This was really too much!

"Patricia happens to know Dr. Loveless quite well," Jack said, trying to keep his voice down. "She'll be working at St. John's for the next year or so. She informs me that there's not a harder-working, more effective and more dedicated minister in this whole conference."

"Poor old Steadman. 'Steady the Yes Man.' The ideal number-two man . . . I guess Belovèd actually couldn't handle it all without him."

"Dirk, the bishop appoints the superintendents—and he can remove them. *He's* the only real boss in Methodism!"

"Belovèd stands between the rest of us and the bishop. He's sold the bishop—exactly as he's sold you!—on the notion that he's just a lowly superintendent faithfully tending his own vine and fig tree. The whole cabinet—except William Pierce Whitley—are his hand-picked cronies."

"Why isn't Whitley?"

"Because he's like you."

"Meaning what?"

"Hes a man of such incorruptible integrity he doesn't know what's going on under his own nose."

"Dirk, I've been in Dr. Worthington's home—"

"Jack, when this man first came to power, he could have had himself sent to the biggest post in the conference. Do you know what he did? He dragged his pregnant wife off to a ramshackle country parsonage where she died in childbirth, and all in order to stage a public demonstration that he had no personal ambitions, was just a meek and lowly country parson like everyone else. He drives a modest car, wears his suits till they're shiny, lives the simple life, and has so fixed in people's minds the image of a mild and harmless little fellow just like themselves that it's taken twenty years for some of them to realize the true facts. Only they've realized them too late."

Jack was beginning to feel pity.

"Dirk, how can you repeat stories like that?"

"I . . . I didn't mean to imply that he deliberately let his wife die. I only meant that an ordinary man—minister or not—could never have taken such a gamble with his wife's first pregnancy. He . . . he's just not like the rest of us, Jack. Oh, I know he started as a reformer trying to oust the old Doffingwell machine. But power corrupts men, Jack. He stops at nothing now. He seizes any weapon from an Easter lily to a blackjack. And incidentally, if you actually are going to marry into all this, I think I should warn you that you're going to be in the lion's mouth. He has a file-card mind, you know. . . ."

"Meaning?"

"What I'm trying to say, Jack, is that if you ever stole a penny from Sunday school as a kid, he knows it."

Jack hesitated. The picture of Dr. Worthington pumping Pastor Elwood and other former ministers of Foxull was unsettling. What would they tell him? There was his father and mother . . . and the fact Gramps had killed a man . . . and there was Mrs. Catlett.

"Anything else?" asked Jack.

"Yes." The crooked grin appeared. "I believe you'll go to Wentworth and preach rings around Kurt Schell and be more help to those folk than he could ever have been."

Jack refused to smile.

"May I ask you a personal question?"

"Sure!" Dirkwell's eyes were guileless, unprepared.

"What harm has Dr. Worthington done your father?"

The bony, freckled face set in hard lines. The strong stubby fingers clenched. Finally Dirkwell said:

"Ever since I can remember I've wanted to be a Christian minister —because my father was. I guess I had a bad case of hero-worship. Preacher's kids move a lot, you know; they lack some things other kids can count on—the same house, the same bed, the same pals at school. . . . But I could always count on Dad. And I'll admit that my thoughts toward Dr. Worthington are not as unbiased as they might be. I only found out last year that Dad had . . . had sold out to him, too! And for peanuts! It happened my junior year in high school. I was quarterback on the football team, and Sis was dating a boy in town. Dad was slated to move. I wanted to play on the team my senior year and graduate with my class; Sis wanted to be with Hal. . . . She cried; I begged. We just knew there was *something* Dad could do to get sent back *one* more year." Dirkwell's face was grim. "There was. He went to Belovèd and offered to throw in with the machine if they could work it somehow for him to stay at Westboro till I graduated. He's been their man ever since, and afraid ever since . . . and I've been ashamed ever since I heard it."

For the first time Jack began to feel shaken.

"Your own *father* is part of this?"

"He votes the slate and sometimes runs errands. He did a little hatchet job once when they made him go tell Oscar Bates to retire. Things get pretty tight in the conference some years, and Belovèd's crowd can't maintain all their pals in the churches to which they're accustomed. When that happens, they sometimes force out one of the old-timers by telling him he's not producing and they can't place him and why doesn't he just save face by offering to retire. Batesey and Dad were always close; Batesey was only fifty-nine and was doing more than plenty of men older than he was. But he was always an independent spirit, and Belovèd evidently decided to make an example of him. Once every few years he likes to put the handwriting on the wall. . . ."

Jack tried not to let his mind race ahead.

"What do you mean, 'He votes the slate'?"

Dirk smiled faintly.

"You are sorta green, aren't you? Well, the Scripture says we're to be wise as serpents and harmless as doves. Look, Jack, I can't possibly give you a cram course in conference politics this afternoon. Walk with me while I hunt for Edwina and I'll do what I can."

As they walked, Jack was aware of a sense of total uncertainty about everything—his church, his vocation, his relations with Pat, his entire future. One hour before there had not been a cloud in the sky!

"Do you know how bishops are elected?" asked Dirkwell.

"I had it all once in school," said Jack hesitantly.

"Well, at least you remember that Methodism is divided into jurisdictions, or large sections of the country embracing many conferences

—North Central, Southeastern, and so on. Every four years the various conferences in each jurisdiction elect delegates who meet and elect bishops and assign old and new bishops to their areas."

"Is Dr. Worthington hoping to be elected a bishop?"

"Not this year. He's laying the groundwork now by supporting other men. Four years from now, in 1960, he's going to make his bid."

"But how can he control what delegates this conference elects? It's a secret ballot."

"It takes only a simple majority to elect a man a delegate. If we had *exactly* five hundred members in this conference, for example, it would only take two hundred and fifty-one votes. The machine votes for a single slate. They pick seven men and agree that they're going to concentrate all their votes on each of them in an agreed order, and they work like beavers getting other people to vote for them, too. The rest of us scatter our votes over thirty or forty candidates. How can they lose? Take that big windbag, Tip Laughlin, they elected Friday. Nobody would have dreamed of sending *him* to represent them at general and jurisdictional conference. But he's got a lot of pals in the machine and they talked the rest of the gang into it; he got one hundred and thirty-four votes, exactly the number the machine controls. After five or six ballots, he had picked up enough extra votes from the ill-informed and uncommitted to put him over! You can't beat City Hall."

Jack pulled his pad of ballots from his pocket. On the back he had jotted down the voting on each ballot. Laughlin—134, then a steady climb. . . . He began to feel a little sick. Dirkwell was going on to some other case, but he did not hear. His whole life was centered around the church; his entire education was invested in it; but most of all, it claimed his heart, mind, and will. But suppose the church was not the bride of Christ? Suppose the entire conference was a corrupt and fallible human organization dominated by a machine and a boss? What would be left to believe in, to love, to serve, to build one's life around?

He *had* believed that Dirk and Prompton and Dan Starr had begun at the bottom simply because they were lesser men. . . . And how idiotically he had preened himself on starting Patricia off next year in a lovely parsonage, when it was she who was starting him!

"Dirk," he said, "surely this many Christian ministers wouldn't just lie down and let somebody walk over them. There would be an awful battle."

"There have been plenty of battles," said Dirkwell, "and the losers have gradually been silenced or have transferred to other conferences. As of right now, the minority that still speaks out is composed of one person."

"Who?"

"Wes Phillips. He's that shaggy-haired old boy in the black suit who's always smoking a chewed-up cigar."

Jack could not remember having seen any such person.

"Wes always casts the lone dissenting vote," said Dirkwell. "He figures that 'One man with God is a majority,' as he puts it. He's fought Belovèd for a quarter of a century now, never held a decent appointment in all those years, and doesn't seem bothered by the way they're making him waste his entire ministry. This is the first year Belovèd has ever put him in his own district. Maybe he thinks he'll charm him into surrender."

They found Edwina lying on the sofa in the ladies' parlor. The three talked the situation over as they walked to the parking lot and stood for a moment under the trees.

"Isn't it disturbing how professional we've become already?" said Dirkwell. "Here's a poor guy who thought his first appointment was arrived at by divine inspiration and the guidance of the Holy Spirit, and he's so out of place we don't know what to make of him!"

"No," said Edwina. "He's like Dan Starr—just in the wrong conference. I begged Dirk not to come back here."

This second allusion to Dan irritated Jack even more than the first. He had always agreed wholeheartedly with the seminary nickname, "Dan the Starry-eyed."

"Edwina," said Jack, "do you believe I was appointed to Wentworth through some kind of political machine?"

"I think Dirk exaggerates their power; after all, they only control about one hundred and thirty-odd votes."

"My wife takes the position," said Dirkwell, "that Belovèd had you slated for the dirtiest job in the conference, but his only child's tears—"

"It's time to go!" snapped Edwina, her small, pointed face furious. She climbed into their battered station wagon and slammed the door. Dirkwell started to follow.

"Just a minute, Dirk. You started this," said Jack.

"Well, Edwina figures it this way: Belovèd has never met the man who was good enough for Patricia, and since he's tough and practical, that would certainly include a green idealist like you. But he's decided that you're going to be in the family whether he likes it or not; so naturally he wants to help you, and he'd certainly have handled the kickoff of your career more cleverly than this. He'd have started you at the bottom, as if you were on the same basis as everyone else, but Pat wanted you in a nice church and conveniently near. Also, Edwina suspects Pat may not care too much for tumble-down country parsonages just on general principles."

"If I thought for one minute," said Jack, his voice beginning to tremble, "that the pastorate of a Christian church had been taken away from a man who deserved it and given to me through family pull and machine politics . . ."

"What would you do, Jack?" asked Dirkwell.

"I . . . I'd give it back!" They both smiled at this. "I'd tell Dr. Worthington to give the church to Kurt and to send me where I actually belonged—wherever that was!"

Both of them were looking at him with sad, bemused faces. Edwina seemed about to cry.

"But what *are* you going to do, Jack?" asked Dirk.

Jack pulled out the crumpled pad of ballots, and suddenly his fingers clenched into a fist.

"I'm going to find out the truth!"

He strode to his car without looking back or saying goodbye, got in, and slammed the door.

At ten twenty-five that night he turned into the driveway of the district superintendent's parsonage and walked across the moonlit lawn and up the wide steps and pressed the buzzer above the neat metal plate marked:

F. J. WORTHINGTON
MINISTER

XI

The Lion and the Lamb

EVEN at a distance of four years, that scene at the district parsonage still filled Jack with confused and painful feelings. For there were so many things he still did not know. So much that Dr. Worthington had said had been undeniable; the man was always so convinced, even in his own self-deceptions, that one could never be certain where honesty ended and insincerity began . . . if, indeed, it ever began. The turning point, Jack still felt, was the threat. But had he actually been threatened or had he only imagined it? The whole thing had been bungled from the instant Patricia opened the door and ushered him into the library.

He must have expected her to look different, so vivid were the images spawned by Dirkwell's ugly words. But they had all looked perfectly ordinary—more so than usual, in fact. They had been gathered for evening devotions when he rang. Patricia had her hair up in curlers, and her pajamas were encased in a shapeless old housecoat. Aunt Katherine, Dr. Worthington's deceased wife's aunt, who had reared Patricia, was in robe and slippers. Dr. Worthington looked chubbier than usual in shirtsleeves; he remarked that he had hardly expected to see Jack so soon, but then young men in love were impetuous. They were just about to have their evening prayers when Jack rang.

"Come, belovèd!"

Before Jack could reply Dr. Worthington had seized his right hand and Patricia his left, and they were all standing around the coffee table with its open Bible. Jack could not remember what Dr. Worthington said in his prayer; he still remembered Patricia's being barefooted, and the sight of her toes digging into the pile carpet like stubby, nervous fingers. He felt absurdly like a thunderous Elijah trapped in the "friendship circle" at a Youth Fellowship benediction. . . .

How had he begun? He vaguely remembered Aunt Katherine's excusing herself, remembered Patricia sitting on the arm of her father's easy chair.

"It . . . it has come to my attention," Jack began, and in the same instant he realized he had planned no way to broach the subject without endangering Dirkwell—and the Schells. He suddenly felt quite unreal, like an actor without a stage, about to recite some false and melodramatic lines to two prosaic people, but he made himself recite them anyway, stumbling along in awkward, roundabout statements that "some people say . . ." and "I am told . . ." His words must all have been ugly, wild, furious, impelled as much by fear as by moral outrage. The only sentences he could remember clearly afterwards were his last ones:

"I should have preferred to receive my first appointment on the basis of merit. I find it difficult to believe that I would have been sent to Wentworth if this were a conference governed by the laws and principles of the Methodist Church."

Patricia's face was pale—bewildered.

"Darling, don't *you* want a good church, too? None of the other new men can preach the way you can!"

Dr. Worthington smiled.

"My daughter may be a little prejudiced on that subject, belovèd. But I think she has perhaps missed the issue that is troubling you." He then proceeded to reassure Patricia, and to remind her that her young man had been brave and honest enough to come straight to them with it all. "Isn't that what you'd have wanted him to do, my dear?"

He looked like a fat little Buddha in shirtsleeves, his bland pink face cherubic and impassive as always. The neat little hand he had put about Patricia's waist was relaxed and casual.

"Naturally, belovèd, if I were able to confront my accusers face to face, in the American tradition, I could easily reassure them. It is rather difficult to deal with attackers who remain nameless. . . ." A pause; Jack compressed his lips and stared back in silence. "I should be most happy to help your informant understand something of how a Methodist cabinet actually does function, since it is rather obvious that he— or she—has never sat in on a cabinet meeting or seen a Methodist bishop in operation. We superintendents actually cannot 'pass the big churches around among our pals like a bag of plums,' as I believe you phrased it, even if we had any such recreant intentions. The big churches today simply refuse to be subject to ordinary appointive procedures. They demand this man and reject that. I am only sorry that your informant has so little faith in my colleagues as to fear some sort of harm through bringing these matters to our attention directly!" Another pause.

Patricia's eyes were turning that intenser blue and her pert mouth had that familiar stiffening which told Jack she was furious. For now he was clearly doubting her father's truthfulness, suspecting him of petty vengefulness, and believing himself a protector of the innocents.

Dr. Worthington, however, only looked mildly distressed.

"Kurt Schell," he said, and the name struck Jack like a slap in the face, "was considered for the Wentworth post. But if, by chance, you feel that someone like Kurt might have been better fitted, what would you have me do now? The conference has adjourned; the cabinet is dispersed; the bishop has left for Europe. Precisely what is it that you are proposing?"

"I don't know!" Jack burst out, feeling more and more like a bumbling schoolboy, his nerves wracked by the possibility that he might be causing incalculable danger to both Dirk and the Schells. And if Edwina were right, Dr. Worthington was probably enjoying having Patricia see how rash and ugly-minded her young man was. "I just know I won't have people thinking I stole a better man's church because Patricia cried on your shoulder!"

"My dear boy!" The round blue eyes grew rounder still. "Is *that* what concerns you—what people may think? I had hoped we were concerned with how best to promote the cause of Christ and to conduct the business of His church!"

Now Jack was being made to look egocentric as well! But, oddly enough, this *had* been his first concern. The superintendent did not press his advantage.

"Belovèd, I do not for one moment deny that I wield some influence on cabinet decisions, especially since the Wentworth appointment is within the bounds of my own district and properly my own concern." Jack winced at having overlooked something so obvious, but again the older man did not bother to press him. "And I am also able to be of frequent assistance to the other superintendents. However, I can scarcely claim that they are my 'hand-picked cronies' or that I 'run them like a bunch of kindergarteners with the bishop thrown in,' as your informant so felicitously expressed it. William Pierce Whitley, to name only one, is scarcely a kindergarten type, as even the most ill-informed should be well aware. My colleagues do joke about my having a 'file-card mind,' and it is a fact that God has blessed me with a retentive memory for detail. But supplying a brother-superintendent with facts and figures about men and churches is one thing. Attempting to sway his Christian conscience for my own self-interest is quite something else!"

"Jack," Patricia broke in, "how can you *believe* such things?"

"I don't know *what* to believe! That's why I'm here!"

Her father lifted a pudgy hand.

"Children, please! We're all tired, and it's late. But if we're going to be in one family, we must learn to live together and to arrive at understandings. Jack has said many things which are undeniable. Let us see if we can separate the facts from our honest differences of interpretation."

He sat up on the edge of the easy chair and spread his hands, counting off on his fingertips as he spoke:

"Fact number one, several other men had more experience and more need, yet Jack was given the appointment. Fact number two, this has probably given rise to much misunderstanding, particularly on the part of Kurt Schell—and Emma—and of others who may resent a newcomer's good fortune. Fact number three," he paused and put his hand over Patricia's two small ones, which were clenched tight, "it was my considered opinion that our young man would be better served in the long run by something a bit more modest at the start. But my daughter's enthusiasm overrode my judgment. Though she did not actually cry on my shoulder, she did point out some obvious differences among the men under consideration."

Jack sat up, dumbfounded. The man was admitting everything! He sprang to his feet.

"Then I refuse to accept the appointment! I demand that you give Wentworth to Schell and send me to Atwood!"

Too late, he realized that his remembering so inconspicuous an appointment was pinpointing Kurt as one of his sources, but this shadow-boxing over names had become absurd. Dr. Worthington smiled at Patricia.

"You are right, my dear. He is a most remarkable young man. In my thirty years of dealing with ministers, this is the first instance in which one of them has demanded a smaller field of service. But I am afraid we could scarcely grant your request for Atwood. That's rather a special problem. Let me see . . ."

It was then that he did it.

He dragged out his battered briefcase from its place by the mantel, put away the Bible, spread some huge yellow worksheets on the coffee table, and whistled soundlessly as he ran the tip of one plump finger up and down the long columns of churches and ministers, many of them much-erased and scribbled over, apparently in the give-and-take of the cabinet sessions.

"Let's see . . . hmmmm . . . well, it seems there's really nothing in the conference that now remains open for a young man in your bracket except the Otha City Circuit."

Jack felt an almost physical sensation of having been struck: The Otha City Circuit was hardly ten minutes' drive from Foxull.

The superintendent's voice was going on, but Jack did not hear. His mouth felt dry and sticky. Dirkwell had said that the man kept files on people, that he dug up everything. He must have got hold of Frank Longworth, the present pastor, and Pastor Elwood, and all the previous ministers of Foxull . . . and from Patricia he would know anyway that Jack had not been home since his freshman year in college, that he had refused to be seen with his parents at commencement, that he had never gone back throughout his three years of seminary. Pastor Elwood had probably been pumped about Jack's childhood, and about the Blalocks, and how Gramps had killed Blackie Detlow. For an instant Jack even wondered whether his antagonist had found out that he had been keeping up a semblance of contact with Foxull through Christine Bannister's letters since she had returned home to serve as nurse and receptionist in Dr. Bannister's office.

Jack tried to hear the older man's voice, tried to focus his eyes on that pink, lamblike face, but he kept seeing the hideous little main street of Foxull, the sooty walls of Harlowe's Mill, the shadowy bulk of the rooming house, and Mrs. Catlett's blazing eyes and wolfish grin as her words splattered over him again. . . . He rubbed his wrists nervously, saw that Patricia was staring at him with surprise, and stuffed his hands in his coat pockets to conceal their trembling.

And now, four years after that encounter with Dr. Worthington and Patricia, Jack still could not decide whether the man had been threatening him. . . . Though it was still beyond belief that the only charge available in a conference of almost five hundred ministers should have been within a stone's throw of Foxull. The mild, casual voice finally broke through again, and for the first time the bright blue eyes turned on his own:

". . . scarcely appropriate to a young man of your abilities, and I still hope you will be gracious enough to discuss it with me before making any final decision."

That was the turning point.

Till then, Jack had wanted to believe Dirkwell's charges, had enjoyed his role of outraged prophet and stern inquisitor, even with all its nerve-racked bumblings. Now he only knew that he must find some sort of common ground with this man who, either by accident or design, had menaced him at a point so vulnerable he could not even bear to consider the possibility of further combat. Jack swallowed hard.

"I only want to find out the truth, sir."

"I knew that you would." Dr. Worthington was putting away the briefcase: "When a man begins to *want* the facts, I can help him."

And the strangest part of all was that they *had* made the final decision simply on the facts! The superintendent reviewed Schell's qualifications, and then proceeded to list Jack's: a good academic record, an outstanding pulpit man, a young man with many of the social graces Kurt lacked, and above all, a man of integrity and courage—as was amply demonstrated tonight when he came "straight to the jaws of this roaring lion of a superintendent and bearded him in his den!"

The small pink mouth pursed impishly and the China-blue eyes gleamed with merriment. Jack flushed. Even Patricia permitted herself a tight smile and an affectionate glance at the lion's gleaming pink skull.

"Tell me, belovèd," the superintendent said suddenly, "how would you compare yourself in preaching ability to your young friend, Dirkwell?"

First, Schell; now Dirkwell! Jack knew that his dismay was obvious, but the man did not need to ask names: He was simply letting Jack know that he already knew them.

"W-what kind of question is that, sir? No man can form a fair estimate of his own sermons! Naturally we all imagine our own ideas and expressions are superior."

"And how about young Dan Starr? There's a brilliant youngster, though a trifle on the naïve and idealistic side."

Jack protested that he had only heard Dan in practice preaching class in seminary, which was not a fair test. Had he heard Kurt Schell preach? Jack grew exasperated, but his antagonist would not let him off.

"Belovèd, I did not raise these questions. You did. You informed me that your appointment had been based on things other than merit. Now, what *do* you think of Kurt's preaching?"

Jack had only heard Kurt once and was forced to admit that he had found him rather uninspired.

"Now, belovèd, I shall ask you to imagine yourself in my shoes and confronted by a choice of two men for a rather nice appointment. One is middle-aged, has fifteen years' service, a wife and four children, is in debt, is rather lacking in social polish and is a most ordinary preacher. The other is twenty-three, with little experience, no debts, no family obligations, but a man of remarkable eloquence, honesty, and courage. Laying aside all thought of public reaction and of family considerations, if such existed, and with a single eye to the best interests of the church and Kingdom of God, which man would you choose?"

Jack threw up his hands.

"That's an utterly unreal choice, and one I could not possibly judge. Anyway, I'm not in your shoes."

The superintendent stood up, his face pinker than usual.

"It is far from unreal! You have come to my home and repeated accusations before my daughter which have shocked and wounded us both. You have questioned my personal integrity, my professional ethics, and my devotion to the churches under my care. You have impugned the integrity of your bishop and his entire cabinet. You have implied that in my position, you would have acted quite otherwise." He paused, the usually mild blue eyes suddenly hard. "As of this instant, the appointment *is* in your hands. I shall be governed by whatever you decide. I feel that simple justice entitles me to an answer."

They were all standing now. Jack felt completely ridiculous. For to insist on his original position now in the face of plain facts would be childish stubbornness; but to confirm his own appointment over Schell would appear outrageously conceited. The only alternative was an appointment scarcely ten minutes' ride from Foxull.

"Dr. Worthington," he hesitated, swallowed, made himself go on. "If the bishop and cabinet feel that the interests of the church would be better served at Wentworth by me than by Kurt Schell, what can I do but accept the appointment?" The superintendent relaxed immediately, but for Patricia something further was clearly needed. "And I should like to apologize to you both, sir, for listening to the sort of thing I heard today."

The superintendent waved a soft little hand, but Patricia only whirled, and walked swiftly out of the room and up the stairs. Her father waited till he heard the door of her bedroom slam.

"Please! No apologies. I appreciate your frankness and courage in coming tonight." He sighed. "Patricia never knew her mother; I am all she has. She takes this sort of thing very much to heart. Over the years I have tried to acquire a thick skin; it seems to be necessary in the superintendency. But I am glad she persuaded me to do for Wentworth what we all want to do in every appointment."

"What is that, sir?"

"To put first the cause of Christ, regardless of how our actions and motives may be misrepresented."

But Jack's eyes were still on Patricia's door.

"Belovèd, is anything else troubling you?"

The question jarred him out of his misery. How could he have accepted all this at face value, when he had in his pocket a concrete proof of bloc voting and political dictatorship!

Dr. Worthington was appalled, of course. He flung up his hands; he protested that he no longer had the inexhaustible energies of youth; he seemed exasperated yet amused. He looked over Jack's pad of ballots.

"Tip Laughlin! Oh, dear, dear, dear! If ever I was tempted to break ranks . . ." He handed the pad back. It all had to be explained this minute? At midnight? With both of them utterly exhausted? Even though Jack had professed himself satisfied with his own appointment just a minute before? Jack found himself sighing too.

"I couldn't go to my first appointment as a minister of the gospel with this on my conscience, sir. If a man like Laughlin can be elected, what can that be but politics in the church of Jesus Christ?"

Silence. Finally the older man sighed and turned toward the kitchen.

"I don't suppose it would hurt your conscience if I warmed a pot of coffee? Good. This may take a little time. You see, it involves the story of my own beginnings."

XII

A Place at the Table

DR. WORTHINGTON plugged in the coffeepot and turned toward the refrigerator.

"You really should know all about me," he said. "You're going to be one of the family. I don't suppose Patricia has told you very much. And, of course, there are many things one cannot make clear to a young girl who imagines that her father is a good man in a simple, black-and-white, easily explainable fashion. . . ."

He set a bottle of milk on the table.

"I was a foundling, you know."

Jack tried not to show his surprise.

"Doubtless your first memories are of a mother's arms and a father's caresses. My earliest recollections are of sitting alone at a little table in one corner of the dining room, while the people on whose doorstep I had been left all sat about a big table together. It seems clear that they could not have had much affection for me. I have often wondered why they kept me . . . whether, perhaps, I was of their own blood in some way I never learned about. . . ."

Jack made a considerable affair of pouring some milk into his glass. Was he being softened up by a sob story? No. Nobody could expose such painful matters simply for effect.

"I do not know what may have transpired during my infancy. Nobody ever told me, and I never asked. From early childhood I can only recall the dining room, and wishing I had a place at the table with the others, and wishing for something of my own—not a toy, necessarily . . . just a little coat or cap, something bought especially for me. But they only gave me the other children's things. I do not even know who the people were, the parents or the children! Now they are only vague blurs . . . presences within me somewhere, without clear-cut features. . . . The woman had me call her "Auntie." Perhaps I was her sister's or her brother's child. I always wanted her to kiss me goodnight as she did the others. One night I remember thinking she was about to. She stood with an oil lamp in her hand and something about her mouth made me sure she was going to. But then she turned and went out, taking the light with her. . . .

"I ran away. I am not sure at what age, but I could not endure the misery any longer. I never saw Auntie again. Possibly she made no effort to have me located. I have some hazy memories of trudging the streets all day and hiding in alleys and railway yards at night. I remember stealing something to eat from a fruit wagon. I think perhaps I stole milk from people's front steps before they were awake in the morning, for even today when I see bottles of milk on a landing—especially in the wintertime, with a certain slant of light on them—it chills me through. I used to find the warm spots on sidewalks or against people's houses, and I'd curl up there in newspapers and sleep, as I saw the tramps do in the parks.

"One night I slept by the chimney of a Methodist parsonage, and when I woke the next morning the minister was standing there in the early light, looking down at me. I shall never forget that look. He had a stern face, but kindly, and he wore a black suit and black tie, and he was rather elderly. I can see him now, with the red brick steeple of the church rising above his head, and beyond that the gray winter sky. . . . I think his look struck me so forcibly because he was the first person who had ever looked at me with genuine interest and . . . and affection. And he called me by a very odd name I had never heard before. He called me 'belovèd.' The old-timers used to do that, you know . . . and out of respect to a good man long since departed, I have continued the custom, though I am aware it occasions some amusement among the younger members of the conference.

" 'Belovèd,' he said, 'why didn't you knock last night? You look half-frozen; I should have been most happy to give you a bite of supper and a place to sleep. Come—don't be afraid.' And he took me into his house and the housekeeper gave me breakfast. He was a widower and lived alone. And a few days later he drove me down to the Methodist Home, the old orphanage that used to be atop the hill just above the new buildings. You've seen the foundations, I'm sure. . . .

"We arrived about dusk, and I must say the exterior was not calculated to inspire confidence, but then I met 'Doctor Charlie' and Mrs. Boyd, and—"

He had been slicing a cold roast for Jack's sandwich, and now he suddenly turned away.

"I was four or five years old. There's some problem about my exact age still." His voice was uneven; he kept stopping. "Mrs. Boyd was a big, motherly woman. . . . I fear my clothes were not the most presentable, though they had given me a bath that morning. . . . It was the first time any woman had ever taken me in her arms and kissed me. It was quite an experience. . . ." He was pouring his coffee, and Jack busily began putting his sandwich together. The voice had become soft and meditative. "Quite an experience . . . it's part of why I cannot explain to anyone else the way I feel about our Methodist institutions. . . . For me they will never be just promotional campaigns and blueprints and bricks and glass. They are the love of God made visible . . . the Word made flesh in the look of a woman's smile, the strength of her arms, the warmth in her eyes.

"But the most unforgettable experience of all came when they rang the bell for dinner that night. Dr. Boyd introduced me to the group just as 'Freddy' because they had not then decided on any last name for me, and then he took me over to a table where Mrs. Boyd sat at the head with nine boys—the boys and the girls ate at separate tables— and one chair was vacant. 'Freddy,' he said, 'this will be your place. You'll sit here for all your meals. Remember this place.'"

He sat down opposite Jack with his coffee. The blue eyes were far away, the voice wistful.

"That was almost half a century ago, but I have never forgotten. I wanted the meal to go on forever—even though I knew nothing to say, and the rest of the boys kept looking me over and whispering to one another. You see, I finally had a place at the table. I wasn't off in a corner at a separate little table any more. I was like everyone else."

He poured Jack more coffee.

"Many orphaned youngsters grow to hate the institutions which to them mean separation from mother, or father, or from some kind of home and love they have previously enjoyed. But to me that Methodist Home was a warm bed, and a roof over me at night, and a place with everyone else at the table; and the bits and fleeting moments of affection Mrs. Boyd was able to parcel out were quite sufficient to fill *one* small heart, at any rate, to overflowing. I suppose there was never any real question as to what I would do in this world, from the first night I lay down in that clean, warm bed—it was only a cot, actually, but I thought it quite grand—and lay in the darkness staring at the fan light over the big double doors of the dormitory. It was a half-circle of stained glass with a figure of John Wesley on his horse, a Bible under his arm, and inscribed on the rim were the words, 'The World Is My Parish.'

"I came into the conference as a young minister thirty-two years ago next October. And now you will see why this background material is significant. An old gentleman named Horace Ovid Doffingwell was at that time the ruler and kingmaker of the entire conference. He literally told the bishop whom to appoint, and he had been in the saddle so long that he had grown lazy and tyrannical, and he abused his powers extravagantly." He smiled faintly. "Which, of course, is precisely what my detractors now like to charge me with. He was a very small man with hollow cheeks and sunken eyes and a scar for a mouth, and I had seen him about and had heard his name but had no idea who he was. But he brought to the floor of the conference a proposal that the percentage of anticipated funds to be distributed to the Methodist Home should be cut in the interest of a hospital project he was then nursing along. It was only a matter of two-tenths of one percent, but I could not have been more shocked had he proposed that we amend the Lord's Prayer. I was just a youngster; I had never before addressed an annual conference. But I rose to a point of personal privilege; the bishop gave me the floor; and I proceeded to give the old gentleman's proposal—and the old gentleman himself—the most awesome raking-over the conference had witnessed in many a day. The bishop actually had to gavel me down and request that I be more temperate in my language.

"I could never remember afterwards half the things that people told me I had said, but I do recall quite clearly my opening remarks: 'Members of the conference, when I went off to public school the boys used to tease me and yell, "He ain't got no mother or father!" and I would yell back just as loudly, "I have, too!" And the boys would yell, "Who? Who?" and I'd say, *"The Methodist Church* is my mother and father!" And the boys would scream with laughter, but my statement is still true and I make it to you this afternoon!'

"I ran way past the time for adjournment, and the bishop postponed further discussion till the next morning. When I finished, there wasn't a dry eye in the house—including old Doffingwell's. For to me he was not simply attacking an item in our benevolence program. He was attacking old Doc Charlie Boyd, and Mrs. Boyd—both of whom were in their graves. I spent the rest of that afternoon and half that night buttonholing strangers and asking them to be sure to vote against the Doffingwell proposal.

"One or two well-meaning souls attempted to hush me up, to tell me what I had gotten into. A big, slow, bull-necked young preacher from out in the hills, a farm boy with fiery red hair and fists the size of country hams, went about with me and publicly joined himself to my cause. His name was Edgar Evans. We got hold of a conference journal and divided up the names, and marked stars by all those who seemed friendly, or interested.

"Oh, there were many stars in our book that night! Edgar Evans came to my hotel room and we talked till nearly daylight—plotting strategy, and congratulating ourselves on all the brother ministers who had shaken my hand with tears in their eyes and complimented me on my courage and wished me well. We had forty-odd 'certains' and scores of 'probables'. . . ."

He downed the rest of his coffee.

"Can you guess how many votes we got the next day?"

"I've no idea."

"Seven."

Jack stared at him in bewilderment.

"What happened?"

"That's precisely what *I* wanted to know. It took me years to understand all the implications of that defeat—and to accept them and begin to use them. I had lots of time to think: Doffingwell was unashamedly punitive. He sent Edgar Evans and me to the most wretched posts in the conference, year after year. Some churches virtually wreck a man's faith in himself and his cause—petty, uncooperative, spiteful, self-righteous; someday you'll know what I mean. It cracked something fine inside Edgar. He somehow never developed, and his potential skills were never given an opportunity to flower. He finally settled into the rut of a narrow but productive rural ministry, and indeed it may well be that he would never have gone any higher, regardless."

He sat for a long time in silence, brooding.

"But *you* went higher, sir," said Jack.

"I had a stake in the struggle that Edgar never had: the Methodist Home. I had absolutely nothing to lose—not even a wife or family Doffingwell could hold over me as hostages. I came back to annual conference year after year to give battle, and each year I learned a little more. I was determined, in the name of the only folk in this world who had ever shown love and kindness to a little lost boy, to restore the two-tenths of one percent in that budgetary item. I think perhaps I was a little obsessed. But the struggle was remarkably educational.

"My original appeal had been mainly to emotion. I got quite a few tears—and sincere ones!—but almost no votes. I came back next year armed with facts and figures prepared by the Home, and between conferences I begged, borrowed, and stole opportunities to speak on the subject. This time I got intellectual assent—but no votes. But that year a wealthy layman to whom I had sent some pamphlets made a bequest to the Home. A modest building resulted, and I was never the same again. If any thought of surrender had entered my mind previously, it was now banished forever.

"I gradually began to realize that Doffingwell had two major weapons: He controlled the opportunities for advancement through his position in the cabinet, and he had an organization. It was probably not much of an organization, and H.O. must have been an extraordinarily clumsy politician. What politician in his right mind would go on record once a year as being *against* a Methodist orphanage? Or let someone create a public image of him as a heartless Goliath annually striking down a defenseless little David?"

The China-blue eyes sparkled, then clouded.

"I had my own handicaps, however. It took me years to accept the fact that the church I loved so much was composed of men who—on the basis of the record—could admire you and endorse your cause, and then lack the courage to stand up and vote their convictions. That very first defeat should have opened my eyes, but I preferred to believe it was due to my not having given them the facts. Surely any minister of the Gospel who knew the truth would act upon it! Then, when they had all the facts, and still refused to stand up to Doffingwell, I decided it was simply that I lacked organization. But here again I was much too idealistic. I was unwilling to face the fact that good men with positive ideals and a certain gentleness and humility of spirit—things especially marked among ministers—find it very difficult to *fight* anyone, especially by organizing. They are, in a word, both too good to submit their individual consciences to the duller conscience of an organized group, and too good to confess the motives which move their opponents and themselves. They did not like to admit—even to themselves—that they could be controlled by a man like H. O. Doffingwell, and by threats to their pocketbooks or status. No, they informed me, things were not so bad as I imagined, and they only wanted to be left alone to do the work to which God had called them.

"So widespread was this inertia, that I discovered to my amazement that Doffingwell was running the conference by default! His men were actually just a minority—and not a very intelligent minority at that.

"At the end, I came face to face with reality. I realized that if right were ever to triumph and evil be dispossessed, I should have to learn to deal with Christian ministers as they were—not as I had imagined them in childhood. I had no influence to sell, no dazzling prospects of advancement or prestige to dangle before them. But I had found the conference honeycombed with disaffected men—some embittered, some outraged, some frustrated, some vengeful. It was a crooked weapon, at best. It took me many years to accept its existence, and more years to take it up and use it. Somehow, it was not the sword of the Lord that this young Gideon had expected. . . ."

He sank into brooding again, and at last a wry smile twisted the thin pink lips.

"But it won."

The man was openly admitting that his whole regime had been founded on immoral methods! Jack realized in after years that this was the point at which he might have ceased listening and assenting, might have turned back forever. Why had he let himself go further? Was it because of the logic, or because his heart wanted to find these strange new ideas logical? He was never certain. . . . He only knew that he could never go back to Foxull again, could not even consider such a nearness as the Otha City Circuit, that somehow he *must* find a way to believe that accepting the Wentworth appointment was moral and defensible.

The casual fashion in which Dr. Worthington had used the word "politician" was profoundly disturbing: Ministers simply did not mention the word in connection with the church! And now he had gone even further!

"Excuse me, sir, but do you mean to imply that you *accepted* help from men who only wanted revenge on someone?"

"Belovèd, they *offered* me no assistance! They were afraid, like everyone else. I sought *them*. I tracked them down, ferreted them out; I deliberately and consciously wooed them into an organized body."

"But if they only wanted—"

"*Only* is a strong word when applied to the motives of men. They wanted to pay Doffingwell back, true. And I was well aware of this, though at times I suspected that some of them were not. But they also wanted to clean up a corrupt and intolerable situation in the church. And they wanted to rectify the business of the funds for the Orphans' Home. And, I might add, not all the men who eventually supported me were men with personal grievances. I had begun to attract a little following. Tears won a few, and logic, and sheer persistence, and personal friendship, and even right and truth had their handfuls. But the weight that finally tipped the scale was just plain anger and pain. And even this, in a sense, was God's doing, for he has so constructed men that injustice outrages them, and woe to him who violates that moral sense."

Jack pushed back his plate. The calm voice went on.

"It was nine years almost to the day from that maiden speech till the hour of victory came. When it did come, it was almost an anticlimax, for we had begun to realize months in advance that the tide had finally turned. We had a new bishop, and new men in the cabinet, and the old regime was tottering. Several of the new superintendents were our men, and the others had seen the handwriting on the wall. I could have written my own appointment that year; the men wanted me to. I had only to express a preference. . . .

"I had married two years before. Pauline came from one of the most distinguished families of this region. Somehow I never quite got over the wonder of it that she could love a man who was nobody and came from nowhere. I had been on country circuits the whole nine years— at first through Doffingwell's hatred but toward the end by choice. I had discovered that having three or four churches instead of one can have its advantages. When you're off at the far end of the conference rounding up votes or mending fences, the folks at one church simply figure you're hard at work at some other point on the circuit." He gazed at Jack with a sly smile. "But you can no more disappear from a station church unnoticed than a goldfish can from its bowl.

"I was literally drunk with the prospect of victory. We had thought of Doffingwell so long as a dictator and a tyrant that I think we had forgotten he was only a man like ourselves. I meant to take a delightful revenge on Doffingwell, to crush and humiliate him utterly, to have myself sent to his own appointment—Asbury Memorial—as a kind of ritual act, symbolic of total triumph. I confided all this one night to

Pauline, expecting her to share my joy. She did not smile. She did not speak for a very long time. She did not even look at me. Finally she said very quietly:

"'But, Fred, how can I love you if you become what you have always said Mr. Doffingwell is?'"

He paused, his plump jowls hardening.

"I left that evil old man at Asbury Memorial till his retirement, and I took a little church out in the mountains, sixty miles from the nearest hospital over rural roads. Pauline was pregnant. She knew what we were going into, but she insisted that now was no time for vengeance and pride but for humility and gratitude to God. We must not discredit the cause I had championed so long. Had I been able to foresee the future, I should never have consented. Never!" The small neat hands clenched into pudgy fists. "Patricia was born in January. Pauline never even saw her or held her in her arms. . . . The roads out in that area were sometimes impassable during winter storms. We had a fine young doctor, but he simply could not get through in time to save her. A neighbor's wife delivered Patsy. Pauline died only minutes afterwards.

"That was over twenty years ago. I was young; I was in such despair that for seven weeks I did not appear in my pulpit. Pauline's Aunt Katherine came back with me from the funeral and cared for Patricia. They thought that the presence of the baby might pull me out, and, of course, it eventually did. But there were days on end when I did not make a single call, or even go outside the house. I simply sat. It never seemed believable that such hard-won victory could be followed by such utter defeat. That I should be there, marooned in that isolated lumber camp—that's all it was, really—bereaved and utterly crushed, while my enemy dwelt in luxury and peace in the house that should have been mine. And all this of my own consenting!"

Then the anger faded, the hardness was replaced by a mild and slightly weary mystification.

"And from these few small seeds has arisen the legend of a mature, cold-blooded, total politician who knowingly dragged his wife away to her death as a kind of political stunt, as a means of cementing his future, if need be, with blood. . . . And who never took time to remarry because his only real love was conspiracy and power. I marvel that some of the older heads allow these things to circulate. . . . The younger men can only believe them because they never knew Pauline."

Jack kept his eyes on his empty plate, thankful that he had not been able to believe such distortions, and troubled that a man as honest and careful as Dirkwell could have believed them and passed them along.

"I stayed in my lumber-camp pastorate four years. I never intended to concern myself in conference affairs again. Thus all my formative years were in little churches among ordinary folk, and that made me what I am at heart today—a country preacher and not in the least ashamed of it. But new issues arose, and men kept coming to me. I suspect now that some came simply in hopes of drawing me out of my shell.

"No organization can continue without positive goals and healthy motivations. Moral outrage is like the starter on a car—it can make the engine kick over, but something more is needed for a long journey. Hatred can overthrow, but hatred cannot govern—not a church! We gradually purged ourselves of the bitterest elements; many fell away naturally; they simply had no interest in constructive programs.

"We still have hangers-on from those early days; and we still attract men with grievances and men wanting power for power's sake. Doffing-well branded us as malcontents, and the stigma still clings after all these years! Would God we did attract men like William Pierce Whitley, and Wes Phillips. But Whitley's too good and Wes is too bullheaded. Oh, I'm heartily ashamed of some of our most vociferous adherents, and I'm often ashamed—in looking back—of my own blunders and follies, though I can truthfully say I have never had cause to be ashamed of my intentions or my ultimate goals. I have kept His Kingdom first. I am aware of the theory that all power corrupts, but, you see, I could never permit myself to become another Doffingwell, however great the temptations have sometimes been. For Pauline died, you might almost say, rather than see me become that sort of person. To surrender now to the corruptions of power would make her faith in me unverified and her death fruitless.

"I have never sought power or the trappings of power; I have no desire to rule anyone or anything; I only want to be known as the little man's friend at court. For myself, all I ask is what every child of the Heavenly Father has a right to—a place at the table. And I thank God that necessity no longer compels me to seek out and pay court to men of questionable motive."

The "no longer compels me" was disturbing. Obviously, what he had done before he was still morally willing to do again.

"What about this man Laughlin?" Jack asked. "How could you pick such a man to represent us at a general conference?"

The mild blue eyes studied him with new interest. Was he pleased to see these symptoms of hard-headed fact-finding, this evidence that the young man had not come completely unarmed?

"Just in the bosom of the family, I should not have selected Tip Laughlin to represent Methodism at a fish fry. His incompetence is spectacular."

"Then, do you know men who'd have been better delegates?"

"Dozens! Almost anyone!"

"Would Mr. Laughlin have been elected if your—your—organization had not put his name on the ballot?"

"I rather doubt it." Smiling.

"Was your conscience at rest about putting him on?"

"I was appalled."

Jack flung his hands wide in exasperation.

"You knew the man was no good; your conscience was shocked when the group suggested his name; you knew dozens of better men for the job; and you *voted* for him!"

"Alas, I plead guilty."

Jack hesitated. The older man smiled.

"You are wondering how I could do all this and still consider myself a Christian gentleman?"

"Well, how could anyone!"

"What is your alternative?"

"Vote your own conscience! Do whatever God commands! I went to the chapel alone, and asked God to guide me, and I voted for the seven men I felt would best represent the interest of the church." Jack settled back. Let him attack prayer and divine guidance!

"How many of your seven were actually elected?"

"Two." Jack hesitated. "I voted for you, sir, and for William Pierce Whitley."

Dr. Worthington smiled slyly.

"I take it that your vote for me was cast before you had been apprised of my true character. So, then, you accomplished two-sevenths of what you had hoped to for the Kingdom of God."

"You *could* put it that way."

"I *do*. Now, let's look at my own batting average. While you were in prayer, I was also in prayer; and I daresay that more of our group were in earnest prayer than even the better advertised saints about us. For we have a sharper spur in seeking to know God's will for these elections."

"What is that?"

"We know we'll win."

The tone was not mocking but almost grim.

"We are only ordinary men like yourself, and ministers of the Gospel, and we want above all else to do God's will. But when I arose from my devotions, I did not rush to the sanctuary to await the first ballot. I went off to a caucus. There I met with other men of prayer and we put our individual consciences together and considered the names we had felt led to suggest. We are all but clay. We have erred in the past. We shall do so again. A considerable majority of these conscientious men of God felt led to our dear brother, Tip Laughlin. He is big, friendly, and wears a smile at all times. I was not aware that he possessed other qualifications. My brethren felt strongly that he did. I opposed them by every legitimate means, but to no avail.

"With considerable anguish of spirit, I wrote his name on my ballots until he was elected, hoping in my heart of hearts that for once the disorganized saints about us would combine their vast numbers to put over some more acceptable man. As is their custom, they spread their votes among half a dozen men—any one of whom I should have preferred—and Brother Tip won in a walk. We had all agreed, you see, on our sacred honor that we would all give our votes to the names we had selected. Six of those names were eminently pleasing to me." He smiled again. His own name had gone in on the first ballot, to lead the delegation.

"Result: I had the satisfaction of seeing six out of my seven choices elected. So, in this instance, I accomplished six-sevenths of what I had hoped to for the Kingdom of God." He placed the tips of his fingers neatly together and stared at Jack across the little arch. "I rather doubt that God ever finds perfect instruments for the execution of his purposes, but still he works in the world. You have your righteousness. I have results."

He rose and began gathering up the dishes.

"How do you feel about it all now, belovèd?"

Jack sat with his chin in his hands.

"I've never been so confused in my life."

"I rather doubted that I could convey to you over two sandwiches at midnight what it took me nearly ten years to learn and then to be willing to act upon. Wisdom seems to resemble a doctor's prescription: unless we pay an outrageous price for it, the stuff does us no good. For your sake and for Patricia's I wish this were not so. I should deeply regret seeing your splendid talents go to waste in the frustrations of small church work, much as I enjoyed it, and seeing your obvious qualities of courage and leadership dissipated among the disorganized and leaderless of this great conference. Our own goodness is not quite as simple as theirs, nor as easy to explain, but I believe it is a far finer thing. It's more true to all the facts. It's actually more righteous, more courageous, more self-sacrificial. To be better, we are willing that our colleagues should think us worse. Some men can bear any cross but that."

The man had an absolute genius for placing his finger on the most sensitive nerve! Somehow, though everything he said was logical, and practical, and persuasive, Jack could not bring himself to face how he would appear to others if he should surrender. Patricia's pet! Her father's pampered favorite! And how could he ever explain to Dirkwell how it happened that he had rushed off to beard the lion, only to come out a few hours later meekly trotting at the lion's heels!

He glanced up to see Dr. Worthington looking at him.

"Young ministers are so jealous of their reputations! They want perfection; they're confident they'll attain it next week, if not today. And they *must* have their sainthood acknowledged by the press. Perhaps a man has to pass forty before he discovers how shallow and fickle spiritual admiration can be, before he begins wanting permanent accomplishment more than a fleeting reputation."

His smile was wistful.

"And every young man coming in sits as a judgment on the rest of us. For we all want to be liked, and thought well of, no matter how long we have steeled our hearts against the wounds of deliberate slander or honest misunderstanding. We see that young man as ourself again, hard and clean and uncompromising, and we want our early self to approve what our later self has become . . . or at least to give us a hearing."

Jack had risen now.

"Dr. Worthington, lots of your ideas seem logical, but they're so strange to me. I need time to think."

"Then give yourself time! Go to Wentworth. Pastor your flock. Learn your calling. And give yourself an opportunity to decide this thing rationally—not at midnight when you're exhausted."

He placed one small hand inside Jack's elbow.

"Why should the forces of evil always be well organized, but never the forces of good? Don't let bunglers like Tip Laughlin play the role God meant for men like you! This world only moves forward when the man with the ideal is also the man with the power. You can remain an isolated idealist—righteous, but utterly ineffective. Or, you can share the forward movement of God's work."

He walked with Jack toward the door, then stopped.

"I'm terribly tired. You'll forgive me if I go on up. Just pull the door shut."

Jack stood by the stairs for an instant after he had gone, somehow expecting that Patricia might appear at the landing. Then he walked wearily to the door.

"Hi!"

He started and turned. She stepped out of the shadows of the vestibule. She had changed to a flowing white peignoir that fell in delicate, statuesque lines, and had brushed out her hair into a fragile gold frame for her face; she had on make-up now, and a warmth glowed in her eyes and suffused the clean, sculptured planes of her cheeks and throat.

"Pat, you fiend! I thought you were never going to speak to me again!"

The mischievous smile vanished. The impish light in the blue eyes was replaced by a darkness, a kind of pain, answering the sudden pain in his own heart. They clung to each other with an abrupt violence, and their lips met almost with terror. After a moment she nestled her head against him and a faint shudder went through the slim, straight shoulders and she said:

"It *was* awful, wasn't it?"

"I kept wondering what had happened to us tonight, and expecting you to come down every minute. . . ."

She burrowed the top of her small golden head against the line of his jaw in a way she had. "Did Dad explain everything to your highness' complete satisfaction?"

"Well . . . quite a few things, but he's a little bit too practical about the ministry to suit me—especially in his belief that ministers do so many things out of ambition—or fear. But he does have some good ideas."

"Gee, thanks!" She took his fingers in her slim straight ones and touched the knuckles with her lips very lightly. "I thought you had wrecked everything when you came charging in tonight shouting and waving your fists—after I had finally persuaded Dad that you were mature and settled far beyond your years." She pushed herself back and studied his face. "You *are* going to Wentworth, aren't you?"

"I told you both I'd accept the appointment. But on some of these other things I've got to have time to think."

She kissed him on the lips.

"Take all the time you want! But I will *not* have you off somewhere on a country circuit living in a shack. Some of those places don't even have city water, you know. And people give you raw milk to drink. You could catch all sorts of awful diseases. I told Dad you could simply *die* and we'd never even *know* about it."

"What did he say?"

"He said they'd have to print it in the yearbook, and that ministers in the country get fat as pigs, and that you had a very capable mother of your own and didn't need me to hold your hand and buckle your galoshes."

Jack stared across the hall, frowning. There it was again. . . . Dirkwell had said the man would dig into everything. . . .

"What does he know about the kind of mother I might have?"

"Dad knows everything—that relates to the church, I mean. I'm dying to see your mother again, and your father. I only got to speak to them a moment, and that was three years ago, remember?" This had been on the morning of Jack's graduation from college, when Christine Bannister had introduced them to her. Pat had been crushed that Jack did not appear at the exercises to receive the Spurrier Award and they had had quite a wrangle over the whole episode. At his graduation from seminary the previous week, Jack had told her his mother's health prevented their coming. "She was so young, and so pretty! We'll have to have them visit us as soon as we have our own home. After all, one of them might have to come live with us someday, and—"

"They won't live with us anywhere! Ever!"

"Jack!" She pushed herself back again and stared in astonishment. "I believe you *mean* that!"

"I . . . I just don't believe in newlyweds living with their in-laws." He tried to make his arms relax.

"That's not what you said." She refused to let him pull her close again. "Jack, we really *must* have a sensible discussion someday about my visiting your family. You've stayed in our home dozens of times; I've never even seen yours!"

"Must we go into all that tonight? Your father got me supper, you know, while you were off pouting."

"I wasn't off pouting. And I shall *never* forgive you for catching me in that perfectly dreadful wrapper, and with my hair up! It was a much worse blunder than those ghastly things you said to Father, you know, because he could defend himself; all I could do was sit there looking a fright."

He kissed her again.

"Pat, I really must go."

"Go where? Surely you aren't going to descend on your new flock at one o'clock in the morning? Your predecessor won't even be out of the parsonage yet! We'll put you in the guestroom for a few days. Go get your bags; you'll have to stay, if only to fulfill Scripture."

"Scripture?!"

"Doesn't the Bible say the lion and the lamb shall lie down together?"

"It does not," said Jack. "It says, 'The wolf and the lamb shall feed together,' which we have just finished doing. That's the trouble with you Religious Education girls: you go off to seminary with ulterior motives; and as a result, you never learn anything about the Bible."

"I did *not* go to seminary to catch a man! I went to protect my interest in one I had already caught."

"How did you know I was already caught?" asked Jack, remembering how he had meant to give her his fraternity pin on college commencement day and then had lost his nerve when he saw Christine introducing her to his parents on the lawn beneath his dormitory window. He had given her her engagement ring only last week, when they graduated from seminary.

"A girl can tell," said Patricia. "Besides, even in college, you used to look at me in Abnormal Psychology in a way that was just too—too normal. And then when you kept brushing off Celeste Rogers in seminary, I knew I was over the hump."

"I never could stand the gushy type."

"I know," said Patricia, "but you were the only theolog who didn't tell Celeste he had prayed over it and that it was the Lord's will for her to marry him and go to Rhodesia or Nyasaland or, anyway, First Church, Yuma. You were awfully rude to her, you know, especially in History of Dogma. She would never have married someone like Paul

Rogers if you hadn't been so rude about Clement of Alexandria. Now get your bags, and no more arguments!"

"Pat, I—"

She pulled his head down and kissed him, hard.

"No more arguments!"

She pulled the door open, and stood with half of her face and body limned in the warm glow of the lamp in the hall, the other half now bathed in the moon's uncertain silver. Jack surveyed her a moment as she stood with hands behind her, head high. He took the ends of the long ribbons tied under her chin and touched the tip of her nose with them.

"There are arguments," he said, "and arguments."

When he returned with the bags, she was upstairs saying something to her father about the guestroom. Jack closed and locked the front door.

"But," he murmured to himself, "I am *still* undecided."

XIII

The Sand Castle

ON WEDNESDAY afternoon Jack met Patricia on the landing of the stairs leading to the balcony at Belfair Church. They were alone for that fleeting moment.

"Pat, we can't keep on like this—"

But she turned slightly to avoid touching him as he stood almost blocking her path, and went on her way down. Jack was shocked at the strength of his own feelings. He went up to the balcony and sat lost in thought while the business session of the conference droned along with an interminable report from the Board of Missions.

It began to seem incredible that he and Patricia had ever been so close; that she had worn his ring from their last year in seminary, from May 1956, to be exact, through September of 1959. It seemed hard to believe they had ever spent that wonderful vacation together at the beach with her father and Aunt Katherine in the summer of 1957.

Jack sighed, and closed his eyes. He had forced himself to relive so many painful memories in the past few hours that he felt entitled to dwell a few minutes on things happy and beautiful.

Jack and Patricia had received their degrees from seminary in June of 1956. Patricia had begun her work at St. John's as director of Christian Education under Steadman Loveless; Jack had gone to Wentworth, only a few miles distant. That first year had been humbling, but he had been determined to show the entire conference that his appointment was justified and that he needed no help or advice from Pat or her father. And besides, Patricia was having her own troubles adjusting to the inflexible schedules and machine-like efficiency of Dr. Loveless. But, somehow, they both got through that first year, and then came annual conference, 1957, and then Jack's first real vacation—two weeks in August at the Worthington cottage on the shore. By then Jack had made his first year's record and felt secure enough to confess some of his fears and problems.

He remembered lying on the beach in front of the cottage with Patricia that first afternoon, and how she had suddenly leaned over and rubbed his forehead and given it a quick kiss.

"Why all the wrinkles? You're supposed to forget all about Wentworth Methodist Church for two whole weeks, and just be pagan and sinful and self-indulgent. And there's not a telephone within four miles!"

Jack gazed up at her, at the clean, bright planes of her face and throat against the stainless blue sky.

"I can't get the knots out of my stomach," he said. And before he knew it, and despite his resolve that they would not talk shop, he was confessing what a staggering burden the pastorate had proved to be. He told her about taking the telegram to the Armstrongs that their daughter had died in a plane crash, about seeing old Mrs. Cottrell almost daily for four months while she died of cancer, about helping Velma Abernathy have her brother committed when he went to pieces one day on the job; about going with the youth group to deliver baskets to needy families at Christmas, and about Thad Manley's family who lived in that tin shack in zero weather with all those children, all their hands and feet blue, and how their eyes never looked at Jack, but only at the basket of food.

He seemed to be telling only the harrowing parts, and to be leaving out all the joys, the successes, the membership drive and the building fund, and the compliments on his sermons, and the thrill of accomplishment in a job so rich and varied that one might grow exhausted but never bored. Talking seemed to untie some of the knots. Patricia listened, nodding; and he knew that it must be an old story to someone who had grown up in a Methodist parsonage.

"And the worst of it is, you can't *tell* anybody!" Jack concluded. "You have to keep seeming calm and secure, and pretending to have all the answers, and sometimes you go back home at night and want to sit down and cry."

"I wish I could help," she said. "I guess I'm only working with the overprivileged and the overhealthy at St. John's."

"You *can* help," said Jack. He was about to say she could marry him tomorrow, but they had agreed to stop wrangling over a wedding date for the two weeks of this vacation. Patricia had been insisting that they must wait and see how things went with Jack in his first appointment, and meantime she could get enough experience at St. John's "not to feel utterly helpless in case anything happened." So Jack only said: "You can tell me what to do with a Sunday school superintendent who's been in for fourteen years and hasn't welcomed a new idea for the last thirteen and absolutely refuses to resign."

"Aha!" said Patricia, her neat red mouth puckering at the corner, "*now* you're talking my language! The first sound I remember hearing from my bassinet was Father telling Aunt Katherine that he had just figured out a way to get rid of the Sunday school superintendent at Tomkins Chapel."

"Say on!" said Jack, feeling better already.

"You can always kick him upstairs," said Patricia. "I mean, create a prestigious job of some sort that would suit an executive neurosis without damaging the church." She drew a line in the sand for this first possibility. "Or, you can whittle him down by having other people each carry off part of his job, like helping somebody with a load of firewood. That's Dad's analogy, by the way." Another line in the sand. "And, of course, though this is rarely done in church circles, you could shower the poor old fellow with appreciation. The year we were at Sentersville Dad softened up the finance chairman by having the congregation present him with a twenty-five-year necktie." A third line.

Jack stared at the three marks.

"Woman, you've been hiding your charms!" He kissed her bare shoulder, already slightly sunburned. It tasted sandy. "Are you ready for the next question, doctor?"

"I'm ready when you are," said Patricia.

"Okay. I met one of these radio preachers last month and made the mistake of complimenting him on his stuff. I thought it was junk, but the poor guy looked sorta forlorn. And he was one of those sweet little fellows, too."

"Those extra sweet ones," said Patricia, "usually stick the longest knives in your back."

"Well, to make a long story short, he's been calling me once a day ever since, wanting to preach at Wentworth Methodist, and I'm morally certain he plans to take a freewill offering. Let's see you get me out of that one."

Jack lay back, folding his hands under his head.

"My dear, dear boy," said Patricia wonderingly. "You are never going to get elected president—or even make it to First Methodist, for that matter—unless you start learning how to pass the buck. Tell your radio friend that you're simply dying to have him, but you've got a super-intendent who's a boor and a snob and he never lets you do anything creative."

"That wouldn't be true," Jack protested.

"I can guarantee," said Patricia, firmly marking her fourth line, "that if you ever allow one of those mike-jumpers inside your church—and to take an offering!—Dad will skin you alive."

"Okay. Try this one: I've got Young Adults who are so old they attend Sunday school in their wheelchairs. How do I get them to move on up into the Men's or Ladies' Bible Class without hurting their feelings? In fact, how do I get half the adults in the church to move on up to their proper age-bracket?"

"You don't," said Patricia, and drew a small, sad little mark. "Dr. Loveless does, but of course he's at St. John's. Dad always said that you run the big churches by the Discipline and the little ones by sanctified horse sense."

"Speaking of the ladies," said Jack, staring out at the horizon, "Pat, I'm seriously beginning to suspect that some of the members of that Susannah Wesley Class come just to pass along the latest gossip instead of to study the Bible."

"Oh, pish-tosh!" said Patricia. "Sometimes you sound just like Dan Starr. And why didn't he marry someone who could explain his con-gregations to him? Martha is as naïve as he is."

"Maybe soft-boiled eggs attract," said Jack. "You're a little on the hard-boiled side, aren't you?"

"Ten-minute," said Patricia. "At fourteen I knew all the things you sweet young things only realize at thirty-five. I had mastered my disillusionments at seventeen, and at twenty-four I'm a good-humored realist and rarin' to go. Which is why you're going to be such a fabulous success. You've got me."

"Then try this one," said Jack: "Mrs. Richardson and Dr. and Mrs. Stanton and George Strackmar and most of the other patriarchs and matriarchs of Wentworth Methodist—and even Miss Mollie!—are determined to do away with our center pulpit and have a divided chancel. They've seen that new chancel at Christ's Episcopal, and they think we can do the same at Wentworth Methodist. I've always felt that when the minister stands up to preach, he should be square in the center, the focus of all eyes. It's the genius of Protestantism. I've had my say; they've had theirs. I know I can rally at least half the church if I make a fight of it, so, if something doesn't give, there's going to be an explosion. Tell me how I can get them to leave my pulpit right where it is."

"It's like the double-wing in football," Patricia said. "You lose a lot of power when you move the pulpit out of the center, but think what you gain in deception!" She poured a handful of warm sand on the center of his chest, and considered it. "For myself, darling, I think you'd be simply terrific preaching from a chandelier, as I practically confessed that first time I heard you do that vespers sermon at Norton's Chapel. The one where you threatened to lay the chastening stripes on the quivering white flesh of sin, remember? It gave me the most shivery sort of feeling when you said that! But if Mrs. Richardson wants that chancel, too, I think we'd better check this one with Dad."

They found him in the kitchen, sitting at the table in a flowered sports shirt and faded khaki pants, copying rows of figures from a report. He listened in silence, the top of his head gleaming pinker than usual in the glare from the beach.

"Young man," he said at last, the neat little hand not pausing in its task, "this sort of thing comes to every minister sooner or later in some form. You are now faced with the choice of a divided chancel or a divided church."

Back on the beach, Patricia added one more line to her series. Jack studied her mocking blue eyes and the saucy mouth.

"One last question," he said. "Are you really this much smarter than I am, or am I correct in assuming that the hands are the hands of Patsy, but the voice is the voice of Dad?"

Patricia tossed her small golden head.

"Are you impugning my intelligence, young man?"

"The only time I ever did that," said Jack, "was in that Ab Psych final, when you missed Frustie Robert's first question: 'Every genuine religious experience contains some objective factor—true or false.' Surely you knew *that* was true!"

"Why, of course I knew it!" said Patricia grandly. "But I didn't think *Frustie* knew it!"

It was a wonderful, happy, unforgettable two weeks. They fished and sailed and lay in the sun for hours at a time; they browsed in the curio shops; they collected a mountain of driftwood to varnish and make things of—and had to leave almost every stick of it; they took picnic baskets and explored miles of the beach; they ate wonderful sea-food dinners at all the places up and down the shore; they saw summer-stock plays; they haunted the art colony and Jack slipped back and bought a seascape she had taken a fancy to and surprised her with it on their last night.

But mostly they talked. About Wentworth, about St. John's, the district, the conference, about everything related to his work.

"Why haven't you told me that before?" he would say.

"I have, darling," she would answer. "Dozens of times. But you never needed it before."

Aunt Katherine spent her time visiting old friends.

And Dr. Worthington worked.

How hard he worked Jack had never realized before. Patricia had bought her father a new surf-casting rig; it stood in the corner by the kitchen range, never unwrapped, while he labored at his makeshift desk covered with statistical reports and mimeographed forms.

"Dad's idea of the perfect vacation spot," said Patricia, "is any place where he can work eighteen hours a day without being interrupted. He comes here every summer to catch up."

One night they tried to get him to go into the village with them to see a summer-stock play, but he was busy at the kitchen table addressing picture postcards. He was still addressing them when they got back at midnight, and he was already up when Jack got up the next morning.

They did not wake the women, but had breakfast together. Afterwards he asked Jack to take the bundles of cards into the village for him.

"Don't mail them anywhere else. I want to be sure they have the local postmark."

The post office was not yet open when Jack reached the village. The bundles were too thick to go through the narrow slot in the door. He snapped the rubber bands and began sticking the cards through, estimating absently that there must be six or eight hundred cards, all glossy scenes of boating, swimming, lighthouses, lobsters, and prize fish held up by gleeful fishermen. One bundle slipped from his hand and cascaded to the sidewalk. As he gathered them up, he saw that all the cards were to ministers of the conference, all addressed in Dr. Worthington's neat, round script, and all bore only a line or two: "Man, what a spot for vacations! FJW." "The big ones are really biting! FJW." "This is the life! FJW."

Feeling guilty, but unable to restrain his curiosity and amusement, Jack began breaking the bands and glancing at random samples as he stood poking the cards through the slot. The man had apparently sent a postal to every minister of the conference, active or retired, every minister's widow, and to quite a number of general board people and miscellaneous church dignitaries. "You ought to see the surf-casting outfit Patsy gave me! FJW." "The fish out here practically jump into the boat. FJW." And "Man, am I having a vacation!?! FJW."

The question mark in the middle intrigued Jack, for it apparently represented an ineradicable respect for truth. And, as he thought about it driving back to the cottage, Jack realized that on not one of those cards had Dr. Worthington specifically stated that he himself was engaged in any of the pursuits so enthusiastically described.

But the most wonderful hours of all they spent at the Point, a lonely projection of rock and sand that jutted into the ocean several miles from the Worthington cottage. Its tip contained a miniature beach, enclosed by a half-circle of high, jagged rocks; and while exploring one day, they found their way into it through a crevice. The view from the tiny beach inside embraced the whole horizon; and on the rim above them a single tree, gnarled and beaten, cast an occasional patch of restful shade on the warm sand.

Jack and Patricia spent endless hours there, and on their last afternoon they took along a basket. After they had swum and basked in the sun, they had their picnic. Then they lay on the beach, not wanting to leave, knowing that tomorrow they would be back in their special worlds again where people's eyes were always on them, and where it was quite impossible to relax and be like other young people in love.

"Well," said Jack, "I guess poor old Steady has gotten another four minutes behind for August during your absence. He's probably got your desk piled high, waiting for his little teammate to return. 'Christianity is teamianity!'" This was one of the more dreadful examples of Dr. Loveless' humor.

"He's not poor, and he's not old," said Patricia. "He's thirty-five, and he never said, 'Christianity is teamianity.' He does say, 'Church work is team work,' which is true."

"He says 'A good churchman has no time to be a martyr,'" said Jack, "because I heard him. And that's certainly true. I don't have an open date to be burned at the stake on between September the first and Easter. Teamianity and Togetherness, that's Steady the Yes Man." He liked to work in the nickname because it always irritated Patricia so. She had pulled the strap of her bathing suit off her right shoulder and was examining the white streak against her tan. Jack leaned over and kissed it, hard.

Patricia jerked the strap back up.

"Go carve our initials on the tree," she said coloring. "We might not come back."

"No knife," said Jack, slapping his trunks. "Do you realize we've known each other six years, and I've never seen you blush before?"

"You never did anything I could blush about," said Patricia, getting up. But she was still blushing. "Let's at least build a sand castle. We ought to make some kind of mark on our place!"

He lay on the beach and pleaded that the tide was about to come in, but she made him get a pie pan from the lunch basket and help her. They built a very respectable sand castle, with a small ditch around it for a moat, and even a low wall around the outer rim of the moat. Jack carried panfuls of wet sand while Patricia industriously shaped and patted it into place.

"Why must you work at everything so?" he asked. "You're worse than your father!"

"He is sort of a beaver, isn't he?" She stuck a scrap of dry seaweed on the tower for a flagpole and then went and stretched out with a sigh on the blanket they had brought. "I used to ruin every vacation by nagging him about it, but now I just let him work away. That's when he's happiest." She paused and looked at Jack, who was sitting on the sand. "He had a coronary once, you know—years ago. I think those were the most awful weeks I ever spent." She plucked at the frayed edge of the blanket, and he was surprised to see that her fingers trembled a little. "Maybe that's why I'm so insecure sometimes. I mean, not just about him, but about you, about life and the future and what kind of churches you'll get, and what kind of house we'll live in."

Jack lay down beside her and clasped one of her hands in both of his.

"I dread annual conferences," she went on, squeezing his hand. "He always overdoes himself. And I live in terror of every fourth one, when they elect the general and jurisdictional delegates. Then he's up till two and three every morning, seeing scores of people, and the tension is simply terrific."

They had also agreed to a moratorium on arguments about her father's political ethics, but Jack was curious.

"Why?" he asked. "He's always on the winning side."

"He wasn't always," said Patricia. "Dad's a terribly insecure person, too, when you get down under the smile and the jokes and the handshake and everything. Maybe it was being a foundling, or being raised in the orphan's home, or that nine years trying to beat the Doffingwell machine, or losing mother when I came. That's probably why—" She stopped suddenly.

"That's why he doesn't like me?"

"But he *does!* He's just got to! But I'm all he has left, don't you see? And he's all I've ever had, except you. You do like him now, don't you?"

Jack was never any good at white lies.

"I'm trying," he said. "But I guess that's an admission, isn't it. He and I seem to be . . . different types."

"I know," she said. "That's what frightens me so. Because you don't seem to realize, dearest, that I'm the same type he is."

They lay for a long while in silence. Jack looked up at their tree. It was gnarled and twisted, its trunk was perpetually bowed against the wind from the ocean, and its roots gripped and dug into the bleak rock like the claws of a bird. It had held on somehow, though winter storms had destroyed all other trees along the Point. It was a solitary, misshapen thing, but beautiful against the blue sky in the afternoon sun.

"I love that old tree," he said, without thinking. "It reminds me of Wes Phillips."

He was instantly sorry he had said it, for he knew that she saw the point of the comparison instantly: her father's machine had rooted out all opposition in the conference except that one unyielding old man. Now Jack had spoiled their tree for her, and at the very end of their two wonderful weeks.

"I wish . . ." she said, and stopped, not looking at him.

"What?"

"I wish you didn't see so much of him." There was an awkward silence. Patricia shivered. "I'm freezing!"

"I'm freezing! I'm freezing!" Jack mimicked. "That's all I hear around this place!" He jumped up and before she could protest he grabbed the edge of the blanket, yanked it across her, and rolled her up tight in it, pinning her arms inside.

"Jack, you idiot! Get me out of this thing!"

He flung himself down beside her, holding her arms tightly to keep her from working them free.

"I can see," she gasped, laughing and trying to twist away, "just how it's going to go when we're married! I'll want the window closed; you'll want it open; I'll be pulling the blankets up; you'll be kicking them off again."

She stopped struggling, and suddenly she was gazing up at him with an almost painful tenderness, only her head sticking out of the blanket and the tips of her fingers holding it away from her chin. In the silence they could hear the slow rhythm of the surf, and from their tree the whisper of the wind off the ocean; and beyond the rocks they heard a seagull's mew, thin and fainting. He released her arms and leaned down and kissed her, and she lay motionless for a long moment. Her eyes were wide, her lips slightly parted, and her hair was tangled and had sand in it.

They were miles from the cottage, and the big rock hid them from the ocean at the spot where he had rolled her, and tomorrow they would be going back. . . .

He had always thought afterwards that it was something in her that had prevented them both from being swept away. But now, remembering it all again, it occurred to him for the first time that the thing that had stopped them might have been in him rather than in Patricia, even though she was the one who always looked so cool and remote, so self-controlled. And that if it had not been in him, they could have been married at any time he chose.

"We'd better be starting back," she said at last in a small, uncertain voice; and after a moment she thrust out her bare arms, and then she had wriggled out of the blanket and was gathering up their things.

He helped her through the crevice, and they both turned, and looked back. Already the shadow of the big rock had darkened part of the brilliant sand; the wind was colder now; the tide had changed; and as they watched, they saw the ripples from the first big breaker reach the outer wall of the sand castle, detach a small segment of it, and melt it and smooth it away.

XIV

Majority of One

JACK was about to leave his isolated section of the balcony at Belfair when he saw Wes Phillips' black suit and shaggy white thatch in the doorway opposite him. Wes lowered his tall, bony frame into the next seat, and they went over their lists together, checking off names of delegates already seen. Then Wes stuffed his list into the pocket of his shiny vest, scratched his head, and sighed.

"How can you talk to a man about his vote in this bedlam?" he asked in his hoarse stage-whisper, waving a big, gnarled hand at the sanctuary below. There the bishop, seated at the table which had been set up for him on the rostrum beside the pulpit, was listening with his inexhaustible patience to a ministerial delegate who had just broken into the crowded agenda for the third time that afternoon on a point of personal privilege. "Well, I'll go down and see who I can catch hiding out in the bookroom." He got up. "How are your feet?"

"Terrible," said Jack. "This is the only spot in the balcony where I'd dare take my shoes off."

"Well, don't overdo yourself this first day. I'll keep the boys working till you get back in shape again."

When he had gone, Jack settled back, smiling. It had been inevitable, he supposed, that he and Wes should have wound up on the same team. . . . And Wes had probably foreseen it from that first encounter when Jack had rashly tackled him on the tobacco issue. That had been on a hot July day in 1956, at the first meeting of the ministers in Dr. Worthington's district following annual conference. Jack had been curious to meet the old man since that conference, when Dirkwell had referred to him as Dr. Worthington's only opposition and had quoted Wes's slogan, "One man with God is a majority."

Dr. Worthington usually rotated these monthly meetings among the smaller churches of his district, being "just a country preacher at heart" himself. Following the morning session, and while waiting for the ladies of Rockmont Methodist to serve lunch, Jack saw Wes standing alone at the edge of the sun-parched lawn before the church. He had the thumbs of his great, gnarled hands hooked in the armholes of his vest, and his head was wreathed in a cloud of cigar smoke. Jack walked up and stood beside him.

So this was Dr. Worthington's thorn in the flesh! He did not look particularly impressive. Jack had found himself irritated by the awe-struck timidity of some of the men toward this crotchety old crusader, and partly from curiosity, partly from irritation, he decided to tackle him on the well-worn Methodist issue of tobacco. They had already been introduced, after a fashion, when the men stood up and identified themselves that morning.

"Brother Phillips—"

"The name is Wes."

Jack coughed as the old man suddenly blew a vast cloud of smoke at him from one corner of his wide mouth.

"Well, Wes, I know, of course, that you took your vows before they passed the tobacco rule, but I was wondering whether you had fully weighed the damage to your personal influence? Smoking may seem a trivial issue but I felt obligated as a brother minister to mention it. We're all in this thing together, you know."

The craggy white brows shot up; the great white head tilted far back; two fierce pale blue eyes studied Jack from head to foot. Finally he removed the much-chewed cigar from his mouth, examined it with care, and said in a rumbling organ tone:

"You know, I never thought about that! Some saintly little old lady might see me smoking this, lose her faith in the ministry, and pitch headforemost into adultery!" He turned to examine Jack again. "Then, seeing that you—a younger and far wiser clergyman—do *not* smoke, she might repent of the fleshpots and come back to the life of virtue and sobriety. Correct?"

"Little old ladies have souls, too," said Jack.

"Tell me, son, how many saintly little old ladies do you suppose there are in this community?" Wes swept the cigar in a grand circle toward the sleepy little village of Rockmont.

"Oh, I don't know. Ten or twelve?"

"And how many rip-roaring, foul-mouthed, hard-drinking two-fisted young men?"

"Hundreds, probably!"

"Good enough. Now, just what do you suppose keeps this last bunch out of church?"

"I wish I knew!"

"I'll tell you." The rumble sank still lower. "They're not quite sure which *sex* we belong to." The shaggy white head nodded vigorously; the ice-blue eyes were guileless. "They can see the preacher ain't a woman. But he doesn't drink, smoke, cuss, gamble, fight, or engage in other male pursuits. So what in thunderation *is* he?" Another cloud of smoke. "Only the good Lord will ever know how many hairy-chested he-men have trod the path of destruction almost against their own will, just because they couldn't place the preacher."

He put one long arm about Jack's shoulders.

"Tell you what: You concentrate on pulling in the little old ladies. I daresay the younger ones will hear you without much urging. I'll pull in the roughnecks—by looking like a fellow who *does* smoke and cuss and who might even think himself just an ordinary human being like they are. You'll have your thousands; I'll have my ten thousands. Is it a deal?"

Jack laughed in spite of himself and shook the proffered hand. The pale eyes glinted; the wide, sardonic mouth shifted the much-chewed cigar further into the corner.

"I'll give you another little tip: next time you're alone with a layman and bark your shin or whack your thumb with the hammer, just say the first thing that pops into your mind—only kinda soft, like you didn't mean to be overheard. You'll be surprised what spiritual benediction it brings you both! You'll have folks in your church that haven't been within shouting distance of a preacher in years."

"They might tell it in the taverns," said Jack, "but I doubt if you'd see many of them in church."

"Hah!" said Wes, suddenly bending down to remove one shoe and pounding its heel on the white fence post beside him. "You follow my advice, young man, and someday you'll be as big a success as I am!"

With one shiny serge coatsleeve he rubbed up the toe of the shoe and put it back on. Then he straightened, stared Jack up and down for a long moment, and said curtly:

"Well, how do you feel now that you've met Belovèd's opposition?"

It was the beginning of a curious friendship.

Wes perceived immediately that Jack was in conflict about the problem of Dr. Worthington's power and methods and he never missed an opportunity to unsettle him further. Jack, for his part, presented the arguments used on him by Patricia and her father as if they were his own, and was astonished to discover that, far from being the blind and self-destroying malcontent he appeared, Wes Phillips was an extraordinarily deep and complicated person. He had a wide circle of friends, most of them laymen, and all sorts of people were forever dropping by his out-of-the-way parsonage to talk to him. He had played chess by mail for years with a Catholic priest and once Jack found him writing his next move on a postcard with a pencil stub and muttering, "There! Let's see the confounded papist get out of that!" He was enormously well read, particularly in the mystics and the devotional classics; he had kept a wry, sardonic gift of humor despite a lifetime of outward frustration and defeat; and he showed a disarming ability to see the two-sidedness of Jack's problems.

And he owned his own soul.

It was this last which kept Jack in turmoil, unable to rest in the arguments put forward by Patricia and Dr. Worthington. For, though Jack was already pastor of a far better church than Wes Phillips had attained in over thirty years, the sight of those cracked shoes and that rusty black suit invariably made him feel uneasy and ashamed.

He had broached the subject of his Wentworth appointment on one occasion, and had confessed to Wes his attempt to beard the lion—and the results. Wes was both amused and admiring.

"That musta given the old boy a turn! Imagine having his future son-in-law charging about all over the conference yelling at the top of his lungs that he'd got another man's church through political pull! No wonder he stayed up till one o'clock in the morning trying to calm you down. Who'd elect him bishop on that kind of publicity? Believe me, boy, if nobody else is praying for you, old Belovèd is! He's on his knees morning and night that you'll save more souls and raise more money at Wentworth than any preacher in history, because if you fizzle, it's gonna make him look like exactly what he is. That, needless to say, would kill *any* politician!"

Not all of Phillips' estimates were this unsympathetic.

"Oh, sometimes I think the man deserves to rule the rest of us," he said one day. "He knows every minister and wife and child in every corner of the conference, and half their congregations as well. He remembers anniversaries, hobbies, and mumps and measles. He travels further dropping in 'accidentally' on parsonage birthday parties than you and I do calling on the sick and dying. He's got every little country parson completely convinced that old Belovèd is his one and only friend at court, because he's just a country preacher at heart himself and always will be—to hear him tell it. He locates a book you've been hunting for ten years and mails it to you for the anniversary of your ordination —which you'd forgotten yourself. He's straight as a die in his personal conduct, makes all his understandings crystal clear, and never breaks a promise. He makes as many good appointments as he possibly can within the limits of holding his own outfit together; and when he does reward some loyal bum with a congregation that deserves better, he does it with a heavy heart and usually tries to make it up to them later on. He's like an umpire: he never admits he called a ball a strike—but he just might happen to call the next strike a ball. He never gets mixed up in controversial issues; he's as safe and orthodox as the Four Gospels; and he loves the Methodist Church with his heart, soul, mind and strength.

"Have you ever watched him at work during an annual conference? You'd think he was quintuplets! One minute he's bringing in a resolution commending Pastor Smith's only child for being valedictorian at her high school graduation, the next minute he's finding a seat for somebody's maternal grandmother. You see him on the rostrum whispering in the bishop's ear this minute, and when you turn around he's helping them haul the wheelchair up the front steps so he can pin a medal on the oldest living lay preacher! How're you gonna beat a guy like that?"

Jack saw Dirkwell only rarely, for he was in a different district. But he had never forgotten Edwina Dirkwell's opinion that Dr. Worthington disliked him, and when the 1957 annual conference had come and gone and Patricia decided to work still another year, he began to wonder if her father had somehow influenced her decision. He began to suspect that she was waiting for Jack to feel that same uncritical idolization toward him that she felt, and Jack's resentment did little to help him accept her justifications of Dr. Worthington's activities. They had many prolonged and emotional arguments.

At the beginning they kept the arguments friendly, and even had fun trying to score points. But the strain of their long engagement began to give things all sorts of emotional overtones. Jack realized that it was in part his own conscience he was attacking, and he sometimes overstated his misgivings in hopes that Patricia could convince him her father's activities *were* morally justifiable. And she frequently did.

Jack realized early that both Patricia and her father regarded his friendship with Wes as a kind of disloyalty, or at least as indicating questionable judgment. This made him even more determined to choose his own friends, especially when he found that many of the district ministers seemed afraid to be seen in Wes's company. The old man's country circuit was only thirty minutes' drive from Wentworth, and Jack fell into the habit of dropping by at the end of the day rather than returning for a bachelor snack at his empty parsonage. Mrs. Phillips, whom everybody called Sue, was a neat, gray little lady with a serene face, cheerful disposition, and a spirit seemingly unaffected by the long series of professional disappointments she and Wes had suffered. They had three girls, all married and scattered afar, and a son still in college.

Jack never confessed to Phillips the full extent of his misgivings or of his differences with Patricia. Rather, he continued to pose as defender of the established order, and one evening at the dinner table in Wes's parsonage he provoked an illuminating discussion of Dr. Worthington's ethics.

"I've decided you're right," Jack said. "Dr. Worthington does deserve to boss the rest of us. He's fair, he's informed, he loves the church, and he works twice as hard as anyone else!"

"Those are not his only advantages," Wes replied, as if thinking aloud. "His biggest advantage is actually moral. He may very well be the only minister in this conference who can deliberately, consciously, and even systematically do wrong whenever he feels it is necessary. To hold an organization in line year after year, to keep it unified in policy and program, and to override the variety of individual consciences that ministers display, you've got to be able to pray with one man, preach at the next, and kick the third in the teeth. And be smart enough to know what goes with who."

"I can scarcely imagine Dr. Worthington kicking anyone in the teeth," said Jack, smiling.

"No," said Wes, "because you couldn't do it yourself, and neither could most of the rest of us. You couldn't have forced Oscar Bates to retire at fifty-nine when older men than he were producing less. But your attitude toward Belovèd may also be a tribute to his own powers of self-deception. He certainly finds punitive actions intensely painful, and he's probably sincere in imagining they're always just 'disciplinary.' He doesn't seem aware of the strength of his own ambition and love of power, but I guess most ministers never are. Isn't it strange that if a man tramples on his wife and children and betrays his conscience and crucifies his self-respect trying to be president of a button factory, we call it sin. But if a preacher does all the same things trying to make it to First Church, we admire the monster and have our kiddies pray for him!

"I'm sure," he went on, "that Belovèd agonizes in prayer over the tough things he sometimes has to do to stay in power; but when he gets up from his knees, he can strike hard and forget it. He's not crippled by any glimpses of his own ability to make mistakes. His strength never seems divided by any suspicion that the will of God could be different from his own. He honestly believes he is only what he seems to himself and to you—a mild, hard-working, harmless little country parson whose one aim in life is to build up the church to the glory of God.

"But by long experience, the men have learned that he'll treat you fair if he possibly can; he'll punish you if he must; and if you come back a second time, he'll crucify you."

Jack stared at the old man's cracked shoes, his shiny suit, frayed cuffs, and unkempt white hair.

"I can't believe," Jack said, "that almost five hundred Methodist ministers would let themselves live under a reign of terror for twenty-five years without rebelling!"

"It's no reign of terror!" Wes replied. "It's only in the last five or ten years that his power began to be so pervasive; you forget that it took him a long time to build this machine. And he rarely has to threaten anybody. Constructive appeals and reasonably fair rewards for seniority and hard work are all you need in handling most preachers. It's like working in a bank or department store. Nobody comes around in a black mustache and cracks a whip over you. The boss is a Christian gentleman, and nothing would offend him more than to think people feared him. But the pressure is always there. . . .

"What makes Belovèd different is that most ministers cannot admit even to themselves that career and status are almost always their first consideration—plus fear of failure. But he looks the facts square in the eye and uses them for all they're worth!

"Lots of preachers," Wes said thoughtfully, "have lived under this arrangement all their lives and honestly don't even seem to know it's there! I keep telling Belovèd he ought to dress the part. 'Wear a diamond stickpin, man!' I told him once. 'Look like the bosses in books! Drive a black limousine; smoke a big cigar; hire a couple of thugs to be your bodyguards. Confound it, man, we have two dozen new men coming up for appointment this year, and not a single one of them will know where to turn. Half of them will probably try to see the bishop, or some other nobody, and let you walk right past under their noses! Take off that disguise,' I told him, 'and play the part the good Lord gave you!' "

"What did he say?"

"Oh, you know Belovèd! He just laughed his merry little laugh and shook his little billiard-ball head, and patted my arm with his warm little hand the way he does, and said, 'Why, Wes, if I tried to smoke a cigar, I'd probably end up in the hospital!' "

He walked down the cinder path to the car with Jack after supper and stood leaning against the gatepost.

"Wes," said Jack curiously, "you seem to agree with your enemy's estimate of human nature. Why have you never joined him?"

"Any fool," said Wes, "can cash in on the weaknesses of his fellow men. I never considered that much of a challenge."

"Well," said Jack, "at least tell me why you haven't transferred to another conference."

"Oh, tarnation, boy! I can't explain my choices to a kid like you! You're of a generation that expects every act to serve some useful purpose."

Wes turned half-about, and Jack followed his gaze as it took in the ancient parsonage and the faded white frame church . . . not the kind of house most ministers were willing to live in, not the kind of church that gave scope and effectiveness to a man with this man's gifts. As they watched, Sue Phillips appeared briefly on the porch. She was always like Wes—calm, cheerful, undismayed—but Jack knew that for a man as sensitive to others as Wes, the hardships his choices had brought upon Sue and the children must have been a crucifying moral dilemma. By all the currently accepted standards of the ministry, Wes Phillips' career was a failure and his gifts wasted, yet Jack had rarely found himself seeking counsel of the men who were successful—the men with the booming suburban churches and the split-level parsonages and the statistical proofs of their prophethood.

"Just what does keep you going?" Jack demanded. "You've been fighting a lost cause now for twenty-five years, and I suppose you were in there battling the old Doffingwell machine before that. Explain yourself, sir!"

The old man closed the rickety gate between them, almost as if he were drawing a line between their generations.

"When I was coming up," said Wes Phillips sourly, "a man didn't have to explain a sense of honor."

XV

Till Death Us Do Part

JACK knew that he ought to be working, not sitting in the balcony of Belfair Methodist pretending to be engrossed in committee reports and resolutions like any other delegate. But the memory of that first breaker rolling in toward their sand castle at the Point seemed now to have been an omen, like the turning of the tide, in his relationship with Patricia. That instant behind the rock had been the high point of their love, before the tides of feeling somehow began to run awry, before those irreconcilable arguments had eroded everything, like the remorseless pounding of the surf on their sand castle. . . .

It was actually not difficult to remember Patricia with fairness, for he still felt toward her now as he had always felt. Indeed, their estrangement only sharpened his recollections of happier times. But with

Thelma it was different. To remember Thelma fairly he had to block off a whole area of later experience in order to remember with even partial accuracy what he had thought and felt at the beginning.

He had first seen Thelma on a mild Saturday afternoon in late September of 1958. He was in his study going over his sermon notes for Sunday morning. Glancing out the window, he saw Ricky Richardson's big, cream-colored convertible stop at the parsonage walk. Rick jumped out, wearing his army uniform. His widowed mother, Mrs. Agnes Stanton Richardson, was the leading laywoman of the Wentworth church. The combined connections of the Stantons and the Richardsons in Washington had been unable to keep Rick out of military service, but they had at least succeeded in getting him a second lieutenant's commission.

A girl was leaning forward on the seat, shrugging out of her coat and putting on make-up in the car mirror. When Jack opened the door a moment later, she was standing very near Rick and gazing up at him with a look of mute, almost awestruck adoration, both hands on his shoulders.

"Gee, Reverend," said Rick, "give us a chance to ring!"

The girl blinked up at Jack stupidly. She had a plump, oval face framed by a mass of dark auburn hair, sulky red lips, and large brown eyes with puffy lids and short thick lashes. She seemed very stiff and ill at ease as she sat down beside Rick in Jack's study, glancing about and blinking again at his diplomas, books, and the portrait of Christ over the desk. It seemed that this was Miss Ross ("pleased to meecha!"), that Rick had only forty-eight hours, and they wanted Jack to marry them—immediately.

"Have you a license?"

Rick handed it over with his irritating grin. Everything about Rick irritated Jack—his insolent good looks, his glittering uniform, his inflection of the word "Reverend." The girl had been sitting with her stubby hands clenched in her lap; her nails were cut short and the polish clashed with her sweater and skirt. She now relaxed a little and permitted herself a timid smile; her teeth were small and white, but she showed too much of her gums when she smiled.

Jack examined the license with deliberate slowness: Miss Thelma Marie Ross was nineteen, had no previous marriages, listed her address as an apartment in New York, and her occupation as waitress.

"I'm afraid your license has no validity here. The law requires that it be issued in the county within which the ceremony is to be performed."

"Oh . . ." Rick's face clouded briefly. "Well, we'll run over to the courthouse and pick up another one."

"You forget this is Saturday. The office is closed."

"Hell, old Carlson will open up for Rick!"

"Mr. Carlson is out of town."

Throughout this exchange the girl sat gazing at Rick with that absurd expression of near-reverence, as if watching his face for the slightest cue as to what she should think or feel. Now at last she stared at Jack, as if he were deliberately attempting to prevent them from marrying at once.

"But . . . what can we do?" she asked in her flat, nasal voice.

"Well, Miss Ross—?" Jack hesitated, suspecting that the name was an Americanization of something—Rossininni?—to judge by a nearly imperceptible accent and something about her coloring.

The owlish brown eyes blinked once under his steady gaze.

"That's right. What's wrong with Ross?" The mouth was sulkier still.

"A good American name!" Again the blink.

"Just say Thelma," said Rick impatiently.

Thelma glanced at Rick, and a faint pink radiance suffused her plump cheeks and throat. Jack wondered if perhaps his being a Protestant clergyman was part of her trouble. . . .

"Well, Thelma, if this is genuine, a few weeks' delay—"

"If!" Rick burst out. "Reverend, this is it!"

"I have no doubt 'this is it,'" said Jack. "But certainly the longer we've known each other—"

Rick rose to the bait.

"We've known each other seven weeks!"

Jack permitted himself a sigh.

"I presume you know each other's families."

"Thelma just has some brothers. And you know Mother, Reverend! Hell, if I gotta please her and the Stantons, I'll die single. Why can't we just skip the family?"

"You may; I cannot. As your mother's pastor—and yours—I feel the same obligation a priest feels to his flock."

Again the blink. That settled the Catholic background. It was almost as if he and the girl had established some form of wordless communication. She turned angrily to Rick.

"Why does *he* have to marry us? Let's go back where we got the license and get a justice of the peace—"

Rick flung the license into Jack's wastebasket.

"Mother's said a dozen times if I ever run off to a J.P., I needn't bother coming home, and she means it. She thinks Reverend Lee hung the moon. Our only chance is to be able to say he tied the knot."

"In that case," said Jack crisply, "I suggest that you take Miss Ross straight to your mother and then to the Stantons and start this whole procedure in a rational way."

Rick dug his fingers into his close-cropped, golden hair. Thelma leaned over and retrieved the license.

"If you really want to marry me like you keep saying, why don't we go ahead and do it today!"

He saw Rick waver.

"I'm a little surprised at Miss Ross," Jack said swiftly. "I should have imagined she would *want* a church wedding! I'm profoundly sympathetic to the Roman Catholic position myself—that it is a holy sacrament." Well, that at least pulled the owlish eyes away from Rick! "It scarcely seems fair to deny her things so dear to feminine hearts—a white veil, candles, flowers, a wedding gown, the joy of kneeling at the altar while someone sings, say, the 'Ave Maria' . . ." Thelma had grown still; her large eyes were fixed on him with a painful hunger; the chubby fingers clenching the license had relaxed. An apostate Roman Catholic, clear as day. Jack went on more slowly, knowing he was winning now. "How different from a mere civil ceremony with a bleary-eyed J.P. in some dingy living room! One could hardly consider oneself married at all!" The license had almost slipped from her fingers.

Jack glanced down at her gaudy shoes with their black satin ribbons crisscrossed and tied at her ankles.

"And if I'm not mistaken, Thelma, it would give Rick's mother great pleasure if you let her take you in to New York on a shopping spree for that bridal trousseau."

Rick studied her mute, imploring face.

"Well, if that's the kind of wedding you want—"

"More than anything in the world!" said Thelma.

Rick jumped up and snatched his hat from the desk.

"Reverend, you're a right guy! I almost thought for a minute there you didn't *want* us to get married. Ain't that a laugh?"

As he shut the door after them, Jack heard the flat, nasal voice:

"Gee, I was expecting some dried-up old geezer! But what made him so hateful at the first?"

He sat down at his desk and dialed Mrs. Richardson; and after a hectic conversation, she finally calmed down enough to hear some constructive suggestions. He put the phone down with a sigh. George Stanton Richardson the Fourth—and a girl who smelled of dime-store perfume and wore a sweater slashed practically to her navel!

That night Jack sat on the sofa with Pat in the library at the district parsonage; her father was out; Aunt Katherine had already gone up to bed. Pat was wearing a simple, severe dress of charcoal gray, almost black. The light from the lamp behind her gleamed dully in her pale gold hair. Her slim, pert face with its chiseled features was amused and the cool blue eyes watchful.

"Jack, stop talking in circles! You *never* call me on Saturday night. You haven't since the first year we were dating. Now, tell Patsy what it's all about."

She leaned back, eyes mischievous, lips slightly parted. The light made a small shadow in the hollow of her throat. Jack suddenly pulled her to him, kissed her hard on the lips and then, impulsively, kissed the little hollow. Then he kissed her throat just beneath the ear.

"Pat—let's get married. Right away!"

The yielding body stiffened.

"Jack, we're *not* going into all that again—and on Saturday night, when Dr. Kramer will be there to hear you preach tomorrow! Have you gone utterly out of your mind? Have you any idea what difficulty Dad encountered persuading a busy superintendent to come out to Wentworth to hear you preach?"

"What's so insane about two healthy, normal young people wanting to get married? I'm twenty-five; you're twenty-four; I have a good salary, a lovely parsonage, and a solid future. Why must we wait till after jurisdictional conference? That's a year and a half from now. We've already been engaged two years and four months without ever getting to the altar! The boys in the district kid me about it—and their wives!"

The small, pert lips compressed, and she colored faintly. He noted absently that her skin seemed dryer and less youthful than Thelma's.

"When we're at Trinity, these child brides will still be on country circuits, and looking middle-aged at thirty, and fawning at your feet in hopes of a good appointment for their husbands because of doctor's bills and too many children and all that. I've heard them. I know."

"Maybe, but there have been plenty of times I'd have traded Wentworth Methodist *and* your dear papa's whole machine just to have what some of those youngsters have!" He knew that the word "machine" outraged her, but she gave no sign. "What can possibly happen to him at jurisdictional conference except that he might miss becoming a bishop? What else can happen? He's got the whole conference in his vest pocket and he has heart failure every time a country preacher says, 'Boo!' " The "heart failure" was in bad taste, but Jack plunged on. "And you're twice as insecure as he is. Believe me, Pat, he'll still be the boss no matter—"

"Stop calling him 'the boss!' "

"He'd *still* be the *boss,* and even if he weren't, so what? Plenty of preachers have led happy and useful lives—and even married!—without a dime's worth of political influence or a chance in a million at Trinity. Why can't we?"

She turned away, folding her hands in her lap, her chiseled profile utterly impassive against the glow of the lamp. She did not intend to contribute to another midnight wrangle—and as always she was being perfectly sensible.

"What did happen today?" she asked at last.

"A couple of kids came by to get married."

He told her all about it, and to their surprise it turned out she had seen Thelma. Rick had taken her out to the Country Club, where Pat and Geneva Nielson had played golf that afternoon. She agreed that the match looked quite unworkable, and that Jack had been justified in calling Mrs. Richardson and contributing his suggestions as to how the young couple could be stalled off till Rick came to his senses.

After she had kissed him goodnight at the door she said, "Isn't it fantastic? That dumpy, unattractive little girl! And Rick always seemed such a sucker for surfaces!"

Jack went to bed immediately on reaching home, but could not sleep. Certainly Thelma's outfit was cheap and tasteless, but how could anyone refer to her as unattractive when she simply oozed at every pore with that vulgar, animal kind of sex? He finally dozed off, irritably remembering Patricia's condescending tone . . . and the little wisp of hair, almost like auburn smoke, behind Thelma's ear.

Mrs. Richardson invited Jack and Patricia over for tea the next afternoon. Jack was moody and irritable; Rick and Thelma had not come to church; the sermon had gone badly, despite Patricia's insistence that Dr. Kramer was impressed.

Mrs. Richardson was a slight, spry woman with handsome features and hard, observant eyes.

"Well, at least this time nobody can claim the dear boy was snared by sex! And that perpetual pout she wears! Oh dear, oh dear. But the problem is, what's to be done?"

What's to be done, unfortunately did not prove to be adequate. Thelma enjoyed the shopping sprees immensely. She got through the teas and showers sometimes without uttering a single word, according to Mrs. Richardson. And when she and Rick came for their counseling sessions with Jack, she would sit with her thigh pressed against Rick's and instead of paying attention would gaze at Rick in that awestruck, humorless, uncritical way as though this very handsome and very spoiled young man in a second lieutenant's uniform were a god turned loose on earth.

The third session proved very difficult, and the last ended almost before it began. Rick came in alone, leaving Thelma in the car. He had begun to have suspicions.

"So damn many things keep happening! Take that dressmaker, Simone: who ever heard of a *wedding* dress not being ready on time? It's got Thelma half out of her mind. And all this counseling!" His white teeth suddenly gleamed against his bronzed skin. "Know something, Rev? Sometimes I think I'm the one oughta be counseling you! You got a cute chick there in Pat Worthington. You two oughta stop stalling. It would solve all your problems, man."

This was too much for Jack. He was horrified to hear himself telling Rick savagely that this match was unworkable! Unthinkable!

"The girl has *nothing* in common with a person of your background! If you have any genuine concern for her, you will help her to face this honestly and courageously—"

Rick jumped up, his boyish face cold and furious.

"I happen to love Thelma Ross, and she loves me. You seem to have read an awful lot of books about sex and marriage, but I'm beginning to wonder if you know what it means to be in love with somebody. Now, in spite of all that you and Mother and the whole damn town can do,

Thelma and I are going to get married next Saturday at two o'clock. Do you want the job or not?"

The rest of the afternoon was a complete loss; that night Jack drove for several hours, brooding, still confused and humiliated. Turning toward home at eleven, he took the short cut across the ridge overlooking the valley. As he crossed the ridge, his headlights swept the parking lot at the overlook and he saw Rick's big, cream-colored convertible drawn up at the edge. A girl's plump, bare arm was sticking up diagonally into the brightness; it did not falter or withdraw, but the stubby forefinger went on drawing imaginary designs in the air; the lights swept past; Jack drove down the hill toward the village.

Animals! Animals without either morals or taste. But after next Saturday they would at least not need to hide in parked cars or cheap motels!

The wedding went off without incident. When it was all over, Jack felt much calmer. He put some finishing touches on his sermon that night, rehearsed it completely twice, laid out his clothes for Sunday morning, took a warm bath, and stretched out in the darkness with a grateful sigh. No more strategy huddles with Mrs. Richardson and Pat; no more attempts to keep a clear mind and a professional detachment toward the two young animals in heat . . . He turned toward the wall and stared angrily into the darkness. Why had everything about the girl simply demoralized him from the first instant he saw her standing in his door gazing up at Rick? He resolutely pushed them both out of his mind and finally dozed off. . . .

The TV programs lately had been reviving the history of Hitler and the Jews. In his dream Jack wore a natty black SS officer's uniform. Two storm troopers brought in a Jewish girl. She sat before his desk, sullen and wordless while he questioned her. At first he remained courteous, trying only to help the creature escape real tragedy; then gradually he lost patience; finally he snatched up his swagger stick, raised it high, and brought it down with all his strength as the auburn head twisted away. . . .

He started awake, sat up in bed, and rubbed his temples with the tips of his fingers, hard, as if he could erase the blazing images by force. How could a civilized person—and a minister at that!—have such dreams? He went down to the kitchen and cut himself a slice of the blueberry pie Miss Mollie had brought the day before, poured a glass of milk, and sat at the kitchen table in his pajamas and slippers, brooding.

That second illustration in his sermon really belonged at the end. You could not simply reason with a congregation. To really sell them, to *make* them believe, you had to close with something that packed a real wallop. He opened the notebook and renumbered two of the pages: he would simply preach page two as page five, then bow his head and go straight into his closing prayer.

He put the plate and fork in the sink along with the glass, snapped off the light, and went back to bed. Storm troopers and swagger sticks! This was worse than that time in college he used to have dreams of flogging Dottie Caldwell for cheating.

Rick and Thelma had been married exactly twenty-seven days when the call came, at two o'clock on a Saturday morning. Jack struggled out of sleep, stumbled to the phone, and heard Trooper McIntosh's voice. He was calling from Waterman, a few miles below Wentworth. Jack remembered picking up a pencil, still half-asleep, and asking whom Rick had run over this time. The next sentence jolted him wide awake.

"No, no, Reverend. Rick Richardson is dead."

Jack was too stunned to speak. Mac was going on about the details and Jack jotted some down: Rick and a companion had been coming home for the weekend; the roads were icy; they had been drinking. Something kept crowding in against the outer edges of Jack's awareness, but he could not get hold of it. Finally Jack said, "Are you . . . Is it quite certain he's dead?" This was a stupid question.

"Windshield nearly cut his head off!"

It seemed that Carl Pryor, the Wentworth undertaker, was coming to pick up the body. Rick's mother was out of town; the housekeeper, Mrs. Hoffman, had answered the phone and was there alone with Rick's wife; she was afraid to wake the girl and tell her; she said Reverend Lee would know what to say.

"And say, Reverend, whatever you do, don't let any of them come to see the body tonight. Carl's gonna need a lot of time on this one."

Mrs. Hoffman had made some coffee, and she put it on the table in the library. Jack gulped it hurriedly as he waited for her to bring Thelma down. Then he ran a comb through his hair again, glancing at himself in the big mirror over the mantel. He had taken a few extra minutes to shave; he appeared composed and well groomed; the dark suit and dark tie looked correct. He had found that the minister's dignity and composure were often a source of strength to parishioners at such times.

Thelma came down ahead of Mrs. Hoffman, who lingered a step or two behind, nervously clenching the lapels of her thick plaid robe and making meaningless faces at Jack as if to inform him that this was the girl.

Thelma had flung on a negligee and was tucking it about her and tying the long, tasseled sash. She paused on the bottom step to thrust her foot more securely into one of her slippers, which had huge, fluffy pompoms that seemed to go with the froth of lace on the gaudy negligee. Her hair was rolled tight in small ringlets all over her head, making her skull look round and her plump face rounder. Her face was pink and flushed from sleep and her skin had a gleaming, oily look, probably from some kind of beauty lotion. She blinked more than usual as she advanced into the brightness of the library, her mouth slightly open and the lips looking pale without make-up.

"What's the matter?" she asked. "Mrs. Hoffman said you wanted to see me."

"It's about Rick, Thelma," Jack said. "I'm afraid we have bad news for you. There's been an accident. Rick got the weekend off unexpectedly and was on his way home." Jack hesitated, wanting to say some more words—any words—to put off the conclusion. "I'm afraid they may have been drinking a little." He had had no intention of bringing this up, but it suddenly slipped out. "Rick lost control of the car and went off the highway—on the bend below Waterman. The boy with him was unhurt. He told Trooper McIntosh what had happened."

Thelma's face paled. She blinked at Jack and ran one hand nervously up the sleeve of her negligee.

"But . . ." Her eyes flicked to Mrs. Hoffman. "What about Rick? Is he . . . hurt very bad?"

Jack had planned the sentence another way, more tactfully, but it came out shockingly direct and brutal.

"He's dead, Thelma. He was killed instantly. I'm terribly sorry to be the one to bring you such—"

Jack hesitated. Her face had turned chalk white and had an eerie waxen pallor under the beauty cream. The plump cheeks seemed to sag as they whitened. The big, squinting eyes grew enormous and much darker, and she sank slowly into the sofa, pressing both palms against the base of her throat. She looked pathetic and grotesque in her frilly negligee, her face a waxy white ball of horror under the skull-tight circle of bobby pins.

Then the scream began.

Her bloodless lips were barely parted, and her horror-filled eyes seemed to be concentrating on something far away, and the noise did not seem to come from Thelma at all. Jack glanced at Mrs. Hoffman, thinking at first that she had made the sound, and was startled to see her lips pressed tightly together and her red-rimmed eyes fixed on Thelma.

It was a toneless, almost perfunctory sound, as if Thelma had been requested by a voice teacher to sound a note. She sustained it as long as she could and then drew a breath and began it again. It filled the huge room with a monotonous "Eeeeeeeeeeeeee" and was so utterly at variance with her staring eyes and look of almost thoughtful concentration that Jack and Mrs. Hoffman exchanged a glance of alarm. Jack controlled himself as long as he could, then stepped forward and touched her shoulder.

"Thelma, we've got to get in touch with Mrs. —"

The noise stopped. The vacant eyes turned up to his face, and suddenly the waxy ball disintegrated in anguish.

"Madre mia!" Her normal voice arose now, resonant with anguish, and Jack felt a momentary relief that she had stopped that unnatural toneless scream. "No! Oh, sancta Maria, no, no, no! Ricky, where are you? Ricky, I'm coming!" She jumped to her feet, her eyes wide and staring.

"You don't want to see him yet, Thelma. They—"

"Ricky! My baby! I'm coming!" She suddenly darted to the door and wrenched it open, standing for an instant in the blast of cold air, her arms flung back, head thrust forward as if searching the darkness.

The act and the gestures were so dramatic, so overdone that they struck Jack as disgustingly false and in terrible taste at such a time. He stepped toward her to close the door, irritated at her play-acting; but to his amazement, she darted out onto the marble porch, which was covered with a thin layer of powdery snow. Jack and Mrs. Hoffman dragged her back. She twisted violently, and flung her head back so hard that the blow bruised his mouth and one of the pins in her hair cut his bottom lip.

"Sancta Maria, what has he done to my Rick? He always hated him! Holy Mary, Mother of God—!"

They struggled clumsily to hold her, bumping into each other, alarmed by her reckless, frenzied strength. She wrenched one hand free from Mrs. Hoffman and struck Jack furiously, trying to claw his cheek at the same time.

"You hated my Rick!" she yelled. "You wanted him dead! You did, you did, you did!"

She spat in his face, and he slapped her so hard that her head bobbed and the hate-filled eyes glazed momentarily.

"Thelma! Stop this play-acting! Mrs. Hoffman, call Dr. Creighton and tell him to get over here with a sedative!"

Mrs. Hoffman ran to the hall, and Thelma sank suddenly onto the sofa, burying her face in her hands and sobbing. Jack stood before her, gasping, and wiped the spittle from his cheek. When Mrs. Hoffman returned, his lip was already so swollen it was difficult to speak properly.

"Bring a coat or something to keep her warm," he said, "and wet a towel in cold water for my lip."

An hour later he pulled into the garage at the parsonage; but instead of getting out, he sat in the car in the darkness, trying to think. He had taken this sort of news to a number of persons in the course of his pastoral duties, but no reaction had ever upset him like Thelma's. She had made all ordinary counsels and reassurances impossible. She had disgusted him with the seeming falsity of her gestures, her stagey shouts, her first prolonged and toneless yelling. But her words . . . these were the most unbearable part. . . .

He yanked open the car door and stood scuffing at the frozen slush with his foot as he irritably pushed the garage doors shut. Then he remained standing in the cold, his topcoat unbuttoned. He stared into the starless night, trying to fight down something that had tried to break through when the trooper's voice had told him Rick was dead.

It would probably never have occurred to him again to remember that fleeting instant—had not Thelma's wild words pinpointed it in a finger of light. . . . For, deep beneath his immediate shock and pity, beneath the instant awe and horror at the violent snuffing out of a human life, he had felt smoulder, had felt struggle to blaze, a split second of wild, ecstatic, undiluted joy.

XVI

A Widow's Tears

TRYING to discover one's true self, Jack decided, was extraordinarily confusing, if only because love and hate and lust and fear were retroactive. They colored one's memory of events that had occurred long before they themselves existed. As he tried to untangle the confused emotions of his Wentworth pastorate, Jack realized that even then he had been aware of pieces of himself that did not fit together. One part of him had seemed then a poised, competent professional man; another part seemed almost infantile, or at least thoroughly juvenile and full of the most abject fears and hungers. Again, he sometimes felt that part of him was striving toward things positive and worth while, but that another part of him was simply running headlong from things utterly unspeakable. Once at a district ministers' meeting, he had broached the subject to Tommy Fredricks. Tommy had majored in Abnormal Psychology in seminary.

"Tommy, I've been counseling a young widow recently who lost her husband in an accident in November. But when I try to help her, I actually feel sometimes as if I had a demon inside that had taken over my reason and judgment! I keep saying the very things that remind her of the accident or deepen her loneliness; even at the funeral I felt once or twice as though I had stuck a knife right in the poor girl, and funerals are one thing I've always felt I did rather well."

"Maybe all of us are handicapped by not fully knowing our own motivations in this business," Tommy answered. "Why do some men become undertakers? How can they endure a daily diet of tears and death—unless something in them *enjoys* seeing people dead or half-crazed by grief? Or take doctors: are money and prestige and the pleasure of healing really sufficient to nerve a man for the daily sight of blood and pain and death—or are these their own reward? What makes a man a state trooper—the desire to protect life, or the chance to take life and not pay?"

This led as usual to a fruitless argument about what constituted normality. Psych majors were all the same: one semester, and they never met another normal human being.

Now, remembering that scrap of conversation, Jack wished he had pursued the matter. For he knew that he had been of real help to Mrs. Richardson in the weeks and months following Rick's death.

"I don't think I could have escaped some sort of breakdown," she had said once, "if it hadn't been for your calls. You always seem so confident and reassuring . . . and you always look so composed and so . . . so impeccable!"

But with Thelma he was never really composed, never sure he was helping at all. This was partly because he was overburdened. He was then in the midst of a building program for the educational annex, and later he was engaged in that complicated struggle with Dr. Stanton and George Strackmar and E. J. Bayliss, Sr., over reorganizing the official board. His days flew away in a blur of committee meetings and administrative duties and community activities and often the real work of the ministry seemed to have been shunted aside.

If Thelma remembered her outburst the night he brought the news about Rick, she never alluded to it, and Jack put it out of his thoughts. He called almost daily at the Richardson home at first, although the burden of his work often limited him to simply looking in for a moment. Mrs. Richardson took the loss of her only child with her unfailing dignity and self-discipline, and attempted, in addition, to shoulder her problems with Thelma, concerning which she frequently sought Jack's counsel.

During the first month Thelma remained almost continuously in her room; she went for days without speaking or even answering direct questions from Mrs. Richardson or the servants. She refused to talk, read, watch television, go for rides, or to cooperate with any attempts to console or distract her. On some of Jack's calls she was still in her robe and slippers at midafternoon and often gave the appearance of not having washed her face or touched her hair. She would stare at him dully from her pillows, or from the sofa in the drawing room, her owlish eyes red-rimmed and vacant, while he tried to draw her out or simply made small talk with Mrs. Richardson. Her figure, always inclined to plumpness, soon became blowzy, for she gorged herself on sweets and upset Mrs. Richardson by going down to the kitchen at all hours of the night for snacks. She could no longer wear any of the extravagant outfits she had bought in New York.

"That," said Mrs. Richardson, "is the one bright spot."

Thelma's appearance finally became so shocking that she herself began to attempt some reforms. She took up knitting and reading, to get her mind off of food, and would walk down to the drugstore to buy stacks of love pulps and paper-backed mysteries, all of which Mrs. Richardson overlaid with copies of *Town and Country, House Beautiful*, etc. The two women also clashed over Thelma's going out in slacks or with her hair in curlers, and playing her radio full blast at two and three o'clock in the morning.

Jack prevented a serious rupture on one occasion. Thelma had insisted from the first that Rick "died for his country," liked to refer to herself as a "war widow," and made Mrs. Richardson promise to ride in an open touring car with her in the annual parade of the local American Legion post. Then one day she came home with a huge white satin banner to be suspended by glossy golden ropes across the picture window overlooking the driveway. It depicted the flag-raising on Iwo Jima in red, white, and blue, bore the Marine Corps insignia in gold, and the purple motto: "My Country—Right or Wrong!" Jack arrived during Mrs. Richardson's explanation that her son "had no remotest relationship to the Marine Corps" and what promised to be a flag day speech by Thelma on how "a person gives their life for their country and even their own mother goes right on like nothing had happened." He was able to convince her that it would be far more meaningful to hang the banner over her bed as the first thing she saw each morning and the last each night.

As Jack's acquaintance with Thelma developed, she became more understandable. The girl was simply lost in Mrs. Richardson's world and had found her safest and least embarrassing defense to be silence; but with him she gradually became more communicative.

"I hate this stinking, one-horse little burg!" she burst out one day, clutching the purple satin lapels of her robe and staring moodily through the picture window in the library. "What can anybody do? Where can they go? A person can't even change their mind without the whole town knowing it. No wonder Rick hated it. Me too—I hate them all! Making cracks in church and in the beauty parlor so a person can't help hearing them. So I bought another Cadillac convertible! So what? Buying things makes me feel better."

"Thelma, they only want to help you—" Jack began.

"Help me! They hate me because I grabbed off their big chance.

They don't come up here because they care anything about me. They just want to have something to talk about. And that big old horsy one is the worst of all—Lib what's-her-name. Always dropping hints about what I oughta wear. If she's so smart, why ain't she married? She's thirty if she's a day."

Thelma yanked the elegant drape shut against the sight of the village, and flung herself down on the sofa, angrily kicking away a thick stack of magazines. *Vogue, Harper's Bazaar*—Mrs. Richardson was certainly trying.

"I'll dress like Ricky liked me to. And I'll read what I want to." Jack had noticed that her feet had big calluses on them, probably from her years as a waitress; and once when he came, she sat on the sofa with the leg of her canary-yellow pajamas rolled up, and shaved at one of the calluses with a razor blade during the entire call. She seemed to have almost no sense of modesty or privacy, especially at the beginning, and frequently received him with her hair unkempt, or in curlers; and on one call she spent the entire time putting up her hair, staring at him and Mrs. Richardson through the wet, straggly strands, the front of her robe and gown splashed with water and shampoo, her plump hands whitened and shriveled.

Strangely, it was in precisely such situations that Jack found himself assailed by a flood of simple animal passion, and the more coarse, indelicate, and slovenly the girl showed herself, the more intense his feelings. He had no intention of giving in to such desires; he timed his calls later in the afternoons in hopes that she would be dressed; he systematically fought down the salacious images that kept bursting through; and he reminded himself that he was in love with Patricia—an exquisite, cultivated, and desirable girl who would someday satisfy every longing.

When Thelma finally did begin taking an interest in her appearance again, however, a new problem arose. Jack noticed it shortly after the Marine banner incident. Mrs. Richardson had thanked him profusely.

"If only the girl would *go!*" she added. "You're the only one who can do anything with her, the only person in Wentworth she . . . likes."

Something in the tone of the word "likes" scratched the swift flow of her words, but Jack did not stop to analyze it. The following week, talking to them both in the library, he suddenly caught Thelma's eyes upon him. She blinked and started, and later he was not quite certain, but for an instant he imagined he saw that same mute, humorless, awestruck look she used to give Rick. He could not get it out of his mind, and, what was more absurd, the recollection of it invariably brought him a kind of warm reluctant glow—as when someone had just paid him an obviously extravagant compliment on a sermon. She rarely appeared with her hair in pins any more, was usually dressed in one of her startling street outfits, came to church every Sunday, and chattered volubly on his calls.

"Now, that's a good story," she said one day when he found her reading a love pulp. "It's all about this girl, see, who loses her husband in the war. And a soldier brings the body back who looks a lot like her husband did, see? Tall and athaletic and all that, see. And guess what! She ends up marrying the one who brought the body back!"

"Amazing."

"Were you ever an athalete? You look real strong even if you are a man of God. I was laying in bed last night thinking how your shoulders are almost as wide as Rick's."

Jack began to make his calls shorter and less frequent, and gradually she drifted back into her former patterns—late hours, slovenliness, moody silences, and overeating. Mrs. Richardson and Jack both noticed the change but neither made any comment as to its probable cause.

Patricia, however, did comment.

Their arguments had been much less good-humored lately. Perhaps, if he had not gone on seeing so much of Wes Phillips, things might have been simpler. For Wes was leading him into deeper and deeper agony of conscience about conference politics, and this affected all his relationships to Patricia. He rarely saw her father, who was almost constantly on the road. But St. John's was only a few minutes' drive from Wentworth, and the district parsonage only a short distance beyond that.

They had both long ago fallen into the habit of taking their eventual marriage for granted, and this had left them free to indulge in little arguments without feeling that their basic relationship was threatened. But lately the arguments had grown in frequency, in intensity, in range.

"Really, my dear," Patricia said, "it's becoming common knowledge that this girl is making a play for you."

"Very common," said Jack. "Lib Bayliss has warned me; Velma Abernathy has warned me; I think Mrs. Richardson has been trying to warn me; and yesterday even Miss Mollie seemed to be working around to the subject. And they are all quite correct. The girl *was* making a play. I gave her no encouragement. She has now stopped."

"Well, don't look so guilty, darling! Nobody imagines you'll find her irresistible!" Patricia's silvery laugh rang out. They were parked at the overlook above the valley, and in the bright moonlight she suddenly thrust her face close to his, letting her mouth sag open and staring up with her eyes very wide. "Gosh! You great, big, strong wonderful man!" The imitation of Thelma's look was startlingly good. She pinched his cheek. "Stop scowling so! I'm concerned about your career, darling, not about Thelma Richardson. If she gets you, too, all the girls in Wentworth will begin blinking like owls, twisting their lips down in a sulk, and wearing knitted dresses that ran out of yarn."

Jack did not quite know why her imitation irritated him so, or her invincible certainty that a person so coarse and unintelligent could not possibly disturb or attract him. He had actually tried to imagine Patricia looking at him the way Thelma looked at Rick and had felt a little disappointed to realize it was unthinkable. The capacity for adoration was obviously a gift granted only to people unobservant and humorless enough to see gods among their frail fellow creatures.

Since that last afternoon at the beach, three months before, Jack had been puzzled more and more about his whole relationship to Patricia. She had originally attracted him, he realized, precisely because she did not exude any such earthen and disturbing appeal. Her beauty was something cool, chiseled, sophisticated; it had a delicacy of feeling, a purity of style and taste, that he had found delightful and satisfying from the first. She both stimulated him and inhibited him; she roused him, and she checked him. She was a marvelously capable person—poised, observant, immensely well-informed about the conference, and concerned about all the same things that concerned him. She knew how to make herself at home in any level of society with a simplicity and naturalness Jack never ceased to envy. By following her leads he was saved from the fear of blundering, and this gave him a comforting sense of polish and security when she was with him.

But something in her, or in him, was making it impossible for them to marry.

The images that tormented Jack with Thelma never entered his mind regarding Pat. Thelma dissolved a kind of tautness in him and left him feeling simple and savage and virile. Pat increased the tautness at the same time she heightened his physical yearning. He frequently imagined their wedding: the most distinguished members of the community were always there. The bishop himself officiated. Patricia was stunning in a gown fragile and snowy and in perfect taste. Her attendants were from the first families. Jack and the best man were in pin-striped trousers and cutaways. . . . He and Pat looked terribly charming taking up half a page in the society section of Sunday's paper.

The honeymoon would be fun, of course, but somehow he rarely thought about it. Possibly he and Pat exhausted their physical hungers in fighting.

"Mrs. Richardson and I," Patricia was going on, "have been a little disturbed at the way you seem to be building up this poor girl's hopes that she will certainly find love again. Aren't you encouraging an unrealistic attitude?"

Jack stiffened. This had become one of the most ticklish aspects, for when Thelma protested that her life was over and that nobody would ever love her again, he found it impossible not to argue the point. Not only because his duty as her counselor required him to strengthen her faith in herself and her future, but because to him she *was* attractive. He was sincerely baffled by the failure of any of the men in his church to betray such reactions.

"As her spiritual adviser," he said, "I could never forgive myself if I let this girl believe that her life is all over. She had a very unhappy childhood. Her mother died when she was only five, and unlike you, darling, she had no kind and responsible father and no Aunt Katherine. She had to bring herself up, so to speak. She had three brothers, all older than herself; and when she was eight, her father disappeared. He must have been the only person in her existence who showed her any genuine affection. It sounds rather like he simply deserted the children, being unable to provide for them. She and the two younger brothers were taken by some relative and the older brother helped provide for them after a fashion. Her education and her advantages—as is painfully obvious—have been limited. She was working as a waitress when she met Rick. Now, after exactly twenty-seven days of marriage, she has been left alone again. The girl is hanging onto hope and self-confidence by a thread. My first duty is to save her from complete despair."

Pat snuggled her head against his shoulder.

"You make me terribly ashamed. . . . I suppose I actually was beginning to think you found her attractive. You know the old saying, 'Drying a widow's tears is the most dangerous occupation known to man.'"

Jack kissed her, and after a moment she said:

"Shall I confess all my fears? I used to be horribly jealous of Christine Bannister when we were in college and every spring I'd see her chasing you around the track. She wore that sweatshirt with the big red fox's head on it, remember? And she was so athletic and had such a terrific figure, and I was never any good at games—not even table tennis. It's an awful handicap in youth work. Whatever became of Christine?"

"She's an R.N.," said Jack. "She's working back home as her father's nurse and receptionist. He's the town doctor."

"Have you seen her since we left college?"

"No."

"Does she ever write to you?"

"Sometimes." It would be impossible to explain that he had to have some way to keep informed about Foxull without actually going back, and that Christine wrote him regularly, and that he wrote an answer on the first of each month.

"Do you answer? I mean, right away?"

"No."

"Good. I always had some sort of feminine intuition that she was after you, too." Patricia kissed his hand which lay on her shoulder. "I wonder what some of our young people would think if they caught the minister of Wentworth Methodist and the director of Christian Education from St. John's parked on this overlook at this hour of the night?"

"They know we're engaged," said Jack. "Everybody knows we're engaged. Darling," he said, "do you know what's wrong with us? We need to be married! I don't honestly believe your father is a power-crazy dictator who's wrecking the church, and you know I don't. It's just that I . . . I want you, sweetheart, and you keep putting us off, and since I can't have you, it makes me want to hurt you."

The small golden head did not stir; the clear blue eyes stared straight ahead.

"No," she said. "It's not just that you disagree with Dad. There's something in the *way* you feel toward him that . . . frightens me. And sometimes, there's something in the *way* you feel about me that's frightening, too. Sometimes I honestly don't think I know you at all! It's as if you had another self, and I'm always afraid that he will turn out to be the real Jack Lee. The first time I felt this way was that day you graduated from college, or were supposed to graduate only you didn't come . . . and your parents sitting there that whole hour, and Christine making all those ridiculous excuses."

Jack removed his arm from about her.

"I thought we'd agreed to drop that subject."

"I haven't mentioned it for ages! But . . . but I can't stop *thinking!* It was so frightening. When you finally came to tell me goodbye, you were like someone completely different from the person I thought I knew. How can you keep asking me to marry someone I don't even feel sure I *know?*"

Jack studied her face, and in the long silence she stared back, her eyes tortured and almost hostile in the dimness. He snapped on the overhead light, but she did not flinch.

"Pat, what in heaven's name is all this talk lately about another *me?* We've been through school together, worked, played, done everything together. You know all of me there is—all of me *I* know. What else can I possibly *do* to convince you that you know me well enough for us to get married tomorrow if we wanted to?"

Pat leaned forward. The single small ornament on the front of her dark suit glittered as she moved, and her eyes were desperate.

"Take me to visit your parents."

"Pat, you already *know* my parents—"

"I spoke to them for five minutes the day of your graduation from college, then Chris rushed them off to meet someone else. Your mother was such a lovely person, and your Dad told us such a funny story—"

"I know, I know! And I give you my word, that's all there is to them. Why drive a thousand miles to prove it?" It was not even that far round-trip, and he was sorry he had exaggerated so.

"Why won't you talk about them?"

"Because there's nothing to talk about."

He snapped off the light, and they drove home in silence. He unlocked the door for her and dropped the key in her palm.

"Jack, is it true that you haven't been home for eight years?"

Jack turned toward the car without answering; when he reached home, he lay awake for hours, then finally drifted off, to be plagued by more wild dreams of Thelma. They were swimming; they were flying; they were dining in a restaurant and fighting over her red nylon handbag with the drawstring mouth, both giggling like schoolgirls.

He slept through his alarm the next morning, and was awakened at nine by the telephone. It was Mrs. Richardson.

"Mr. Lee, could you come over at once? Something—oh, just hurry! And please don't ring."

He had never heard her voice like this. He pulled on his clothes, trying to think what could have happened. Why had she urged him not to ring? Had something happened she wanted kept from the servants?

Mrs. Richardson met him at the door.

"I sent Mrs. Hoffman and the maid downtown," she said, closing the door behind him. Her voice trembled and she kept swallowing and pressing her hands to her cheeks. "I think . . . something may be wrong with Thelma. She often sleeps till noon, but this morning, for some reason, I looked in on her. She doesn't seem to respond. . . ."

Jack was already halfway up the stairs. He flung open the door of Thelma's room and saw the pill bottle on the night table. It was empty. Thelma lay sleeping, the light from the morning sun falling in bars across the bed from the venetian blinds. Her lips were slightly parted and her breathing was almost imperceptible. He could not find her pulse. Her hands felt cold and clammy. Her skin had a strange splotchy color.

Jack grabbed wildly for the phone on the night table, but someone had apparently moved it off. He jerked the table away from the wall, spilling cigarette ashes, magazines, bobby pins, and the empty bottle. The phone was not on the floor! For a brief instant he thought he might still be dreaming one of his crazy dreams of Thelma. Then he saw the neat round hole in the baseboard and the ends of the wire taped to the wood. He raced to the door.

"Mrs. Richardson! Where—"

She was already at the top of the stairs, placing her hand on her lips to signal him to silence. Was the woman out of her mind? What could it matter what the servants knew at a time like this?

"Where in heaven's name is the phone? Call Dr. Creighton!"

"We had to remove all the upstairs phones," she answered, still whispering. "She eavesdropped, you know."

"Well, call Dr. Creighton!"

"I hadn't wanted to call him unless it was absolutely necessary—"

"Necessary!" Jack almost shouted. "Mrs. Richardson!"

Again she pressed her hands to her temples.

"Mr. Lee, you don't know what it is to be prominent! If the papers—"

Jack pushed her aside and took the steps three at a time. He had to dial twice because he could not control his shaking fingers.

After summoning Creighton he raced up the stairs again and found Mrs. Richardson putting a stack of Thelma's magazines into the wardrobe. One of them fell to the floor at his feet; he kicked it savagely aside, too furious with the woman to speak, and sat down by the bed and began to massage Thelma's wrists and to slap her face with sharp, short slaps.

"Open the window!" he snapped.

"But—"

"The girl is *dying!*"

Mrs. Richardson rattled with the blind, finally got the window open.

"Wider! All the way!" Jack was nearly shouting again. "And come rub her ankles!" He found himself praying under his breath, wildly, passionately. He slapped the white cheeks again, and glanced over his shoulder at the clock. What could be keeping Creighton?

"I had no idea it was so bad," Mrs. Richardson was saying, her face paler still, her hands jerky. "And we really don't know. She drinks sometimes . . ."

"She got those tablets at the drugstore yesterday. I saw her!" Jack glared at the bottle, which lay where it had fallen, clean and gleaming except for a dusty whiteness in the bottom.

"She's so cold!" Mrs. Richardson's eyes were pleading. "Is she . . . going?"

"I won't let her go!"

Jack saw astonishment mingled with the fear in her face, but it seemed unimportant. The important thing was that Thelma had to live.

Creighton arrived within minutes and an hour later he came out of the room, closed the door, and smiled at them.

"If you'd called me five minutes later I'm not sure we could have saved her, but—"

Jack did not hear the rest. He averted his face, kept it turned away from them as he descended the stairs, and walked out the door without speaking or looking back.

Three weeks later, Mrs. Richardson closed the big house and left for Europe, and Thelma went home to New York.

XVII

The Voice of the Hireling

JACK returned to the Middleton Hotel ahead of Wes on Wednesday night, exhausted, but too keyed up to sleep. Belfair Methodist had been a madhouse on the first day of conference. In the midst of arrivals and registrations and the necessary preliminaries, Jack and Wes and the rebel group had found it difficult to locate specific delegates and to talk to them. And they kept running into questions concerning the motives of some who had joined the rebel cause. DeForrest Garrison, in particular, was suspect, and a few had even raised doubts about Dan Starr. The doubts about Garrison were probably only too well grounded. . . . Jack sat by the window brooding and waiting for Wes to come in.

The Starr-Garrison episode had occurred at annual conference the year before, in June 1959, when conference met at Epworth Methodist Church. Jack had been present on the Saturday morning in question, at the final business session of the 1959 conference. Dan Starr had presented a report on the floor of the conference on that Saturday morning a year ago. Dr. Garrison, who would normally have made the presentation as committee chairman, had appeared briefly, looking pale and haggard, to say that he was unwell and to ask permission for Dan to read the report. The material Dan chose to single out for special consideration had to do mainly with the church and juvenile delinquency. He was a slender boy with wide shoulders and a clear, bronzed face. He had a shy, almost girlish smile, direct blue eyes, and a wholly unself-conscious simplicity and charm. He was twenty-four, but his curly blond hair and athletic grace made him look much younger, especially when he became impassioned in speaking—as he did on this occasion. The delegates, who had been sitting through three days of uninspired committee reports, were obviously moved by his sincerity and eloquence; there had even been a burst of applause from some teen-agers in the balcony at the close, and the bishop himself took a moment from the overcrowded agenda to commend the young man for his presentation.

At the end of the business session Wes had joined Jack at lunch in the church basement.

"Stand by for fireworks," Wes rumbled. "Garrison must be trying to bring your friend Starr to the bishop's attention direct—without going through Belovèd. This is the first time in years anybody's hatched up a trick like that. Better tell Starr he's in for trouble."

"Dan's not the plotting type," said Jack. "Besides, Dr. Garrison was ill—you could see that."

"Garrison's never yet been too sick to rise and shine before an annual conference. Something's up."

They had argued briefly. Wes maintained that Garrison had "stomped on the most exposed nerve in Belovèd's whole body—his ability to keep himself between the bishop and the bulk of the ministers." He predicted an immediate and violent reaction. Jack found the whole idea amusing, but that night Patricia confirmed this diagnosis.

"I really think perhaps you should warn Dan and Martha that Dad and the other superintendents feel Dan was going over their heads."

"Do you believe such nonsense?" Jack demanded.

"It—it doesn't seem quite like Dan. But Dad's almost never wrong about why people do things."

Jack got up early the next morning, which was Sunday, and drove out to Shiloh Methodist, a historic little church on the edge of town where Dan and a group of other young men were to be ordained by the bishop and the cabinet at eight o'clock. He found Martha with Dan in the narthex.

"Dan," said Jack, "when you presented that report yesterday morning, did you know those teen-agers from Macedonia Church were in the balcony?"

"Gosh, no! I was really floored when they applauded! And did you hear that little bouquet the bishop tossed me?"

"And guess what!" Martha broke in. "The pastoral relations committee from Macedonia was there too. We heard that they were asking the bishop to send them Dan instead of Dr. Burnham. Wouldn't it be fantastic if he should!"

Jack felt uneasy. Patricia had not mentioned this.

"Dan, you don't want to go to Macedonia. It's one of those dying inner-city churches surrounded by a slum. Those places are preachers' graveyards!"

"Who cares! It's got all the problems we're interested in. Martha did social case work before we married. It's got a terrific potential in youth work—they're literally swamped with delinquency down there, and just about everything else. And with all due respect, Dr. Burnham is ready for retirement; he'd just be out to pasture at Macedonia."

Just at that moment the ordinands were summoned to the basement to be given their final instructions, and Martha hurried off to get a seat in the small and crowded sanctuary. Jack stood in the narthex trying to think. He had never been able to take seriously Wes's insistence that Dr. Worthington could be brutally vengeful, but if the superintendent actually imagined Dan was in on some sort of attempt to go over his head to the bishop, the matter ought to be cleared up at once.

Just at that moment the ushers opened the doors, the congregation rose, and the processional hymn boomed out:

The church's one foundation is Jesus Christ her Lord;
She is his new creation, by water and the word.
From Heav'n he came and sought her to be his holy bride,
With his own blood he bought her, and for her life he died.

Jack caught a glimpse of Dan's face as the double line of young men swung past him. The bright curly head was lifted, the wide shoulders squared, the girlishly beautiful blue eyes exalted as the men moved down the aisle followed by the cabinet and then the bishop, his face remote and withdrawn, as if he too were both oppressed and inspired by this supreme hour in the lives of the young ministers under his charge.

Jack stood against the wall in the rear. The chancel of the beautiful little church was much too small for all the superintendents to stand comfortably or to move about conveniently, and suddenly Jack realized that Dr. Worthington was no longer visible and must have slipped out by one of the side doors after the preliminaries.

Jack found him in the basement, walking up and down in the cool dimness, among the long columns of pillars and additional supporting timbers.

The basement was no longer in use, and was covered with dust and festooned with cobwebs, and here and there the janitor had stored boxes of seasonal items or tools. Jack stood with Dr. Worthington by the stairwell leading to the chancel overhead, and they talked and argued; and between times the bishop's voice floated down, clear and distinct, but with a hollow, ghostly quality. Jack kept trying to establish the point that Dan Starr was incapable of any sort of trickery to promote his career, that he was so naïve and idealistic as to have been subject for jokes in seminary, where someone had nicknamed him "Dan the Starry-eyed." His eagerness to serve a dying inner-city church in a slum was irrefutable evidence that he had a thoroughly nonprofessional approach to the ministry, for most ministers fled from such appointments.

They paused and bowed their heads as the bishop read the opening prayer in the ordination of the deacons, who went to the altar first.

"Almighty God, who by Thy divine providence hast appointed divers orders of ministers in Thy Church, and didst inspire Thine apostles to choose into the order of deacons Thy first martyr, St. Stephen, with others; mercifully behold these Thy servants now called to the like office and administration . . ."

After the prayer Jack tried several other angles, all in vain.

"Sir," he said at last in exasperation, "I should be curious to know what you consider was the actual course of events!"

Dr. Worthington's round pink face reflected a slight boredom.

"It's nothing very difficult to fathom. Dr. Garrison, as you may have heard, came into the ministry from the legitimate theater. He is known to be able to turn pale simply as a parlor trick, and over the years his occasional 'illnesses' have begun to be suspect. He came to us with only a college degree, had never had any seminary training, and was extremely sensitive on the point. I was fortunate enough to be able to persuade one of our Methodist institutions to honor him with the degree of doctor of divinity."

Jack had heard that Dr. Worthington was extraordinarily acute in ferreting out a man's fondest dream—or greatest terror.

"Unhappily, Dr. Burnham was bitterly opposed to this harmless little gesture. He may be somewhat limited professionally by a dry speaking style, but he is a scholar of repute and holder of three earned degrees. He intervened with some of the college trustees and very nearly prevented Dr. Garrison from receiving his degree.

"DeForrest Garrison is far too wrapped up in himself to think very long about harming anyone else. But he has never forgiven Sid Burnham for almost causing him to live out his days with no more notable title than 'Reverend.' He knew that Sid was slated for Macedonia this year; he knew that the church was unhappy with the appointment; he knew that nothing else in Sid's bracket was open right now. I therefore assume that, simply in hopes of embarrassing Sid and possibly causing him to suffer a humiliating step-down in his last appointment before retirement, he staged his little drama yesterday morning. It *was* a drama, you know!"

From the stairwell they could hear the voice of the bishop as he went down the line, laying his hands upon the head of each ordinand:

"Take thou authority to execute the office of a deacon in the Church of God; in the name of the Father, and of the Son, and of the Holy Spirit. Amen. . . . Take thou authority . . ."

Jack tried to control his mounting anger.

"Sir, is it Dan's fault if he's attractive to those young people? Sending them an elderly man of Dr. Burnham's type is almost like deliberately turning them over to dope and delinquency! Everybody knows he'd retire tomorrow if he didn't need those extra service-years on his pension."

The pink face looked genuinely perplexed. The China-doll eyes were rounder than usual.

"But I thought I just said there was nothing else open in Sid's bracket!"

"Then let him drop down a few dollars! Isn't it only the number of years that affect his pension? The salary has nothing to do with it."

"My dear boy, the church moves forward because her ministers have dependable goals to aim at. To ignore the long-term needs of her professional ministry and to think only of the short-term needs of an individual church would bring only confusion and disaster to any human organization. For almost forty years now Sid Burnham has given unstintingly of himself; he has taken difficult posts without complaining; he has observed the strictest propriety toward his superiors and colleagues and the boards and commissions; he has pushed the total program even when it differed radically from his own desires; he has been in the highest sense of the term a team man. Who can possibly calculate the effect on his spirit and morale if all these things brought no reward? Or the effect on the hundreds of ministers in this great conference? What would be left for them to live for?"

"There's always people."

"I'm serious! And young Starr—consider the effect on him if we should thus publicly encourage his belief that the church rewards trickery and deceit!"

"Sir, you're *assuming* that Dan—!" Jack suddenly realized that his voice might be carrying up the stairwell. The service for deacons was now concluding; Dan would be coming forward next with the elders. They listened in silence to the bishop's prayer:

"Almighty God, the father of our Lord Jesus Christ, who thought equality with Thee not a thing to be grasped, but emptied Himself and made Himself obedient, even unto death on the cross, behold, these Thy servants. They kneel before Thee in humility, laying aside every sin which might hinder or embarrass the glorious ministry whereunto they are called. They bow before Thee in meekness and lowliness of heart, consecrating every gift and every aspiration wholly to Thy service. They ask not to be ministered unto, but to minister. As Christ knelt in Gethsemane, so kneel Thy servants with but one plea: Not my will but Thine be done. In Jesus' name. Amen."

"Excellent!" murmured the older man. "Beautifully done!" He raised his head and returned his gaze to Jack. "I would not give ten cents for the minister with no ambition, but your young friend will have to realize that he cannot get to the top in a single jump. If he is willing to wait his turn like everyone else, no post will be too high for him to aspire to."

Jack had wanted to go upstairs and see Dan ordained, but obviously he was not getting through to Dr. Worthington.

"Sir, if Dr. Burnham really meant his own vows when he was ordained, why can't you just ask him to accept whatever church is available and tell him you've found a man who can do a better job at Macedonia than he can? After all, it's certainly not a very desirable post right now, even if it does happen to be in his bracket. In fact, why can't the bishop send any minister where he's needed, even if it involves cutting his salary in half? Isn't that what the word 'minister' means—someone who serves other people?"

Dr. Worthington had been pacing slowly up and down. Now he stopped and gazed up at Jack, his face plainly troubled.

"Ordination is one of the highest moments in any minister's life. But it is like the stained glass and the Gothic arches and the beautiful music upstairs: The whole structure rests on things not quite so attractive to behold, but solid and necessary. And unchanging." He placed the tips of his plump, tapering fingers on the dusty side of one of the huge upright timbers. "This building was originally a rather modest structure, but the congregation grew in numbers and affluence and one day decided they simply had to build the tallest steeple in town. But the added weight brought dangerous strains and they were forced to add so many timbers in the basement that part of this room became unusable.

"You might ponder this as a sort of parable, if you like. Possibly the first Christians *were* as selfless and unworldly as is generally assumed; certainly they were few in number, their organizational structure was quite modest, and they anticipated the end of history at an early date. But time went on, the church grew, its shadow lengthened, and the motives which had empowered a band of lay preachers in a temporary world soon proved insufficient for the full-time professionals of an on-going organization. So title and rank and salary and seniority had to be wedged in among love and sacrifice and faith." He patted the rough timber. "These are not very attractive, I grant you. But without them you would have no church at all."

Overhead they heard the cadence of footsteps as the elders came forward. Dan would be at the altar now. The bishop was reading:

"Jesus said . . . I am the good shepherd: the good shepherd giveth his life for his sheep. But he that is an hireling, and not the shepherd, whose own the sheep are not, seeth the wolf coming, and leaveth the sheep, and fleeth . . ."

Dr. Worthington raised his voice slightly.

"Belovèd, your proposal would require that every minister be as selfless as Christ. But suppose we suddenly assigned a distinguished member of the conference to some lowly post simply because it happened to fit his particular gifts and he could thereby advance the Kingdom of God. How could one explain such an appointment? His colleagues would know he had not requested it. They would assume that we were glossing over some scandal or breach of discipline. The man himself would feel sure he was being punished for some crime he had not committed."

Jack stared at the dusty floor and said:

"Then you actually can't put the Kingdom of God first, and the Holy Spirit has no place in a cabinet meeting."

"Of course it has a place! I've seen problems unraveled which could only have found solution through a wisdom more than human. I've seen the whole cabinet stop dead for prayer. I've seen superintendents in such agony in their desire to be fair to every man, not to penalize or hurt any man, that they broke down and cried."

"But if a big church—"

"Oh, come, come, belovèd! Everyone knows that the Holy Spirit has nothing to do with the big church appointments—those are all settled by wealthy laymen. But the Spirit certainly does exercise an influence in the medium and lower brackets."

Jack's mind suddenly went back to Pastor Elwood sitting in his neat, plain study in the Foxull Methodist Church, saying: "Unless we bear the cross, we cannot wear the crown."

"But don't you believe that any minister ever thinks of his ministry just in terms of service?"

"They all do! After the question of the bracket has been settled. Perhaps every man thinks of his own status and advancement as the necessary lever by which alone he can lift his fellows. I honestly don't know. But I do know one thing:

"I know that all my years in the superintendency I have never yet had a man deliberately seek out a church beneath his salary bracket simply because it offered a greater opportunity for service or happened to fit his special talents. Steve McCullen did ask for Elm Avenue when it meant a cut of almost a thousand dollars, but that was because he saw the terrific potential. I remember he told me at the time, 'If I can't double that budget within three years, I'll eat my shirt!'

"We have plenty of dying textile mill towns within the bounds of this conference, and mining towns where poverty and unemployment have intensified every human need. But the men who come to me never inquire about 'opportunities' like that, or fields of service that are 'wider' in that particular way. I don't mean they refuse to tackle a difficult job for the Kingdom if you challenge them with it and show them it needs doing. But they're not *thinking* of their ministry in such terms; they never *ask* for that sort of job; it usually comes as an unhappy surprise—like rain in the middle of a ball game. The men who come to me never have but one question: 'What does it pay?'"

"You surely can't believe they're preaching just for money!"

"Not money as such. Salary is only an index: it tells the world you've built a bigger church than the next man, or won more converts to Christ, or can preach a better sermon. And, of course, a cut in salary proclaims one a *spiritual* failure. Ambition and fear, or both: these just about exhaust the basic motivations. The rest is window dressing—or self-deception."

"Well," said Jack, "that doesn't leave much to believe in."

The older man looked perplexed.

"It leaves everything—because it leaves the truth! Belovèd, I beg you for your sake as well as for Patricia's to face up to what the church is and what her ministers are made of. They are old pros, playing for money, who like to imagine that they still have their amateur standing. I daresay Wes Phillips is the only man in this whole conference who's still an amateur at heart, but the ineffectiveness of his entire career is a genuine tragedy. These youngsters upstairs today are not of his caliber. Give them a few years in the unrewarding hardships of rural work, a few years in the spotlight of a competitive organization like ours, or just a wife and children and a few unpaid bills, and they will be asking about their next church only what all the others ask: 'What does it pay?' "

"Well," said Jack, "if a man's theology is any indication—"

"My dear boy, where salary is concerned all clergymen have the same theology."

Jack was deeply wounded—far more than he would have expected—by the implication that he fell so far below Wes in courage and integrity. From above they could hear the bishop's voice as he moved down the line of young men kneeling at the altar. In his mind's eye Jack could see the little half-circle of black-robed figures as the bishop and several superintendents gathered about each man in turn, their outstretched hands resting upon his bowed head:

"The Lord pour upon thee the Holy Spirit for the office and work of an elder in the Church of God. . . . And be thou a faithful dispenser of the Word of God, and of His holy Sacraments. . . ."

When Jack felt he could speak without emotion, he said:

"Then what's to become of Dan, sir?"

"He is being assigned to the Carsten Circuit."

Jack stared at one of the dusty uprights and said:

"So a young man who could really help young people goes to a country circuit to pastor old folks, and a loyal old fuddy-duddy goes to Macedonia, and all this comes under the name of promoting the Kingdom of God on earth."

"You will be pleased to know," said the superintendent mildly, "that the bishop was much disturbed by your young friend's shocking descriptions of the state of youth today. He insisted we do something about the situation at Macedonia. He also shared your unfavorable opinion of Dr. Burnham. Thus Dr. Burnham *will* be forced to take a church somewhat beneath his bracket." He paused. "You will be further pleased that we are sending an extremely able man to Macedonia."

"Who?"

"Dr. DeForrest Garrison."

"Dr. Garrison! To *Macedonia?!*"

The round blue eyes were artlessly surprised.

"Why, yes. Weren't you just now advocating that the man should be picked for the job regardless of bracket or morale or prestige?"

"But . . . but that's a cut of three thousand dollars!"

"Thirty-two hundred."

"But Dr. Garrison has been holding the most distinguished pulpits in the conference."

"For twenty years."

"So . . . so he's being punished, too!"

"He may possibly take it so. By your own standards, it is an excellent choice: He is a tremendous drawing card; he's attractive to all age groups; they've heard him; they want him; if anyone can reactivate Macedonia, he can. And it should make an interesting test of your theories."

"Dr. Garrison is not a typical minister of the Gospel. He's a prima donna!"

"He is facing what you insist every minister desires—an opportunity to serve human need in its most extreme form, and incidentally to give up a suburban home and a charming congregation for a house and a job in the slums."

"It's not a fair test."

"Well, perhaps not. All the same, I regret that it would be improper for you to accompany Mr. Hoffner when he informs this latter-day St. Paul of his call to Macedonia."

Jack made no answer, but walked slowly away down the long dusty aisle between the columns of ugly timbers. He was almost afraid to let himself begin thinking through what this meant for his relationship to Dr. Worthington and to Patricia and to his whole future. For this meant that Wes Phillips had been right. This meant that Wes Phillips might also be right about all those other things they had argued over.

For this was vengeance.

Brutal. Naked. Deliberately unmasked.

Jack decided to speak to Hoffner. He and the other superintendents might be able to bring enough pressure to bear to save Dan—and even to soften Garrison's punishment. As he came up out of the shadows into the brilliant sunlight again, he realized that the congregation had already begun the closing hymn.

> *There's surely somewhere a lowly place*
> *In earth's harvest fields so wide,*
> *Where I may labor through life's short day*
> *For Jesus the Crucified.*

He stood on the sidewalk in the shadow of the soaring steeple, its white spire pure and dazzling against the clean blue sky, and the chorus of the hymn rang out:

> *I'll go where you want me to go, dear Lord,*
> *O'er mountain or plain or sea;*
> *I'll say what you want me to say, dear Lord,*
> *I'll be what you want me to be.*

XVIII

A Call to Macedonia

ALFRED HOFFNER was a big, kindly, horse-faced man with shaggy gray hair and a lumbering walk, who was now serving his third term as a district superintendent. Jack had found him a good friend and candid adviser and had no hesitancy now in approaching him about Dan. They had sat on a little stone bench beside Shiloh Church after the 1959 ordination service, the superintendent setting his worn and bulging briefcase on the grass before his feet. He offered Jack no hope whatever that the decisions on Dan and Dr. Garrison might be reversed.

"We sat up till past two this morning trying to make Fred Worthington see that Garrison isn't brave enough or interested enough to form some kind of power bloc of his own. Honestly, sometimes I don't understand Fred at all!" Hoffner stared absently at the crowd, many of whom had remained to congratulate the ordinands and were milling about chatting and laughing. "He's gifted and informed and a born administrator. He's a good man, and he deserves to be a bishop more than any man I've ever known.

"But, once or twice a year he suddenly goes stone blind and crazy from simple *fear* and makes me ashamed to be called a member of his team." Hoffner kicked the briefcase. "There's something terribly wrong with Fred. I've wondered if never having known his mother or father has something to do with it. He says that the Methodist Church was his mother and father, but he says it too often. And when he gets it into his head that someone is threatening him, well, I just plain pity the man!" Hoffner plucked a blade of grass and chewed on it. "So now I've got to tell DeForrest that we're sending him to a big empty barn that's on the skids financially and every other way—and that we're giving First Church, Claremont to Leonard Foley—and *I'm* the one who promised I'd help DeForrest get First!"

"Why don't you ask Dr. Worthington to send him back to Central for one more year?"

"Fred's beside himself! He's determined to make an example of Garrison and Starr. Anyway, Garrison blew Central wide open this year trying to sell them on altar boys to light the candles ahead of his grand entrances. The pastoral relations committee told me that under *no* circumstances would they take the great man back." He sighed. "I suppose every conference has at least one DeForrest Garrison, but why did the good Lord put him in *my* district?"

"Then get the rest of the cabinet together! Get the bishop to reverse all this!"

Hoffner shook his head.

"It's not that simple. Fred's convinced the bishop that Garrison is the only man who can save the youth of Macedonia and that this is a case where we've got to think of the Kingdom of God regardless of salary and conference standing." Jack gave a short, jerky laugh and Hoffner glanced up, then went on. "Fred has done us all favors when he could. Nothing really out of line, you understand, but . . . well, every superintendent naturally wants the best possible men for his own district and doesn't always consider the welfare of the conference at large. So now Fred wants us to do *him* a favor that's not completely proper. We have to keep our relationship with him intact if we hope to accomplish anything next year. We've got almost five hundred other preachers to provide for, and somebody has to serve Macedonia!" Hoffner grinned a little wistfully. "I'll admit the bishop should have seen through this one, but he's only human and can't know all the facts about every appointment."

"Then inform Garrison! He's telling anybody who will listen that he's slated for First Church, Claremont."

The long horse-face looked suddenly haggard.

"I'm not a very brave man, son, but I've taken bad news to a lot of preachers in my time, and thank God most of them are good Methodists and believe that God does have a part in all this, and so do I. And the funny thing is, this appointment could be God's will, if DeForrest were willing to take it that way: Those folks in the slums need Christ, too."

"Then tell him so at once!"

"I'll inform him; that's his right under our system. But I'm going to give it to him short and quick, just before conference is over." A wry smile. "DeForrest is an actor. I honestly don't think he'll consent to die unless the Lord allows him an audience and a good line for his exit. He makes big scenes that tear you all to pieces. He says things you spend years trying to forgive and forget."

Jack protested that he could not possibly wait till just before the bishop read the appointments that afternoon, and ended by threatening to tell Garrison himself. To his surprise, Hoffner amiably agreed: Someone was sure to tell him anyway; it might as well be straight and factual.

A short, stocky man in a tight-fitting suit had been lingering by the church, glancing at them from time to time.

"Here comes Claude Waddell," Hoffner said rapidly. "He's been hounding the life out of me for days. He's on the pastoral relations committee from Macedonia, but he doesn't know the big news yet. He's been hunting all over for Garrison. Maybe you should take him along. With a layman standing there admiring him, DeForrest won't dare let his hair down."

Waddell was a muscular little man with an earnest, leathery face and a boyish grin showing teeth in need of dental repair. He looked uncomfortable in his very new suit, and he gestured vigorously with stubby, calloused hands which much scrubbing had not freed of the black grease around the nails. He pronounced it "Waddle, like a duck," and was delighted at Hoffner's explanation that Jack was going to see Dr. Garrison and would be glad to help Waddell present the needs of Macedonia. Jack did not mention that the appointment was already settled for fear of Garrison's reaction to any sudden and joyous congratulations.

Hoffner had said Garrison was across town at Wesley Memorial, putting on a demonstration of his "Bible Teaching Through Drama," and Jack drove over with Waddell.

Jack was well acquainted with Garrison. He had worked a week one summer in a camp for intermediates, and Garrison had driven out each night to give the inspirational addresses. They had had several long talks.

"I was on the stage, you know," Garrison had said. "Mostly bit parts; one good role in a comedy that never got beyond the Shubert in New Haven. Then one Sunday night I filled in for a friend who was supposed to be Stephen in a one-act play at my church. I was never the same again. I felt . . ." he glanced at Jack almost shyly, "that I actually *was* Stephen. That I *was* laying down my life for Christ. And the congregation felt it—tremendously! I was never content from that moment to spend my years and talents creating butlers and detectives when I felt I could help create the Christ. Maybe I am just an actor at heart, but aren't we all?

"You're new in the ministry, Jack. You haven't yet preached the same sermons in your third or fourth pastorate. But even the second time is acting. The original mood, the sense of the importance of the issues, even your belief that you'll accomplish something big with that sermon —all of these have to be brought back to life by artificial respiration. So you rework the thing and update your illustrations and practice it till you feel everything you felt the first time—except the complete sincerity. . . . In short, you're actor."

"I'm already doing those very things," Jack had confessed wryly. "What will I be like at forty!"

"And at fifty-three!" Garrison self-consciously ran one hand over his impeccably groomed white hair. "Because one also loses faith in *oneself*. I have sometimes actually thought that the greater one's gift for preaching Christ publicly, the smaller one's remaining energy for following him privately. Ethel used to have to keep the children out of my path on Mondays—as if I were some sort of prima donna!" He ran the fingertips of one delicate hand over his flamboyant tie. Conference gossip had it that all his ties were hand-painted for him in New York. "I suppose you know the legend that actors have no souls. They can only be *other* people. Themselves they never quite discover or get control of. So they are forever hearing themselves say things to people they'd give their right arms to unsay. Result: they have very few friends."

That had been two summers ago, but Jack had never forgotten the pathos of that roundabout little plea for friendship by an immensely talented and popular man.

At Wesley Memorial they found that Garrison was holding his teaching-through-drama class in a small auditorium in the basement. Jack and Waddell found all the seats taken and watched from the rear door while Garrison arranged one of his "control groups" of children about a long, low table on the little stage down front. They were mostly eight- and nine-year-olds and a titter rippled through the crowd as Ethel Garrison separated two boys scuffling for the end chair. Jack guessed that the spectators were mostly Sunday-school teachers who enjoyed seeing a "control group" do the things their own classes did back home.

Garrison smiled at the audience.

"You must forgive the sons of Zebedee. It seems they are always with us. Now, boys, what did the Savior say when two of *his* best friends started a squabble over the head chair?"

The boys looked mystified. A pink-faced moppet at the other end shot up her hand.

"He made them go to the foot of the class!"

"That's exactly right, Lucille. He said if we want to be first, we have to put ourselves last. And what did he do to *show* his twelve friends what he meant by this lesson?"

The apostles fidgeted, biting their lips and scratching their heads, and finally Garrison said:

"He put on a little play for them, didn't he? He acted out a part for them—just the way we've been doing today." Garrison's voice had suddenly taken on a simple, childish quality, and his face seemed to have the untroubled and transparent candor of their own. "Now, you just watch, and I'll show you the one he put on for his friends when they argued about getting the best place at the table."

The children poked each other and whispered, their eyes shining with anticipation, and a stir ran through the audience. Waddell nudged Jack.

"He can play any part he wants to, and he makes you think it's really them. It's like he really *was* them. Sorta gives you a funny feeling. . . ."

Garrison turned toward a summer camping tableau at the rear of the little stage, consisting of a tent and cot with imitation campfire and a stone altar surmounted by a rustic cross. With almost disdainful adroitness he stripped the sheet from the cot, draped it about him with a few deft movements, tied a towel about his waist, and had one of the children get some water for the little white wash basin on the box at the head of the cot.

He *should* have looked absurd.

Jack expected him to, as he approached the children with his florid necktie peeping through the folds of his flowing white sheet, his tan and white shoes standing out in somehow utterly unexpected contrast —was it because Jack had unconsciously expected sandals?—his cuff links glittering, and most of all, the skimpy towel barely reaching about his somewhat plump waistline.

But he did not look absurd.

A total hush fell upon the children as they gazed up into his face, and in the audience not a person stirred, not a whisper sounded. In spite of himself Jack felt for the first time in his life that now he actually had an impression of how Jesus must have looked. For everything about Garrison had undergone some subtle change—his walk, his posture, the movements of his hands, the lines of his face. A gentle radiance and peace seemed to flow in his motions, in the turn of his head, the sudden uplifting of his eyes. Jack heard the little man beside him swallow noisily in the silence and let out a small, hushed explosion of breath. Even Garrison's voice was different, as if someone else were speaking through him.

"For I am among you as one that serveth. He that would be great among you, let him make himself the least and the servant of all. He that exalteth himself shall be abased, and he that abaseth himself, the same shall be exalted."

The faces of the twelve children were mute, hypnotized, their small pink mouths slightly open, their eyes wide. They gazed up in wonder, entranced by the translucent love that shone down upon them with an almost physical presence and warmth.

Garrison knelt with the same easy grace that had suddenly possessed all his movements, simulating the act of dipping his hands into the basin and washing the feet of the first child.

When the demonstration was finished, Mrs. Garrison took over the instruction. Jack had Waddell sit in a chair by the basement entrance, and then caught Garrison's eye.

Garrison did not remove the towel or sheet, but came up the narrow aisle and out into the hall with the same new, grave walk, carrying the basin and seemingly unaware of the startled glances of occasional passers-by. This was something Jack had not anticipated. It was as if Garrison were still immersed in his role, unable to break free of the personality that had enveloped him. He shook hands, still holding the basin.

"I had the water put in it," said Garrison, noticing Jack's glance, "to compel me to walk as Christ would have in those circumstances."

"DeForrest," said Jack, "I . . . dislike people who carry rumors. Especially about appointments. But I happened on something this morning I felt you were entitled to know."

"Well, what is it?" Still the same calm voice, the same disturbing sensation of echoes.

"Leonard Foley is going to First Church, Claremont."

Garrison's melodious laughter was so spontaneous that Jack felt his face redden.

"You dear child! Surely you must be aware that—in all charity—he's one of our less scintillating pulpit personalities. Not to mention the fact that he's much younger than he appears. It would be years before they'd dare boost Lennie to a pulpit like Claremont." Garrison rarely used terms like "appointment" or "church"; it was almost always "pulpit." Again the musical little laugh as he ran the tips of his fingers over his exquisitely groomed white hair.

"I have this straight!" Jack snapped.

"Tell uncle. I shan't breathe a word!"

"I had it from Mr. Hoffner just one hour ago."

The glancing lights in the gray eyes vanished, but no other light replaced them. The mischievous expression on the handsome pink face disappeared, but no other expression came. Slowly, perceptibly, the pinkness gave way to white. When the voice emerged at last, it too was strangely devoid of expression.

"You're sure this is First, Claremont—not some other First?"

Jack nodded.

The expression came now, deep in the large gray eyes, like something dimly discerned at the back of a misty cave. It came in the voice too, chill and frightening in its intensity.

"Alfred Hoffner sat in my house, at my table, on the twelfth of February and told me with his own lips that First Church, Claremont, was *mine!*"

Jack started to speak, but Garrison went on:

"I followed him once, you know—at Chapel Heights—and I added more members on profession of faith my first year than he took in by all means during his entire pastorate there. I see now that he has never been able to forgive me. And as a D.S., of course—"

"Mr. Hoffner never wanted to return to the superintendency this last time, but the bishop—"

"The bishop! What does the bishop know about this conference? Only what Belovèd tells him—no more, no less."

Before Jack could answer, he suddenly noticed Waddell approaching and tried too late to motion him away.

"Dr. Garrison, I'm Claude Waddell—waddle, like a duck, you know? I'm from Macedonia. I'm on the pastoral relations committee you talked to Friday, remember? You told our chairman for us to come hear that young fellow, Starr, and we did and we thought he was terrific, but they told us he didn't have enough experience for Macedonia." Well, that settled Garrison's part in it: he had planned on Friday to be ill on Saturday so Dan could speak. But Garrison scarcely seemed to be listening. Waddell was sweating, and his voice was unsteady. "You preached a revival at our church two summers ago. I've said ever since that if Dr. Garrison could knock sense into a sinner as far gone as Claude Waddell, he could knock it into anybody. But maybe you don't remember me?"

"You're very kind," said Garrison. "I'm happy that you're continuing to go forward in your Christian experience."

"DeForrest," said Jack, "Mr. Waddell has been looking for you everywhere. I said I was sure you'd give him a minute."

"It was most gracious of your committee to want me back so soon," said Garrison. "But I'm booked up on revivals through next summer."

He turned away and spoke to Jack. "I've just been trying to figure out *when* they decided this. My guess is Hoffner knew it already when he was sitting at my table and eating my food. He knew I'd tell everyone—"

Waddell skirted around Garrison's outthrust elbow, to avoid making him splash the water from the basin.

"We want you for our *pastor*, not just for a revival!"

Garrison was plainly astounded.

"Surely your committee must realize that's utterly out of the question, Mr. Waddell! I'm flattered but . . . you understand." He smiled for the first time, briefly.

Waddell's round face hardened. A dull red showed under the leathery skin above his too-tight collar.

"No, sir, I guess I don't understand. I feel like the Lord put me on this committee to do a job, Dr. Garrison. The other two members got disgusted and went home. I got to tell our folks *something*. Mr. Hoffner said to see you."

Garrison compressed his lips.

"Very well, Mr. Waddell. Exactly what is Macedonia prepared to offer?"

"Everything a preacher could want! There's taverns and dives, and the new throughway has jammed all kinds of people in there. There's no playgrounds. The kids just run wild in the streets. We got more sinners in a mile of our church than in all the rest of the city put together!" Waddell's round face grew rounder as he grinned, his eyes shining. The minister stared back in polite bewilderment.

"I daresay that's an understatement, Mr. Waddell."

"But you can handle them, Dr. Garrison! Just like you done these kids in here!" He jabbed a muscular hand toward the auditorium, where Ethel Garrison was lecturing her group.

Garrison carefully shifted the basin to his right hand to avoid Waddell's enthusiastic gestures, loosened the knot of his hand-painted necktie with the tip of one finger, and gazed briefly at the ceiling.

"Nothing else, Mr. Waddell?"

Waddell scratched his thinning hair, then grinned.

"Nothing but sinners, Dr. Garrison!"

"You haven't, by any chance, had any recent meetings of the Commission on Stewardship and Finance?"

"They got nothing to meet about! Everybody with a decent job or any money has left us for the suburbs."

Garrison stared down at the flowing white folds of his robe and thoughtfully smoothed the impromptu lapels with the tips of his beautifully manicured fingers.

"Mr. Waddell, we do not seem to be talking the same language. Possibly the defect lies in me. I have just had some rather distressing news and fear I am really not myself." His eyes wandered from Waddell's hands to the water in the basin, then hastily away. "The entire conference is painfully aware of the tragic dilemma of the inner-city church, of which Macedonia is certainly a *prime* example. Naturally, it goes without saying that as a minister of the Gospel, my sole desire is to go where my limited gifts can be of use."

"I remembered that from your revival, Dr. Garrison. I told the committee, 'Dr. *Garrison* don't care what kind of a parsonage Macedo——' "

"However," Garrison went on, "I am sure we are all agreed that Christ was never concerned over a man's outward appearance—what kind of clothes he wore, that sort of thing."

"I told them that's how you'd feel—"

"Yet, in our own day, Mr. Waddell, many devout Christians—some of them colleagues of mine!—would seem to imply that the white-collar man and the professional man and the well-to-do have no *right* to hear the Gospel preached!" He stared hard at Waddell, who made no answer. "The Scripture tells us that '*whosoever* believeth on him shall be saved!' Whether in slum or in suburb. Right, Mr. Waddell?"

"Yes, sir."

"Naturally you are concerned that friends and neighbors of yours shall find him, too—persons whose heartaches and joys and ways of living you know best. But I am likewise touched, Mr. Waddell, for those among whom God has seen fit to place *me*."

Waddell scraped one foot against the other.

"Well, I never had too much school. Does that mean you *will* come?"

Garrison permitted himself a sigh.

"I am attempting to say, Mr. Waddell, that a number of my colleagues might feel a call of God to your type of situation. As of this moment, I myself do not."

Jack stepped hastily forward and seized Waddell's arm.

"Dr. Garrison will consider it, Wad."

"I have considered it!" said Garrison, staring at Jack. "This man needs to get busy exploring other possibilities. The appointments will be read this afternoon at two and it is already past ten! Sir, my answer is *no!*"

"He'll think about it," Jack repeated, dragging Waddell away a few steps and whispering, "Get out before you ruin everything! You've almost got him. Get out. *Get out!*"

But he was too late to shut off the radiant smile Waddell cast at the minister as he turned and walked away with his buoyant, bouncing stride.

"Jack, why in Heaven's name didn't you tell the man they can't have me?" Garrison's fine eyes seemed to focus on Jack attentively for the first time. "And how could Hoffner possibly be too chicken-hearted to tell him flatly that Macedonia could scarcely be considered in DeForrest Garrison's bracket?"

Garrison stopped dead.

He had been gesticulating angrily with his free hand, shaking his beautiful white head in irritation.

Now all movement ceased.

Even his breathing seemed to stop.

The flashing gray eyes went hard as stone, then slowly they came to rest on Jack.

"Jack," his voice was almost inaudible, "why . . . did you bring that man to me?"

"I told you," said Jack a little too hastily. "He was asking everyone where to find you."

Jack was shaken by the other man's terrible intentness, by the appalling extent of his vulnerability to pain. Waddell had been mostly bone and muscle, and—for all his green illusions about the Christian ministry —lived reasonably close to the rocky facts about others and himself. But Garrison was all naked nerve-endings. The fact leaped out in the fineness of his features, in the soft unmuscular body with its flowing white robe and towel, in the delicacy of the fingers that held the little basin.

"Did he ask . . . you?"

The man had become clairvoyant. Why had he noticed the way Jack phrased it?

"No."

"Then why did *you* bring him?"

Jack realized now, staring into that bloodless face, why Hoffner had wanted to put off telling him. He decided that if Garrison guessed the truth, he would admit it; if not, Jack would seek some less painful way . . . possibly let Ethel Garrison break the news. . . .

"Well, I just understood he was inquiring, and I was coming here. You asked me once to look in on your drama group."

"Inquiring of whom?"

"He was asking Mr. Hoffner." After all, the little man had told Garrison he'd been talking to Hoffner. But now Garrison fitted all the pieces of the puzzle into a new, more meaningful unity.

"But that's not really why you brought him."

"Well . . . not exactly."

"You'd been talking to someone else."

"Yes."

"Who?"

There was no way òut.

"Dr. Worthington."

The gray eyes had been staring so long that Jack was almost startled when the lids suddenly appeared. They sagged shut for a brief instant, but jerkily. Garrison drew a long, deep, shuddering breath, his nostrils flaring, his shoulders rising. A wave of crimson swept up his throat and cheeks, and the veins in his temples throbbed as if his heart were beating visibly in his face. The gray eyes stood out, blazing; the smooth high forehead seemed almost purple against the whiteness of his hair, and his lips writhed back, forming the whispered syllables so painfully that they almost seemed to stand carved in the air before him:

"*Macedonia!*"

The tin basin clattered to the floor, bouncing and ringing as its contents rippled out across the composition tile.

"He did this to *me!*"

His face contorted, like that of a runner lunging at the tape. He slapped both hands several times into the heaving folds at his chest, yanking the material out stiffly in his clenched fingers, then crushing it against him, his voice a raw whisper of pain and disbelief:

"To me! Meeee!"

Jack was too unnerved to speak, as if he were in the presence of a trapped animal, mad with pain and capable of slashing at anything that moved.

"Where is he!?" said Garrison suddenly, in something more nearly resembling his normal voice.

"I don't know."

Garrison whirled, took one swift lunging step, and nearly tripped over a trailing corner of the sheet. He stared down at himself in amazement. With shaking fingers he tried to undo the knotted towel, finally yanked the corners apart and then flung the looping folds of the sheet from him, half-kicking his feet free and vanishing down the corridor with swift, purposeful strides.

The session in the auditorium had ended. With a buzzing murmur people began moving out into the hall. The little blonde girl named Lucille came darting through the group. At the doorway, she stopped, gazing down, and her wide clear eyes fixed on the spilled water, then moved to the overturned basin, and came to rest wonderingly on the sheet lying soiled and trampled on the floor.

XIX

Pastoral Call

IT WAS after twelve Wednesday night when Wes came in. He wearily pulled off his shiny black coat, loosened his tie, and came over to stand beside Jack's chair at the window.

"Any luck?" asked Jack.

"Trying to find anybody at Belfair Methodist Church on the opening day," said Wes, "was a waste of shoe leather. The few I did see all gave me the same routine: they just want to be left alone to do the work the good Lord gave them."

"Same here. What did they think of our slate?"

"They all agreed on William Pierce Whitley. One of them thought Whitley was on our team and was ready to join up, but I had to explain that we're not trying to elect ourselves to something, we're trying to elect capable men who're *not* on Frederick John Worthington's team." Wes glanced out at the lights of Middleton below them. "Whatcha doing?"

"Trying to remember," said Jack grimly. "I even went and stood on the curb in front of Belfair. I can remember everything up to that instant, even to stepping off that curb on Monday morning. But the next thing that comes back is being on that train from New York and hearing the conductor call Middleton. The nineteen hours between is still a complete blank. I even tried hailing a cab and going off a few blocks. I did everything Dirkwell said he saw me do except hire a woman in a black dress to get out of the cab and then get back in with me and drive away."

"You're sure it couldn't have been our Miss Pat?"

"Patricia Worthington hasn't spoken to me since I got to Middleton —not here at the hotel, not out at Belfair."

"Well, let's turn in." Wes unbuttoned his vest. "We need to start early tomorrow morning. I told Starr and Adams to have the boys meet us at the church at eight o'clock." He wound his big, old-fashioned pocket watch. "A lay delegate was asking about you today—name of Hummaker."

Jack sat by the window in the darkness after Wes had gone to bed. Christine had written him in May that Fred Hummaker would be the Foxull delegate, as he had been every year since he retired from the barber shop. Jack could still remember his first haircut, and how his father had sat in the shoeshine chair, thumbs hooked in his vest, cigar stuck out at that cocky angle, and had multiplied six-digit figures in his head for that hair-tonic salesman. Jack wondered whether his father still did his mathematical feats in the barber shop. He remembered how Gramps Blalock had tried to flatter Bruce Lee about them that night when the old man brought the proposition from Harlowe's Mill. Jack could hear again his father's reply:

"My son's not going to be a clown, Gramps. A man with a gift from God needs to live among people he can talk to. . . . When a man's got nobody to talk to about what he knows, the waste and lonesomeness of life run him crazy. He . . . does things he'd never do in his right mind. . . ."

The words came back now with hurting sadness. Jack could never seem to remember anybody or anything related to Foxull without getting entangled in a swirl of pain and confusion. Even when Christine had written him in March that Oley Larsen's mother had died, he could not remember anything about Oley Larsen except meeting him on the street the morning after Jack had fled from Mrs. Catlett and slept all night in the culvert . . . and how Oley kept grinning that senseless, idiot's grin.

For the first time it occurred to Jack to wonder whether it could have been Christine Bannister who got out of the cab before Belfair Methodist Church that past Monday morning. She was forever slipping things into her letters about his parents, especially about his mother's health—not actually saying them, but writing them between the lines. Could something have happened to his mother? But if he had gone off with Christine, they would have gone to Foxull, not to New York. . . . Jack tried to recall whether he had ever seen Christine in a black dress with white accessories.

His principal recollection of her clothes always centered on that awful sweatshirt with the grinning fox's head and the words "FOXULL HIGH SCHOOL" emblazoned over it. High school stuff was simply not worn in college, but it even attained a certain measure of fame on the campus as the "lucky sweatshirt" which accounted for her occasional modest victories on the girls' track team. At the close of one meet she even gave an interview to the college paper about Foxull.

"Jack and I were practically the whole track squad," she had said, suddenly hooking her elbow through his and preventing him from going in to the showers. "If one of us got sick, half the team was missing!"

"Foxull had a very respectable track squad!" Jack told the reporter angrily. "We placed second in the state in the mile relay one year."

The boy put this down, his notes fluttering in the wind.

"We would have taken first," Christine added, "if we hadn't been short of equipment. Passing on the baton was no trick at all, but passing on the spiked shoes was murder!"

The college annual had printed a cartoon showing Jack and Christine in Foxull track uniforms, each wearing only one spiked shoe and having the other foot bare. They had long bushy fox's tails, and Jack wore a clerical collar. The cartoon struck Jack as disrespectful of the ministry at the time, and he had even cut it out of his annual, but now he suddenly found himself wishing he had saved it. . . .

Christine had also humiliated him in those days by reading the Foxull weekly paper aloud on the steps of the girls' dormitory every Friday evening. She read the social column, the poetry corner, the church news (Collection at Forked Stick, $1.84), the editorials, and even the advertisements. *The Foxhorn* was as well known on the campus as *The New York Times*—possibly better. She called it the Foghorn, of course—the inevitable label back home.

"Why," he had asked her angrily during track workout one day, "did you have to read the poetry page in Dr. Summerfield's lit class? 'Ode to My First Crocus,' by 'Twinkletoes!' You know very well 'Twinkletoes' is nobody but Miss Martin. You did it just to make me ridiculous!"

"Everything that's done in this universe doesn't relate to you, Jackie Lee, unbelievable as that might seem. I did it so I could write Miss Martin that I'd read her poem in our college poetry class. Not half as many of us are thinking about you night and day as you seem to imagine!"

"Who said—!" Jack began, but she jogged away without even waiting for his reply. Her answer made him furious and stuck in his mind for weeks, as did the sight of her lean, tanned face and the shock of her gray-green eyes meeting his with such pert indifference. . . .

She had had tiny beads of perspiration on her upper lip that afternoon. . . . Jack stared down at the lights of Middleton beneath his hotel window, remembering how, on another afternoon long ago, he had tried to kiss her when she had been fixing supper for him in the kitchen and had turned from the sink with milk on her upper lip. The memory brought an unexpected pain, as though it had been only yesterday instead of in another world, happening to another self.

Christine had never missed an opportunity to poke fun at his new manner and bearing after that vespers sermon in the spring of his sophomore year. She had resolutely refused to accept his new self, had implied that it was utterly false, some sort of artificial creation which he could simply take off like a suit of clothes if he so desired. And, strangely, he had on rare occasions felt that there was an element of truth in her opinion . . . as on that first call he made on Thelma after she had moved back to New York from Wentworth. . . .

He took the red plastic button out of his pocket and studied it for the hundredth time, trying to associate it in some fashion with a woman in a black dress getting out of a taxi, with that terrifying blankness from which he had emerged nineteen hours later to find himself sitting on a train from New York, pulling into Middleton, his legs aching, his feet bruised and bloody, his socks wadded into balls and stuffed in his coat pocket, and with them a red button apparently torn from a woman's jacket or coat. And the button was not like Christine Bannister; it was like Thelma. Vulgar, cheap, flashy!

Even now he could feel again that sudden demoralizing relaxation of will, that dreadful uncertainty which had frightened him so badly as he sat in Thelma's apartment that sultry July afternoon in 1959.

Thelma and Rick had come to his study the first time in mid-September of 1958, and Thelma had gone back to New York the following March. She had written Jack several times, asking him to be sure to stop and see her if he ever came to New York, but his replies were so brief as to be barely civil. He had rigidly fought down the flood of salacious images that seemed always threatening to rise and engulf him whenever he thought of her. Even the sight of her letters did something to him—the round, childishly precise handwriting setting down so carefully on the perfumed pages the most atrocious blunders in spelling and grammar. Somehow, just because they were ungrammatical, the letters demoralized him!

He had gone to New York shopping that day in July, had finished early; and as he fumbled in his coat pocket for some change, his hand came out with a letter he had received from Thelma the day before. She got off from the restaurant every day at six, got home by six-thirty. On an impulse he stuffed the letter in his pocket and turned back toward the subway.

Thelma had just got in. She opened the door the width of the brass chain, still wearing her white uniform, and then burst into smiles and unhooked the chain.

"Of all people! I was just thinking about you today! Know what? You're the first person to come see me in my new place. I'll change and be right out."

She bustled into the bathroom, still chattering, and Jack sat down in the small easy chair by the window. The tiny apartment reflected Thelma's personality perfectly, from the slovenly housekeeping to the stacks of love pulps on the floor beside him. A record player by the kitchen door was piled high with discs. They would be the latest hits sung by a young man in a golden suit who strummed a golden guitar.

One of Thelma's white shoes thumped against the half-open door and bounced out onto the carpet beside the bed. The living room and bedroom were combined, with a bath and a tiny kitchen-dinette, both opening off it toward the rear.

"Ten hours in that stinking restaurant! My feet are killing me." The other shoe bounced out.

"How long have you been here?" asked Jack.

"Ever since I left Wentworth."

Three and a half months—and he was the first visitor. He remembered the story of her friendless childhood. . . . Perhaps Thelma could be forgiven if she chose to flee from barren realities now and then to a world where people wore golden suits and drove up in golden cars. . . .

"Quick as I wash my girdle, I'll be out."

She splashed and thumped about the bathroom, chattering about her employer, her hours, high rents, and asking an occasional question about Wentworth. The flat, nasal voice, and the slovenliness, the bad grammar and the absence of privacy or modesty, even her familiar love pulps with their lurid covers—all did something to Jack, relaxed something deep inside him.

"When did you say your train goes?" she asked.

"Eight twenty-two."

"I'll fix us a snack. That way you won't have to buy nothing. Whatcha say?" She appeared suddenly in the familiar quilted housecoat with the loud satin lapels and stood on one bare foot flexing the arch of the other and wriggling her toes, which had several corn plasters on them.

In Wentworth the answer would have been automatic. A minister avoided even being seen alone with a young woman in his car, much less dining alone with one in her apartment. But the automatic self he had always assumed to be his real self had suddenly lost its precision and promptness. He was vaguely aware of her feet. Her eyes were bright and casual, but her foot, the one resting on the arch of the other, was rigid. She was terrified he might not stay.

"That would be wonderful!" he heard himself say, and saw her plump cheeks dimple.

He had bought a paper, and sat by the window trying to fix his mind on it while she chattered and banged about in the kitchen.

Back home in Wentworth yesterday, he had felt completely secure as he stood in the doorway of the parsonage gazing down the hillside at Miss Mollie's neat little cottage and at the rows of neat little houses beyond it, each with its carefully trimmed hedge or small white fence. Old man Gregory's snowy thatch bobbed along the sidewalk, indicating that it was four-thirty and the afternoon mail was in.

But here, suspended in a tiny steel and plaster cell high above this boulevard of swarming strangers, Jack felt suddenly that his ordinary self might be nothing but a convergence of others' expectations, an intersecting of shadows from the church and post office and school and all the neat cottages. Here, removed from its setting, that shadow self seemed unreal and powerless and pointing in no certain direction. For back home those expectations told him instantly when to smile, to frown, to sigh, and best of all, what to *feel*. In Wentworth he responded to a drunk or a dirty joke or a sexy-looking woman in prompt, exact ways he could anticipate. But the drunk on the subway today had called up no response at all, and the joke he'd overheard in the elevator had struck him as funny! And Thelma . . .

Jack suddenly felt terrified, defenseless, like an invincible knight pulled from his mount and stripped of his armor. During the meal he tried to play his familiar role of compassionate minister; he said all the usual things in his usual voice, but nothing seemed to have any sincerity of feeling. Once, glancing up, he saw in Thelma's owlish brown eyes the dawning of something familiar—that unthinking, doglike adoration with which she had always gazed at Rick, and with which later she had seemed to be gazing at him once at Mrs. Richardson's.

She blinked and lowered her eyes, and the familiar creamy translucent stain turned her plump cheeks and throat a glowing pink. The wild thought kept trying to form that whatever he might do here would have no connection with his church or career, because here he was not himself. He was someone else . . . someone who lived in a shell and had been mistaking the shell for the real person.

He helped her wash the dishes in the tiny sink, and when they had finished, she turned suddenly and stood almost touching him, reaching up for the pull chain on the light, her face only inches from his own. In the living room he stood with his back to her, gazing down at the boulevard twelve stories below, his fist knotted in the cheap, gaudy material of the drape. He could not seem to breathe.

Terror won.

Sheer, blind, paralyzing terror.

At the time he had been sure it was terror of sin. But now, remembering it all again, he had the curious feeling that it had not really been fear of sin at all! It was related most deeply, in some fashion he could not grasp, to having his armor-self fall away completely and forever, leaving him facing something or afraid of something past all bearing. He rubbed his wrists.

"I—I just remembered something I must do before train time. I must run."

She implored him to stay, and stood very close to him again at the door, the puffy-lidded brown eyes larger than usual and beginning to grow bright. He could scarcely restrain himself from running down the hall to the elevator, and on the street he did run, plunging through the crowds and racing down the subway stairs as though pursued.

On the train, settling back in his seat, he remembered something, got out the envelope bearing her address and tore it to shreds and started to fling them under the next seat. He hesitated: his trash would be one more thing for the clean-up boy to bother with. But why must the smallest act always become a moral issue? Angrily he drew back his hand to throw, could not, and finally walked the length of the car and put the stuff in the slot under the water cooler.

He could still remember the feeling of calm certainty with which he had stuffed the bits of paper through the slot and then returned to his seat and his evening paper. He had been perfectly, completely, and finally certain that on that July afternoon of 1959 he had seen Thelma Ross Richardson for the last time.

XX

A Prince Has Fallen

THE MIDDLETON HOTEL was downtown near the railway station; and when Jack had finally gotten to bed that Wednesday night, he lay in the darkness listening to the sounds of the city—and to Wes Phillips' stentorian snore. He wondered whether he would ever have gotten into this reform movement had it not been for the old man's gadfly tactics during Jack's long friendship with Dr. Worthington.

That friendship had reached a turning point during Jack's long argument with the superintendent in the basement of the Shiloh Church in June of 1959. Dr. Worthington was ordinarily an acute observer, yet he had seemed startlingly unperceptive that day. For some reason he did not seem to realize how shaken Jack had been by the punitive appointment of DeForrest Garrison to Macedonia, or how shocked and angered Jack had been to see a long-time friend like Dan Starr relegated to the Carsten Circuit. Otherwise, Dr. Worthington would scarcely have entrusted Jack with so delicate and explosive a business as that offer to Edgar Evans, barely three months after the Starr-Garrison outrage in June.

It was almost as if—

Jack opened his eyes and lay staring into the darkness.

It was almost as if the man had been deliberately trying to goad him into revolt! He surely knew that Jack's relationship with Patricia was already strained to the breaking point and that most of the tension came from their inability to agree about Dr. Worthington himself. Which might explain why the man had sent Jack—young and inexperienced as he was—to take Edgar Evans the proposition about St. Luke's. For if there was any single act which could be said to have triggered the whole rebellion, it was that offer to Evans.

"You need the experience," was all Dr. Worthington had said. He was in the hospital at the time, ordered there for "a rest and a checkup." Jack assumed that he had pushed himself to the verge of another heart attack; his doctor had forbidden him to use the phone or to transact business. It was a Sunday afternoon in August; Patricia had called Jack to say that her father wanted to see him at once, and that he should arrange to be absent from the youth program at Wentworth that night. Her father was sitting up in bed, but looked pale and depressed.

Harry Wilson, the brilliant young minister of St. Luke's, had died of a heart attack that morning; Jack was to drive out to Talcott Springs and inform Evans that the superintendent was offering him the appointment. Jack was not to attempt to influence Edgar's decision, simply to make sure he understood the offer was no mere gesture.

On the long trip to Edgar's remote rural circuit, Jack brooded over this astounding development. He had made no attempt to conceal his dismay. St. Luke's was a historic little church that had been enveloped by a sprawling suburb. It had one of the loveliest sanctuaries in the conference, and its membership was largely of the country club variety. Edgar Evans had pastored rural circuits all his life. Even as an interim appointment the offer was incredible, but Evans had been Dr. Worthington's first supporter in his battle for the orphans' home thirty years ago. They had both been sent to country charges by the vindictive kingpin of the conference in those days, H. O. Doffingwell; and Edgar had never gotten any higher. Then, when Dr. Worthington finally came to power, many other men were demanding rewards, and Edgar was never the demanding type. And so the years had slipped away.

But there was an irrational element in this decision. Dr. Worthington was ill and depressed, and Jack wondered if he feared he might die without ever having repaid Edgar's ancient loyalty. Or perhaps he had lately become confident he would be made a bishop in 1960 and wanted to take care of Edgar before being transferred to some distant area.

The superintendent surely must have known that this would bring cries of "politics" and "cronyism." A vacancy like St. Luke's would normally involve a small step up for a whole chain of men, and Jack could think of at least half a dozen who would be outraged if Dr. Worthington picked up Evans from a country circuit and jumped him over them all. Clarence Motherly, in particular, had believed himself in line for St. Luke's two years ago; but Harry Wilson had come back from graduate school with a Ph.D. just then, and St. Luke's had asked for him instead. Now Clarence would doubtless imagine his promotion to St. Luke's a certainty.

Clarence and Edgar had carried on a friendly feud in district ministers' meetings for a number of years. Edgar ridiculed Clarence for wearing "a shawl and a petticoat" in the pulpit and for "dressing in the dark and getting his collar on backwards." Clarence would reply that Ed thought the divided chancel was invented so farmers could pile their pumpkins in the middle for the Lord's Acre program. He never tired of recounting how he had gone to Ed's study one day to retrieve a Bible dictionary, "and where do you think we finally found it? On the floor, under a sack of fertilizer!"

Evans had two small country churches; on his arrival three months before, he had set up his usual man-killing arrangement of preaching four times every Sunday—a morning and evening service at each church—in an effort to build interest and attendance. The schedule Dr. Worthington had given Jack indicated that on the "first and third" Sundays, Edgar was at "Sharpe's Chapel, 9:45 A.M. and 6:00 P.M.; Talcott Springs, 11:00 A.M. and 8:00 P.M." Jack glanced at his watch. He could sit in on the close of Edgar's first service, have a bite at the parsonage and present Dr. Worthington's offer, and be on his way back before the eight o'clock service began.

Sharpe's Chapel was a small, white frame building set at the head of a narrow valley. A hand-drawn poster tacked on the weatherbeaten front door indicated that tonight was "Youth Night," with a special program by the pastor and his wife. The churchyard was full of automobiles and pickup trucks, and the congregation contained a large proportion of young people. Ed's sermon, which Jack had heard once before at a summer youth camp, was the type of thing most ministers did on God versus Mammon, the treasures of earth versus the riches of spiritual contentment, and so on. Edgar was almost done when Jack took a seat on a back pew, but Jack knew what had gone before: the story of Edgar's poverty-stricken boyhood on a farm, his burning determination to be a success and make money—"big money, fast!"—his successful beginnings as salesman for a farm-machinery agency, and the prospect of a life of security and comparative ease when he took over his uncle's agency at some future date. Then came his call to the ministry and a long and tormented struggle with fears of the hardship and poverty he had known so intimately as a child. And this conflict was made more painful by his love for Blanche Waterman, "only daughter of none other than A. G. Waterman, Sr., of Waterman's Department Store!" Should he risk losing the girl he loved, answer the call to a profession with few earthly rewards, or should he fight on toward "the golden idol of America, the Almighty Dollar?"

"Do you know the Devil's favorite word?" Edgar lifted one huge fist toward the bare, white-painted ceiling. "Success!" The big voice boomed in measured rhythm as the big fist crashed down on the pulpit in time. "Suc-CESS! SUCCESS! SUCCESS! These big men want salvation—sure! But they want money more. They want Jesus Christ—of course! But they want power more. They have their fat salaries and fine cars and big houses—true! But Edgar Evans has the Savior of the World!"

Edgar was a giant oak of a man, with bristly white hair that had once, so Dr. Worthington had said, been fiery red. He had considerable charm, a homespun eloquence, and a rugged, obvious honesty.

His voice was inclined to be flat and twangy, but it was also capable of an affecting warmth and resonance.

"Of course I had no peace! I was fighting the Lord God of Hosts." He shook a huge fist at the ceiling. "And the man who does that has no more peace than a heifer with a burr under her tail!" But those who want the good things of a perishing world might as well know that, "This world is just like a vicious old sow: If you're gonna be one of her litter, and go after what she's offering, you gotta lay right down in the mud and slop beside her!"

Jack kept trying to imagine this great, ham-handed man in his shiny, ill-fitting serge suit making the dainty little journey from the lectern to the pulpit in fashionable St. Luke's. Clarence Motherly, yes. Clarence, with his pale narrow face and saucer eyes, his Adam's apple bobbing inside his clerical collar, his narrow shoulders draped with a white satin stole. But Edgar?

Jack saw now that Dr. Worthington had doubted his own arguments that the older laymen of St. Luke's were men of Edgar's generation, that they had been ill at ease under Harry Wilson's vocabulary, that with nine months to go before conference the church might accept Edgar and then learn to love him and even ask for his return. For just as Jack was leaving the room, the superintendent had called him back, sitting up a little in the bed.

"Jack—"

"Sir?"

"*Pray* that he won't accept it."

Edgar towered over the plain little pulpit now, his great arms flung wide, his big palms turned up, his huge body somehow conveying an impression of infinite peace.

"The cross we dread, dear friends, turns out to be our peace! Gone were the fears, gone were the worries about a big house and a big car—big me, and little everybody else. And when I told this dear lady beside me on the platform what I had decided, do you know what she said? She said, 'Oh, Edgar, I've been praying for weeks that you'd give in to your call.'" Edgar leaned one elbow on the pulpit, his rugged face and deep-set brown eyes transfigured by the recollection of his victory.

"It was just thirty years ago next April that Edgar Evans turned his back forever on the madness of this vain world with all its silver and its gold and set out on the lowly road of the Methodist ministry. And he's never regretted that decision for one minute."

He poured himself a glass of water from the pitcher on the pulpit, drank it down noisily in the silence, wiped his mouth with the back of one big hand, and added:

"Not for one minute."

Edgar turned, and his wife came forward to stand with him. Their daughter, Bea, a tall red-haired girl, went over to the piano. Blanche Evans looked almost too young to be Edgar's wife; she had a trim figure and a heart-shaped face with enormous, expressive dark eyes. She dressed with simplicity but with style and taste, and a single streak of gray at her temple only added dignity to her obvious warmth and charm.

Edgar put his arm about her waist, and Bea struck a chord. Jack was surprised to find that Edgar sang passably, and Blanche blended her clear, powerful voice expertly with her husband's.

> *I'd rather have Jesus than silver or gold,*
> *I'd rather be his than have riches untold,*
> *I'd rather have Jesus than houses or lands,*
> *I'd rather be led by his nail-pierced hands*
> > *Than to be the king of a vast domain*
> > *And be held in sin's dread sway.*
> *I'd rather have Jesus than anything*
> *This world affords today.*

When their duet was concluded, Edgar took a seat at the back of the rostrum, and Blanche addressed the congregation. Her part of the program consisted of a brief "postscript" to her husband's sermon, in which she described her childhood and youth as the only daughter of a well-to-do businessman. She had originally had ambitions for a career as a concert singer, had been given an elaborate schooling, and her "big chance" had just come when she decided instead to marry Edgar. Her parents' fears that she was unprepared for the hardships of the ministry were apparently only too well founded, and Jack felt that she must have left many things unsaid in her brief, humorous, and tactful references to a town girl's adjustments to rural living. She displayed a considerable dramatic flair, particularly in her description of dropping the letter in the corner mailbox informing the agency that she had decided to give up her prospective tour in order to marry a Methodist minister.

"It *is* difficult, isn't it, to let go the good things of this world!" Her voice, always musical and expressive, was clear and compelling as her eloquent eyes swept the upturned faces of the young people. She held one dainty hand aloft, her fingers gripping the imagined letter. "But God made it easy for me to give up all the foolish things I imagined I needed for happiness. For when the mailbox banged shut on that letter, it opened the door for me into a whole new world. I found rest from my silly, selfish ambitions and discovered that my life had a meaning and purpose." Her fingers flew open. "Let go, young people! Oh, I beg of you to let go and let Christ enter in!

"When I put on this wedding ring," here she held her left hand high for an instant, "to take up the duties of a minister's wife, I did not find everything easy and pleasant. But it was joy, not labor. I had given my life to God, not to gadgets!" She studied the ring for a moment with a tender smile. "I discovered that the abundant life consists not in possessions, but in others! Thinking of others, working for others, living in others. Edgar and I have enjoyed few material advantages as the years have come and gone, but when we look back, we have our reward!"

The brilliant, dark eyes grew misty. She gazed over the heads of the rapt congregation. Her voice was warm.

"We see faces! Faces reflecting lives changed, sorrowful hearts comforted, men and women freed from enslavement to money and things. For, you see, our reward is in people!" She flung her arms wide, advancing to the very edge of the low rostrum, her gaze melting and compassionate. She seemed to be restraining herself almost by force from going down into the congregation to gather them all in her arms. "*You* are our reward, our wealth and security. You . . . and you . . . and you . . . you are our treasure in Heaven!"

Bea struck a chord at the piano; Blanche remained standing with head back, face flushed and exhilarated, her voice pure and powerful.

> *In the cross of Christ I glory,*
> *Towering o'er the wrecks of time!*
> *All the light of sacred story*
> *Gathers round that head sublime.*
>
> *When the woes of life o'ertake me*
> *Hopes deceive, and fears annoy,*
> *Never shall that cross forsake me;*
> *Lo, it glows with peace and joy!*
>
> *Bane and blessing, pain and pleasure*
> *By the cross are sanctified,*
> *Peace is there that knows no measure,*
> *Joys that through all time abide!*

After supper at the parsonage in Talcott Springs, which was twenty minutes' drive from Sharpe's Chapel, Jack and Edgar climbed the hill to the little cemetery behind the church and sat on the low stone wall as the moon rose, listening to the seething of the crickets and the occasional faraway tinkle of a cowbell or bark of a dog.

"I'm sorry our boy wasn't home," said Edgar, taking out a big pocket-knife and selecting a stick to whittle. "Don's courting a girl down the valley. I'd sorta hoped he might feel a call to the ministry, but Blanche keeps telling him, 'Get that engineering degree and the big corporations will be fighting for you!' "

Neither Ed nor Blanche had asked the reason for Jack's appearance at this out-of-the-way spot on Sunday evening, though Jack knew they must have wondered. Edgar was shocked and stunned when Jack now told him of Harry Wilson's death that morning.

"Poor old Fred," he said at last. "I wonder who he'll ever find to follow Harry at St. Luke's. . . ."

"You, Ed," Jack answered.

Edgar laughed.

"That church would fit me like socks fit a rooster. I guess he'll send Clarence; he was in line before Harry came back from graduate school."

"Ed, I'm trying to tell you: Dr. Worthington is offering you St. Luke's. It's yours if you want it. He would have called or driven out himself, but his doctor has ordered him to have complete rest for a few days."

Edgar turned sharply. The moon had now risen, huge and orange, at the end of the valley. In the dimness under the trees Edgar studied Jack's face for a long moment, then suddenly tossed away the stick and put up his knife. He got to his feet, one big hand half-raised as if to shield himself. Jack got up too, disturbed by the expression on Edgar's face.

"Get away from me!" The deep-set eyes, normally friendly and ingenuous, were hard and hostile. "I've found out where I belong. A man finally gets some sense knocked into his head after thirty years. I'm through with all that! I'm at peace!"

Jack was startled as much by Edgar's face as by his words. He tried to protest, but Edgar would not let him. Jack finally thrust out his hand.

"Okay, Ed. I'm sorry to have upset you so. I thought you'd be pleased!"

Suddenly the big, contorted face relaxed; the wide grin flashed; Edgar seized his hand in a bruising grip.

"Forgive me, boy! I don't know what came over me. You go back and tell Fred it's nice to be remembered, but he'd better give St. Luke's to somebody who can handle it." He hesitated, fleetingly. "I mean, *really* handle it."

There was a sudden, constrained silence. Jack was startled to see that Edgar was sweating, though it was cool in the shadows of the trees. As they walked back, Edgar suddenly stopped halfway down the hill. Jack followed his gaze as it wandered across the jumble of glimmering headstones, the crooked path down the hill, the peaceful valley, and came to rest on the neat little white frame church. The confusion and bitterness faded from Edgar's eyes.

"There she is—the mother of ministers! No matter how high they climb, they all start off at her knee." His voice was soft and meditative. "When a young preacher's eye first lights on her, no matter how lonesome and run-down she looks, he stands for a minute not daring to go in yet, and says to himself, 'My first church!' But it's really *the* church to him, because she gets a man when he's still teachable, when the ministry is still a high and holy calling and not just a job to be done. She reaches him before his heart gets calloused to people's troubles and sins.

"He's so sure he's gonna make all these poor folks over by next Sunday and get promoted to the city by next June! But four years later he can't hardly preach that farewell sermon for the lump in his throat, and he knows his little country church has made him over instead. He thought religion was a bunch of ideas from a classroom, and then she took him around from house to house and introduced him to poverty and loneliness and pain, and showed him how to lay in a sickbed for twenty years, and what death is, and how to do the best you can with what you've got, like a man said to me once when I caught him plowing a mule and a horse together."

Edgar swept a big hand toward the moonlit valley and the lights of the farmhouses in the distance.

"Sure, I know you couldn't get a new idea through their skulls with a post-hole digger, but Christianity woulda been plowed under long ago if the country church could be turned sideways by every wind that blows out of Boston. *Somebody's* got to comfort the widows and the fatherless while the professors are making up their minds whether God is even real at all!"

"Oh, I've heard all the big preachers laugh about that first church paying them off in corn and potatoes because the folks didn't have any money. But I've noticed that when one of them gets down to that last paragraph, and is through slinging the big words, and wants to make sure everybody knows what he's talking about, he always ends up telling about some little old lady in a poke bonnet whose doctor had just told her she was dying of cancer. And he tells how she preached him the greatest sermon on faith he ever heard, just talking about how if the preacher liked blueberry jam, she probably wouldn't be needing all she'd put up, and how she'd just finished setting out her bulbs and hoped she'd at least see the first crocuses, come spring . . . just sitting there in a creaky rocking chair in her plain, bare room, like somebody watching the last coals burn out in the fireplace. . . ."

They stood awhile listening to the crickets. From somewhere far off a dog barked. Edgar's voice was peaceful now, and confident:

"I love country folks. Maybe that's why God has kept me with them."

Jack had just climbed into his car when Blanche appeared from the doorway of the church. She was sorry about the supper; they hadn't expected company.

"Is anything wrong, Edgar? You both look . . . Has something happened that I should know about?"

Jack told her about Harry Wilson's death. Again the stunned surprise, the pity. Then:

"But . . . has it something to do with us, Edgar?"

Edgar found his voice at last:

"Now, sweetheart, don't start getting any ideas. Fred sent to ask if I was interested in St. Luke's, just as a little gesture. Jack's got to get back, and we've got another service." He was talking much too fast.

"Was it only a gesture?" Blanche asked Jack. Her dark eyes were suddenly quite expressionless, and her voice devoid of its warmth and music.

Jack started over the whole thing again, but cars kept arriving for choir practice before church. Blanche finally suggested that they discuss it in Edgar's study, a tiny room which had a salt-box roof and was built onto the rear wall of the church. Blanche snapped on a bare, overhead bulb and stood with her back to the weatherbeaten door. Edgar slumped down on an old church pew against the far wall; Jack remained standing by the rickety desk, which was piled high with leaflets and seed catalogues.

"Well, Edgar, weren't you even going to tell me about this? I think it also concerns me and the children. It's the kind of appointment you've always talked about."

Edgar banged his big fist on the cracked seat of the pew.

"That was talk. This is reality. It's like saying you're not afraid to die and then having a gun stuck in your face."

Blanche pressed her hands together; Jack realized that they were not actually dainty, as he had imagined, but strong and muscular, with the nails cut short and square. Her vivacious, heart-shaped face now had an odd kind of inflexibility.

"This is the first time I ever heard going to St. Luke's compared to dying. I must say, I think the children and I could stand that fate quite well after some fates we've put up with lately."

Jack wanted to escape, but Blanche insisted that he stay. Their voices rose occasionally, despite the sound of the choir practicing just beyond the adjoining wall of the sanctuary. Edgar kept insisting that he could not possibly handle "that country club crowd. They'd walk out in a body the first time I opened my mouth." Blanche maintained that human nature was the same everywhere; Ed had always said so himself. This was the chance of a lifetime; he had been complaining about getting tagged as a circuit preacher; Belovèd was giving him a chance to break out at last. Why not trust the superintendent's judgment?

Edgar shook his head.

"That's what's so crazy about this!" he said. "Fred never misjudges a man—at least, not his weak points."

He peeled off his rumpled serge coat, hung it carelessly on the arm of the dusty pew, and sat gloomily studying a pair of muddy brogans by the door, his damp shirt clinging to his massive shoulders.

"That's the kind of shoes the Lord meant me to wear," he said suddenly, "and Fred Worthington knows it. I carry them in my car, so if a man is milking, or baling hay, or digging potatoes, I can pitch right in with him. Sometimes I wear 'em getting up a sermon, just to make me keep my feet on the ground and not go slinging a lot of fancy words. . . ."

Edgar spread his big, calloused hands and studied their sunburned backs and the reddish hairs now turning white. His voice was almost boyish in its pleading.

"Blanche, I've just got a couple more appointments left. Why can't I work with the kind of people we know I can help? I'm old . . . old and tired. I'm . . . tired of being *afraid*."

Blanche sat down beside him and seized one of his big hands. Her voice held a note of alarm.

"You've never been afraid in your life!"

Edgar studied the streak of white at her temple, the blouse that Jack now saw had been washed and ironed too many times, and the neat little pumps that had been polished too many times.

"I've been afraid all my life, sweetheart." Well, he had not been afraid in the early years, but every year at conference time he got the shakes; then he began getting them between conferences . . . afraid of the bishop, afraid he'd "say something dumb" at a ministers' meeting, afraid for her and the children.

Blanche looked bewildered and disbelieving.

"But why didn't you ever *share* it with me?"

"It's bad enough to be a failure when you've promised a girl the moon. Especially when she's given up big things for you."

"Oh, nonsense! I might have been a complete flop! Surely you haven't been fretting over that all these years!"

The room was unbearably stuffy. Jack propped open the window with a stick lying on the sill. He tried not to listen to their voices. From the shadows outside he could hear the crickets again; and from the road the crunch of tires on gravel as the congregation began to arrive. Beyond the flimsy wall of the sanctuary the choir was practicing another hymn:

> *Jesus calls us o'er the tumult*
> *Of our life's wild restless sea . . .*

Edgar mopped his face with a wadded handkerchief.

"Wanta hear something funny? I used to lay awake in my hotel room at conference afraid the big chance would never come, that I was tagged, stuck for life in one bracket. But these last few years I've been laying awake afraid the big chance *would* come!" The craggy, reddish brows shot up in an expression of quizzical amusement at the desperate absurdity of life; the wide mouth grinned crookedly. Blanche bit her lip, her big dark eyes suddenly brimming.

"And this last annual conference I knew it was now or never for me, and when the bishop read us out for Talcott Springs, I said to myself, 'Well, old workhorse, why not face it?'" And lately he had begun to feel again that peace he'd felt in his first appointment, "just like a little brown thrush in my chest was ready to bust out and sing." He had begun to think that maybe this was where God wanted him after all, "talking to folks about crops and the price of hogs," and knowing he was doing "what none of them fancy degree boys could do." And that's when he began to be afraid the big chance *would* come.

"Oh, I liked to dream a little still, and complain a little, but I really dreaded them offering me something good, because then I'd have had to admit to Blanche and the kids what I really am—just a country boy without sense enough or manners enough to handle a city appointment if I got one."

They sat in silence for a time, listening to the hymn:

> *On Christ the solid rock I stand*
> *All other ground is sinking sand . . .*

Finally Blanche spoke in a soft, slow voice, like a mother explaining something to a small child.

"Darling, do you remember that rainy day on our honeymoon when we went inside to look at that church with the white pillars? And how just for fun you climbed up in the pulpit and looked down at me and said, 'Blanche, how do I look?' Do you remember what I said? I said, 'It's where you belong!'" Edgar nodded, a rueful smile tugging at his mouth. "Darling, I married you because I love you and have faith that you want to be somebody. I didn't mind those early years, not really. No matter how terrible things were, I always told myself, 'Edgar will get out of here. Edgar will do big things someday!'"

She ran her fingertips over his brow, playfully attempting to smooth away the wrinkles, and touching the bristly white hair at his temples.

"We're not as young as we used to be, Edgar, and the big chance took a long time to come. But you always said that loyalty would pay off someday."

He jerked away from her, and the eyes he turned on her bulged from their sockets in his desperation to communicate.

"Blanche, can't you *see?* That approach to the ministry is what's been wrong with me from the start. That's every man against the other, tooth and claw. I've had thirty years of that. I'm old now, Blanche, old! Old and tired. Why can't I just be *myself* and do my work for the few little years I've got left—just be what the good Lord made me?" He seemed about to seize her, as though impelled by some physical impulse to break through the things that entrapped him. "I'm *not* a big man, Blanche. I'm not. I'm *not!* Why won't you help me to . . . to face it?"

They stared at each other across a widening chasm of incomprehension. The pain and bewilderment were so intense Jack turned his head away and gazed at some stacks of mimeographed material on the floor by Edgar's desk. They were programs from bygone revivals and summer camps, their jaunty colors faded, their once clear captions now barely readable: "Christ or Career?" "Week of Power—Edgar Evans, Evangelist!" "My Utmost for His Highest." Edgar was standing in the middle of the room.

"It's not that I've lost faith in myself, Blanche; it's that I've finally begun to see myself, to know where I belong. And where I belong is . . ." The firm voice faltered as he flung his arms wide, and the fierce, hard light in his eyes wavered as he gazed about him at the stuffy little cell with its peeling walls and dusty books and ill-assorted furniture. It was clear that he could not take the final step alone, that he was pleading for someone to confirm all this, to seize him roughly and say:

"Yes! This is the place. This is the job. Your life is a product of justice, not of ingratitude. Face it. Take your wound—and be healed!"

Jack wished that Pastor Elwood were here to lead Edgar that last step. Jack might have had the courage had he been alone with Edgar. But Blanche was gazing at her husband in anguished disbelief, her eyes brimming, her fingers knotted together. Whatever the world might see in Edgar Evans, whatever he might see in himself, Blanche saw something more, for she looked through eyes of love.

Edgar sank down by his wife on the dusty pew. Somewhere in that silence the moment of decision had slipped away, and for him the granite features of truth, so nearly glimpsed in their wholeness, had vanished again—perhaps forever—in the swirling mists of his own self-deception and his wife's blind faith and pain. From the sanctuary they heard the beginning of another hymn:

> *I must needs go home by the way of the cross*
> *There's no other way but this . . .*

Blanche stared at the wall, her voice remote, puzzled.

"Darling, I've stuck with you from the beginning and I will to the end, no matter what you decide tonight. But if you pass up a chance like this just because you're tired and overworked, and because you've had such a long, hard fight, I just don't think I'll be able to stand it. I hauled water a quarter of a mile at Cartersville, and we didn't have any decent furniture at Wade's Chapel. You know the kind of schools we've seen the children go to, and how I've tried to fill out the gaps in their education. I've made all of Bea's clothes from the beginning, and she's always the best-dressed girl in her class. I'm not complaining, but if you do love me, and if you do love the children, how can you let this opportunity get away? You *would* be tagged then, and we'd all three begin to think the tag was true!"

The warmth and music vanished from her voice:

"When I *think* of the plums they've given to men without half your talent, without half as good a record! And when I think of some of the boys Bea has dragged home with her. . . . I've lain awake at night, absolutely terrified that she had run off and married one of them. And

I've thought, 'If only we could get out of here before it's too late! If only Bea could meet some boys from the right kind of homes, so she'd have something to *compare* people with!'

"And I never stopped believing! Even that winter at Ferriston in that awful barn of a place where the pipes would freeze and I had to keep the children in bed just to keep them warm, and they were sick all winter and you were never home. I didn't mind—not really! Because you were out building up the churches and making a record, and in a few years your work would be appreciated. And we'd start getting good appointments, and the children would have a nice house to live in, and a doctor who could recognize appendicitis before it killed your little boy."

Evans closed his eyes, and his face turned ashen under its tan.

"Blanche, *please!*"

She was sitting with her feet placed neatly side by side and her hands folded in her lap with a careless composure so out of keeping with her statements that Jack felt uneasy. On the rostrum she had seemed almost youthful, with her brilliant eyes, flushed cheeks, and trim, erect figure. Now, under the glare of the light, Jack saw the fine, severe lines about her mouth; her eyes were remote and dead, her cheeks colorless, and the proud shoulders slumped. She looked shockingly aged, like an actress who could no longer bear the cruelty of a close-up.

"Well, I made up my mind from the first day that I would never be a millstone around Edgar's neck like some preachers' wives. Only God knows the things I've been through and the thoughts I've had. But it's been quite a little struggle these thirty-odd years, because—"

Suddenly her voice cracked.

"*I hate them!*" She averted her face from Edgar. "They don't sing—they yell. They don't change—you destroy yourself against them." Then the tears appeared under the dark lashes. "I've prayed till my knees had sores on them. I've begged God to help me understand them and love them." She bowed her face in her hands; Edgar, stunned and bewildered, timidly raised one big hand toward her trembling shoulders. At last she lifted her head, dabbed at her eyes with a tiny handkerchief, and gave Edgar's knee a reassuring pat. "Poor Ed! No . . . I don't really hate them, but maybe I've been needing to say I did. I feel better now. One can't hate them more than two days in succession. They're like big, stubborn, lovable children; one day they drive you to despair and the next day they do something so beautiful you almost cry. Edgar knows what they're thinking before they do, but I'll never understand them."

She paused, as if surprised by her own thoughts.

"Maybe I've really never tried. . . . I suppose I've actually been thinking for the past thirty years that rural work was just . . . just temporary!" She stared at the faded weatherboarding of the sanctuary wall opposite her and suddenly laughed, a chilling, mirthless little laugh that sounded exactly as if she were crying.

She turned her gaze on Jack.

"Is it a sin to want a robed choir—just once in your whole life? And a church that looks like a church inside, instead of like a cracker box or a town hall? Would it be wrong just once to have an organist who could open with Guilmant's 'Pastorale' or Schumann's 'Adagio' from the *Second Symphony?* Sometimes I think I could have endured all the rest of it quite easily if it hadn't been for wanting my music . . . my music."

She lowered her eyes to her wedding band, the fingers of her right hand twisting and turning it on her finger.

"But thank God I never suspected it would all be for nothing. Thank God I never realized a man could do a thing like this to someone he really loves, and to his own children. How can one's entire life just be thrown away like this? How can God let such things happen to those who've tried so hard to serve him?"

This time her sobs were dreadful, racking her whole body. Edgar reached up several times to pat her shoulder with a clumsy, almost fearful bewilderment. But when at last she straightened again, she seemed strangely composed.

"Well, it's almost eight. We'd better go in."

But Edgar was not listening.

Jack could literally see the decision as it formed.

He could see it in the line of Edgar's jaw, in the squaring of his big shoulders, in the deepening of the crow's feet about his narrowed eyes, as if they were measuring something in the distance.

"Well, sweetheart, this *is* the big chance. You've never been wrong about me in the past. Maybe it is where I belong, and no matter how it comes out, once I've been at St. Luke's, I'll at least wear a different tag."

Blanche did not smile. She studied him fiercely for a long moment, then collapsed against him.

"Thank God! Oh, thank God, thank God, thank God!"

Before they parted Edgar asked Jack to join them in a prayer; he and Blanche always had prayer at the high moments of their lives. They knelt together, but Jack's mind and emotions were so exhausted that afterwards he could recall only one fragment—Edgar's plea that in their new parish he and Blanche might "bring peace and rest to dear people tormented by the passions and ambitions of this world."

Jack's car had been blocked by a pickup truck, but the keys were in the ignition. While he was maneuvering it cautiously backwards, he could hear Edgar through the open windows of the church:

". . . apologies for this slight delay in beginning our evening service, but 'A prince and a great man has fallen this day in Israel.' We have just had word of the tragic and untimely death of Dr. Harry V. Wilson . . ."

When Jack got back into his own car at last, he slammed the door, and then paused. Through the open doors of the church he gazed down the length of the aisle and saw Blanche Evans coming forward to stand at the edge of the rostrum, trim and erect, arms flung wide and head back, her face and eyes radiant as her marvelous voice rang out clear and compelling through the summer night:

> In the cross of Christ I glory,
> Towering o'er the wrecks of time!
> All the light of sacred story
> Gathers round its head sublime
>
> When the woes of life o'ertake me
> Hopes deceive, and fears annoy,
> Never shall that cross forsake me;
> Lo, it glows with peace and joy!
>
> Bane and blessing, pain and pleasure
> By the cross are sanctified;
> Peace is there that knows no measure,
> Joys that through all time abide!

XXI

Portrait of a Man

"Boy, what in thunderation are you chuckling about here in the middle of the night?" Wes's gravelly rumble from the other bed startled Jack out of his musings.

"I thought you were asleep," said Jack. "Oh, I was just remembering that talk we had the morning I drove Belovèd to Lake Leisure to see the bishop."

"Well, stop laughing; you scared the daylights out of me. And stop this infernal digging into the past and get some sleep. Tomorrow's Thursday, and we'll have plenty to do when we get up." Wes groaned mightily, but just before the old man resumed his snoring Jack heard him chuckling in the darkness too.

The situation had had its amusing aspects. . . .

Jack had seen Blanche and Edgar on Sunday; Dr. Worthington had been released from the hospital the next afternoon; and on Tuesday he had Jack drive him to Leisure Lodge. On his way to the district parsonage, Jack went by to see Wes, who happily forecast that the Evans appointment would be too thick even for the bishop. It was certain to outrage the conference from one end to the other, and a delegation of angry laymen from St. Luke's was rumored to be on the way to Lake Leisure this very day.

"These bishops can be tough," Wes remarked, grinning. "The final say is in their hands, no matter what any lowly superintendent tries to pull over them; and they're jealous of their power. You're always asking how Belovèd manages to keep the bishop under control. Well, he's gonna need all the tricks in his bag today; they tell me the bishop is roaring like a mad bull, and I'd say that our plump, pink matador is about to get himself gored at last."

If the matador was aware of his danger he gave no sign when Jack picked him up that morning. He enjoyed the drive, especially when they began to get into the mountains, and chatted volubly.

"I was the first member of his cabinet the bishop picked himself," he was saying. "All the rest he inherited when he came to our area. Naturally that gave me a position of responsibility and trust."

Naturally, thought Jack, not taking his eyes off the road as it wound along the steep mountainside, and that also gave you an inside track with a bishop who knew nobody, who was the victim of whatever information you chose to give him, and who has been putty in your hands ever since. But you're about to get gored, matador!

"I suppose people read many ugly things into our relationship," the cheerful voice went on, "simply because I was instrumental in swinging a crucial bloc of delegates to him at his election. What they forget is that I could have swung my bloc to half a dozen other men, a number of whom would have been far more inclined to grant me favors afterwards, but I did not. I gave them to the man I felt best qualified to be a bishop in the Methodist Church. He's humble; he's fair; and he's objective."

This was probably sincere. Wes had once said almost the same thing: "It's all a matter of interpretation. You can call it favoritism, or you can say that Belovèd felt our bishop was the best man for the job." But could even the most impartial bishop escape having his judgment affected by the presence of a cabinet member who, at precisely the right moment, had delivered precisely the right number of votes for victory?

Far off down the gorge they could see the lodge at last, set into the mountainside at the head of the lake. The cheery voice rattled on.

"People would value our bishop even more highly if they realized that courage and impartiality are not built-in attributes of the episcopacy. The best of them are only too human, and in Methodism their office carries temptations of prestige and power, which an Episcopalian or Roman bishop could not imagine. Our bishop had his campaign conducted with integrity; he refused to make deals with interested groups; the votes we finally cast his way were given because he had just rejected an even larger bloc that had strings on it.

"After all, consider the way some men have got themselves elevated to the episcopacy! Morgerson's delegation went off to conference four years ago pledged on their most sacred honor to back Freddie Friston. But what did Morgerson do? The minute he got there he forgot he ever had a sacred honor; he had friends working night and day lining up votes for himself; and poor Freddie never even knew what hit him!" He paused, gazing out over the water and humming a snatch of a hymn. "Look—look at that trout! Three pounds if he's an ounce!" Jack turned his head too late to see more than a white splash on the sky-blue mirror of the lake.

Jack had never seen Dr. Worthington so ebullient. Probably his favorable cardiogram was responsible. Jack wondered whether the man could possibly be unaware of the fate awaiting him. As they neared the lodge he rambled on about the power of wealthy laymen he had known. It seemed that their ability to pay the church debt or buy a new organ was much less significant than their habit of command, their talent for administering big programs, and—in the case of a difficult financial campaign—the magic of a big name throughout an entire district or even a conference.

As they pulled into the parking lot, he added:

"Big laymen can become virtual dictators in a local church. But the funny thing is, without such men a church is crippled!"

Jack noted with amusement how out of place Dr. Worthington's car looked among the rows of gleaming monsters and small, exotic sports cars that crowded the lot. While the superintendent went to the desk, Jack waited by a pillar in the vast, low-ceilinged lobby, watching the residents come and go and hearing snatches of conversation. The air-conditioning felt delightful. Jack had talked to Wes for nearly an hour in Wes's garden that morning, standing in the broiling August sun while Wes hoed and weeded. ("Gotta get Sue some beans to can! Last winter the congregation got behind on my salary and I thought I'd never get outa debt to the grocer.")

Two tanned, bony young women in bikinis came by from the pool just below the Lodge: ". . . told her, 'Darling, if the dampness bothers you, why don't you and Herb buy a place in Arizona—just to knock around in between seasons?'" Then a hairy-chested man with a towel about his wet trunks, gesturing to a friend in a lurid robe: ". . . voted thirty thousand shares we picked up at the last minute, and they never had a chance . . ." Three fat men, all very sunburned: ". . . trouble with those characters that hang around the White House. 'Just who the hell,' I said, 'do you think put you in the Senate anyway?'" The voices eddied about Jack's pillar till the superintendent returned.

Stepping into the elevator, Jack saw the operator's eyes wander over Dr. Worthington's rumpled blue suit with ill-concealed disdain. The bishop's suite was at the end of a long corridor on the third floor. One room had been taken over by his secretary, Miss Tillery, as a reception room. Four men and two women were already waiting, all middle-aged, all together in a line along the wall, and all sitting up very straight. Dr. Worthington nodded and smiled. Only one of the six smiled in return, and Jack concluded that they were the delegation from St. Luke's.

"Ah, Miss Tillery! For your collection!"

From a bulging pocket the superintendent produced a diminutive tiger carved of yellow stone. He had written a missionary in India for it, and Miss Tillery's rather plain face was radiant as she examined the gift and chatted. It seemed that the bishop was sitting for some final touches on his portrait; the job had been commissioned by his alma mater and was to hang in the college chapel. While she was announcing their arrival, the superintendent stood by the closed door and remarked carelessly:

"I must say, I *dread* approaching the bishop with church problems while the poor man is trying to snatch a few days' rest. One usually gets the exact reverse of one's desires."

Jack saw the uneasiness in the faces of the delegation at this remark, then Miss Tillery reappeared, her eyes much rounder and darker behind her spectacles:

"He's been *expecting* you!" she whispered. "Good luck!"

The main room of the bishop's suite had oak-paneled walls, and big, rough-hewn oak rafters; on the side overlooking the lake, casement windows from floor to ceiling ran the entire length of the room. The bishop was sitting in a high-backed chair at the far end, with his back to the big stone fireplace. The artist had his easel between the sofa and the windows; the bishop's chair was on a raised platform, and the hem of his long black robe trailed over the edge; the gold and purple hood mantled his shoulders, and one hand held a Bible on his thigh, finger thrust into place as though he had paused in reading. For some reason he looked much bigger than Jack had remembered him. His rugged, handsome face, framed by its mane of iron-gray hair, was toward the windows, and he did not turn his head or move when they entered, but his voice boomed down the entire length of the room.

"Fred, what's all this I hear? This Evans business cannot possibly be allowed to stand. You seem to have forgotten that it is I who must sign these appointments and bear the responsibility!"

The artist—a squat, swarthy man in a polo shirt and slacks—calmly stirred some paint on his palette. Jack had never seen the bishop betray anger before; indeed, he had marveled at his infinite patience in conducting the complex and tiresome business of the annual conferences at which he presided. His voice did not soften as they approached.

"Honestly, Fred, I'm disappointed in you—and I'm embarrassed. This thing involves half a dozen men and several districts besides your own, yet you did not even do me the courtesy of a phone call! You know as well as I do what some people are saying in this conference, and this is precisely the sort of thing that lends an appearance of substance to their charges. I am embarrassed that you compel me to remind you, Fred, that I am still bishop of this area and nobody can bear my responsibilities for me."

Dr. Worthington did not answer immediately. He went to the sofa and sat down very slowly and deliberately. He was breathing hard; and when he finally replied, his voice was low and he kept pausing between sentences.

"Forgive me, Bishop. . . . The fact is, I haven't had a telephone available. . . . I'm afraid I've been going at it a little too hard lately. . . . Doctor put me in the hospital for three days. . . . Refused to let me transact any business." He paused, drawing several deep breaths. "You remember Jack Lee, of course. I had Patsy get hold of him and sent him out to see Edgar and Blanche for me. . . . He can give you their feelings at first hand. . . ."

The bishop hastily came down from the platform.

"In Heaven's name, Fred, you shouldn't have driven up here today! Flo! Flo, come here at once! It's Fred."

"Jack did all the driving. I felt you would want me to report on the matter personally, Bishop. I'm terribly sorry if I've embarrassed you. I'm all right now . . . really."

The bishop's wife appeared from the next room. She was a slender little woman, even smaller than the bishop. She was quite plain, but had a charm and naturalness that put people instantly at ease. Jack had heard that her family connections had often stood the bishop in good stead and formed part of his much admired judgment in matters where national issues affected his area.

All attempts to persuade the superintendent to have the house physician summoned were unavailing. He insisted that he was all right, that the altitude had simply left him a little short of breath, and he finally consented to lie down in the middle bedroom for a time.

The bishop resumed his pose in silence, his eyes straying from time to time to the bedroom door. Jack sat on the sofa and heard the superintendent talking to the bishop's wife about matters of health. He kept recurring to persons he had known—mostly prominent churchmen—who had broken under overwork and responsibility. The bishop's wife finally came out and sat gazing through the casement windows at the lake and looking depressed. When Dr. Worthington appeared, he looked tired and sank down on the sofa by Jack with a grateful sigh.

"Well, Bishop," he said, "you have every right to be angry with me."

"I'm not angry, Fred, but . . . well . . ." The bishop kept stealing uneasy glances at his superintendent. The health issue had upset him, and Jack realized that the matador had side-stepped the opening charge and that the bull was now cautious and puzzled. "I have never doubted you had sound reasons for considering Evans. . . ."

"No, Bishop. It was a blunder. I don't deny it. I was ill, and I kept thinking about Bishop Morgerson, and poor old Guy Tompkins, both better men than I, and both struck down at the very peak of their powers. I'm just a little man, Bishop; I don't have the impartiality for bigness. I suppose in many ways Edgar is a poor choice for St. Luke's, but he's never had a chance to prove himself to himself, you might say. I figured I could talk Jerry Millstead and some other key laymen into giving him a try, just till conference. I suppose I was actually afraid something might happen before I could reward a man who came and stood by me when I was friendless and unknown."

If the bull had been pinked, he gave no sign. He glanced sharply at Dr. Worthington.

"Now! That's more like it! When you start pulling those sob stories on me, Fred Worthington, I know you're feeling like yourself again. You *never* do things for mere sentiment, and you know it. If you had reasons for the Evans appointment, I should be most happy to hear them." The bishop glanced at Jack, who could not restrain a grin.

Dr. Worthington's merry laugh rang out, but Jack thought he detected a note of discomfort. Score one for the bull.

"Well, I confess I did have a problem in conference morale. Edgar is much beloved. He's become something of a symbol to the little men in this conference. I've thought of him as their hero and their spokesman in many ways." Jack appreciated the respect for truth evinced in the 'in many ways,' for Edgar was no conference hero or spokesman in any ordinary usage of the terms. "I reasoned that many little men cannot help asking themselves, 'Why should I be loyal? What has a lifetime of loyalty brought Edgar?' I wanted to show them that in one conference of Methodism, at any rate, a lifetime of sacrifice is not lightly regarded."

Jack noted that the superintendent did not mention that his action had left the "little men" angry and resentful. The bishop frowned, obviously sensing the gaps in his own knowledge of the little men.

"But," Dr. Worthington went on, "I know nothing about the conference. You see all the districts; I see only my small corner."

"Oh, tommyrot!" the bishop slapped the arm of the chair, then replaced the hand in its proper pose. "You know every pig track in every man's district and without you we'd all be lost! You're forever pleading the case of some country parson whose own superintendent scarcely knows he exists!"

"I do like to think of myself as the little man's friend at court," said the superintendent gravely. "After all, I'm only a country parson at heart."

"Oh, tommyrot!" said the bishop again. "You're no more a country parson at heart than Flo is. In fact, you're less."

This time it was the bishop's wife who laughed, and Dr. Worthington simply sat with his hands folded over his plump waistline and grinned slyly at them all. Jack scored another for the bull.

"Well," said the superintendent at last, getting slowly to his feet. "I'd better call Edgar. He certainly knows every Methodist appointment is subject to the bishop's judgment. It's only fair that I should be the one to tell him."

The bishop's gaiety was gone. The pain and frustration in his face were obvious.

"Sit down, Fred, in Heaven's name! It's not as simple as a phone call *now*. You've told Evans. He thinks the church is his. He considers it the just reward of a lifetime of labor. But what about Clarence Motherly? I promised myself that that poor man would never again be subjected to the kind of humiliation he experienced two years ago when we sent Wilson to St. Luke's after virtually committing ourselves to Clarence. I'm shepherd of all these men, Fred—not just a single district. And when things like this come up, I sometimes don't think I can bear the load another day."

He closed his eyes, mopping his face with a handkerchief. Dr. Worthington suddenly smiled.

"Oh, before I forget, I had a call last night from the West Coast." He fumbled through some notes and letters. "It was from Chet Krutcher.

He's got a youth assembly in full swing out there at Asbury Meadows on the lake; he had Bishop Blackman booked for five days beginning tomorrow morning at eleven, and now Blackie has canceled on him with some kind of virus he picked up in Asia. Chet asked if I knew anybody of that stature who could pinch hit, and of course I thought of only one name."

"Quite impossible. Tell Chet I'm flattered and so forth, but we've a planning meeting Thursday to set up that fund drive for Higher Education. You're one of the conference chairmen; you could have told him all that when he called." For the first time the bishop smiled. "Fred, you're the best fund-raiser in Methodism, but aren't you getting overconfident? How could you forget a drive for three million dollars?"

The superintendent's blue eyes gleamed, and he ducked his round, pink head in acknowledgment.

"I, for one, would be willing to double up, and so would Bill Whitley and Steadman Loveless, I'm sure. Steadman's a bachelor; he's got plenty of time. We can all double up if our handling of that sort of drudgery would bring spiritual benediction to a thousand young people none of us could interest for five minutes!"

This last brought instant protests, but Jack scarcely heard. Patricia had said that her father had spent half the night on long-distance. . . . Youth work was the bishop's first love and greatest talent, the one thing that might lure him out of his area for a few days, while the superintendent got things back under control. Dr. Worthington must have spent a small fortune calling all over the country in search of just some such last-minute cancellation. But the bishop was not falling in line.

"No, that's quite out of the question with this Evans business to be settled. Besides, that's tomorrow morning. I could never *be* there by then."

"You could take a jetliner at six; I'll have Jack drive you both down in my car."

"Drive us *both* down!" exclaimed the bishop's wife, sitting up straighter and laying her magazine aside.

"Why, of course! I told Chet I wouldn't even trouble the bishop with his offer unless he'd throw in a ticket for Flo. I reminded him you were one of the best-informed people in Methodism on world missions, and that you'd be a standout as a discussion-group leader on missionary vocations for young people. After all, Chet's got foundation money for just that sort of thing."

A lighthearted argument ensued, but it was clear that the superintendent now had the bishop's wife in his camp. Jack had forgotten that matadors had toreadors to assist them.

"You've turned my wife against me," grumbled the bishop.

"This will be an excellent boost for your books on the West Coast," the superintendent went on. "I told Chet you'd expect to see them in the book display and that an autograph party might not hurt."

The sweet, persistent voice was going on, but Jack was remembering something Wes had said once. They had been discussing Dr. Worthington's seeming ability to bend the bishop to his will, and Jack had asked, 'Just what's he got that the bishop wants so badly?' To which Wes answered dryly, 'Money.' At the time Jack had taken this to be a reference to the superintendent's legendary prowess as a fund raiser.

Now he gazed about at the big suite and suddenly wondered how the bishop could possibly maintain himself in this style for a full month out of every year. He recalled hazily some sort of reference Patricia had made once to the bishop's being a trifle straitened financially. . . . Wes had said that at one time bishops used to charge even for the customary functions of their office—one hundred dollars to dedicate an organ, two hundred dollars to dedicate a church, etc., until the general conference forbade such practices. What would Krutcher pay for those five days —five hundred dollars plus travel? Plus a chance for the bishop to plug sales of his books. . . .

Jack had once heard Dirkwell complain of his inability to bring an urgent matter before the bishop:

"Plenty of bishops are at their desks and on the job twelve months a year, except for absolutely unavoidable outside engagements. They work at the job of knowing their men! But Belovèd keeps our bishop booked up solid with high-priced speaking engagements all over the country, and he's so busy making money in other episcopal areas, he doesn't know what's going on in his own!"

Jack had retorted that the bishop was promoting causes he believed in, which was certainly true, and his success as an inspirational speaker was phenomenal. But now Jack stared at the three people before him in sudden uneasiness. . . .

Dr. Worthington was discussing the stairstep of small promotions involved if Motherly should be sent to St. Luke's, thus leaving his own church vacant for the next man below, and so forth. He was plainly counting on the bishop's known distaste for desk work, administrative detail, and sticky ethical issues. And he was pushing to the breaking-point the bishop's obviously limited power to endure seeing anyone hurt.

"Blanche is going to take all this much harder than Edgar," the superintendent was saying. "Wives always do. There's no question it's a sticky appointment, Bishop, but that's the kind you're good at."

"It's the kind I'm worst at!"

"I deny that categorically. And certainly nobody could have handled the Bakersville situation without hurting someone."

Jack winced; the Bakersville affair had been recounted to him once by Wes. The bishop's wife averted her eyes. The bishop's face turned pale.

"Fred, I can scarcely believe you wish me to beg your forgiveness again for what was as much ignorance as vanity on my part. Had I deferred to your judgment, the church would not have split. But I was new; I had not yet learned that the title of bishop conveys no gift of omniscience."

Dr. Worthington raised his small, plump hands in protest.

"Tom! Please! Every member of the conference admired the bigness and humility with which you went to those folks afterwards. I don't know of an act during your entire first quadrennium that made you more beloved!"

The bishop's eyes remained fixed on some distant point beyond the wooded shore of the lake. When he spoke again, his voice was somber.

"The night of my election to the episcopacy my father was present. He was a very old man then and had given half a century to the parish ministry. He shook my hand without smiling and said, 'Tom, I'm going to pray for you as long as God spares me—harder than I've ever prayed before. Because now you'll never go hungry or hear the truth again.' But at that moment I had no idea the prayers would be necessary."

If the matador had meant to give a grievous wound, he had plainly succeeded. After a pause the voice went on:

"It's all been so different from what I expected. I have almost five hundred pastors in this conference alone! When can I sit down in their living rooms and meet their families and hear their problems? A Methodist bishop cannot be a friend and father-confessor to his ministers, like an Episcopal or Roman bishop who tours a compact little diocese and even confirms the children of the churches. He's one vice-president in a vast bureaucracy, an errand boy for the general boards, a man who—precisely because of what he is and where he is—can seldom know what's actually going on at the grass roots. Or in other spheres around him!"

For the first time Jack found himself sympathizing with the bishop's absences from his area. Self-indulgence, yes; but it was also a chance for a vital and compassionate human being to shrug off the entanglements of the bureaucratic process and get back in touch with people.

Plus five hundred dollars and all expenses paid. . . .

"How can a man stay humble and sane in this office? He has more power than any frail mortal should be entrusted with; he's elected for life. Is it any wonder we become so enamored of our own self-importance that people dare not even mention our blunders or follies? A bishop would go quite mad were it not that each of us has someone he can trust, someone not afraid to tell home truths." He smiled faintly. "Yes, I did go down to Bakersville and stand in the pulpit and confess I had erred. But after almost twelve years in office I doubt that I shall ever have that much humility or courage again. . . .

"It's not just that one can so rarely assemble all the facts necessary to achieving truth and justice. It's the realization of one's *moral* limitations! I actually used to think a mere man could achieve total objectivity—even surrounded night and day by people who have something to gain from him. But in spite of all my efforts and prayers I find myself prejudiced against this man, inclined toward that church. Take Clarence Motherly: superbly educated, hard worker, considerable experience. Yet that eternal smile has made it virtually impossible for me to *think* of the man without irritation. And that biases me *for* him today, which can be as confusing as a bias against him. . . . People seem to forget that a bishop is only a man."

The artist had been listening, motionless.

"Well," he said unexpectedly, "we might suggest that the college just hang the canvas like a Rembrandt or a Botticelli. You know—'Portrait of a Man.'"

Dr. Worthington filled the abrupt silence, rattling on about a spectacular youth meeting the bishop had staged, etc. The pathway to possible frustration and pain had been sketched; now the sure road to satisfying accomplishment was envisioned. Then, somehow, the superintendent managed to get off onto the new golf course at Asbury Meadows, and the bishop's wife broke in to ask her husband when he had last played a round of golf, and this turned into what was apparently a long-standing family debate. Jack wondered whether either of them realized just how the problem of health and overwork and responsibility had gotten into their awareness that afternoon. The superintendent listened in respectful silence, then finally brought the conversation around to St. Luke's again.

"I suppose it's really poor old Jerry Millstead I've been worried about. You remember how upset he was when we sent Harry Wilson to St. Luke's. Jerry never knew what that graduate-school theology was all about; to him Harry was just another smart-aleck college kid spouting big words. In fact, I once heard Jerry say that one more highbrow in the St. Luke's pulpit would end his active membership. So, naturally, I hesitate to think what he'll say when Clarence waltzes out in that white satin stole and tees off with the Sursum Corda. But, after all, Clarence is a good money raiser, and Edgar rarely meets the askings."

The bishop smacked his free hand against his knee.

"Jeremiah Millstead is a crotchety old conservative with a sixth-grade education who made a million dollars running a fish cannery and thinks that qualifies him to run the Methodist Church. He's named every pastor to St. Luke's except Harry Wilson for the past forty years, and it's about time for *some* Methodist bishop to remind him that he has not yet been elevated to the episcopacy!"

The superintendent's wispy brows expressed pious dismay.

"I have always preferred to regard Jerry as a devout layman who has consecrated his considerable wealth and executive ability to God. After all, Peter was a fisherman!"

The bishop raised his eyes to the raftered ceiling.

"Fred, please! You know perfectly well that any resemblance between St. Peter and the chairman of the board of Millstead's Mackerel is purely coincidental."

Again the ringing little laugh.

"Well, Bishop, I confess Jerry is not the most beloved layman in Methodism. And, as you say, we've got a big push coming up, and Clarence is certainly the man for a key spot in the district like St. Luke's."

Silence.

"Now, just a minute, Fred." The bishop's sonorous tone was suddenly muted. "Whatever our personal opinions of Jerry, every layman in the conference respects his business judgment. We've got this overseas relief drive on our hands already, which Jerry doubtless puts in the same category with foreign aid. He's never really been sold on higher education—or any education at all. . . . Just what did you mean about Evans and Jerry?"

The superintendent frowned and rubbed his chin.

"Why . . . it was more an intuitive sort of thing than any rational analysis, Bishop. I just had a kind of hunch that Edgar is what Jerry thinks of when he forms his mental image of a *bona fide* man of God. Jerry was born on a farm. He likes to see a preacher kneel in the pulpit . . . that sort of thing. Actually, though, I haven't heard Edgar preach for several years."

The bishop picked up his cue instantly. The deep-set eyes fixed on Jack. Jack had been determined to say nothing that might promote the superintendent's campaign, for though he liked Edgar, the appointment itself was unthinkable and could only bring humiliation to the man and problems to the church. But under the bishop's rapid-fire questioning he found himself trapped by the truth. The very things that had shocked and upset him about Edgar now proved his greatest recommendations. The bishop then questioned him about Motherly, and again he was trapped. When the questions ceased, Jack added:

"I'd have to agree, sir, that Edgar would have quite an appeal to someone from a rural background. I'm sure his effect on Mr. Millstead would more than offset the loss of a few suburban young people."

Although this problem was not in a class with Millstead's far-ranging influence, it obviously caused the bishop further thought—and gave Jack the satisfaction of jostling the quick-footed matador.

"Well," said the bishop suddenly, "Motherly is out. That much is certain."

"Bishop, I—" the superintendent's voice reflected anxiety and protest, but the bishop simply lifted his hand.

"Please, Fred. That's my decision, and it's final. We've almost exhausted the good will of laymen all over this conference because of the way the education drive was mismanaged some years ago. We've got to have Jerry on our side! It may be true that Edgar rarely meets his askings, but have you considered what the effects might be across the entire conference if the merest whisper got out that Jerry Millstead regarded this push as unsound? I know it's distressing to have to sacrifice a church to the foibles of one layman, but this thing is bigger than any one church. Our colleges are in trouble! We've got to have a man at St. Luke's who can get Jerry behind this thing and make him push it! And from what Jack tells me, Edgar's first sermon should more than persuade Jeremiah Millstead that Methodism is still the church of his fathers."

The superintendent finally agreed. He had been taking the short view, like all superintendents, and thinking only of how Clarence might boost his own district's contributions. That was the great strength of the episcopacy, having someone who saw all the effects of an action throughout all the districts of the conference. And so on, and on, and on . . .

Well, the bull had been slain, or rather, had been respectfully permitted to run himself onto the sword. Now the only unresolved detail was that of shipping the remains to the West Coast while the matador tidied up the arena. And, of course, there was still that delegation of laymen from St. Luke's in the waiting room.

Jack got up and wandered over to the tall casement windows. Down at the pool a man was practicing full-gainers off the high board while most of the bathers sat under umbrellas sipping their drinks and watching. Along the wooded shore two people on white horses picked their way down the bridle path.

The talk drifted to the high cost of living, thence to ministers' pensions, and thence to the fact that this would be the bishop's last year before retirement.

"We're thinking of buying a little place down at the old campground," said the bishop. "Just enough for the two of us, with a spare bedroom for the grandchildren in the summertime."

Dr. Worthington straightened.

"You haven't put any *money* down!"

"Why . . . why, no. But certainly we must act soon."

"No, no!" Dr. Worthington kept starting to speak, then hesitating. Finally, he said, "I should advise you to hold off a while . . . by all means."

"Fred Worthington, what are you up to now?"

The superintendent sat back and folded his arms.

"I have no idea what you're talking about."

The bishop kept staring at him and then exchanging a look with his wife. Finally, Jack realized what it all meant: the superintendent had some sort of movement afoot in the conference to buy the bishop a home for his retirement. Twice during Jack's years in the conference there had been spontaneous "love offerings" for the bishop and his wife, who were immensely popular. Jack had helped collect the donations on one of these occasions and had been touched by the unfeigned pleasure many a hard-pressed parsonage family took in contributing. Wes Phillips had taken a slightly different view. He had handed Jack a quarter and two nickels and had said: "When I was nineteen and practically broke, I once kicked in five bucks to help buy a big-league shortstop a touring car that he took and wrapped around a live oak tree the first time out. Can I do less for the bishop and his wife when they're scraping along on twelve thousand five hundred a year and doing a lot more for mankind?"

"Fred," the bishop was saying, "I positively forbid this, do you understand!"

"Bishop, I have no power to stop people from loving you!"

They finally returned to the subject of the West Coast trip, and Jack wondered whether the bishop himself was even conscious of the precise moment at which he began talking about the series of speeches he would use for the young people. For the decision to go was not actually made by him; it was the spontaneous outgrowth of a mood of warmth and congeniality and mutual trust. It simply rose up about him and enveloped him like the beauty of this summer day beside a mountain lake.

Once the decision had been made, Jack noted a change in the bishop. He became brisk, alert, commanding. He curtly declined the offer of a chauffeur to the airport; he called in Miss Tillery and gave her notes covering all sorts of contingencies for his absence; he dictated a series of penetrating suggestions for the campaign steering committee; and he sent his wife off to ready their things and to call the airport and verify the reservations which the superintendent was having held for them pending his decision.

All this he did without changing his posture or moving his head. Even the artist seemed infected by this sudden decisiveness and finally proclaimed himself satisfied, and everyone gathered round and studied the tremendous personage on the canvas.

"Magnificent!" Dr. Worthington beamed. "It really gives meaning to the old phrase, 'a prince of the church'!"

"Oh, tommyrot, Fred!" said the bishop.

Jack waited in Miss Tillery's office while the bishop and Dr. Worthington explained the situation to the delegation from St. Luke's.

Through the half-open door Jack could hear their voices. The bishop was gracious but inflexible: The interests of the whole church were involved here; it was only an interim appointment; surely they would not withhold their cooperation. The delegation finally came trooping out, their faces grim. Dr. Worthington appeared a few minutes later. He was brisk and cheerful, but underneath the bland exterior Jack thought he looked terribly tired.

In the hall, waiting for the elevator, Jack said:

"Really, sir, you shouldn't have undertaken this so soon after leaving the hospital."

The older man's voice was slow, measured, almost chilling.

"I have never known what it meant to have brothers or sisters, or even mother or father. Only friends. I value mine. Edgar was the first. He wants a try at St. Luke's. He's going to St. Luke's if I have to pave the way with my body."

They rode down in silence. While Dr. Worthington was resting a few minutes in an easy chair in the lobby, Jack strolled into the gift-shop and bought a glossy picture postcard of Leisure Lodge on which he scribbled a brief, unsigned message to Wes:

"The bull never had a chance."

XXII

Cloud of Witnesses

WHEN Jack finally broke with Dr. Worthington, the break came suddenly and unexpectedly, at the district ministers' meeting the Monday following the visit to the bishop.

The day started routinely enough. Jack got out Steadman Loveless' advance materials on the Kingdom Commitment Crusade, threw the bulging manila envelope onto the back seat of his car, and went by the Wentworth post office for his mail. The only first-class item was another small, pink envelope from Thelma Ross Richardson. She had been writing him once a week since he dropped by her apartment in July, even though he never answered, and this was September. He stuffed her letter into the glove compartment without bothering to read it.

He picked up Wes on his way to Mount Gilead, which was Clarence Motherly's church, about thirty miles from Wentworth. They arrived early and sat in Jack's car talking and watching the other ministers drive up. They discussed Dan Starr's probable reaction to being punished for DeForrest Garrison's attempt to bring him to the bishop's attention at annual conference in June. Dan had not appeared at the July or August district meetings, although the superintendent frowned on absences.

"He mighta broke an axle," said Wes. "Those roads out on the Carsten Circuit are pretty rough. . . ."

Clarence Motherly came over to greet them. To Jack's astonishment he apparently believed that Edgar Evans had pressured the superintendent into giving him a try at St. Luke's. Jack tried to explain that Blanche had overridden Edgar's better judgment, but Motherly's big, fawnlike brown eyes stared at Jack coldly. He kept pursing his small, thin-lipped mouth, and his Adam's apple bobbed inside his clerical collar.

"It was the payment of a long-standing political debt!" he snapped. "But Edgar Evans will live to regret the day he stole an appointment from me."

He returned to the church to finish preparing his devotional for the meeting. The parking lot was filling up; Dr. Worthington's car pulled in, then several others.

"Say, there's Dan!" Jack exclaimed.

They saw the slim, athletic figure come swiftly between two cars to intercept the superintendent. They saw the familiar flash of white teeth against the bronzed face as Dan stooped and seized the heavy briefcase from the older man's hand. As the pair disappeared into the church, Jack and Wes turned to stare at each other in stunned silence.

"If that had been some bootlicker like Clarence Motherly," Wes said at last, "I coulda believed it." He shook his shaggy white head. "Dan Starr! Carrying the boss's briefcase and grinning like a mule eating briers . . ."

But Jack was too shaken to comment. Presently they got out and went to stand on the steps, where most of the ministers had now gathered, waiting for the sound of the opening hymn. Steadman Loveless pulled up to the side entrance in his station wagon; Patricia was with him and helped him carry in some materials for the visitation campaign he was presenting. She had on a pale-blue pleated skirt and a white blouse with frilly cuffs and a froth of lace at the throat. She did not glance in Jack's direction and he did not join the handful of men who went around to help. Their relationship had been worsening all summer, especially since her father's action against Dan Starr, whom they had known since seminary. Last night they had argued till past midnight, and this time the differences had begun to seem irreconcilable. When they parted, they were still angry . . . and beginning to be frightened.

The men watched in wry ill-humor as Loveless carried in his stacks of mimeographed materials. They all had the thick manila envelope of his advance mailing in their hands, and some were shuffling through the multicolored pages while they waited.

"This is the biggest one Steady ever mailed out," grumbled Wes, "but now he's hauling more in a truck and bringing his secretary to help him unload it on us."

"The Ringing Challenge Telephone Hour!" snorted Thompson, a gangling country preacher. "How can you challenge somebody if you can't get the party line?"

Edgar Evans was standing in a cluster of men under the shade of the portico. He had on a natty new suit whose padded shoulders made him seem even more tremendous than he was.

"Look at these visiting hours," he was saying. "The big-city bureaucrats who dream up this stuff never heard of milking time. And stock to be fed." Obviously his recent elevation to St. Luke's had not lessened Edgar's identification with the rural ministry.

"It's not milking time that gets me," said Tommy Fredricks gloomily. "I'm in a mill town, and the mill is running two days a week. How can we push for bigger financial commitments right now?"

"It's the same all over the mining section."

Jack could not remember ever having heard so much dismay and resentment. Many of Steadman Loveless' prefabricated programs had been brilliantly successful, but a few had been unqualified disasters.

"We've just finished one big push. Why can't they give us a breathing space?"

"This might work in other districts, but it ought to be drastically modified here—or junked."

"We've just spent six weeks working out a program tailored to local needs. If Steady insists on this one, it will wreck the morale of some of the best laymen in my church."

"I'll go through the motions, but they can't make me put my heart in it."

"It's this inflexible regimentation that's turning rural folks against Methodism."

"It's a sinful waste of two whole weeks, that's what."

"Personally, I haven't the strength for another lockstep program right now."

This went on till they heard the sound of the hymn. Jack saw Merrill Adams drive up just then and waited outside to hear his comments. Jack and Adams had once had a long talk on power politics.

He saluted Jack with a multicolored pamphlet.

"How do the men feel about this one?" he asked.

"I've never seen them more bitter and frustrated."

Adams cocked a thoughtful eye toward the church, from which the sound of the opening hymn floated down.

"Well, I suppose we'll all register our conscientious scruples, and then let the big boys ram it through as always." He stood staring into space. "I've been doing a lot of thinking lately, Jack. About ambition. I've always been an ambitious man, and everyone has always assured me that's a virtue, and I've done rather well—by keeping my mouth shut and by pretending not to notice things. Belovèd always says he wouldn't give ten cents for a minister with no ambition, but why? Why should *he* say that? Isn't it because such a man would be unmanageable? Would refuse to endorse programs he felt were contrary to the interests of the Kingdom or the needs of his own church? If a minister wandered into this conference who had no personal ambition for his own career and advancement, what would he need to be afraid of? What could you bribe or threaten him with?"

"He'd be like Wes," said Jack.

"Exactly. Wes only wants to promote truth and right. We want to promote truth and right—*and* our own careers. It's that 'and' that makes all the difference. He has singleness of heart, and peace; we're all double-minded and live in hell." He smacked the manila envelope with the back of his hand. "What makes us so timid in the pulpit, so afraid we'll offend some rich little old lady who needs a few home truths? Ambition. What makes us more afraid of failure than we are of sin? Why are most of us scared to death of controversial subjects?"

"We do seem to be," Jack admitted. "Yet look how many of our greatest pulpits have been filled by men who spoke out on just such things."

"Maybe we underestimate the people. And the Lord." As Adams turned toward the steps he suddenly paused and smiled his rare smile. "And why are we always preaching against ambition?"

Jack knew that Wes had been working on Adams for years, but apparently something had now brought him to a crisis of conscience. . . . Probaby the St. Luke's business. . . .

Jack was about to follow him when Dan Starr appeared, ran lightly down the steps, and over to Loveless' station wagon. When he returned bearing some manila folders, Jack met him just within the cool shadow of the building and they argued briefly.

"Why didn't you talk to me at conference!" Dan snapped. "You might have had the guts to tell Martha and me what that ham actor Garrison was getting us into!"

"Dan, I spent an hour arguing with Dr. Worthington the day you were ordained. I did everything I could for you!"

The girlish blue eyes widened; the familiar-unfamiliar smile flashed against the tanned young face.

"You *all* did! You *all* did everything you could—short of getting involved yourself." He suddenly glanced up at the big window in the wall of the sanctuary beside them. "You know something? It gives a man a new slant on life when he's been slugged and thrown in the ditch and the good Samaritan never comes along—when his oldest friends just pass by on the other side. He sees everybody from a new angle. He sees what this Christian ministry really is—a jungle. A stained glass jungle, maybe, but a jungle just the same, with every animal against every other, tooth and claw!"

The words were childishly dramatic, but they stung.

"Well, you surely can't believe this is the answer—carrying the boss's briefcase! Running errands for the number-two man!"

Dan flushed to the roots of his bright golden hair.

"I'd heard Emma Schell talk about 'Patsy's little lap dog,'" he snapped, "but refused to believe it—till this last conference. Up till then you were my idea of what a man of God was supposed to look like and act like, Jack Lee. But from a ditch you don't look quite the same. So listen: I know my talents; I know where God wants me to use them; and if a machine controls all roads that lead there, then I'll join that machine. And I can't see that I'm doing anything that you haven't done—only you did it quicker."

Clarence Motherly had almost finished his devotional when Jack walked in and sat down on a back pew, still trembling with anger and humiliation—and with fear. For he knew that he would never be able to live with himself now, or with the blazing scorn in Dan's eyes. He did not know yet what he would do to erase that scorn, but he knew himself well enough to know that he would be compelled to do something, whether rational or irrational, helpful or completely self-destructive.

Motherly was wearing a white satin stole over his black robe, and against the rich oak paneling of the pulpit his pale forehead and saucer-eyed face had a stern, almost monastic gravity. Even his voice was different, sounding almost masculine as he wound up his brief devotional message:

". . . that Christ is calling us today as men of God to rise to the heroic stature of these men of old who through faith stopped the mouths of lions, escaped the edge of the sword, were tortured and refused to accept release, suffered mocking and scourging, chains and imprisonment, were stoned and sawn asunder and went about in skins of sheep and goats, destitute and ill-treated—of whom the world was not worthy! Therefore, since we are compassed about by so great a cloud of witnesses, let us also lay aside every weight, and the sin which clings so closely, and let us run with patience the race that is set before us, looking unto Jesus, the author and finisher of our faith!"

Following Motherly's devotional, Harry Washburn, president of the district group, disposed of the routine business and turned the meeting over to the superintendent. Jack decided that Dr. Worthington must have been preoccupied with conference politics when he let Loveless' committee push through this impractical program. But, as always, the superintendent now resembled Coach Nelson, exhorting the Foxull football team at half-time. Coach Nelson was also round and bald and he, too, had a bottomless reserve of artificial enthusiasm and a sublime faith in the magic of "teamwork"! It seemed that there had been "some misunderstanding" of the program throughout the conference. Hence its author, "our own Dr. Loveless," would "speak to us today" in order that Dr. Worthington's district might be "*first* to report, *first* in persons rededicated to Christ, and *first* in financial commitments!"

Steadman Loveless' presentation was more that of a school teacher than a coach. Patricia sat on the front pew and handed up the proper items to him at the proper time, but Jack tried not to think about her, or Dan, or her father, or anything but Loveless' silly program. Watching that gray, colorless man with his squarish face all sketched in flat lines and unbending planes, Jack recalled something Wes had said: "Steady's an omen: If a born bureaucrat without one spark of emotional fire can rise to our highest pulpits, then maybe we're no longer the church of the warm heart."

Loveless was holding up a yellow file-card:

"Let us now turn to the Electronic Kingdom Commitment Card. Note that I am rubbing the electrographic pencil so as to black in the square directly to the left of the words, 'I commit myself to the practice of daily prayer.'" He indicated a number stamped in the upper left-hand corner: "The first three code letters designate the district, conference, and jurisdiction; the first numeral indicates the pastoral charge; the last five digits designate the individual prospect. Use of code numbers instead of proper names for prospects enormously simplifies the computation of results. Thus, when prospect has recorded his commitments in this fashion, pledging himself to pray, to read his Bible, to attend church, etc., the card is forwarded to campaign headquarters and within a matter of hours we are in position to flash the word to the most distant charge in the conference as to its precise standing, its district's comparative status, and various items of interest to the pastor, such as the median number in attendance at midweek services, etc."

The man beside Jack was doodling absently on his electronic card and had drawn a huge zero in the space at the bottom marked "Pastor's Loyalty Quotient." When Loveless reached the end it was almost lunchtime and his final request for further questions was met with dead silence. He stepped back and stood by the turnover chart.

"Mr. Chairman, this is the program adopted at annual conference and it is therefore mandatory for all districts. However, there have been misunderstandings about it, and I should like to move that the ministers of this district give it a unanimous vote of confidence and approval."

Motherly and Dan Starr both rose to second the motion.

Dr. Worthington had risen when Loveless stepped back, and now, forgetting that he was not the presiding officer, he absently called for the vote. A scattering of unenthusiastic "ayes" sounded across the room.

"All opposed, and it is so ordered."

Jack had intended to vote "no" out of sheer mulishness. Throughout the meeting he had been unable to stop recalling "Patsy's little lap dog," and for some reason Dan's angry blue eyes had reminded Jack of Mrs. Catlett's molten black ones when she was screaming those unspeakable things at him. And Patricia had said something last night that popped into his head now: "After all, my dear, you're not another Wes Phillips!"

"Mr. Chairman!" Jack was on his feet.

Washburn started, realizing that Jack was addressing him. He rose, his heavy, lined face looking slightly flustered.

"A point of order. Although the chairman was present, he did not preside. Nor did I hear a call for discussion. I request that this action be ruled null and void and that we take the vote again—*with* time for discussion."

There was a dead silence.

Several of the men looked around, as if they expected to see Jack smiling and to discover that this was some sort of prank. Dr. Worthington's mild round eyes flashed a piercing, intenser blue, and his pink lips tightened. Then he blinked, smiled, and inclined his head very slightly.

"Jack is entirely correct, Mr. Chairman. I fear that your superintendent was a small church pastor so long he still thinks of our district simply as a brotherhood rather than a sitting of parliament."

The motion was repeated, and the second—this time by Motherly alone—and Washburn called for discussion. Jack picked up his materials and went down to stand beside the first pew while Loveless stood beside his turnover chart at the altar.

Jack could not remember later how he began. It was like that college vespers sermon all over again: he could only hazily recall the words but could never forget the mood—a mixture of anger and fear and moral outrage. Dr. Worthington revealed only his unvarying courteous interest. Patricia kept pretending to be sorting and arranging her materials, her eyes lowered, her small golden head bowed. Steadman Loveless kept adjusting his shaded spectacles with the tip of his middle finger and meeting each argument in turn with that same bland superiority with which the born bureaucrat greets every practical exception to the master plan.

But Loveless' unruffled composure was not as disturbing as the effect of the discussion on the assembled ministers. Jack kept glancing at them, particularly at the rural men, expecting some nod or indication of agreement or smile of encouragement. Their faces were completely expressionless, but under the silence, under the unnatural absence of the smallest movement, Jack could feel the enormous anxiety. He began to wish he had waited for some better occasion. Then his glance lighted on Motherly, whose saucer eyes were dark with misery that this dreadful embarrassment to the superintendent and Dr. Loveless was occurring in Mount Gilead. Jack let his anger boil over.

"Dr. Loveless, when this material was conceived I presume you had in mind a large, well-organized church in a fair-sized city. Possibly your committee had no representative from the rural areas or the mine fields?"

"In point of fact, we did not." Loveless somehow made it sound more like a virtue than a lapse.

"Yet you insist that the testimonial dinner be at six o'clock sharp. Farmers have many chores at about that time; very few come in from the fields by a stop watch."

"How *do* they come in?"

"When it's *dark*."

"Then the rural pastors will have to inform their congregations that all these schedules were finalized and sent to the printer months ago. If the pastors show genuine enthusiasm, every phase of the program will prove workable."

"*Every* phase?"

"Every phase."

Jack snatched up a pink mimeographed sheet.

"Step Two here calls for the chairman of the Official Board to call on the church school superintendent. Correct? But what about a small church I know in which the chairman is also the superintendent? Does he call on himself?"

Loveless blinked once behind his shaded spectacles. For the first time he made no reply. Jack seized another page.

"The Victory Worship Hour is to be at eleven o'clock on the final Sunday, with the pastor reading the prepared sermon without deviating, correct?"

"Correct. We find that where pastors are permitted to improvise their own sermons, the campaign themes are often forgotten—or even deliberately omitted."

"Then tell me this: If a country preacher has four churches instead of one, with preaching hours staggered through the day, how can he possibly read this junk in all four pulpits at the same hour on the same Sunday?"

Loveless ran one hand over his gray hair. The calm, rational eyes showed at last a flicker of discomfort.

"The committee is not insane, Jack. But may I remind the brethren that the value of a united effort does not lie in the separate activities which compose it. Taken out of context, some of these may at times seem pointless or even absurd. But when we carry them out in a vivid awareness that tens of thousands of fellow Christians are doing exactly the same things in exactly the same way at exactly the same instant, *then* they become an unforgettable mountain-peak of spiritual experience."

Jack realized from this rhetorical flourish that Loveless now considered his part in the discussion ended. He whirled on the group, determined to elicit some similar trace of emotion from those eerily blank faces. He tried to recall exact words and phrases, and even the tone and manner in which each man had expressed himself scarcely two hours before.

"Mr. Chairman, I contend that this program is a sinful waste of two weeks' time. We haven't the strength for another lockstep program right now. We've just finished one big push; we need a breathing space to tend to local problems. This thing will wreck the morale of some of the best laymen in our churches. Our pastors may go through the motions, but you can't make them put their hearts in this. It should be drastically modified or junked." One or two of the men blinked, but most continued to stare with that bland, unreadable blankness. Finally, exhausted, and unable to recall any further quotations, Jack said:

"I'm aware we can't reject this program, but we *can* demand it be adapted to our needs. In the name of simple honesty and for the welfare of our churches, I ask you for an expression of no confidence in this program."

Jack kept expecting that someone—Wes Phillips, at least!—would speak out. But it was one of the new men, a tall gaunt youngster named Perriman, who finally stood up.

"I think Jack is right." He glanced apologetically at Dr. Loveless. "My laymen say it'll never work on a circuit." He paused and swallowed. "I've got four churches."

Had it not been for that one thin voice speaking those few words Jack would almost have doubted his own sanity or wakefulness. He walked back to his seat. The man beside him did not look at him.

Dr. Worthington stood up, his voice mild and pleasant.

"I have long been an admirer of Jack's frankness and courage. I am confident he had no thought of dividing the body of Christ or of undermining the spirit of unity and teamwork which has been the great strength of our connectional system. Mr. Chairman, I suggest that we give Dr. Loveless' program a standing vote of confidence!"

He was smiling, but he remained facing the men, his bright blue eyes wandering over them one by one.

"Any further discussion?" Washburn nervously adjusted the knot of his black tie, glancing at Jack to see whether he would accept the open vote. "All those in favor—" He stood on tiptoe, jabbing with his pencil as he counted. "Thirty-seven *for*."

The men sat down.

"All opposed, by the same sign."

Jack stood, feeling terribly tired. Wes was standing. Perriman was standing. Adams was standing.

"Opposed, four."

Jack slumped down and put his materials into the envelope while Washburn closed the session. Five men were absent, and the chair had no vote, so there had been no abstentions. The men stood and Washburn lifted his hands:

"Now may the peace of God, which passeth all understanding, keep your hearts and minds in the knowledge and love of God, and of His Son, Jesus Christ our Lord. Amen."

In the basement at lunch Jack and Wes sat alone; nobody claimed the other four seats at their table. The other men seemed absorbed in their customary raillery as they waited for the Mount Gilead ladies to serve them following the grace. Wes saluted Jack with a stalk of celery.

"Welcome to the Choir Invisible!"

The voice was bantering, but the ice-blue eyes were grave under their craggy white brows.

"Where were you when the rats were leaving the ship?" Jack snapped. "You could have said *something!*"

Wes tucked the paper napkin in his shiny black vest.

"Look, boy, Grandpa ain't gonna be here forever. If you intend to start fighting for the right, you've got to get used to doing it alone—so alone you wonder sometimes if you're in your right mind." His voice softened somewhat. "I've seen this coming for a year, but it still gives a man a bad feeling to be partly responsible for getting a fine brave kid into this kind of trouble."

"I'm still shaking," Jack confessed.

"You'll get used to it. I shook the first ten years."

Jack glanced up and saw that Patricia was helping serve tables at the far end of the room. She looked pale, and she did not glance in his direction. Jack forced himself to eat. Finally he said:

"I figured at least a few of these yes-men would thank me for expressing their convictions!"

Wes sloshed some cream in his coffee.

"You crazy? The boss is running for bishop and wanting his district to raise more money and save more souls than all the others put together. You do your best to torpedo that. You try to force his preachers to admit their private principles in a public place. You endanger their careers and wives and kiddies. You give them all a guilty conscience. And now you want them to carry you around on their shoulders while Belovèd's eating his pie!"

Jack winced. Wes was gazing at him with concern.

"Look, boy, they all admire your guts, even if they don't want to be seen eating with you. Don't be too hard on them, son. Lots of these men are living in a perfect hell over issues like this. And, after all, you smoked out Adams when I'd been nagging him for years and never got him to come clean. Everybody knows the Perriman kid didn't know what was involved, but all the same you got four votes out of forty-one! Were you expecting to flatten the hosts of darkness in the first round?"

As the men straggled out after lunch, Jack found Patricia untying her apron in the kitchen.

"Pat, we've got to have a talk right away."

"What's left to talk about?" she asked in a choked voice and turned toward the stairs, one hand over her face.

"I'll see you tonight!" Jack called after her.

He found Wes sitting on the front steps, blowing smoke rings at the toe of one dusty, high-topped black shoe. Jack angrily dashed the rings with his Homburg.

"Let's go. I've got sick calls to make and a PTA devotional to get up for tomorrow. Tell me a text for parents and teachers." He deliberately made his voice casual, refusing to let himself think of Patricia.

"Ain't you gonna wait?"

"For what?"

"The congratulations!"

Wes jerked his thumb toward the superintendent's car, just turning into the highway beyond the cemetery. Jack caught a glimpse of Patricia sitting close beside her father.

"I said let's go!"

Wes got to his feet, grumbling. As they reached the bottom of the steps Motherly, Thompson, Farmer, and half a dozen other men came down the sidewalk from the basement entrance. Motherly laid one hand on Jack's arm.

"Jack, God didn't make me the fighting type, but I want you to know I was with you this morning—all the way! We all were! Naturally understand that we're not in the same position you are—I mean, single and no responsibilities." The fawnlike brown eyes were pleading. Several other men walked up. All the faces were friendly but hesitant. "You understand, don't you, Jack?"

Jack did not smile. He continued to hold his hat in his right hand so that nobody could shake his hand. He looked around the little circle for a long moment, studying each face in turn. Then he turned and pushed his way through, still holding the hat.

"Yes," he said. "I do understand."

XXIII

Never Marry a Minister

THEY argued for over an hour that night in the library—a dreadful wounding argument that gripped them both in a kind of relentless logic and emotion neither could surmount. Dr. Worthington was out; Aunt Katherine was upstairs with a book. Patricia sat in her father's big chair; Jack sat on the opposite end of the sofa. She was wearing a flowered dress he had not seen before, with a tight bodice and full skirt. The blue-gold pattern in the material made her eyes an intenser blue and deepened the pale gold hair that framed her taut, sculptured features. She tried to appear relaxed, but he noticed that the slim, tapering fingers folded so carelessly in her lap were rigid. There was something different about her hands, and suddenly he realized that she was not wearing his ring.

The knowledge that this was probably the end goaded them both to desperation in their efforts to understand themselves and each other and to communicate, but the differences were now too deep. Jack thought Loveless' electrographic pencils hilarious; Patricia saw nothing amusing. He felt he had no choice but to speak out against the dreadful program; she felt her father had no alternative but to push it through. He could not describe the annual conference appointments of Garrison and Starr except as neurotically vengeful; she had implicit faith in her father's estimate of the men and events.

And under it all ran a curious sense of desire *not* to arrive at understandings—a desire to wound irrevocably, to make reconciliation impossible. Jack sensed it in himself; he suspected it in her. As he saw her now slipping away from him, he remembered again that he had been attracted to her at the outset precisely because she did not attract him physically the way Christine did . . . because he did not want to possess her physically. He wanted merely to enjoy the pride of possessing something rare and exquisite and valuable. . . .

His eyes traveled wonderingly over her as they argued—her small hands clenching and unclenching in her lap . . . the bent knee peeping from under the hem of the graceful skirt as she sat with one foot tucked under her. She was a beautiful and interesting woman, yet she had a tautness, an inability to relax into complete femininity, to yield herself completely to her love. Was this what had drawn him to her in the first place? Had he wanted to shield himself by seeming a normal young man in quest of love, yet using a pretended love to escape love?

In his desperation to get at the causes of their long engagement, Jack even tried to imagine the possibility that it was he who had prevented their marrying. Had he not been able to win her because he had never wanted to? The thought brought him a devastating shame and he pushed it away. He could not possibly decide now that he had simply *used* this exquisite and sensitive girl to run from his own fears and problems!

No! It was Patricia who was to blame for everything! He had loved her and wanted her terribly, completely, all these years. Then why had his imaginings never got beyond their wedding, with the bishop himself officiating, and the smart chapel crowded with distinguished people? Under the surge of their words he forced himself to imagine her coming to him on their wedding night: she would be wearing that filmy white peignoir . . . he would untie the satin streamers and she would let the garment slip from her . . . they would sink down into the soft bed together, the clean line from her throat to the tip of her shoulder broken only by the strap of her gown. He would . . . His mind stalled. He forced it to go on. He would be skillful and masterful and know exactly what to do . . . or would he? His mind stalled again. He glanced up.

Her eyes were fixed on him: irritated, cool, amused.

And they *would* be!

They would be!

He would do something stupid or grotesque, and her silvery laugh would pierce him like a knife!

He did not know what they had been saying. Their angry words died in the air as he half-rose, staring into her eyes. His sudden self-understanding seemed somehow to communicate itself to her, to snap something tight inside them both.

"Pat, I'm not sure I understand everything about us, or why we've done these things to each other. But I do believe that we love each other—or have, and can again! Maybe everything has been my fault. What I did this morning was stupid and dangerous, but it had to come sooner or later, in some form. Surely you've known that someday you'd have to make a choice between your father and me!" She nodded mutely, beginning to tremble. He moved down to the end of the sofa near her. "Then choose me! That's the normal thing, the sensible thing any girl would do. There's nothing to be afraid of."

Her eyes were tormented. Her voice emerged thin and small.

"Nothing to be afraid of! You don't ever seem to realize that a woman wants to face life with someone she can understand—not with a wild stranger who jumps up on an impulse and smashes it all into bits— without even consulting her in advance! I just want to have some idea what our life will be like, and what roof we'll have over our heads and what we'll eat. You can end up like another Wes Phillips if you want to, but I've lived that life—all my life!—till Dad became a superintendent." She lifted her eyes to his; they were anguished, but implacable; her voice hardened: "I've lived that life—but no child of mine ever will."

She studied his face for a moment, and her own face became wistful. She turned and gazed musingly at the big bronze firedogs on the hearth.

"I'll never forget that night you spoke at the vesper service. After *all* poor Aunt Katherine had said! After hearing her tell me a thousand times, 'Never marry a minister!' The minute you began to speak, I knew somehow my goose was cooked. I actually wanted to burst out laughing, it was so ironic! With four hundred boys on the campus I finally had to go home and confess that I'd fallen in love with a ministerial student. And, oh, how I kidded myself from the first instant.

"I was going to eat my cake and have it, too. I knew from that first night that you were wild and crazy, but I told myself you'd have splendid appointments from the beginning and go straight to the top, and our children would have *complete* security!"

As she talked, Jack kept gazing at her curiously. It seemed desperately ironic that they should finally be beginning to understand each other after all these years—now that it was too late! For now he realized clearly for the first time that Patricia had obviously never thought of clergymen as anything but religious career men, competing with one another in a subtle web of spiritual and professional relationships utterly unknown to laymen. Things that shocked and dismayed Jack were as uneventful to her as rain on a cloudy day. The stained glass jungle was her native habitat, and she no more expected ministers to be like Christ than she expected her Greek grocer to quote Euripides.

She was gazing at him wonderingly, affectionately, seemingly lost in her own thoughts, but the words she was saying suddenly pierced him through:

"And I even sold *Dad!*" She laughed aloud, a ringing little laugh from lips that did not seem curved in the right directions. "At first he was absolutely furious. He said the most awful things: 'I tell you the boy's neurotic! He's a perfectionist with a martyr complex. He's so wrapped up in himself he doesn't even know other people exist. How could he make you happy? How can he judge people and handle them when he doesn't even know they're out there? He's blind to his own sins and that's why he can't understand or forgive sin in anyone else. He just wants to star; there's no place in the church for men like that—'"

At last his face seemed to register on her. She paused in mid-sentence, the bitter amusement vanishing from her eyes. Jack turned his head away, but she seized his arm.

"Darling, please don't look so stricken. That wasn't his final judgment. It's just that I'd never been serious about anyone before, and I'm all that he has in the world, and here you were taking me away from him! Naturally he fought back!"

Jack nodded, trying to believe it was so, wanting her to speak of something else—anything else! Patricia seemed to realize his need.

"And I even persuaded myself I'd get a mother in the bargain! She'd be young and beautiful and everything my own mother had been. And while we were engaged I'd visit in your home, and she'd come in and sit on the edge of the bed and we'd talk till all hours of the morning! And she'd insist that I call her 'Mother' from the very first day."

Jack did not look up. When her voice resumed, it was quiet and mild.

"But then I finally realized that you weren't ever going to fulfill that little dream of mine, that you not only weren't going to have me visit your mother—you weren't even going to *talk* about her!

"And, of course, I finally had to admit that you weren't really the safe, secure type at all and I was just kidding myself to believe so. Oh, you put up a good front and made a very nice record at Wentworth for a first appointment. But I've known all along it wasn't anything permanent, that it wasn't the real you—whoever that may be! Dad said so too. He'd been expecting something of the sort you pulled this morning for a long time."

"I'm delighted that your father understands me so thoroughly, because this morning I finally understood him for the first time. I mean, what he *is*."

"And what *is* he?"

"A cynic!" The word burst out with such finality that it startled Jack himself. "I've been excusing him and admiring him for the past three years as just being honest and realistic about the evil in men, as knowing more about human nature than the rest of us. But a realist tries to see *all* the facts—not just the ugly, evil, selfish, greedy side!"

"My father has been observing people for thirty years—"

"And he's been manipulating their weaknesses so long he's forgotten they have good in them too."

"He has more actual facts on file—"

"Facts! What kind of man files only the dirt on people? It's a fact that DeForrest Garrison faked a little illness to boost along a talented young preacher he liked. But to your father that turns out to have been a try at overturning the whole conference. It's a fact that Dan Starr was so green and unprofessional we considered him downright funny. But to your father he's suddenly a scheming, two-faced career man in cahoots with Garrison, and he crucifies him! And you call that being observant? It's a fact that Oscar Bates was doing more productive work than plenty of men older than himself, yet your father forced him to ask for retirement. Why? Because he's never yet observed anything good in a man as independent as Oscar Bates."

"Dad didn't create the human race!" Patricia's face was dead white; she was trembling. "He's just trying to do the best possible with people as he finds them."

"But he does create! Look what he's made of Dan Starr in three short months—a cynic and a slugger like himself! Maybe most of our men aren't as good as Dan was, but at least there's a fight going on inside them. But people like your father help evil to win by shouting from every housetop how irresistible it is, by ridiculing the very existence of integrity and sincerity. Then they pretend they were merely reporting on human nature when the truth is they've been helping transform it. They stir up an atmosphere of suspicion and fear that brings out the absolute worst in everyone!"

"Dad's real sin," Patricia said icily, "is refusing to admit that at least one of the younger men is in the same class with Wes Phillips."

This was so nasty and stupid that Jack was almost beside himself.

"His sin is ambition!" he almost shouted. "He's so insecure he'll never feel safe till we're all made over into the image of Steady the Yes Man."

"Oh, Jack, honestly! Sometimes I think spiritual jealousy is the occupational disease of ministers. What kind of superintendent could fail to use a man of Steadman's judgment and ability?"

The smiling superiority was insufferable.

"What kind of father keeps stalling his daughter from marrying someone she says she's in love with till he breaks up her chance to find happiness and a home of her own?"

"And what kind of son," her voice suddenly slashed across his, "is so brutal and ungrateful he refuses to invite his own mother to see him ordained?"

Jack felt the blood drain out of his face.

He tried to meet her eyes, but could not.

He turned his face away.

For something in her eyes told him that this was not the only thing she knew about him and his parents. She knew everything. She *had* known everything from the beginning, from the first instant he had refused to discuss them. She had gone straight home to confide it all to her father, and he had called up Pastor Elwood, or Longworth, or half a dozen men who had held the Foxull appointment. He had dug out everything . . . everything. . . .

There was something that did not fit in—an off note in this some-where. If she had known from the beginning, how had she been able to conceal her hatred and contempt for him, why had she kept on pretending to love him? But his humiliation was so devastating it blotted out all such contradictions in one enormous anguish.

"Well," he said shakily, "at last we're finally getting down to the real reasons. If my people aren't good enough for you, why didn't you say so long ago and stop this insane stalling!"

"I've never had a chance to *know* your people! You won't talk about them; you won't take me to see them; you freeze up when I mention them. You have some sort of dreadful problem about them that you won't share with me, so that I feel I don't even know half of you at all, yet you expect me to *marry* you! How can I marry someone whose own mother was afraid to come and stand with him when he was ordained a minister of the Gospel?"

"She was *sick!*"

"She was *afraid!* I begged and pleaded with them by letter and by long-distance to come, to stay with us overnight, and they both wanted to come. But your father's even more afraid of you than she is. What have you done to them? It actually makes *me* afraid of you!"

Jack bowed his head.

"I can't explain it," he said at last. "I honestly can't. I've tried. I do love you, Patsy, more than anything in the world. But I can't seem to be any different from what I am. And I can't see things the way your father does. That's just a fact. Let's accept it and not tear ourselves to pieces trying to deny it or escape it."

She was silent for a long time. When her voice did come, it was small and tremulous.

"And your mother . . . and father. Is the way you feel toward them also something I've just got to accept without understanding or questioning?"

"It's part of *me*. If you marry me, it goes with me."

"Do you think it might ever change?"

"No."

Silence.

"Well," she said at last, "maybe we ought to face the facts about me, too. Because I can't change the way I feel toward Dad. I think he's good, and honest, and sincere, and willing to be misunderstood in order to get things done that he believes are right. I'm all he has in the world, and till you came along, he was all I had." Her voice began to shake. "Maybe you don't quite know what you're asking when you want me to leave him and go off with someone who feels toward him as you do. I *love* my father. If I had ever known my mother, I'd have loved her, too. You're asking me to hate him and hurt him, just because you can do such things to your parents. But I don't want to be like that."

She turned her eyes away and shakily ran her fingertip down one of the gold threads in the pattern of her skirt.

"Father always felt that he had failed you. He feels himself a pastor to all the young men in his district. He felt he should have been more help to you about your parents, but you never asked his advice. Naturally, it's been a little hard for him to understand how anyone who does have parents could treat them the way you do yours."

Jack realized even then that she was trying to tell him she already knew everything, that she was willing to talk it through with him. And he wanted desperately to seize this opportunity; but even then, with the whole thing almost out into words, he could not make his voice speak to Patricia about these things. Glancing sidewise at her, he realized that she, too, knew this was the last possibility for them both. He saw the color come and go in her cheeks, in the delicate veins at her temple. . . .

At last she rose, took the small velvet box from the mantel, glanced briefly at the ring inside, then placed it exactly in the center of the sofa cushion beside him.

"I even kept the box," she said in a small, tight voice. She tried to laugh, but the sound was more like a sob, and she walked out of the library and up the stairs on swift, stumbling feet, and he heard the door of her bedroom close in the silence.

XXIV
The Keeper and the Beast

WHEN he left Patricia, Jack drove out to the parking area beyond Wentworth, on the bluff overlooking the valley. Below him the moonlight lay softly on the folded hills, and to the west he could see the village glowing like a bed of dying embers. The September night was cool, and he sat behind the wheel trying to think.

The seeming unnaturalness of his own reactions impressed him, even at the time. He knew that he should be feeling complete despair over losing Patricia, but instead he felt only a curious emptiness . . . and fear. Perhaps they had both known for months in advance that a breakup was inevitable. . . . And the day had brought so many shocks and humiliations that by the time he and Patricia parted he had probably exhausted his capacity to feel.

He sat in a stupor for a long time, with disconnected images of the past drifting before him. . . . The first time he had met Patricia . . . the things they had done together . . . the endless plans they had made . . . that vacation at the shore . . . And beneath all the images, like a faceless gray mist in which they floated, was fear.

But what did he fear? He did not know. It was not simply the fear of professional failure, or loneliness, but something deeper . . . something of which these were mere symptoms. He tried vainly to seize this nameless something, but the mist slipped through his fingers.

He kept seeing the expressionless eyes of the men as they stared at him at the district meeting that morning. How could he have been so stupid? Patricia's father was right, of course: Jack could not lead men if he had no idea what they were like. But if they were only what her father believed them to be, what was there left in the ministry worth living for? Jack had seen dozens of rubber-stamp votes during the past three years, when the men apathetically endorsed handed-down programs in the hopeless conviction that one could not resist a bureaucracy. But this had involved a clear-cut moral issue—the welfare of the district and the churches in their care!

Perriman was the only bright spot . . . well, Adams, of course . . . but Adams had never looked at Jack the way Perriman did, with something almost akin to reverence. Hero worship, that's what it was. . . . Why had he thought of it as reverence? His mind kept jumping crazily. He saw Foxull again with the main street dark and empty and himself stumbling down the railway tracks to escape Mrs. Catlett's hissing voice and iron hands . . . yet never having escaped at all, after all these years. For he was still pursued by her laughter, and by Fred Hummaker's loud guffaw, and by Oley Larsen's idiot's grin. And now, unable to stop thinking of what Patricia's father had said of him, Jack felt the same pain all over again. The man was blind to the good in people, true; but those round, China-doll eyes never failed to see through pretense and self-deception.

When Jack remembered how he had wallowed in that smiling little man's outrageous flattery, his pain and humiliation seemed to rise and choke him, like a deadly gas filling his lungs and throat and threatening life itself.

The foliage under the trees suddenly lit up; Jack heard the sound of tires on the gravel; a convertible stopped at the opposite end of the parking area. He could hear the strains of a radio mingled with a girl's laughter, saw the boy's head bending low. . . . Rick's convertible had been parked almost at that spot the night he had seen Thelma's plump arm thrust up into the glare of his headlights, her forefinger drawing insolent designs on the air. He could see the brown, puffy-lidded eyes gazing at him across the dinner table in her New York apartment that past July, could feel again that ridiculous warm glow as he glimpsed the dawning of that mute, doglike adoration. . . .

From the other car Jack heard a shrill giggle followed by a choked little scream. But to his surprise the resentment and moral censure that would ordinarily have risen in him seemed to turn listlessly awry and dissolve even in the act of forming. If ministers were only what Dr. Worthington had always insisted—fearful, ambitious, self-seeking—what was left of the church to fight for, to sacrifice oneself for? People did not actually revere and adore ministers. They despised them! And all the days of his life he had wanted to be a minister—had held his imagination in a strait-jacket and had crucified his body's longings in order to think himself worthy!

Far down the valley he saw the serpentine length of the 10:20 for New York, its brilliant blue-white spots gleaming through the moonlight as it snaked its way among the hills and grew larger, more brilliant. Finally, as it glided past directly below him, Jack saw the glare of the windows racing alongside the right-of-way, effortlessly leaping all obstructions, plunging through all pitfalls, speeding toward some ecstatic consummation amidst the soaring spires and jeweled canyons, the scintillating vastness of the city.

On an impulse he opened the glove compartment and took out the letter from Thelma he had tucked away that morning. He ripped open the scented pink envelope, assuring himself that he did so simply to satisfy an idle curiosity and not because he would be unable to avoid seeing her address. In the light of the bulb in the glove compartment he read it and stuffed it in his coat pocket. He should write her at least occasionally. He had been inexcusably rude.

He pressed the starter, backed in a half-circle, and saw that the car at the far end was not a convertible at all. Why had he been certain it was a convertible? As his car rounded the shoulder of the bluff halfway down, his eye wandered idly along the tracks below, gleaming like silver arrows in the moonlight, flying swift and straight. . . . The angry red of the block signal changed as he gazed, suddenly glowing against the ethereal beauty of the landscape like a bright new gem—brilliantly clear and green. Then all was hidden by trees again. . . .

The main street of Wentworth, deserted and dark except for a few naked, pitiless street lights, reminded him for some reason of Foxull. He drove slowly past his church—a little church with a clique of moneyed people and therefore quite a nice plum for a beginner in the ministry. Well, he could now rest assured of a lifetime in churches even smaller than this, on Main Streets where the store windows also advertised bake sales and county fairs. . . .

He passed the railway station, idly read the schedules of arrivals and departures, and checked his watch by the big clock over the ticket agent's desk. At the parsonage he left the garage doors open, but only because he often left them open.

Inside the kitchen he dropped his hat onto a chair by the door instead of hanging it up, and in his study he removed the New Testament from his coat, took the small gold cross from his lapel, and shoved them both across the desk. He did not permit himself to imagine any reason for these things. He enjoyed doing them simply because if he actually should perform certain intentions—which intentions he did not even take seriously enough to formulate clearly—these little activities would be the enjoyable preliminaries.

Usually he bathed and shaved in the morning, but tonight he soaked awhile in a warm tub and then shaved, using a new blade and doing a leisurely and meticulous job. In the bedroom he rubbed up his shoes, laid out his clothes, and selected the splashy flowered tie Thelma had sent him one Easter. It was so vulgar he had never worn it before. He set the alarm for six-thirty and stretched out between the cool sheets, still tingling and glowing from his bath. His coldness and fear had mysteriously vanished, and he felt quite relaxed, which seemed strange, because he had not been able to hit on any acceptable solutions to the problems facing him.

Normally he put his wrist watch on the night stand by the bed, but tonight he kept it on and lay in the darkness glancing at it from time to time. Suddenly a sound brought him bolt upright in bed: It was the distant rumble of a train, mingled with the blare of the diesel's horn! He flung back the sheet, snapped on the lamp, and lunged at the chair where he had laid out his clothes. With a single wrench he ripped his pajama jacket open, and as the top button went spinning and bouncing against the baseboard across the room, the meaning of the sound suddenly registered:

It was the 10:54 *from* New York.

From!

He turned, weak and shaking, and picked up the overturned chair. As he straightened, he caught sight of himself in the mirror of the bureau: The face was pale, the jaw set, the eyes wild and staring. Dazed and horrified, he turned away, sinking down on the edge of the bed.

He had actually intended to go!

And with this realization came an awareness even more appalling: He *still* intended to go.

Even as his mind foundered under the impact of this staggering fact, he found himself glancing at the clock and rising from the bed and taking a fresh shirt from the drawer, for the other had been rumpled when the chair overturned. Then he lay staring into the darkness. . . .

He had been aware that the life of an unmarried minister is subjected to pressures not felt by laymen, but he had thought of his own life pattern as a mighty dam, trebly reinforced by the deep-sunk foundations of a total life view, the weight of long-established habits, and the buttresses of public opinion. And he had always assumed that a break, if it did come, would be preceded by ear-splitting cracks and strains, with ample time to take measures.

It had not happened that way.

Jack had pondered many times later as to when the actual decision had been made. It seemed unthinkable that one could decide something without being aware of it, or without admitting it to oneself, yet he had finally become convinced that the actual moment of decision had come when his car rounded the shoulder of the bluff and he saw the railway signal turn green. That horrifying instant before the mirror was simply the point at which he became aware of what had already been decided.

But even then, in the shock of that awareness, the dam did not seem to break. It did not even crack. Slowly, majestically, with a dreamlike aura of utter unreality, the dam simply rose with stupefying gentleness all in one easy, continuous motion, all in fragments. And in the very act of dissolution it was buried forever under the long-awaited ocean that came flooding in, sweeping him away in a tide of voluptuousness that engulfed him to his depths.

With sudden curiosity he got up, snapped on the lamp, took Patricia's photograph from the bureau, and sat on the edge of the bed studying it. Once, ages ago, those pert, clean-cut features and direct eyes had struck powerful, responsive chords in him. But now their music was tinny and patternless, while deep within him sounded the first faint notes of a new music, earthen and savage as the throbbing of a jungle drum.

At the station he carefully rolled up the windows of the car and locked the doors, but when he glanced back from the train window as the station glided away he saw that he had left the headlights burning. He realized he should never have brought the car downtown as a public announcement that he had gone out of town that night, but none of these problems seemed worth bothering about. The train gathered speed; the shacks along the edge of town swept past. He was not *going* anywhere, after all: he was being carried by something outside himself. For from that first moment before the mirror, when he had realized that he would go, all his intentions and actions had seemed part of an enormously complicated machine that he had built somewhere, somehow, in secret and long ago—but had never meant to use. Then something had tripped the starter and the whole thing had sprung into life—smooth, purring, automatic, and irreversible. For he could no more turn back now than he could jump from this speeding train into the darkness.

A stocky woman diagonally across the aisle was trying to reach her coat on the overhead rack. Jack got it down for her and returned to his seat, automatically averting his eyes as she thrust her feet and legs out onto the opposite seat and threw the coat over them.

The last farmhouse in the Wentworth area was the Strackmars'. The engineer blew for the crossing and the train swayed on the long curve. Jack was startled by a rough hand on his shoulder.

"Sorry to wake you, sir."

"I wasn't asleep!"

"Sorry, sir, I spoke to you twice. Ticket, please."

Jack fumbled for the money, unable to believe that he had not even thought to buy a ticket. . . .

The train swayed; the rotating landscapes might almost have been covered with snow, so brilliant was the moonlight, as barns and houses, distant hamlets and fields glimmered amid the silver filigree of the forests. He remembered that curious feeling of being about to dissolve into a central emptiness when he had sat in Thelma's apartment the past July. The feeling returned now, but stronger. There the restraining armor of his usual self had begun to teeter and loosen when removed from the context of its daily scenes and people, and he had rushed from her in terror of those disintegrating pulls. But now the flying landscapes seemed to loosen the armor gently, to disengage it piece by piece with soft, pale fingers, hurtless and efficient. . . .

The towns were growing larger now, the scenes more disconnected: meadows and factories, exquisite suburban homes and converging highways, glaring billboards and silver filigree . . . He responded as the stimuli appeared, without control or selectivity, relaxing in sudden enjoyment at not having to pass judgments any more. He settled back, tilting his hat over his eyes and resting his shoes on the starched white seat cover opposite him.

A billboard shot past, a tangled ravine, two jangling crossing lights that seemed almost to brush his shoulder. In the shadowy mirror of the window he saw the sleeping woman across the aisle. The coat had slipped from her legs. He turned slightly and from under the shaded hatbrim gazed through half-closed lids, his eyes moving down her body to her rumpled skirt which had worked up to reveal a few inches of white, blue-veined flesh at the backs of her thighs just above the tight roll of her stockings. A diamond winked at him from her ring finger. In his mind's eye he pushed the skirt higher . . . they were making their way to a Pullman compartment somewhere. . . . The woman stirred and opened her eyes, and Jack pretended to be asleep.

How could he possibly endure the hours ahead? How could he last another minute after all these years of waiting, of controlling his thoughts, of turning his eyes away, of pretending not to notice, of saving himself for someone who proved at the end to be a cheat and a fraud? How could he endure this coachful of naked women all the way to New York?

He grinned and chuckled, half-dozing, his mind a muddy, direction-less river ablaze with phosphorescent eddies. He could see Patricia lying down tonight in her cool white gown complete with all her emptiness and fear, while he and Thelma sank into a warm, deep bed naked as sin and shameless as goats or monkeys! He had burst from his prison at last! But how had he got into prison anyway? It was all some sort of ghastly mistake that began somewhere or other . . . in a church? Yes! When he had preached that vespers sermon his sophomore year in col-lege. *That* was where he had put the armor on. But there was no turning back now. He half-opened his eyes in astonishment, aware that he had no intention of leaving the ministry.

He lay back again, hugging himself, blissfully wrapped up in the cozy warmth of a whole new way of thinking: after all, there was no real contradiction between the ministry and Thelma, between this coachful of women and that churchful of women he preached to every Sunday. The district ministers might have refused to confess his lord-ship that morning, but Perriman had confessed! The reverence shining in his eyes had been unmistakable. And Thelma had confessed at Rick's funeral, for her tears were really tears of ecstasy at how virile and heroic he was in the face of death. It wasn't that preaching was a sexual activity, exactly. The point was that it *meant* the same thing to your heart of hearts whether your congregation bowed down and worshipped you or Thelma lay down and embraced you. . . .

But all this might be difficult to explain to laymen. Tomorrow he would get the whole armor of God back on somehow. The important thing now was to make up for those lost years, those lost women. . . .

He must have slept, for he was aware of an ache in his neck and shoulder. He shifted, glanced at his watch. Beyond the window more factories flew past, more tracks and highways all converging faster and faster, more weed-grown lots. He snuggled down again. Yes, that's what he was—an empty lot that things just happened *on*. In the morning school children trooped across it; in the afternoon boys played ball or rode bikes; but at two in the morning the wild dogs had their turn, rending each other in the darkness for the favors of some waiting bitch. And certainly nobody could impute responsibility to a weed-grown lot!

But vacant lots couldn't *see* themselves, while he saw himself con-stantly, studied himself, analyzed himself. Maybe the lot had a keeper who let the school children come and the boys play and then turned the wild beasts in and got them safely back offstage by schooltime next morning. . . . Anyway, the keeper was only trying to teach Patricia a lesson. . . . And it was Patricia, of course, who would have to answer to God for anything he might do tonight, she and her lamb-faced father who fancied himself a judge of human nature! For the keeper would punish them all—and himself, too. He would punish that prudish ministerial self that had made him waste these precious years. For now he would think all the thoughts he wanted to think, say all the words, fling wide the doors and drag temptation in by force! He would throw himself away cheaply, degrade himself totally, humiliate the self that had humiliated him so long. But best of all he would pay back Mrs. Catlett for having the audacity to pretend he was "no different than anyone else!" He grinned and hugged himself, listening with his ear against his shoulder to the singing roar of the iron wheels that were carrying him to so marvelous a consummation.

As the train began to get into the city he went to wash up and tried to smooth some of the wrinkles out of his coat. In the subway, the last bits of the armor fell from him, smashed and pounded into fragments by the hurtling roar. Seated opposite him were a great, shapeless, dough-faced woman and a hollow-chested man. In Wentworth they would have been members of his church and he would have spent hours listening to her dreary vexations and inquiring about the man's cough, persuading himself that he was deeply concerned about both these dreadful creatures. And *believing* it! But now he realized that all those things were simply part of the shining, professional self this journey had pounded to dust, and he stared contemptuously through them both and wondered how two such misshapen animals could copulate.

When he got off at his transfer point he realized that he should be exhausted, but instead he was filled with a fierce, raging energy that would not let him relax. He felt almost as if he were possessed by an incredibly potent and creative force of evil that endowed the external things about him with their power: His eye ferreted out the one obscene magazine on the rack, the one vulgar poster on the wall, the one provocative woman boarding the car, seized them all and greedily enlarged, intensified. . . .

He stood grinning and chuckling as he heard the roar of his approaching train, and when the headlight finally emerged from the tunnel, his bliss and excitement were almost past bearing. For he was coming at last to that moment he had long anticipated somehow, somewhere, in some unknown part of himself, from that very first afternoon in September, almost exactly a year ago, when Thelma Ross had appeared at his parsonage with Rick. The moment had drawn a giant step nearer when the state trooper's voice on the telephone that night in November had said Rick was dead. The moment had almost burst through into realization this past July when he had stopped by her apartment in New York.

And now—!

Now in a matter of minutes she would unlock the door and turn up her face to his, the sulky lips parting as they curved, the plump cheeks still flushed from sleep and bearing the warm crease of her pillow, the doubt and wonder in her eyes already yielding to glory. . . . And at last the flickering lamp of God and right and conscience which had seemed so real, whose light had deluded and misled him for so many years, would be extinguished forever in a passionate darkness by her soft and blissful sigh.

Forever.

XXV

The Faithful Steward

AT FIVE O'CLOCK on Thursday afternoon, just before adjournment of the business session at Belfair Church, the tellers announced the election of two more delegates—Sid Burnham and Terry Halstead, both machine men. The rebel bloc had kept ranks throughout the day, but twenty-two votes were simply not enough to start a man moving up the ladder of ballots.

Jack went outside to get a breath of air. The rebels were to hold a strategy session in the tower room at five-fifteen. Just as he turned to re-enter the church, Jack saw Edgar Evans standing before the steps. His shoulders looked a little too big for his new, tailored suit, and his rugged, leathery face had lost some of its tan during the nine months since Jack had talked to him and Blanche about St. Luke's. Edgar had remained friendly and cordial to Jack, unlike many of the men, who had turned cool overnight once Jack's leadership of the revolt had become public knowledge.

"Well, Edgar, how's it going now that you're the minister of a booming suburban church?"

"Great, Jack! Never better!" Then Edgar grinned and ran his fingers through his bristly, reddish white hair. "I'm lying, and you know it." He fumbled in his coat pocket. "I've got to get a glass of water somewhere." He pulled out a small glass cylinder, uncorked it, and dumped two thick tablets into his huge palm. "Stomach trouble," he said, smiling sheepishly. "Oh, I guess I do all right with some of the older men. Half of them were born in the country, just like Blanche said. But . . ." He hesitated. "I don't sleep like I used to, Jack, out in the country. Maybe I tried to make this shift too late in life. You know the old saying, 'You can get the boy out of the country, but you can't get the country out of the boy.' I'm having a lot of trouble—especially with the preaching part of it . . . and the young people . . . Blanche has been a tower of strength, though. She practically writes my sermons now, and tells me what not to say to who and all that sort of stuff. Which is funny. . . ." He stared down at the two tablets in his palm. "Out in the country I always had to tell *her*. Even after thirty years she never seemed to catch on to country people's ways. Now, she's telling me. . . . The folks are so crazy about her they'll put up with me, I guess. She's working at this thing around the clock. I don't know where she gets the energy, but she never even seems tired. Just walking on clouds! Well, it's what she's always wanted. We made it at last!" He gave Jack a smile that seemed forced, almost bitter, and slowly walked away.

The tower room above the choir loft was much too inconvenient to be used by any of the conference committees and hence afforded an ideal location for the rebels' caucuses and strategy sessions. The meetings were usually hurried, with some of the men not even bothering to sit down; the number present rarely exceeded fifteen or eighteen; the furniture consisted of a rickety lectern and two dozen reed-bottomed chairs, obviously relegated to this spare classroom from the new educational annex. Opposite the small tower window hung a yellowed photograph of the original church, its dusty glass cracked and the ornate gold-leaf frame tarnished and blackened by time.

The fellowship, like the room, had a certain stripped, almost bleak severity. Here Jack had noticed a curious shyness, a tendency to understatement and even gruffness that stood in sharp contrast to the saccharine fellowship so often characteristic of the ministry. Yet the comradeship was almost painful in its intensity; the depth of feeling so intimate and so fierce it had to be held in check by a deliberate casualness. Clarence Motherly seemed quite a different person—more confident, more manly. Even DeForrest Garrison seemed to have been touched. His bitterness over the Macedonia appointment seemed less caustic, his preoccupation with his own misfortune less intense. Jack himself frequently climbed the steep, dusty stairs to this little room feeling shaken and exhausted, to leave it half an hour later invigorated and secure.

The men were seated about in various postures of thoughtfulness or dejection.

"It's the inertia that gets me!" said Perriman, his gaunt young face even more haggard than usual. "They've all seen things this way so long they figure it's hopeless."

"All I hear is the same refrain," said Thompson, staring at a much-marked list of names. "They just want to be left alone to do the work God gave them. They don't want to get involved. They've got too much at stake. What do they think we've got at stake?"

"If we had as many men working as Belovèd has," Dirkwell rejoined, "we could change a lot of that talk."

"It's not the talking that does it," said Wes. "It's the power. All we can offer is a chance for a man to show some guts and maybe bust up his career. They can offer better appointments plus opportunities for service on a dozen boards and commissions. And they're also able and willing to scare the daylights out of anybody they can."

The discussion turned to the lay delegates, but it was agreed as always that the ministerial delegates could not wash all this dirty linen before laymen. The rebellion would have to stand or fall on clerical candidates elected by clerical votes. This relieved Jack immensely, for he knew they would have expected him to talk to Fred Hummaker, the lay delegate from Foxull, whom he had been avoiding throughout the conference.

"If we could ever start a man with fifty or sixty votes," said Adams, "we'd give them a run for it."

"We'd *have* fifty," Jack said, "if William Pierce Whitley would endorse our slate."

"What we need," said Dirkwell as the meeting ended and he followed the men out, "is one of the old-timers everybody loves who could tell Whitley the facts of life in King James English."

Jack paused at the top of the stairs.

Pastor Elwood!

The old man had been in poor health, but he was due at conference today or tomorrow!

The registration desk informed Jack that Pastor Elwood had arrived that afternoon. Jack tried his hotel, then spent a while canvassing the church, and finally gave up and went to dinner.

Jack was surprised to find that memories of Foxull and of his parents had been coming back with increasing frequency in recent months. Since his affair with Thelma, even though that affair was over and done with forever, Jack had experienced a mellowing of all his judgments of other people. He kept remembering how Christine had accused him in college of refusing to let himself think about what his extravagance was doing to his mother's health. From Christine's letters it was clear that his mother was still in the cloth-inspection room in Harlowe's Mill. His parents must have gotten more deeply in debt during his college and seminary years than he had realized. . . .

One day, sorting through some notes from his freshman year at college, he had come across a snapshot of his mother standing beside the house, with his father's boxwood gardens in the background. Jack sat for a long time holding the snapshot. She had squared her shoulders and lifted her chin that way as she stood in the doorway of his room so long ago and told him goodbye. . . .

After dinner Jack returned to Belfair, certain that Pastor Elwood would not miss the inspirational address at the church that night. He had gone seeking him a dozen times just this way in the years the Elwoods were at Foxull, especially that day the offer of the chemistry scholarship had arrived. He could feel again the transformation that always came over him in Pastor Elwood's presence. He could see the bronze cross on the minister's desk, the calm, squarish face and direct, close-set eyes, even the starched white collar and the black shoes, could hear the sonorous voice again as it had sounded that day:

"Do you believe you can serve God *and* Mammon?"

"Oh, no, sir!"

"Then it's clear that you are confronted with a choice, aren't you? Either take this exciting offer and commit your life to money and things, or turn your back on the world and the kind of success it promises and seek real peace and security through obedience to God . . . unless you bear the cross, you cannot wear the crown. . . ."

"But, sir, Mother's sick, and Dad's in debt . . ."

"What shall we eat? What shall we drink? Wherewithal shall we be clothed? My dear boy, the Christian life is a venture of faith! . . . Are you a follower of the Lamb?"

"Yes, sir."

"Then follow him!"

Jack found Pastor Elwood in the balcony of Belfair, just as the evening's program was getting under way. Mrs. Elwood had felt tired and had stayed at the hotel. They retreated to the tower room for privacy, but Jack was sorry he had made Pastor Elwood climb the extra stairs, for he seemed much older than at conference the previous June, and Jack tried not to notice the occasional twitch of his knee. But the clear, direct eyes were the same, and the voice still had some of its resonance. Jack was thankful again for Christine's monthly letters, for although Pastor Elwood had left Foxull in 1949, he asked about many Foxull residents Jack would not have expected him to remember. He was especially distressed to hear that Mrs. Larsen had died. "Poor Oley! I suppose now they'll have to put him in an institution. . . ."

The conversation came around at last to the present situation in the conference, and although Jack knew that Pastor Elwood had been ill, he was startled at how little the old man seemed to know about events of the past twelve months. He questioned Jack at great length, the clear, direct eyes intent and thoughtful as Jack tried to outline the story of his own involvement:

"When I entered the conference in '56, Dr. Worthington took Kurt Schell's appointment and gave it to me because of Patricia. I rushed off to the district parsonage and accused him of it, but he talked me out of the whole thing. I suppose I'd finally have joined the machine, but Wes Phillips kept needling me. Then last year at conference Dr. Worthington crucified Dan Starr and DeForrest Garrison, and he followed it up in August by giving St. Luke's to Edgar Evans just for old times' sake. That did it. I attacked him publicly at the September ministers' meeting, and . . . and that kicked off this reform movement. . . ."

For one wild instant Jack fought the impulse to add: "And Patsy gave me back my ring that same night, and I plunged into an affair with a woman in New York and only broke it off about six weeks ago, and if I don't confess it all to somebody I'm going to go out of my mind!" For if there was anyone in the world to whom Jack could have unburdened himself, it was Pastor Elwood. But the impulse vanished as it formed, and after a moment he pulled out one of the slips of note paper on which the rebel slate was listed.

"Now: there are still five jurisdictional delegates to be elected. The machine took all the general ones, but actually it's jurisdictional conference we're concerned with, and we can still split the delegation, even if we only get two or three men on it. Naturally, we want you to vote for these men in the balloting tomorrow. But the main thing we need is somebody to talk to William Pierce Whitley!"

Jack handed Pastor Elwood the slip of paper. The old man laid it on one of the reed-bottomed chairs beside them. A lock of hair fell across his forehead just as Jack had seen it fall a hundred times, but now the lock was white and the hand that pushed it back was palsied.

"Young people are so impetuous," Pastor Elwood said slowly. "I've never concerned myself with conference politics, but from what I've heard, things have been this way a good many years. Although I must say in all fairness that Fred Worthington has been a real friend to the little ministers of this conference. He sent Mrs. Elwood a very lovely card only last week."

"I know," said Jack irritably, "but about Whitley—"

"My dear boy, I doubt that William Pierce Whitley could even connect my name and face."

"Pastor Elwood! There's not a minister in the whole conference more honored and loved than you!"

"By you, son. Only by you." The wide mouth set in a weary smile. "Oh, I suppose most of the brethren know in a vague sort of way that I exist. And, I've had my days! I've puffed up the statistics the way we all do. But the real conversions, the lives actually changed forever, I could almost count on one hand." He surveyed Jack from head to foot, and the watery eyes took on a glowing pride. "I was just forty-one when I came to Foxull, Jack. As you can imagine, it was scarcely the appointment we had been hoping for. But I stayed longer and accomplished more than in any other pastorate. God has called only one young person into the ministry under my thirty-five years of preaching, but that one has made it all worth while. Because what I dreamed of doing for God when I first entered the ministry so long ago, you *will* do!"

Jack turned away, unable to reply.

"Jack, listen to me." The once resonant voice was subtly changed. "I know very little about conference doings, but I know some things

I pray God you will never know! I know how it dulls you and narrows you to serve the little churches year after year, where the young folks all move away and the old-timers never change. It makes your entire life just a holding action, with not one taste of victory."

He got up, his knee twitching, and seized Jack by the shoulders and gazed down at him:

"*You* were my taste of victory. I've remembered you in my prayers morning and night through all these years. If you still respect my judgment even a little bit—"

"Pastor Elwood! You *know* how I feel about you!"

"Then *don't destroy your ministry!*"

Jack could not have been more shocked if the old man had struck him. "Wh-what did you say?"

"Give this up! Stop while there's still time to salvage your career! Everyone is convinced that you're doomed. I've scarcely been able to sleep since I heard what you were about. It's worse than when Greg was sent home—"

The Elwoods' only son had been expelled from college for cheating and had later run away from home.

"There's no comparison!"

"I didn't mean it that way." The old man sat down again, pounding his knee with a trembling hand. "It's the local church that matters. That's where we build the Kingdom. I've been in this conference all my life without getting mixed up in conference politics. All I've ever asked was to be left alone to do the work God gave me."

The phrase sent a chill through Jack.

"Is *that* how you imagine these appointments are made?" Jack was suddenly more frightened than he had been since the entire struggle began. "Pastor Elwood, I am only trying to be the *kind* of minister you taught me to be. You taught me that our church has a marvelously wise and fair form of government, but surely you know that the church has been corrupted—"

"I know nothing of the kind! We know only this one conference—one out of a hundred!"

"I apologize. But this one conference has almost five hundred ministers in it, and it's the only one God holds me responsible for. Please talk to Dr. Whitley. Just tell him the facts. He does know you exist."

Jack realized he was talking faster and faster to escape something in Pastor Elwood's face.

"Jack!" The old man pushed himself out of the chair, his pale, squarish face tormented. "Stop! Please stop!" He was breathing hard and making an odd little sound in his throat. He leaned forward and spoke slowly and carefully, spacing his sentences:

"I am *not* going to Dr. Whitley. I am *not* going to anybody. I am *not* getting involved! Have you actually lost your mind, as some people say? I am five years from retirement and I am not a well man. Mrs. Elwood and I have no savings. We own no property. All that we have in this world is my pension, and the possibility that we shall be accepted in the conference home for the aged. How can you dream of asking that after all these years I should antagonize the powers that be?"

Jack sprang up, too, his voice hoarse:

"And how can you talk about pensions at a time like this? You taught me that a Christian takes no thought for tomorrow; you said only God can give us real peace and security! I've quoted you a hundred times!"

"Jack, be reasonable. You're young and have no responsibilities. You can transfer to some other conference and begin all over. I assure you all this will look quite different when you are sixty. Pensions are calculated on the basis of how many years a man has served, and I *need* these next five years. Oscar Bates never wanted to quit at fifty-nine; didn't you know that? They just told him they had no church for him, and why didn't he just gracefully request retirement. They could force me out today! Mrs. Elwood and I have nothing—nothing! How do you expect us to live?"

"What shall we eat?" Jack snapped. "What shall we drink? Wherewithal shall we be clothed?" He wanted to seize the old man and push him up taller, make him strong and hard and uncompromising again. "Were all those things you told me just meant for children, or for laymen?"

Pastor Elwood sighed, and suddenly he passed his hand across his eyes as if to shut out the memory of something.

"I knew that night at the revival," he said slowly, "when you came down and announced for the ministry, that you needed help . . . needed to go deeper. But when you said you wanted to be a minister like me, it was as if my own son had come home. The first thing Mrs. Elwood said when we got back to the parsonage that night was, 'Did you notice how much he looked like Greg?' So I kept one little sheep for myself, instead of leading it straight to the only Good Shepherd. . . . You looked at me, son, the way many young folks looked at the picture of Christ that hung behind the pulpit."

"Aren't people supposed to admire the minister?"

"Not that way. That's idolatry. But you were like that, somehow. You seemed to idolize everyone you believed in. Christ loved sinners; you love saints. It's beautiful, but it's disturbing, the way you take perfectly ordinary people and read into them all sorts of qualities they never can possess." The direct eyes suddenly wavered. "Never."

The last word, spoken with such quiet finality, blew away the past as a breath of wind might topple a seemingly immovable landmark. And now the past itself had suddenly become a mirage, and the future trackless sand.

Jack fumbled for questions, not because there was anything left to argue, but because he hungered for some explanation of this devastating loss.

"But . . . but you always said we had to put first God's kingdom! You said we had to bear the cross or we couldn't wear the crown."

"Jack, please stop quoting me as if *I* invented our whole faith! Can't you really see how unoriginal those phrases are? They're all from books, or from Scripture!"

"But your sermons were turning points in my life!"

"It was *you*, son, not my sermons. The poorest sermon ever written is the voice of God to the man God is calling. When He laid His hand on you, I happened to be the pastor of your church. It's that simple."

"But . . . didn't you really mean all those things you said? Shouldn't we practice them ourselves?"

"I'm not a conference politician! I just want to be *left alone* to preach the Gospel. Why is that so terrible?"

Jack gazed at the empty chairs in the little room, remembering the grim faces of the rebels that morning—Wes, Thompson, Adams, young Perriman, Farmer, and the rest.

"It's terrible, I guess, because a voting majority of the men in this conference say it. And because only a handful refuse to say it." Jack stared at the floor, wishing it would all end. "If I'm afraid to speak up to the boss or the bishop at conference, I'll be afraid of some rich little old lady in the front pew back home. I'd rather go to a smaller church with a bigger message. You always said a minister must renounce everything."

Pastor Elwood struck his chest with his fists, so that the cross on his watch chain trembled in the light. The reedy voice grew shrill:

"Can't you understand that it was Christ who was perfect and who bore the cross and who died—not you or I? Our job is not to be Christ Himself!"

"What exactly is our job?" Even in the midst of his despair, Jack felt genuinely curious.

"We are called to be stewards of a mystery. A steward is just someone put in charge of something; he doesn't own it; he didn't create it; he cannot even understand it, much less duplicate it. Our first job isn't to be brave or original or even sincere. It's to be *faithful,* to transmit to our flocks the faith once delivered to the saints. When God sent me to your little village, I did not preach myself but Jesus Christ and Him crucified, and it was He who called you to His service. My sin was that I let you identify me with the Word made flesh."

They stood in silence. Finally Jack said,

"I was drawn to Christ because I saw Him in a particular individual who carried a little penknife and wore high-topped shoes and looked at me in a certain way. It was your voice God spoke to me with and your hand He laid on my shoulder when you prayed for me by the back steps. I can't separate the minister from the message. It's not like a suit of clothes he can put on and off. And I don't believe we'll ever change this world by faithfully preaching things we don't intend to practice."

"Well, son," said Pastor Elwood, "the older I become, the more unattainable Christ seems. I have no doubt that many people in your own parish imagine you to be somewhat better than you are, and that helps to give your words weight and to make you a real source of strength. I do not wish to pry, but have you actually attained this perfection you speak of?" Jack felt his whole body stiffen. He was thankful that Thelma was of the past, yet even in the midst of his worst degradations he had been unable to relax the standards he had set for the ministry. It was like the time he had debated about calling Thelma because the dime in the phone booth did not belong to him. How could one person contain such fantastic contradictions? Pastor Elwood was tactfully looking away as he spoke. Now he turned back, and the close-set eyes under the wispy white brows fixed on Jack with something of their old command:

"I suppose it's almost impossible for any of us to understand the adults we idolized in childhood, but look at me, son. Please!"

He stood squarely before Jack as if he were trying on a suit before a tailor, his bowed shoulders flung back a little, his arms hanging straight down.

"Can't you honestly see what I am? A little person, a very ordinary person—not a hero or a martyr! I do hope you may someday find yourself able to love me again, *with* all my sins, and to accept me for what I am. Not a big man or a brave one, but your former pastor and your friend."

Jack's thoughts were too painful for expression, and he suddenly seemed to be gazing on a miniature of someone he had known—a perfect reproduction, from the stiff white collar down to the neat black shoes, yet not life-size, not genuine. Even the familiar gold watch chain dangling on the dark vest seemed now small and false, and its cross only an imitation.

The old man saw that Jack did not mean to reply and he straightened a little and no longer trembled as he turned to the door. As Jack watched him descend the stairs to the balcony again, the service ended, the doors opened, and the congregation began streaming out as if impelled by the tide of organ music that flooded up. As the white head vanished, Jack had an almost physical sensation that something had burst—a gigantic, iridescent bubble through which he had viewed the ministry and this man.

For, despite all the professional disillusionment of the past four years, and the shocks and reverses of this past week, something deep inside him had remained unscarred—a heritage from a world of childhood peopled with heroes, saints, and martyrs, all larger than life, all quite without blemish or stain. But now the prismatic colors had vanished, the lenslike power to magnify was gone, and he found himself staring at life in black and white, devoid of distortion and of magic and depth. It was almost as if a kind of radiance had been taken from the air. For when the mantle of prophecy slipped from the old man's shoulders, it left the church no longer the church Jack had loved. Suddenly her music was flat, her temple only a building, her traditions empty of power. And her mighty host of flaming ministers seemed only a gathering of junior executives, crusaders in business suits whose sword arms were weighed down by the armor of seniority, and whose hearts were shielded by thick sheafs of pension papers both from the scimitar of an infidel world and from the cross of Christ.

XXVI

Postscript to Ecstasy

JACK turned away into the little room and closed the door. He sank down in a chair by the wall and sat staring at the ancient photograph of Belfair Church opposite him. Nothing seemed certain now, and under the dreadful emptiness was a still more terrible emptiness, a loss of faith in himself.

A more capable, objective person might have found some way to win the old man, but Jack, as always, had muddied the waters with emotional charges, and had erred disastrously in his estimate of Pastor Elwood and of the pressures upon him. He bowed his face in his hands. Why had he ever imagined he could lead? Why had the rebels offered him the leadership in the first place—after that fiasco at the district ministers' meeting when he had mustered only four votes against Loveless' ridiculous program! He should have stuck by his original refusal. That, at least, had been based on cold facts . . . brutal, ugly, undeniable facts that could still come back to destroy them all. For even now, with nothing to show for the rebels' courage and sacrifice but systematic defeat, ballot after ballot, that episode from the past could still bring upon them all an additional, undreamed-of humiliation! Of course none of them had been able to conceive the real reason he had at first refused when they appeared at his parsonage that Tuesday night.

Their appearing had given him an awful fright. But, after all, it was the evening after that first night with Thelma, and he was scarcely himself.

He had awakened that morning to find her already dressed for work. "Pssst! Wake up!" she whispered, sitting down on the edge of the bed and kissing his ear. Her eyes were mischievous and possessive. "You better get out before everybody gets up." Beyond her the light of morning, gray and watery, filtered through the paper shade. "I'm already late. Hurry back. I'll never be able to wait!"

Jack ate at the all-night café across from her apartment building, then walked down to the subway entrance and turned to stare for a moment at the vast cliffside of windows, his eye counting up to the twelfth floor and noticing that he had forgotten to raise the shade masking the tiny opening.

At Grand Central Station he realized that he had bought only a one-way ticket. This seemed past all understanding, but he bought another. His mind did not seem to be functioning properly this morning. There was some reason he had to rush right back—but what was it? He sat waiting for his train, turning his ticket over and over and reading the name, WENTWORTH, and suddenly he found that he could not connect it with anything! He frowned, trying desperately to fill out the name with a railway station—it would *have* to have a station—and streets and houses and people and a church—there *must* be a church! Nothing came.

Fighting off his panic, Jack tried imagining himself getting on the train and approaching the town by the stations along the way. But the tracks curved away into blankness! He jumped to his feet, colliding violently with a man coming around the end of the bench with two large bags.

"I'm terribly sorry!" Jack exclaimed.

The man nodded irritably, pushed past him, and the spell was broken. Wentworth appeared out of the blankness, and all the stops along the way. Jack sank down, dazed and frightened. He was supposed to see a cabinetmaker about the communion table at eight; Ted was to meet him at Heatherly's for lunch at twelve; Miss Mollie had been sick, and he meant to call on her some time that afternoon; at four he was supposed to give a devotional for the PTA in the library reading room at the high school. He recited these facts to himself a number of times, half-expecting them to slip into blankness, but they remained sharp and clear. He got out his billfold and reassured himself that the name and address on his identity card were correct. For some reason he half-expected to see no name. . . .

Well, it was already too late for the cabinetmaker and the luncheon engagement, and in this irrational condition it might be wiser to get home too late for the devotional. Suppose everyone walked out the instant he appeared? This was senseless: he had been alone on the platform at Wentworth. He had been alone again at his subway transfer point. He was the local minister, and they would appreciate his devotional as always, but it would simply be more prudent to tackle it at a later date.

The voice on the loudspeaker was calling his train. He jumped up and strode quickly out into the street to escape that horrid noise. He walked for a while, sat on a park bench for several hours, dawdled over his lunch for an hour, then rode a bus for an hour, dozing occasionally. This would never do. He would have to make a choice: either go back home and face them or give up the ministry itself. But his mind and will seemed stupefied. In the block ahead he caught sight of the spire of a cathedral. He pulled the bell cord. Leaving the ministry was out of the question; he must somehow get himself together.

As he started up the broad steps, a young woman pushed open one of the massive doors and crossed the wide flagstone walk. Out of the corner of his eye he followed her down the sidewalk, wondering how she compared with Thelma in bed. . . . In disgust he jerked his eyes away. How could he excuse such thoughts when his body was utterly dead and desireless?

He walked the length of the vaulted aisle in the empty, radiant dimness, knelt at the altar, bowed his head on his clenched hands, and tried to pray. But a new and enervating sense of unreality enveloped all his acts and thoughts. In the past he had resisted God at various times, had struggled with God, had even doubted God's power or concern, but the felt reality of his unseen antagonist had been beyond question. Now he felt no reality there at all, forced his petitions out into mere emptiness. He whispered aloud, hoping to give his prayer greater reality by making it a thing apart from his muddied mind and spiritless imagination, but his whispered insistence that he was forsaking the hideousness of sin was a lie: for though he was aware that last night *should* seem ugly and immoral, it actually seemed neither.

It had not been as indescribably beautiful as he had expected, or as ecstatic. In fact, it had been a disappointing anticlimax compared to the raptures his imagination had anticipated, but Thelma had seemed happy. She seemed a different person, no longer awkward and hesitant but relaxed, graceful. . . . Even her flat voice sounded richer, more expressive. And he had proved to himself that he was normal, and the tremendous relief and satisfaction of this discovery made it sheer hypocrisy to kneel at an altar and pretend to be repentant.

He sat down on the first pew, gazing up at the rose window but not feeling its beauty in the slightest. Now he no longer needed this form of beauty: all he needed was the warmth of Thelma's adoration, for that at least had not been an anticlimax. He wondered whether it was this that had made him so wildly jealous of Rick from the first moment. . . . Perhaps it had not been a physical attraction at all. Perhaps it was this that made her body so seductive, infusing it with the promise of a completeness of surrender which other more attractive women might find impossible.

He stood up.

Well, he now knew himself normal and capable of a satisfying marriage, even though at the beginning last night he had proved unexpectedly shy and she had almost had to woo him. The thing to do now was to return home, take up again the only life he knew, and try to forget this entire business. In due time, no doubt, his sense of the reality of his calling would return. He walked slowly out of the church and down to the corner bus stop.

His resolution faltered when he heard the speaker calling his train again, but this time he forced himself to get on. He watched the city slip away in the afternoon light of a tall, slightly overcast sky. Was it only last night that he had ridden in? Yesterday seemed part of some other world entirely, and he felt now that some other self must have gone to the district meeting yesterday morning and then argued with Patricia last night and later boarded the train for New York. He must have been utterly beside himself, mad, bewitched by dreams and visions! He had removed the tiny gold cross from his lapel—and then left his car parked beside the station with the headlights burning!

He kept retracing his actions step by step, over and over: he had been quite alone on the platform, which meant that nobody from Wentworth had got on with him. He had been quite alone at the subway transfer point, which meant that even if someone had managed to jump on at the last split second in Wentworth, and *had* for some reason followed him across on the shuttle train and in the subway, they had certainly lost him then . . . unless they had hidden somewhere at the transfer point. But that was quite impossible. He *had been alone*.

He squared his shoulders, staring out at the changing countryside as the factories and power lines gave way to meadows and little stone fences, feeling his normal self gradually being reconstructed as the objects beyond the window became more coherent, more pleasing to gaze on.

The familiar stations were drawing him closer and closer to Wentworth. At last it was the next stop. Jack found his mind disorganized by sudden irrational images: the cinder platform crowded with his entire congregation, their eyes lascivious and knowing, their lips mocking, their fingers pointed accusingly. . . . This would never do: he *had* been alone! He jumped to his feet and walked the length of the car, forcing himself to stare into every face. In the men's room he splashed cold water over his face. As he stood combing his hair and adjusting the ghastly necktie with its screaming colors, he was startled to see his eyes and lips coolly self-possessed, his expression almost arrogant!

The train swayed on a steep curve, the speaker suddenly filled the room; they were passing the Strackmars'.

He stood on the shifting metal between the coaches as the train pulled in, his shoulders back, head high, wondering whether all other outwardly confident people were likewise trying to reassure themselves that no one could possibly suspect . . . The flagman flung the door back with a shattering crash; the familiar outlines of the streets and houses burst in on Jack through the glimmering dusk with frightening unexpectedness. The parking area was deserted except for his car; at the opposite end of the station three or four loafers lounged against the baggage wagon.

Jack pressed the starter button of the car again and again as the train pulled out. Something seemed to be wrong! Furious, he was aware of Willis, the station agent, trotting toward him and just as the eager, anxious face thrust itself upon him, he remembered. He sat motionless under the torrent of self-important words, shocked and humiliated that he had wanted to run from this nosy, bald-headed little man, still more painfully humiliated that he had to force himself to meet the round excited little eyes.

"I thought you were just meeting somebody, Reverend," the grinning little mouth was saying for the tenth time, "and when I looked out again—bang! Nobody there! I tried to turn your lights off, but you had the car all locked up." (Also for the tenth time . . .) "I tried to open your window . . ." (On and on and on . . .)

"I had an emergency call," Jack interrupted at last; "you know how it is in the ministry." Being compelled to lie to this gossipy little busybody was exquisitely bitter, and implying that he knew anything about the ministry was still worse. Willis beamed as he turned toward the station.

"Hey, fellas! Come push the minister's car!"

The loafers shambled out of the gloom under the wide eaves, surrounding the car and grinning at Jack. He pretended to be interested in the ignition and the shift. One of them, Thad Manley, always grinned this way, persistently and senselessly, and was never completely drunk but always on the verge. Jack was intensely humiliated to find his own eyes waver under that bleary gaze. Was the man smiling *more* than usual? It had been raining lightly, and the men slipped and struggled as the car moved forward, then burst into shouts of laughter. Glancing back to wave his thanks, Jack saw that Thad had fallen flat in the middle of the street. The engine caught, and as he pulled away toward the garage at the end of the street, their laughter followed him.

But was it really Thad they were laughing at? And why had Willis called Jack "Reverend" so *many* times?

Jack had just opened a can of soup and cracked two eggs in the skillet when he heard the knock. He turned the burners down before going to the door, exhausted and irritable. Now what?

His first thought as he yanked open the door and saw them all standing there in the gloom—Adams, Dirkwell, Perriman, and the eight others, with their faces so solemn and determined—was that it was a conference committee of investigation. Everything was already known by everyone: they had been sent immediately to present him with charges and to suspend him from all ministerial services pending a trial. He would end like Gary Fullersbee, who had gotten involved with a woman in his congregation, had been put out of the ministry, and was now rumored to be an incurable alcoholic.

These conjectures were so ridiculous that the sudden terror evaporated even as it began to form, and Jack snapped on the lights and invited them in. They insisted that he go on with his supper, and he was relieved to have an excuse not to face them. It seemed past belief that he had had the courage only yesterday morning to blister them all so unmercifully at the ministers' meeting.

Dirkwell, Adams, Farmer, and Thompson followed him to the kitchen and sat around the table while he made an elaborate business of fixing the meal. Surprisingly, he noticed that he felt less uneasy before his brother ministers than he had before the station agent and the town drunk. He felt certain that the congregation to whom he had played counselor, judge, and savior for the past three years would

be quite without mercy or understanding. But a number of his colleagues had at various times expressed willingness to forgive a minister
gone wrong, to allow him a second chance. Such leniency had always
shocked Jack profoundly—in the past.

He turned the eggs over briefly, dished them up, and set them on
the table, keeping his eyes on them and suddenly remembering the
empty plates and scraps of food on Mrs. Catlett's table that night . . .
and the way his father had avoided his eyes. . . . And for the first time
in nine years he thought of his father without hatred.

The men had been making small talk. When Jack sat down to eat,
Thompson came suddenly to the point:

"Jack, this conference is ripe for some changes. I know we left you
feeling a little lonesome yesterday, but you've got friends. Some of us
went home from that meeting to do some soul-searching. We've got to
the point where we can't live with ourselves any longer unless we take
some kind of action, no matter how dangerous it may be. Harriet and
I have been talking about it and praying about it for months. Last night
we agreed you had given a sign to the whole district and the only thing
I could do was to come tell you that on the next issue you'd have my
vote too."

The others nodded. Farmer, a squat, red-haired man, clenched his
fist and said:

"I never really knew what the rest of us looked like till you stood
up and spoke out that way—absolutely fearless and uncompromising."

"We heard about it this morning over in our district," said Dirkwell.
"Edwina told me if I didn't get over here the fastest way I could, she'd
never speak to me again."

Jack already knew what was coming, but the situation struck him
as so desperately funny that he wanted to hear them say the words.

"Jack," said Adams, "all this conference needs is someone with nerve
enough to step out and lead. We think you're that man."

Jack wanted to laugh. He stirred his soup.

"Not interested."

He spread some jam on a bit of toast with careful exactness amid
the confused outcry of disbelieving, self-justifying voices. They obviously thought his refusal the posing of a prima donna who had been
piqued and must now be begged and wheedled.

"The man you want," Jack said at last, "is Wes Phillips."

"Wes is a ten-time loser!" Adams snapped. "We've got to have a new face—somebody young and smart and aggressive. Somebody whose courage is beyond question, somebody who's proved his integrity under fire. Jack, I don't deny that lots of men have envied you, and some have feared you, but they know this business yesterday morning was no act and that you threw away things most of them would give their eyeteeth for." He smiled: "And they know you can't back out now."

"Besides," said Thompson, his pale eyes shining, "you've been on the inside! You know how he operates. You're the break we've been waiting for!"

The men from the living room had come out now and stood crowded about, all talking at once.

"The answer is no!" Jack almost shouted, pushing back his plate and getting up. If they had only come last night—even at eleven o'clock! How could he ever explain to them now that he could never attack anybody again, much less invite a counterattack from that mild, smiling, deadly little man whose conscience permitted him to use any weapon he could ferret out? Jack stood in the middle of the circle and saw that his fingers trembled slightly as he pushed his knife and fork more nearly into the center of the empty plate. He knew that he must seem unbelievably spiteful and childish, but any impression would be better than having them glimpse the truth.

"I can't explain how I feel about all this," he said at last in a low voice. "I'm sorry. Your offer comes too late."

They were profoundly shocked. One or two started to speak, but Adams and Dirkwell herded them out with meaningful looks and little movements of the head. As Jack watched the cars drive away down the rainy street he knew they would be back. He snapped off the lights and slumped down on the sofa and sat staring into the darkness, utterly crushed by the fantastic irony of this visit.

He had left Thelma imagining she would see him again, and soon. . . . He would drop her a line in the morning and explain the whole situation as best he could, although that was certainly going to be tricky after all those things he had told her last night. He must have been utterly, utterly *insane!* But how could he risk having all this floating about in a letter, all down in black and white? Besides, a letter would be so cowardly. The honest thing would be to have it out with her face to face, where he could make it unmistakably clear that such an affair was out of the question, had already proved disastrous beyond his wildest forebodings.

He forced himself to sit up and began unlacing his shoes. Yes . . .
he would go down in a couple of weeks . . . maybe even wait a month
. . . and have a good, long talk with her face to face.

It was the only honest way. . . .

Face to face . . .

XXVII

One Hundred Dollars

THURSDAY night Dirkwell came up to see Wes and Jack at the Hotel
Middleton and they talked till past midnight. Jack fell asleep almost
before Dirkwell had gotten out of the room, but he had terrifying
nightmares and woke about two o'clock covered with a cold sweat and
trembling all over.

He had been having nightmares every night since he got back to
Middleton from New York. In them he was usually fleeing some unknown danger, his lungs bursting with terror and exhaustion. But why
should that be—unless he had done something violent or terrible in
New York, something which had caused a curtain of amnesia to descend over those nineteen hours?

He went to the closet, got the red plastic button out of his coat
pocket, examined it by the light in the bathroom, and ended with the
same sterile thoughts as always: it was the kind of thing Thelma would
wear; the scrap of thick red material on the back showed it had been
ripped from a coat or jacket. But he had never done any physical violence to Thelma, except, of course, that he had slapped her that night in
Wentworth, when she became hysterical on getting the news of Rick's
death.

Could he have harmed someone else? Paulo? Or someone like that
creature called Harry? For, if there had been any kind of weapon
handy on that counter . . . Jack shivered. Of all the shames and degradations, that had been the worst. It had been even worse than the
rending moral struggle, a struggle that had dragged on for eight
months—from September of 1959 till the end of April, six weeks ago,

when he had finally made everything clear to Thelma and ended the whole affair. He had fought it from the first day, but the tide had never really turned in his direction, till that business of the negligee brought him to his senses.

It had happened on the fourth Monday in November in '59, the night following the Sunday of the fund drive for overseas relief. The train fares to New York, the extra meals, the gifts for Thelma had become a serious strain on Jack's finances. His conscience would not permit him to cancel his tithe to the church; the publicity materials sent him for the fund drive had depressed him terribly—photographs and reports of half a world living in hunger and rags, starved faces of little children staring up at him from leaflets and posters, mothers whose babies had arms like matchsticks and bellies swollen by famine. . . . He put in an additional ten dollars out of his own pocket on the morning of the appeal, to which the response of the congregation had been excellent. Jack had acted as treasurer for the children's donations, so that the act of giving the money to the minister at the altar might make the occasion more impressive for them. He could still see the parade of little faces, features dreadfully serious, nickels and pennies clutched tight in childish fingers. Several children and two adults had given him more money later, and he still had that with him—$23.28—and planned to turn it over to the general treasurer on Tuesday.

He and Thelma had argued about money almost from the beginning. She had somehow managed to squander Rick's insurance, had been unable to keep up the payments on her car, and now barely managed to make ends meet. She invariably felt that his refusal to buy her something foolish or extravagant indicated he no longer loved her. Last time it had been perfume. But today there would be no bribe; they would have an understanding, once and for all, about the value of money.

How had their relationship ever come to this? It was becoming nothing but a genteel prostitution. Buy me such-and-such, or I won't be "in the mood" . . .

At the beginning it had been glorious, ecstatic. They had needed nothing but the wonder of their own bodies, had been engulfed in a torrent of long-repressed passion. To Jack's surprise, Thelma seemed to know almost nothing about the arts of love, and as they learned these together, they also explored other facets of one another's personality. For Thelma this obviously brought a deepening and enriching of love. For Jack it brought a deadly boredom.

Thelma was constantly plaguing him to take her out. But Jack did not dance; he could not endure the thought of sitting at a table in a dim-lit night club watching other people drink and dance. He dared not take her out to any public park or amusement area for fear of running into someone from Wentworth. Sometimes they went window shopping late at night, or ate snacks in hole-in-the-wall restaurants near her apartment building. Occasionally they went to a late movie, usually a double feature of Thelma's choosing, and sat in the darkness in the balcony with other couples. Her choices were unfailingly dreadful, but Jack sat through them with dogged patience. Anything was preferable to the possibility of a chance meeting with someone from his church.

He knew that the fear of such a meeting in a city the size of New York bordered on the neurotic. He was not even sure what would be proved. Thelma was a widow now; they had known each other in Wentworth; surely he could call on her or take her out without someone's imagining things! And when he refused to take her out, she could be very difficult, though this was probably not always deliberate. He suspected that her doubts and insecurities simply froze her, so that she *could* not respond.

But she responded to gifts!

She was quite childlike about them. They unlocked her heart, relaxed her doubts, left her utterly self-abandoned to love. Perhaps this was because in her childhood at birthdays and Christmas there had never been any mysterious and exciting boxes tied with brilliant ribbons and bows. Sometimes Jack had to turn his face away from the pathos of her shining eyes and trembling fingers. And on these occasions she was not only more delightful in bed; she rarely argued about going out. So Jack studied her tastes and wishes, but as he began to exhaust the possibilities of aptness and surprise, he compensated by sheer costliness.

When he slid his key into the lock of her apartment door, his hand trembled. She left the chain unhooked for him on Mondays now, for she was working from midnight to eight and was often asleep when he came. This time she was lying on her stomach with one arm under the pillow, and her sweater had worked up above her waist. Jack sat down on the edge of the bed and planted a long kiss in the small of her back, between the waistband of her slacks and the hem of the yellow sweater. She drew a long breath, squirmed, and opened one eye; then she closed the eye again, hugged the pillow with both arms, and churned her legs about on the rumpled bedspread.

His breath caught short, and for an instant he could not remember what it was he had meant to take up with her. She rolled over and sat up, blinking and rubbing her face where a crease in the pillow had left its print on her plump, flushed cheek. Then she kissed him lightly and padded off to the bathroom, and he heard her splashing water over her face and brushing her teeth. When she came back, she was pulling her sweater down and gazing about the room, her eyes shining.

"Well, where is it? Oh, Jack, please don't make me hunt!"

Jack lay with one elbow in the pillow.

"Where is what?"

She kissed him hard, nuzzling his cheek and giving him a little bite on the lobe of his ear.

"Please! I can't wait another minute! Where is it?"

Jack tried to wrestle her down, but she broke away and was peeping under the chair and the bed.

"Thelma, what *are* you talking about? Look at me!"

His tone brought her up short; her smile vanished.

"Didn't you get it?"

"Get what?" Was this some sort of anniversary for them?

"What you promised."

"But *what* did I promise?" He must not lose his temper.

"It doesn't mean anything if I have to tell you." She flung herself down in the easy chair, pulled one bare foot up, and examined her calluses.

"Thelma, darling, let's try to be reasonable. It's been two whole weeks. Do you know why I couldn't come last Monday? Simply because I had no money. And I thought that train would never get here today!"

She touched a big callus gingerly, not looking up.

"I've been waiting, too. But I thought your promises meant something. You're a man of God."

"Don't start that 'man of God' business! Just tell me what I promised. Please."

"If you have to tell a person their promises, they're not really promises."

Jack ran his hands over his face as if he could brush away the cobwebby effect her mentality always had on him.

"Darling, I've had a rough two weeks, believe me. This fund drive we've been in was a killer. In addition to that, I've had a man in the hospital with an acute coronary and I've been down there at all hours of the night for the past four nights. I should be there right now. I'm tired. I've had a lot on my mind. I'll just have to confess I honestly don't know what this is all about; but if I did promise something, I'll do whatever I promised."

"It's probably too late now. The store will be closed."

"Some of them are open till nine tonight. Which store was it?" Jack glanced at his wrist watch. Six forty-five. He could ride the subway, that would leave him roughly seven dollars.

Thelma pulled up the hem of her sweater, examined her navel, and stroked out a bit of yellow fluff.

"Maxine's."

"*Maxine's!*" Thelma had forced Mrs. Richardson to let her buy some trousseau items there, but even Mrs. Richardson had remarked on the prices.

"You promised to buy me that negligee."

For the first time she raised her head. The owlish brown eyes were dead serious, the sulky lips unyielding. Jack had to control himself not to burst out laughing.

They had been window shopping and had seen the negligee, a hideously vulgar froth of orchid rosettes and lavender mesh that would have looked absurd on anyone so short and plump, and as a little joke he had remarked:

"Now there's something you'd look good in! I'll have to pick it up next time I come in."

"Darling, you're wonderful!" She gasped.

"Gosh, it's past ten! I'll have to run!"

Her response had been so apt he still could not believe she had actually taken him seriously.

"Thelma, you knew perfectly well I was joking! Besides, that thing probably costs a small fortune."

"Ninety-nine fifty. Plus tax. I asked next day." She padded over to the bed and flung herself down.

Jack sank into the easy chair. There was no point in shouting that it was a joke, joke, *joke!* Of all their differences—food, clothes, books, movies, music, everything—the most impassable gulf had been humor. Jack's was ironic. Hers was slapstick. Once he had laughed aloud at a reprint of an ancient *New Yorker* cartoon, and Thelma had come and leaned over his shoulder.

"Whatcha laughing at? You never laugh any more."

Jack showed her the cartoon of a mother urging her small son to eat, with the caption: " 'It's broccoli, dear.' 'I say it's spinach, and I say the hell with it.' " She took the magazine out of his hand, sat down on the bed, and studied it for a long time in silence.

"What's so funny about it?" she asked, frowning.

"I don't know. It just struck me funny, that's all. People laugh at different things."

This had become his stock solution.

"Was it really broccoli?"

"I don't know. What difference does it make?"

"Why do you laugh at something you don't even know?"

"Because that isn't the point."

"What is?"

"I honestly can't explain it. There's just something funny about a child saying such a thing, I suppose."

Thelma read the caption again, her sulky lips silently forming each word: ". . . and I say the hell with it."

"I don't see why a man of God would call it funny for a child to talk like that. His mother ought not to let him."

Jack had subsequently made a determined effort to keep his humor obvious and literal. The negligee joke had been his first blunder in weeks. He knew that her failure to realize he had been joking could trigger a whole chain of resentments in Thelma. She had realized early that these various differences were partly what made him so evasive about the possibility of marriage, and as a result very small irritations could sometimes plunge Thelma into a sullen unresponsiveness. She would then insist on his taking her out or would do one of the many things she knew exasperated him—would call her friend Carlotta and talk for thirty or forty minutes on the phone, would play the same popular record over and over, would force him to talk to her about the church or the ministry or what a minister's wife did or about Patricia, invariably referring to her as "Patsy" because she knew that had been one of Jack's pet names. Or she would keep calling him a "man of God," or would say, "Fix me a drink, will you, sweetie?" because she knew that particular chore humiliated him more than any other and she always had to instruct him again on some part of the process he had forgotten.

She often did things that were deliberately crude and offensive just "to drag you down off your high horse once in a while." But she had a pathetic craving for the very things she ridiculed and never tired of asking, "Do you think I'm a lady?" At the beginning she had tried to question him about his family, and he knew that she was humiliated by his silence and probably felt he considered her socially or morally unworthy to discuss his mother and father.

Jack sometimes wondered how they managed to continue in spite of so many barriers. One reason was, of course, that her very vulgarity made him desire her more. It probably did not occur to her that Jack might find her inferiority relaxing or that he might have felt inept and insecure with Patricia. But the thing that brought him back to her again and again despite the fantastic impossibility of the entire affair was her love. He wallowed unashamedly in her doglike adoration and in the knowledge that—barring upsets or misunderstandings—she was his for the taking, utterly abandoned, without shame or restraint. The past two weeks of wanting her had been torture. They had only a few hours before she left for work. They *could* not fight now!

Thelma sat up and yawned, stretching luxuriously.

"I feel lousy. I think I'll soak in the tub a while and then we could eat out and take in a movie before I go to work. Whatcha say?" The puffy-lidded eyes were guileless.

"Thelma, listen, please. I haven't got a hundred dollars. I think it would be immoral to spend that much on a negligee, but that's beside the point. I'm just plain broke."

"Forget it. I have already. I just thought a man of God was supposed to keep his promises like anyone else."

"Thelma, I've got exactly seven dollars and twenty-one cents with me." He did not mention the relief money; that belonged to the church. "I drew out my savings months ago. I have about five dollars in my checking account. I'm in debt. I've already drawn my salary through the end of next month. How am I supposed to raise a hundred dollars in a strange city at this hour?"

"How do I know? I never went to college."

"Thelma—"

"Oh, go away! You make me tired." She flung herself on the bed with her face to the window. Jack sprang up.

"I'll get the damned negligee!"

"I don't want it now."

"I'll get it anyway—if the shop's still open!"

She rolled over toward him, hugging the pillow.

"Ask for Helen. It's all wrapped and everything." She gazed up at him sideways, her dark auburn head sticking up above the pillow.

"You *devil!*" Jack burst out.

The beginning of her smile vanished.

"I don't like anybody calling me that."

"I was only—" Jack could think of no substitute for the word "joking." He snatched up his hat and topcoat and slammed out of the apartment.

As he stepped out onto the sidewalk a blind panic swept over him. Suppose the shop had closed? He yelled at a taxi, jumped in, and sat on the edge of the seat while the swerving vehicle seemed to crawl through the crowded streets.

Helen proved to be a tall, bony girl with an exhausted face and platinum hair. She was obviously impressed by Thelma's "boy friend."

"I'll write you a check if I may," he said, pulling out his checkbook as she set down the box. The total was $102.48. His fingers trembled slightly at the beginning, and he reminded himself again that he would figure out some way to cover this as soon as he got home tomorrow, and that tomorrow was quite unimportant anyway.

"Have you any identification, sir?"

He knew everything would be marked "Reverend" or "clergy."

"I'm afraid I left my billfold at Thelma's."

They refused the check.

He managed to seem only casually distressed. He knew that Helen would be disappointed to lose the commission. He told her that Thelma was upset, and that the negligee was a peace offering. Could she possibly—as a personal favor to Thelma—take the box home with her and let him bring the money later that evening? Helen's big, brilliant eyes surveyed him again.

"I shouldn't. But . . . well . . . Okay."

In a phone booth Jack went through the yellow pages with shaking fingers. "Churches, Methodist." Surely, from the hundreds of men he had known in college and seminary—

"Fairmont: . . . Paul A. Rogers, Asc. Minister!"

He dialed the number, searching frantically for the name of the girl Paul had married. . . .

"Celeste? This is Jack Lee, remember?" This chummy opening was outrageous, since he had snubbed the girl repeatedly at school; but her familiar giggling voice reflected only delight. It developed that Paul was at the church but would be back in a few minutes.

The subway helped calm Jack a little. He knew very well that by eleven he would see Thelma with clear and jaded eyes. Then why this insane conviction that he was rushing headlong to some lasting consummation? Why this quaking terror that Paul might not have the money, that Thelma might have to leave for work before he could return, that Helen's place might be deserted? Was he really running toward Thelma at all? Or was he running away from something else? He knew she could never send him away permanently, yet her "Oh, go away!" had made him almost irrational.

At the end of the line he checked his appearance in the restroom mirror. The gray topcoat, gray gloves, and the Homburg were perfect; he wished he had not worn the sports coat, a gift from Pat. But it was so obviously expensive that it might add just the right touch. He rubbed up his gleaming shoes with his handkerchief and dashed up the stairs.

Celeste had not changed a hair or a giggle. She phoned the church, gasping, "He's here!" and then conducted Jack on a gushing tour of their new parsonage, a split-level home in an exclusive suburb. When they got back to the living room, Jack sank gratefully onto the sofa, stealing a glance at his watch. Eight forty-five. Celeste gushed on. She simply could not wait to tell Bess Thornton that Jack was still single; and he had not gotten fat or bald like so many ministers. Jack wondered just what Celeste had been expecting after only three short years.

Paul arrived at last, and after more endless gushing and reminiscing, Celeste finally went to the kitchen to fix coffee, and Jack explained that he had come in on business and had lost his billfold. ("Isn't that like a country parson come to town?") He had to have one hundred dollars at once, and hoped to make the 10:10 afterwards. He saw that the story was getting too elaborate and stopped. It turned out that Paul and Celeste had only thirty-seven dollars in the house. Paul finally decided to have Jack write him a check for fifty and to step down the street to Mr. Woodall's where Paul would borrow the other thirteen. This was so absurd that Jack was beside himself, but Paul had always been the timid type and his bland pink face clearly indicated that he had already gone the second mile. Fifty dollars was almost worse than nothing, but Jack knew that he absolutely must seem casual. His entire story might have struck Paul as highly improbable. . . .

"Fine!" Jack said. "You're both terribly kind. I'm sure I can raise the balance somewhere."

Woodall proved to be the laughing Rotarian type and lived in the palatial home Jack had noticed walking up from the subway. Jack had to bite his lips to keep from blurting out as he watched Woodall's plump fingers separating the crisp, clean edges of the bills in his wallet. Woodall was sure that it never hurt anybody to be a good Samaritan, though you never could tell about these preachers!

"He might be in town playing the ponies!" Fulsome laughter from Paul. "He doesn't look much like a country parson to me!" More laughter.

On the subway at last, he counted the money. He had $5.81 left after the cab, phone call, and upcoming subway fares. Paul's $50.00 plus the $23.28 relief money belonging to the church made a total of $79.09. The negligee was $102.48. He glanced at his watch in despair: nine-fifteen. That seemed odd. Surely he had been delayed by Paul and Celeste for at least an hour! He held the watch to his ear but could hear nothing above the roar of the subway. But the sweep hand was moving—

Pawnshops!

He had learned by chance that the watch had cost Patricia one hundred and twenty dollars. He would ask thirty and have money for a taxi and a meal before train time. . . .

Jack had only chaotic recollections of getting from Paul's to the pawnshop district. He could still remember hurtling along in the subway, then running down filthy sidewalks with faces streaming past him— coarse, brutal faces of shambling men with bloodshot eyes, curious faces of slatternly women, dirty faces of children who skipped out of his path. . . .

The shops were already dark!

Then, halfway down the block, he saw one with a light still burning. He broke into a run, knowing that he was too tired to run, too tired to care whether he got to Thelma's in time or not, too tired to desire her any more, but absolutely compelled to push this insane venture through to the end. Wild images danced before his eyes. Mrs. Catlett's grinning lips . . . Patricia's amused, observant eyes . . . Dan Starr staring at him with blazing contempt . . . His feet pounded on the littered pavement, his heart pounded, he had a pounding in his brain. . . .

The little man in the frayed vest was trying to close the steel gate across the shop front.

"Please! I've got to have some money!" Jack seized the gate, gasping and hanging on to keep from falling. "Please!"

The pawnbroker gazed at him over his dirty, steel-rimmed spectacles. "I am closed. They don't let me do business this late." He gazed down sideways at Jack's topcoat and shoes. "If you make it quick . . ."

They descended the three steps from the street level, and Jack followed him to the rear, where a single light still burned. The disarray of objects overflowing the shelves and counters merged into a hazy tunnel, like the packing in a rat's nest. The man went behind the counter, looking up at Jack from his sallow, grizzled face, the light overhead glinting in the lens of the jeweler's loop at his temple.

Jack laid the watch before him, and the man turned down his loop. In the silence Jack could hear the conflicting ticks of the different clocks on the walls, and the man's wheezing breath. After an eternity he snapped the back onto the watch again and stood staring at it through his thick lenses. Finally his black fingernail doodled a figure in the film of grease on the counter top.

"Fifteen dollars."

Jack turned cold all over.

"Fifteen dollars!" His voice sounded strangled. "I only got it Christmas! I happen to know it cost—"

"I know." The pawnbroker turned up his loop, and in the watery light his eyes traveled from Jack's trembling fingers up his arm to his face. "I am closed. Please." The wheezy voice was toneless with fatigue.

"Give me twenty-three sixty-nine and you can keep it!" Now the man knew what he needed, but Jack's mind, like his emotions, seemed out of control.

The man gestured toward the shelves and counters.

"Who redeems anything? Fifteen dollars."

Jack snatched off his hat and slapped it down.

"How much?"

He did not even pick it up.

"One dollar."

"It cost eighteen dollars!"

The man sighed, coughed, and shoved one hand inside his shirt where a button was missing, his face wrinkling into pain and distaste. He nodded toward the front of the shop. A man in rumpled, sodden clothes was peering in at them, stooping low and swaying and grinning.

"Will Bennie ask me for a Homburg?"

Jack felt a terrible momentum building up, building up. . . . He pulled off his topcoat.

The man dragged it across the greasy counter.

"Four dollars."

This time Jack made no attempt to conceal the anger. He pushed his gloves and muffler across and stood with fists clenched, drumming. The beady eyes lifted briefly; the black-nailed hand shoved the articles into the pile.

"Fifty cents."

Jack tried to add the jumbled figures in his head, laid his fountain pen and pencil on the counter.

"Fifty cents."

A dreadful despair began to steady him; he unfastened his cuff links and tie clasp.

"Twenty-five cents."

The amounts were so outrageous he wanted to laugh—or cry—or both. He shrugged out of his sports coat and took the New Testament from the inside pocket. The pawnbroker felt the rich, hand-loomed fabric while Jack turned back his flapping cuffs.

"Two dollars."

It was the end: he was short forty-four cents.

Jack leaned on both arms and began to laugh. Then he stopped, ripped out the title page of the Testament on which Wes had scrawled, "For Jack on his ordination day. Welcome to the Christian ministry!" and shoved it across. The man touched the Morocco binding dubiously.

"What is it?"

Jack stood with his head between his shoulders, supported by his arms, his chin almost touching his chest, and chuckled, tried to speak, chuckled again, his eyes fixed on the man's black skullcap.

"A New Covenant!" he finally gasped out. "With the God of Abraham and Jacob! And Isaac! Let's not forget old Isaac! How much for the word of God, eh?"

The pawnbroker's eyes were uneasy; he pushed the Testament away; Jack pushed it back, furious.

"How much?!"

"No one will buy it, but I give you ten cents."

"Make it forty-four cents!" Jack chuckled again. "Or just make it thirty pieces of silver—eh? Add it up! Add it up! I figure it twenty-three thirty-five."

He unscrewed Jack's fountain pen, added up the figures on a scrap of pasteboard, shoved a pawn ticket at him, and turned his back. In the opening between his elbow and his side, Jack saw the drawstring neck of the dark cloth bag. He felt his right hand twitch uncontrollably. The trembling extended to his whole arm, to his whole body. If only he had some kind of club . . . He drew a deep breath—

"Harry."

The word broke the silence so unexpectedly that Jack started. Its tone was mild, remote, weary. Jack's eyes locked with the pawnbroker's in the dingy mirror.

A fist pushed aside the sleazy curtain at the rear of the shop. The fist was holding a spoon, and a man appeared with a bowl of steaming soup in his other hand. He advanced slowly, carelessly, blowing on a spoonful of soup and splashing some on his yellowed undershirt. His enormous shoulders were covered with dark fuzzy hair and his eyes, looking out of misshapen eye sockets, were too placid. The dim light gleamed on his bald, sweating head, and the position of the bowl showed that he meant to fling the contents into Jack's eyes. Jack was aware that the pawnbroker had his hands on something under the counter.

Harry stopped. Jack was facing him squarely. The pattern of the ticking clocks was unaccountably clear and sharp. Jack slowly and carefully turned his palm up and stretched it out toward the pawnbroker. "I'll take my money."

He saw the almost imperceptible relaxing of the fuzzy shoulders, counted his money, and walked out. As he stepped up onto the sidewalk something struck him violently between the shoulders and on the ankle and he lunged sprawling, his right foot hooked behind his left ankle. The silver rang on the sidewalk and several coins rolled off the curb into the gutter. Jack whirled over on his back with clenched fists, but Harry had already slammed the steel lattice between them. A passer-by stepped across his feet without even glancing down, and from the shadows Bennie grinned, swaying.

Jack got to his knees and began picking the coins out of the mud and filth, trying to wipe them off and then shoving them down deep in his pocket beside the bills.

In the subway he found a raw bruise on his left forearm, the left knee of his trousers was torn, his palms were red and scratched, and he had an ache between his shoulders where Harry had struck him. When he reached Helen's apartment, the clock in the foyer showed ten-forty.

Helen made no comment when she opened the door, but her eyes widened and for an instant he thought she did not recognize him. A soldier and a girl glanced up from the sofa, then put their lips back together. Another soldier watched from an easy chair as Helen led the way to the bedroom. The box was on her bureau. Jack picked it up as she bent over to count the money on the bed, sighing and shaking her platinum curls, which were disheveled.

"You're short thirty-four cents!" Her long bony fingers clutched the money; she straightened and her brilliant, angry eyes traveled up his body to his face. Her big, expressionless smile flashed on unexpectedly, "I'll just throw that in for your peace offering!"

Jack swayed slightly and stared at her, befuddled. When the door of the apartment had closed behind him, he sagged against the wall and saw with numbed surprise that his grip had burst open one corner of the box. He heard Helen's voice, ugly and rasping:

"Didja notice that guy? He came in tonight just before closing time, dressed to kill, with that smooth oily pitch they all give you, and tried to stick me with a bum check for a hundred dollars! Now he comes back looking like a tramp and gyps me out of thirty-five cents."

"Why'dja let him have the package?" A man's voice.

"Hah! You shoulda seen his eyes when I told him he was short. He's on dope or something; that kind will kill you. I could feel goose pimples pop out all over me."

"That's funny." The man's voice. "I can't feel a one of them now." Laughter. "What was in the box—heroin?"

"That negligee I showed you, Fred, remember? I told the buyer we'd never unload it in my lifetime, but this wild man bought it, just like Thelma said he would."

"Say, I gotta meet this Thelma!"

"You wouldn't look at her twice. The guy is nuts."

Jack stumbled toward the elevator. Filthy animals! When he emerged from the subway entrance before Thelma's apartment, he saw the myriad windows glowing through the cold night air, tier on tier. It was almost eleven; she would have to leave for work very soon; the whole thing would be hurried and joyless; he did not even want her any more—now that he knew he could have her.

But he knew that he would go through with it.

The logic of the whole evening required it. The logic, and something else. Something beyond reason, deep and blind and relentless that often brought him to New York when the demands of the pastorate had left him too exhausted for desire. Sometimes it seemed that instead of his body dragging his spirit into sin, it was his spirit which flogged his jaded body on beyond its furthest cravings, lashed his weary imagination, goaded his desireless flesh to yet one more joyless grasping at joy.

When Thelma had left for work he lay in a hot tub, trying to soak the soreness out of the bruise between his shoulders. She had been shocked by his appearance and dismayed by the story of his activities, but enormously flattered. She insisted that she would not only redeem his things when she got off in the morning but would bring him the money to cover the bad check. No doubt this would be from Carlotta.

Jack still could not believe that he had actually considered grabbing the moneybag and making a run for it . . . to be shot down like a mad dog before he reached the door . . . or to be caught and held by passers-by till the police arrived. He could almost see the blinding flash-bulbs in his face and the lurid front pages of the papers back home. And the fear in the pawnbroker's eyes, he realized now, had not been of physical harm; it was the uneasiness all normal men feel in the presence of a man possessed.

When had his sanity returned? Only when he lay in bed at last and saw Thelma coming toward him, smiling, wearing that hideous lavender and orchid garment.

"Golly!" she had exclaimed over and over, "I never dreamed *you'd* do anything *wrong* just for me!" Her much-repeated announcement of his fall seemed to contain an unmistakable note of satisfaction. "You're all worn out," she said. "You just lie still and I'll dance for you."

She snapped on the bed lamp and selected a popular record. Normally, she was quite awkward, but when her fears and insecurities were dissolved, she became astonishingly graceful, lithe, and relaxed. She had first danced before him simply to irritate him, as a kind of joke. But they were both surprised to find that it added something to their relationship. For her it was a means of self-expression, an escape from her inarticulate vocabulary. For him it was a release from the unending propriety of his daily life and appeased a startling hunger for things earthy and obscene. Her movements were a mixture of things she had seen on television, at night clubs, or in movies. They were both elegant and crass, charming and obscene, prim and brutally lascivious. And when he was tired, they helped bring his body up to the compulsive demands of his will.

Jack lay in the tub with his eyes closed.

One thing was certain: the affair must end.

He knew he had made this resolve before, and that visions of Thelma would torment him again, for she had never been more transfigured and impassioned than tonight. He suspected that for the first time she had become completely and finally secure in the conviction that he loved her.

And that was supremely ironic.

For a new factor had been secretly working its way up into place alongside his varied and contradictory reactions to Thelma. First had been unalloyed passion; then shame; then boredom; then fear and horror at the kind of person this affair was making of him. But now something additional appeared, something frenzied and violent that exploded inside him like the searing flash of a pitchy log that bursts into hissing flames:

It was hatred.

XXVIII

The Promise

JACK did not see Thelma again for four weeks—not till Christmas Eve. She wrote him three times, asking what was wrong and imploring him to come, and Jack grew frantic at the possibility the postmaster would recognize her handwriting. He knew he must see her and make her understand that they simply could not go on any longer; this opened the door again to desire; and he was appalled and miserable to find that his mushrooming hatred for the person herself seemed powerless to diminish his enslavement to her body.

Then, on Christmas Eve at the Santa Claus party in the church basement following the vespers and carol sing, he received a gift envelope containing one hundred and twenty dollars. This was almost double the previous year; the treasurer must have passed the word that the minister was in a pinch. The pounding that night had also been exceptionally generous. They had hidden four big cardboard boxes in one of the Sunday school rooms, and the men lugged them out and put them on a table after Santa had distributed his gifts and gone.

A group clustered about Jack while he went from box to box, lifting up jars and cans and packages and reading the cards and the notes scribbled on the bags. Velma Abernathy giggled when he came to her earthenware crock of baked beans. ("Just warm them in the oven.") Mrs. Richardson had put in a baked ham. ("For your bachelor sandwiches.") Sara Armstrong had made one of her fruit cakes. Mrs. Alliston had a loaf of nut bread all wrapped in gold paper. Mr. and Mrs. George Strackmar and Gloria had their names on a huge bag of canned goods. Miss Mollie had put in four jars of her famous plum jelly. Pross Williams had baked him a slightly lopsided cake. ("I should have bought one; but after that wonderful sermon Sunday I felt I just had to do something that required real effort!")

Jack was wearing a new suit that three laymen had bought him that week, and George Strackmar insisted on taking some pictures of him standing at the lectern in the sanctuary. The choir decided to have their picture taken too and went trooping upstairs to put on their robes again. George stood about on the pews, sent for floodlights, and took forever arranging the candles and poinsettias on the altar and adjusting the stoles on the choir vestments.

Jack obligingly struck various poses. He would make a run for the 8:55 as soon as George was finished, would pick up a farewell present in a shop at Grand Central, they would have one final night. . . . Then tomorrow he would somehow get it through her unreceptive mind that everything was over. George hoisted his camera for the tenth time:

"All right, choir, sing! We want this to look natural."

Their voices rose once more, "Silent night, holy night, all is calm . . ." while George frowned and squinted.

Thelma had been pressing Jack more and more in recent months about the possibility of marriage, and her ideas of what a minister's wife did in the church and community were grotesque. He had done everything he could think of to discourage her, short of a sledgehammer frankness, but the broadest hint was quite wasted on that stubborn, armor-plated mind. Sometimes he felt trapped almost beyond hope in a kind of gluey web stuck together of her abject adoration, her physical endearments, and her impenetrable faith that they would someday be "Reverend and Mrs. Lee—don't that sound cute! And sometimes when you're standing up preaching, I'll be thinking to myself, 'If these old biddies only knew what we were doing *before* we got married—wow!' And I'll give you a little wink, you know?"

George flashed his bulb at last.

"Hold it, everybody! We want a shot of the minister reading. Just a few lines, Reverend—and move a step to the left. I want those organ pipes in this."

Jack glanced down at the open Bible and read:

"And there were in the same country shepherds abiding in the field, keeping watch over their flock by night . . ."

He made the 8:55 with only seconds to spare, and during the trip he brooded over the fact that he simply could not keep stalling off the men who were urging him to head a reform movement in the conference. They had been after him since that district meeting in September. Even Dan Starr had reversed himself barely a month after the meeting, and had also been pleading with Jack to lead. Jack had finally agreed to meet with nine of them at Merrill Adams' parsonage on January 4, and he knew that they considered this tantamount to acceptance.

But first he must break off with Thelma. To undertake such a fight against a man like Dr. Worthington and at the same time to continue this affair was unthinkable.

As he had suspected, she had a tree set up with her gifts for him already under it. He was glad he had taken time to buy some extra things, for her tiny tree in this lonely apartment in this tremendous city sent a pang through him after the small-town warmth and long-standing friendships of the church party in Wentworth. Thelma was sitting on the floor by the tree staring up at him.

"S'matter? You look kinda sad." She jumped up, kissed him, and disappeared into the bathroom without waiting for an answer. Jack wandered over to the window. Her face had looked so radiant in the dim light of the little tree; she was so delighted with that tiny collection of gifts. . . . How could he possibly tell her at Christmas? Below her window he saw the dim-lit, jumbled rooftops of the slums that began on the opposite side of the boulevard and far beyond, on the horizon, was the blaze of the city again. Thelma had escaped somehow from that swamp of tenements and hovels. Small wonder that to her this tiny flat and her monotonous existence were quite endurable.

She suddenly appeared from the bathroom wearing the lavender negligee. The remembrance of everything he had gone through trying to raise the hundred dollars for it struck him all in a single blow. That decided it: They would open the presents tonight, and tomorrow he would tell her.

When they finally got to bed, Jack reached over to snap off the lamp and saw some stamped envelopes on the night stand. They were apparently Christmas cards, and the top one was addressed to Mrs. Richardson.

"I thought I oughta write her how I was getting along," Thelma explained. "Since Rick was killed in the war and all. And I wrote Mrs. Hoffman because she used to sneak my magazines back in when she found them in the trash. Mail them when you go tomorrow, will you, sweetie?"

"But you can't send messages like that for three cents."

"Oh, pooh! They never check at Christmas time."

"But you can't *do* that!" He snapped off the lamp.

"Why not? It's only four cards. They wouldn't send a policeman all the way up to the twelfth floor for four cents."

"That's not the point. It's like stealing. It's wrong."

"How can it be wrong if everybody does it?"

"You don't decide right and wrong by how many people do it. I preached on that very thing Sunday and used Christmas postage as one of my examples. I couldn't sleep at night if I sent even one sealed message without a four on it, and I forbid you to."

"Oh, don't be so fussy."

Thelma gave him a little biting kiss on the ear, and he turned and pulled her close and then his heart seemed to explode, as if the horrifying knock on the door were a monstrous, icy fist smashing him in the chest out of nowhere.

"Sis! Hey, Sis! Wake up—it's me—Paulo!"

The hoarse, drunken voice seemed already inside the room. Jack started violently and felt Thelma's body go rigid. They lay frozen with terror while the hammering and shouting increased. Finally a hall door opened somewhere, an angry, imperious male voice took over, and Paulo's voice moved away, grumbling.

Jack rolled over on his back, weak and trembling. Thelma's brothers worked for a trucking firm on the other side of town; they were usually on the road, and Thelma kept up with their whereabouts through the girl in the dispatcher's office. Tonight she must have forgotten to inquire. He could hear her shivering breath as they waited for the clang of the elevator door.

But it did not come.

Instead, they heard a drunken mumbling at the end of the corridor, which jutted out past the outside wall of Thelma's room, forming an L with it. Then came the stiff, sliding sound of the hall window opening, which looked across the angle of the L into Thelma's window, scarcely five feet away. Her shade was pulled down, as always, and Jack realized later that Paulo had simply seen the janitor's push-broom left in the hall and had reached across with the handle. But at the time he had an appalling vision of a drunken figure climbing out onto the narrow, icy ledge of the corridor window twelve stories up and trying to step across the angle.

At the sudden, spine-chilling sound of that knock on the glass, Jack flung out his arm in horror. His wrist struck Thelma's bottle of sleeping pills and sent it clattering across the floor.

And a moment later Paulo was back at their door.

"Lemme in! I heard you!"

"Who is it?" Thelma's voice was thin and feeble.

"Me—Paulo. Lemme in!"

While she pulled on a robe over her gown, Jack grabbed up his clothes and shoes, closed the bathroom door softly behind him, and with an ecstasy of clumsiness shoved the tangled mass behind the curtain of the little alcove used as a linen closet. Then he stood frozen as Thelma called out in a coarse, rasping voice he had never heard before:

"I'm sick. Whatcha want?"

"I'm hurt. I'm cut. Open up! You gonna take all night?"

"Okay, okay, okay. I'm coming."

She snapped on the light; Jack stepped behind the curtain of the linen closet, wanting to slip on his clothes but terrified of making a sound.

The lock clicked, the chain of the night latch rattled, and the thick voice filled the air.

"Christ almighty! I thought you'd never wake up. Don't you know it's Christmas Eve? Why ain't you up celebrating like everybody else?"

"I'm sick, I tell you. Whatcha want?"

"I want a bandage, whaddya think I want? I'll get it myself." Jack heard the voice approaching the bathroom.

"Let me see the cut!" Thelma's voice rose almost to a scream.

"Jesus, you do look bad. You're white as a sheet, kid."

"It's only a scratch. Sit down and I'll get the kit. You don't know where nothing is around here."

She pushed the bathroom door half-open, stepped inside, and snatched up the first-aid kit. Jack saw the shock and bewilderment on her face as she glanced about, and he realized that the glossy pattern on the curtain behind which he was hiding made it opaque under the bright light, though he could see her perfectly. Then she closed the door again.

"You and Pietro are like babies. Why don't you be a man, like Bart? He'd never come crying and waking me up at two o'clock when I'm sick."

Jack glanced down at his wrist and realized he had forgotten his watch on the end table! There were goose pimples all over him, and he had to clench his teeth to keep them from chattering. Thelma had strung a clothesline in the narrow space between the curtain and the shelves; it was hung with her wet stockings and underthings, and these clung to his back and shoulders. From the apartment behind him, beyond the wall of the closet, he could hear the strains of a radio and the voices of carolers: "O little town of Bethlehem, how still we see thee lie . . ." then Paulo's hoarse voice again:

"Th' hell with Bart and Pietro. Where were they when I was getting cut on?"

"Drunker than you are, probably. There! Now get out and let me get some sleep. You wanna get the flu too?"

"The flu! Why didn't you say you had the flu? I'm going."

Jack let out a pent-up breath and was about to pull the curtain aside when he heard Thelma's agonized scream:

"That's the bathroom!"

The door burst open and Paulo stumbled in.

"I know what I'm doing!"

He was a short, swarthy, powerfully built man with a pock-marked face and close-set black eyes with almond-shaped lids. His greasy hair was blue-black and curly and glistened with particles of melted snow. He stood with his back to Thelma and the door, staring straight at the curtain only a few feet away, while he unbuttoned his black leather jacket. Jack clenched his teeth and drew in tiny, suffocating, noiseless breaths.

Paulo's thick lips curled back and a drop of moisture formed on the hanging lower lip and he wiped it away with the back of one thick, grimy hand. He was having trouble getting the jacket off over the fresh white bandage on his wrist.

"Theresa heard you had a boy friend again."

Silence. Paulo gouged at his jaw teeth with a black fingernail, pulling his wide mouth far around in a rubbery grimace, and spat in the commode. Then he turned away at last, letting the jacket fall to the floor, and began washing up at the basin with his back to the alcove.

"It better not be no black Prod. You stick to your own kind from here on, understand? Them black Prods mean nothing but trouble to a Catholic girl, understand? If we ever catch you even looking at one of them again, we'll knock *all* your teeth out this time, understand?"

Through the open door Jack saw Thelma standing by the bed.

"Have I gotta hear how you're taking Papa's place every time you get drunk? Go preach to your buddies at Vito's."

Paulo splashed water over his face, rubbed it vigorously, and straightened, groping for a towel.

It all happened so quickly that Jack decided later he must have been planning his act all the time he stood there, naked and trembling and half-suffocated. Paulo swung in a clumsy half-circle and put out his left hand, palm high and turned toward Jack, like a baseball player about to catch a ball, his dripping fingertips reaching for the curtain. He stumbled as he came and almost fell into the alcove.

Jack enveloped him in the curtain in one big lunge, snapping the twine it was hung on as he hurled him backwards across the narrow tile floor. The back of Paulo's head slammed into the door jamb and he went limp, but in his terror Jack held him up and banged the bobbing head against it once more before he lowered him to the floor still muffled in the curtain. Then he stood up, trembling violently, his body shaken by convulsive gasps.

Thelma had sunk to her knees beside the bathroom door, both hands over her mouth, her eyes bulging.

"Is he dead?"

Jack knelt, still gasping, and felt his chest.

"No, just out."

He flung his clothes into the bedroom, shoved the unconscious man aside, and locked the door. He dressed frantically, stopping only to get his watch from the end table. Thelma stared at him with growing terror.

"What are you doing?"

"Getting out, you idiot! He didn't see me. He doesn't know who I am. I've got to get away before he comes to."

Thelma seized him by one arm, her face ashen.

"You can't leave me alone with him. They'll beat me; they'll make me tell them where to find you!"

They heard a low moan. Jack hesitated.

"You'd better get out, too."

"Are you crazy? I got no place to go; I got no money; where could I go on Christmas Eve?"

Jack stuffed his tie into his coat pocket and jammed his arms into the coat, trying to think. Another moan, then something bumped the door. Thelma's eyes were enormous and her mouth was sick with terror. This was the end. Jack had known from the start that the whole thing would burst out into the open in just some such irretrievable disaster. They would get his name, his address; they would appear in Wentworth— The moan turned to a garbled voice. Jack seized her by both arms to keep her from collapsing. She could have dressed and run to Carlotta's, but now it was too late.

"Listen," he whispered fiercely, "whatever you do, don't tell them who I am. Just remember that I love you and that we're going to get married. Do you understand? We're going to be married. That's a promise! But you mustn't tell them *anything!*"

Thelma clung to him briefly with a wild, incredible strength as the bottom panel of the bathroom door suddenly bulged horrifyingly under the splintering thud of Paulo's boot. Her white face was unflinching.

"Never. Not even if they kill me."

The elevator was standing where Paulo had left it; at the street floor Jack blocked its sliding doors with a coat-tree so that Paulo would have to take the stairs, then ran across the icy boulevard toward the subway entrance at the end of the block. He heard the roar of an approaching train as he ran down the steps.

Forty minutes later he emerged on the sidewalk before a department store. The wind whipped his topcoat about him and the air rang with chimes and carols from the store's main window. There wise men and shepherds knelt before the manger; the star of Bethlehem gleamed in solitary purity; and from the amplifier the voices rang out in the empty street:

"Holy infant, so tender and mild,
Sleep in heavenly peace. . . ."

Jack turned away and stood leaning against a lamppost. Within seven hours he would have to stand at the altar in a black robe while the congregation knelt for Christmas communion. . . . It might be the last time he would ever have to face those encircling eyes, for to the killing daily weight of guilt and hypocrisy was now added the crushing possibility of immediate exposure—lurid, sensational, and violent. It might even be the last official act of his ministry, for whether Thelma talked or managed somehow to keep silent, all the possible paths before him now led only to tragedy.

Jack sank slowly to the curb, his body stalled and foundering along with his mind. He slumped sideways against the base of the post and sat staring vacantly at the frozen slush about his feet. The icy wind slapped a crackling undulation of torn Christmas wrapping paper briefly against his ankles, and above the chimes, and above the splintering thud of a heavy boot that kept pounding in his brain, he could hear his own fierce whisper:

"We're going to be married. That's a promise!"

XXIX

Consider the Lilies

IT WAS ten o'clock Friday night. Jack was standing in the doorway of one of the smaller banquet rooms of the Middleton Hotel, waiting for William Pierce Whitley to arrive. The evening session of the conference at Belfair Church had ended at nine, and tomorrow morning would probably see the end of the balloting. The tables had all been removed from the banquet room, and the chairs were set up facing the small stage at one end, on which a dance band had left some of their music stands. He counted the rebel group—twenty-one, plus himself. All present. Then he counted the newcomers again—all seated in a body on the left side of the aisle. Forty-five! Twice as many as they had hoped for!

Clarence Motherly got up from his seat among the rebels and motioned Jack to follow him out into the hall.

"Jack, I've been talking to some of the boys. We're afraid this thing is going to backfire. We must have been out of our minds to let you talk us into it."

"What have we got to lose?" asked Jack. "There are only three more delegates to be elected anyway, and not a single name on our slate has gone in yet—except that we had William Pierce Whitley on ours too, of course, like everybody else. But if Whitley stands up there tonight and endorses our slate, it will turn this conference upside down."

"*If!*" said Motherly, his thin, pointed face puckered with anxiety. "Jack, these men you inveigled here tonight think Bill Whitley hung the moon. He's their ideal of the Methodist ministry. But he's *not* a politician!"

"So?" Jack glanced again at the elevators.

"So this foxy trick of luring all his admirers here by telling them he'd have a statement is exactly the kind of political trickery Whitley detests. He'll denounce you, Jack! And if William Pierce Whitley brands you as a cheap trickster, it will destroy everything we've accomplished thus far."

"Whitley *will* make a statement! I asked him to come and hear our side of this thing, and to ask any questions he wanted to, and then to give us his position. I tell you, I'm going to make him see the light. Wait and see."

"Jack, you look like you're about to drop in your tracks right now!" Clarence seemed almost frantic. "You admit you haven't slept four hours a night since conference began. How can you match wits with one of the best minds in the conference at this hour of the night?"

"What's the alternative?"

"Call off this crazy stunt! Tell these men there's been a mistake and Whitley's not coming after all. Do anything! It's all over, Jack. Belovèd's got his delegation. Those last three delegates mean nothing. If you have any feeling at all for the rest of us who've followed you, admit defeat gracefully while you can still salvage something."

Jack looked at him sharply.

"We caucused on this at the church this afternoon, Clarence. We voted unanimously to give it a try. What's got into you, anyway? Are you trying to tell me something?"

The man looked utterly miserable.

"Jack, I want you to know that whatever happens, I've felt cleaner and better these few months working with you than I have in years. I'll never forget you. But I've been talking to some of the boys. If you win Whitley tonight, we'll go with you on the floor of the conference tomorrow morning all the way, win or lose."

"And if not?"

"We'll go back to Belovèd for whatever we can get."

Jack stared at him in a daze. That would mean breaking ranks on the final ballots. The entire conference would know they were done for.

"Who is *we?*"

"Thompson, Garrison, Farmer, and myself."

"Okay, Clarence."

"Jack, don't look that way! You have no family, no responsibilities. I'm forty-three years old! Garrison is past fifty. Men our age could never come back—"

"I said okay, Clarence."

Just then the elevator doors opened.

"Here comes Whitley," said Motherly.

William Pierce Whitley was a slim, erect man in his sixties. He was of medium height with pleasant, clean-cut features and an infectious smile. He glanced over the crowd, smiling and waving briefly, and took a seat on the front row. After an opening prayer, Jack placed his notes on one of the music stands and described briefly the political situation within the conference and read a statement of the aims and purposes of the rebel group.

"We believe," said Jack, reading from the rebel statement of principles, "that the church establishes both a vertical relationship between individuals and God, and a horizontal relationship among its various members. This last involves programs and policies determined largely by numerical majorities rather than by isolated individuals acting alone. The machine holds power by sacrificing the individual conscience to the conscience of its own majority, by voting as a single bloc for a single slate of candidates, and by controlling others through their hopes of advancement, fears of failure, or their indifference.

"We believe that an organized machine can be defeated only by an organized opposition, also willing to vote as a bloc for a single slate. This opposition will not find it easy to preserve in group action the level of integrity possible to them as individuals, nor will they find it easy to take up the sword of political activity without danger that the weapon will shape the hand of its user. All power corrupts, and those who would resist power with power must be willing to risk their own integrity in quest of a larger integrity for the church as a whole.

"Such methods are at best a necessary evil, but the alternative is a continuation of virtual dictatorship.

"Even the legitimate ambition for a wider field of service is also exploited by the machine; and, for this reason, some of us must renounce our own legitimate aspirations if we are to dispossess the tyranny which threatens all. While it may never be possible to make it easy to be good and hard to be bad, it should at least be possible to create an atmosphere in which the limited courage of the average minister can express itself, and in which independence and integrity are not suicidal.

"I believe we are all agreed that the situation in our little corner of Methodism has become intolerable, and surely all of us desire to restore in our conference that form of government by duly constituted authority which is one of the glories of Methodism. The only issue that divides us is *how*.

"Our final problem is actually one of character. The church at large can be redeemed only if it has within it a courageous and self-sacrificing minority willing to accept the principle of an ongoing Gethsemane and a continuing cross. We have preached this Gospel as valid for the world about us; it is now time to apply it within our own world of professional Christianity."

Jack then read out the names of the men who had signed the statement of principles, and yielded the floor to Burl Avery, who was to be the spokesman for the newcomers. Avery came forward, surveyed the group, and ran one of his thin hands over his thatch of snow-white hair.

"In my forty-seven years of service to the Master," he said slowly, in his reedy old man's voice, "I can truthfully say that I have sought counsel of him and him alone. I never imagined that the day would ever come when I would seriously consider letting any man—or group of men—tell me who to vote for in an annual conference of the Methodist Church."

He suddenly stopped dead, and Jack saw his eyes wander over the rebel group one by one. Jack winced as his own eyes met the beautiful, bitter gray eyes of DeForrest Garrison, the round, staring eyes of Clarence Motherly. He knew what Avery was thinking: men whose own ambitions have been blighted by the machine. But Jack felt his spirits revive as he saw Wes sitting there on the front row with his shiny black suit and frayed cuffs; and Adams with his pale, unflinching eyes and solemn face; Bradley, a tall, cadaverous man with bushy hair; Haycox, built more like a fullback than the thoughtful and scholarly type he was; and young Perriman and Alan Dirkwell . . . and Dan Starr—men with little to gain and everything to lose in a fight they knew to be well-nigh hopeless. Hopeless, that is, until tonight.

Avery finally went on:

"I know that these principles Jack read are not Scriptural, and they're not the religion *I* was raised in. But . . . but they're *true!*" He blinked and stared about him in genuine bewilderment. "My father and my father's father rode these plains and valleys on horseback to build up this conference as an arm of God's kingdom on earth. I can't see it run this way any longer. I couldn't face them in Glory!" He flung his trembling hands wide, still clearly apprehensive and confused. "I've already talked to most of the men sitting over here." He indicated the newcomers. "They're looking for an answer, too. We understand that Bill Whitley has been doing some thinking along these same lines and has a statement to make."

Jack rose quickly, hoping that none of the rebels had overstated the situation to get out a bigger crowd. Whitley's face showed no indication of irritation or resentment.

"Our main argument tonight," Jack said, "is a mathematical one. I shall first ask all those who have already signed our statement of principles to stand."

The twenty-one rebels stood almost as one man.

"Now, I shall ask our visitors a simple question: If Dr. Whitley *should* decide to endorse these principles and to approve a slate of candidates selected by the entire group of persons present in this room now, would you be willing to vote as a bloc for that slate?"

Jack studied the newcomers, saw little indications of encouragement and approval, and took the plunge:

"If so, would you stand."

Avery stood first, then the man directly behind him, then a whole row, then others singly or in groups, till at last all forty-five were on their feet. Shelton, who had been sitting against the wall in the rear, was one of the last to stand. Jack found this grimly amusing, for he was almost certain that Shelton had come as an informer for the machine.

Jack turned to Whitley.

"Dr. Whitley, you see before you sixty-eight men who will vote as one—if you give the word. The machine controls a solid core of not much greater dimensions. And if we add to that the psychological impact of such a move, and the fact that your own name and prestige would swell this group by a third or a half, you see what we have before us: an opportunity to take all three of the remaining delegates and eventually to destroy the organization which has dominated our conference for the past twenty-five years."

When the men were seated again, Whitley rose and stood at the edge of the platform, obviously shaken.

"Gentlemen, I confess that this was a type of argument I had not anticipated—and a brilliant one." Here he turned to smile at Jack. "But I am sure we all rejoice that the church in our day is producing young men clever enough to out-general their elders. I for one admire tremendously the courage and persistence with which Jack has stuck to his guns during this conference."

Jack caught Motherly's eye as they got over this first and most dangerous hurdle. The whole rebel group relaxed visibly.

"Now, Bill," Wes grumbled, "nobody ever maneuvers you into anything unless you want them to! You just *claim* you gave up all those shenanigans you learned in business, but nobody could raise the kind of money you do just by prayer and fasting."

Whitley joined in the laughter.

"You're wrong about that, Wes. I found out by chance that prayer could make some of my former associates jar loose. Just after I'd sold my business and taken my first church, I dropped by the club one day and was talking to an old friend from my days at Harvard Law. I'd heard he'd recently made a killing on the market, and the bishop was after me to raise some money for a hospital at that time. I thought Joe might come through with a few dollars because it was tax-deductible." He smiled his infectious smile, and Jack noted how the entire room grew more at ease under his good-humored self-possession.

" 'Joe,' I said, when I saw I wasn't getting anywhere with the old skinflint, 'why don't we just pray about this thing?' We were sitting all alone in the gunroom, and nobody was within earshot, but the man actually turned pale. 'Bill,' he said, 'you're not going to pray right here?' 'Why not?' I said. I knew Joe was shocked at my appearance and at the dreadful news he'd heard about my new way of life, but evidently this was too much." Whitley was rumored to have only two suits and was said to lead an austere life even in the most fashionable appointments. " 'Bill,' he said, 'a man who would pray *here* would stoop to anything!' And right then was when I began to realize the possibilities of prayer. 'Well,' I said, 'if you won't pray with me, let's just sing a hymn together and I'll be going. What about a couple of stanzas of "Amazing Grace"?' The poor fellow set down his martini and reached for his checkbook, and we dedicated an entire wing of the hospital to the memory of his mother, who would have been even more shocked at all this than he was!"

He stood, relaxed and affable, till the laughter died away. Then his face sobered as he got down to the business at hand. To Jack's astonishment, he quietly agreed with the rebel estimate of corruption within the conference, even though, as he put it, "Some of my colleagues in the cabinet would prefer circulating the fiction that I am either too ignorant or too pious to see what goes on right under my nose."

Jack was startled to realize that he himself had uncritically accepted this very fiction; it struck him now that the machine feared Whitley precisely because he *did* understand them.

"This conference has heaped honors and advancement upon me, but many men have been shunted aside whose labors were far more deserving. I run little risk in appearing here tonight, but I am humbled that many of you should have endangered your opportunities for future service in hope of some word of clarification from me." He did not glance at Shelton, but Jack was certain he had spotted the informer.

"To be frank, this whole problem has been an agony of conscience to me, too, and I came tonight partly in hopes of discovering some morally acceptable solution. I should therefore like to direct a few questions to Jack Lee, as leader of this reform."

Jack's exhaustion had almost overwhelmed him once the outcome of the entire struggle seemed out of his hands, but now he rose and came forward.

"Jack, let us assume that I 'give the word,' and that you do take those three delegates and disrupt the machine's operations. Will that machine disappear?"

"No, sir. Its leadership is most resourceful—and unscrupulous. I assume they would fight back hard."

"My estimate exactly. The conference would then be divided into two warring factions?"

"That's better than a dictatorship!"

Whitley remained calm; it was clear he was not trying to treat Jack as an opponent, only to get at his views.

"And how would you designate the new faction?"

"I've no idea. Rebels. Young Turks."

"Not a machine?"

"Certainly not!"

"But how will it differ from the group we now refer to as a machine?"

"In everything! In character . . . in purpose . . . in goals and motives. We're not trying to rule this conference; we just want to keep it from being ruled—to clean house!"

"But if the machine fights back, the housecleaning might go on for years. You would have to strengthen and consolidate your own position year after year till the machine was finally destroyed."

"I suppose so."

"Just as the old Doffingwell outfit was destroyed?"

"There's no parallel!" Jack was instantly sorry he had shown his exasperation. He saw Adams and Wes watching him with concern. Whitley looked sympathetic, but pressed on.

"But is it not a fact that at least the *leaders* of the present machine began with praiseworthy intentions, but after years of power their own motives have become as suspect as those of the men they dispossessed?"

"I'm afraid that's true, but I'm not sure their leader is entirely aware of all his own motives."

Whitley's eyes fixed on Jack with new appreciation.

"That's most generous of you. And most perceptive, in my opinion. But to continue: You are asking us to take up the morally ambiguous weapons of political activity—meeting in secret, voting as a bloc, surrendering the individual conscience to a group conscience, binding oneself to vote for an agreed-upon slate of all too imperfect men, and all the rest of it. You justify these dubious means on the ground that our motives are pure, our opponents' motives are not. But then you admit that they began with good motives too. Assuming that all your men are pure and single-hearted now, can you guarantee that time and power will not also make *them* blind and cynical and corrupt?"

Jack wanted to sit down but forced himself to remain on his feet.

"Dr. Whitley, some men stay *out* of political activity for selfish reasons—from fear or self-preservation." This was a blunder; no purpose could be served by attacking the motives of Whitley's admirers. Jack passed one hand over his face and tried again. "I mean, *all* men's motives are suspect to some degree. Evil will never be dispossessed by any man who waits for a band of angels to do it with. I think our little group is immensely superior to their opponents in honesty of purpose, but even if they were only slightly superior, I'd still feel an obligation to jump into the fight on their side with all my heart and soul."

He paused, fumbling for ideas. Wes suddenly spoke up.

"We all know that if you had wanted power for yourself, Jack, you coulda got it by inheritance. In another five years, Bill, he could have been *telling* you, not asking you."

Whitley smiled, and the tension was broken by murmurs of appreciation. Jack tried once more.

"I'll grant that time and power corrupt, but all a man can console himself with is that he began the fight in singleness of heart and refused at that moment to yield to the whispers of self-preservation or advancement. The future is in God's hands; all he expects of us is to cleanse the temple in *our* day. Personally, I had rather risk my own integrity in the corruptions of combat and power than to stay aloof and see the church I love growing daily more corrupt under men more evil than myself. And for that matter, there are some men in the machine this minute who are morally more admirable than plenty of those outside it who condemn them. Maybe they fell from grace, but at least they fell fighting with their eyes on some goal higher than their own halos!" This was all bad, bad, bad. He was too tired to control his irritation. He had always respected Dr. Worthington more than he had these lily-whites, and now these lily-whites were his only hope of victory. They were the balance of power in the church, and he now realized for the first time, they had always been!

A man named Bonner stood up, obviously pinked by this thrust. He had a round, pious face and was one of those who wore pin-striped suits because Whitley did.

"Speaking for myself alone," he said in a resonant, ministerial tone, "I suppose that some of the things you've referred to actually do go on in this conference. But here's one minister of the Gospel who doesn't believe he can build up the Kingdom of God by answering a call to become a church politician! I don't know anything about politics and don't intend to find out. All I ask is for those people to leave me alone to pastor the church God has given me."

Jack sighed. What an absolutely typical summing up of the whole lily-white position! And how much more realistic and subtle Whitley was than these admirers of his.

"It's not that simple, Ned," said Whitley. "But let's get back on the main line. Jack, don't you agree that resisting power with power may in the long run produce worse evils than those it intends to destroy?"

"It did seem to in the Doffingwell fight."

"But isn't it possible that this was not simply an exception? That in the very nature of the case right is forever on the scaffold and wrong forever on the throne?"

"Could you restate that, sir?" Jack's mind seemed fuzzy.

"I mean to say that a scaffold is of necessity a very lonely spot, and perhaps integrity can only reach its full flower on a scaffold—or a cross. For if you put the good man on the throne, surrounded by the instruments of power and the necessities of implementing his goodness in very complex situations, he begins at once to be less good. And he may end by building scaffolds for other people. I'm asking if that isn't the very nature of life and goodness in this world?"

"I suppose one could make a case for it. But I stand on these principles," Jack said stubbornly, placing one hand on his notes. "Permitting evil to grow and spread is a far greater wrong than using slightly questionable tools to uproot it. Why should the forces of evil always be organized, but never the forces of good?"

He saw instantly that Whitley recognized this as one of Dr. Worthington's favorite statements and wondered whether his opponent would now make him look ridiculous by indicating its source. But the older man only blinked once and said:

"Now, Jack, I have only one or two more questions. Are you certain that the votes in this room, plus my supposed influence, could damage the machine?"

"I am! People don't realize how *few* they are! They run things by default. Your belief that no imperfect human being tells you how to vote is an illusion: every four years your refusal to act in unison is what enables them to elect their own hand-picked slate. So you *are* being told."

For the first time Whitley seemed stung.

"The test of Christianity, Jack, is not simply that 'it pays.' It *can* bring seeming disaster. I believe that if we submit to God's commandments in obedience and faith, he will bring the results he desires in his own way and in his own good time. 'Vengeance is mine, saith the Lord.'"

"Well, I believe," said Jack, "that He wills those results through specific people—however imperfect—and that He is using me and this handful of men to carry out His providential plans. Why can't He use an organization? Why can't a score of men praying and thinking and acting together come closer to His will for a complicated situation than the same twenty men functioning as separate individuals?"

Whitley seemed lost in thought. Finally he said:

"Well, gentlemen, if I had thought this were a simple, open-and-shut case, I should not have bothered coming tonight. Perhaps I can best explain my thinking by my own history, with which most of the older men here are already familiar. I had a stint in business before I became a Methodist minister; I did rather well and was on my way to doing even better when I came to that fortieth birthday that gives so many men something to think about. I began to wonder about the meaning of my existence, to seek some goal beyond self and security.

"I have always been of a practical, logical cast of mind, but when I tried to apply logic and practicality to the problem of life's meaning, I came up with nothing. The puzzle simply did not yield to that approach.

"I finally began seeking the answer in the New Testament, and possibly I would never have gone too deeply into this religious aspect of the quest had it not been for a very great personal tragedy just at this time." Whitley's voice wavered for an instant. "Our only daughter had spent almost her entire life in dreaming about the foreign mission field and in preparing herself for service there. She was on her way to join her husband at an overseas mission station of which he was medical director. Our two grandchildren," here the pleasant voice wavered again, "were with her. The plane was last reported on course and with no indication of trouble. It was never heard from again."

He paused. No sound broke the silence.

"What previously had been simply a matter of curiosity now became almost a mania with me. The absolute ethic of the New Testament had always seemed to me offensively simple-minded, impractical, unworkable. But my despair and grief had become so intense I could endure them no longer. In the end, I made a sort of contract with God, agreeing that I would surrender my doubts and reasonings and would accept as valid all the seemingly irrational claims of the New Testament, if He would, in turn, remove the emptiness and give my life a sense of meaning. And from that day to this my life has been filled with a peaceful strength and sense of direction which I find quite impossible to explain, something far too deep for words—like death or love—something I can only marvel at, be grateful for, and try as best I can to win others to believe in. I can only conclude that God has ways, resources, methods, or whatever you care to call them, which are beyond our grasp but which are effective nonetheless. These are our true source of vitality and influence; they alone can give meaning to these little lives of ours, spent in erratic wanderings between the dark-nesses of birth and death."

He paused for a moment, then glanced at Jack.

"Now comes my good friend, Jack Lee, and urges me to return to that dark and meaningless world of human wisdom and contrivance which I renounced almost twenty years ago. 'Tear up your contract with God,' he says in effect, 'and I will show you a more excellent way.' Now, we all realize that he has no such thought in mind, and that his courage and sincerity are beyond question. But from where I stand, that is precisely what his proposition amounts to—and I confess that it has kept me awake nights.

" 'Come,' say the rebels; 'the church is a jungle where the larger animals are devouring the small. Join us in making it an even deeper jungle, where the large devour the large. The wisdom of God is foolish-ness,' they say. 'The words of the Savior have no application within the church. Why must the forces of evil be organized, but never the forces of good? Let us fight power with power, and lo, the Kingdom of God will be at hand.'

"But, don't you see, this is precisely the view I had to reject in order to accept the plain teachings of Scripture in the first place! These are the very principles that make the world of business such a jungle, and the world of politics, and the whole secular world!"

His voice rose, he seemed for a moment like a man attempting to persuade himself. He took a slim, gilt-edged New Testament from his coat pocket and held it aloft.

"These are my principles—even when I cannot understand them.

These are my cleverness, my methods—even though they do not always bring the results *my* heart might desire."

He began to turn away, as if he were finished. Jack saw the newcomers nodding their heads, nudging each other; even some of the rebels looked shaken. In another instant the whole battle would be lost.

"Dr. Whitley! How can you possibly maintain that you are doing God's will by permitting the church to continue in the grip of evil and corruption, when by the mere lifting of a hand you could save her!"

Whitley's face was somber but unflinching.

"I honestly *do not know*. I only know that the words of Christ are simple, clear, direct, childlike, tinged with no evil. His instruments are creative and healing. Yours bring deeper diseases in the very act of attempting a cure. I cannot use your means when the only word of God I know commands me to rely on faith and love and trust, to resist not evil, to turn the other cheek. I am nearing the end of my ministry; I cannot deny now all the principles that rescued me from doubt and despair; I cannot and will not substitute the wisdom of man for the plain commands of Christ. What would he do in this situation? Would he connive, plot, hold secret meetings, resist power with power, cash in on the mixed motives of his fellow men? 'Consider the lilies of the field,' he tells us, and assures us that if we have faith, God will also care for us."

Jack saw that it was all over. But exhaustion made his mind stubborn and ungraceful.

"Dr. Whitley! Good men like you have allowed evil to rule us unopposed for a quarter of a century, and tomorrow, if you persist in this view, all hopes of reform will be utterly destroyed again. I beg you to be sensible! Don't you *want* to be on the winning side?"

Whitley smiled, his face relaxed and peaceful.

"This world has produced plenty of men more sensible and practical than Jesus of Nazareth, men like Julius Caesar, for example. But where are Caesar's followers tonight? My dear young friend, I *am* on the winning side!"

Jack snatched up his papers and thrust them at the man.

"Dr. Whitley, I beg you to save the church! Please—please sign these principles!"

Too late, he saw his error. Whitley simply extended his New Testament and stood silent and motionless.

"You have your principles," he said at last, "and I have mine."
And he turned and walked silently from the room.

Jack sat in a stupor as Whitley's group broke up. A number came by the platform to shake his hand or wish him well, then they all straggled out, some in silence, some arguing, till only Avery remained, and the rebels. As the last of the newcomers left, Motherly also walked out, not looking at Jack, and after a moment Garrison and Farmer followed, then Thompson. Nobody seemed to attach any significance to their action, and Jack made no comment.

Avery finally got to his feet.

"I'd like to sign the paper," he said. Jack laid it on the seat of a chair at the edge of the platform, and the men watched in silence as the old man slowly wrote his name, his white hair and stooped figure limned in the harsh glare of the light above his head.

"I know it's all over now," he said in his reedy voice, "and I should have come at the first of the week when Wes asked me to. I guess I should have done *something* years ago. . . . If you men still intend to vote as a bloc tomorrow morning, I'd appreciate a list of your candidates."

Jack had intended to ask the men what they wanted to do now, but Avery's request seemed to please them, so he said:

"We shall be honored."

The men got to their feet almost as if at a signal. This was the end of the long struggle, but nobody wanted to put that fact into words. They did not come by to shake Jack's hand, for that would have been a symbolic admission of defeat. Instead, they filed out just as they had from other caucuses that week, as if this were not the last.

Finally only Jack and Wes remained. Jack explained why Motherly and the three others had left earlier. The lights overhead seemed dazzling; Jack felt giddy; he folded up the statement of principles and stuffed it clumsily into his inside pocket. Well . . . just as at the district meeting, he had not measured up. He had wanted a chance to prove himself; and tonight a capable, objective person might have snatched a tremendous victory from the very brink of disaster. But Jack Lee was not such a person.

Wes was standing with one high-topped black shoe on the edge of the rostrum and one elbow on his knee.

"Consider the lily-whites," he muttered. "They vote not, neither do they caucus, but they've kept this machine in power for a quarter of a century." He stared at the cracked instep of the shoe. "I wonder what Clarence got as his thirty pieces of silver. He probably made old Belovèd pay some gosh-awful price for those four measly votes."

"Such as?"

"Oh . . . you know how Belovèd's mind works better than the rest of us. He must have figured out some sort of offer he knew we couldn't match—or wouldn't."

"Well, he always told me you had to figure out what a man especially feared . . . or what he wanted so much it was an obsession." Jack straightened, and he and Wes stared at each other. "St. Luke's!"

Wes nodded his shaggy white head, his wide, sardonic grin changing slowly to an expression of pity.

"Pore old Edgar Evans. Belovèd is giving Clarence his church and sending him back to the country."

But Jack was already halfway to the door. Wes caught him as he stepped into the elevator.

"Boy, where are you going at this hour of the night? You look awful —you're plum glassy-eyed!"

Jack punched the button.

"Suite 1138! I've never won an argument with that man in my life, but he's not going to do this to Edgar!"

XXX

Children of Darkness

PATRICIA had not spoken to Jack since the conference began, but when she opened the door of her father's suite he was so completely wrapped up in his rage that her sudden appearance seemed unimportant. He shoved past her, staring about the room.

"Where's your father?"

"He's lying down. And I don't want him disturbed again." She was tying the sash of her robe; her eyes stony.

"Get him up."

"It's almost eleven. He's had a dreadful day—"

"Are you going to get him up or am I?" Jack yelled. The left bedroom door opened before she could answer, and even in his rage Jack was shocked at the man's appearance.

His face was pasty, the circles under his eyes were an ugly blue-gray, and his shirt and trousers were rumpled. His cuffs were unbuttoned, and his tie hung in two long streamers. For an instant he considered shouting the whole thing out before Patricia but realized that her ignorance might be a usable card.

"I'm here about Clarence Motherly."

The superintendent nodded to Patricia, and she turned reluctantly toward her room.

"Dad, *please* don't let him excite you." Her door closed.

"You must forgive Patricia's rudeness. She still cannot accustom herself to the physical rigors of conference."

Jack had intended to stand, but the man's appearance was so disturbing that he sat down, whereupon the older man sank into an easy chair.

"I presume Shelton has told you Whitley's decision."

The blue eyes did not even blink at the informer's name. Apparently he did not mean to prolong this by a single word.

"Yes."

"And now Clarence is leaving us and taking Garrison, Thompson, and Farmer with him."

"Yes."

"Wes and I figured out his price-tag." Jack had meant to trap him somehow into admitting the price, but now, staring into those impenetrable blue eyes he decided to gamble on the older man's exhaustion and willingness to deal at once with the facts. He spoke almost casually, hoping for a bigger shock:

"Clarence has wanted to be pastor of St. Luke's ever since he entered the ministry. Now you're planning to take the church away from Edgar and send him back to the country. We know this has been a tough fight, but we don't think it should be carried that far."

It worked.

There was no observable change in the pale, composed face or the pudgy hands folded in his lap, but they both knew it had worked.

Jack leaned back, waiting for the acute, factual analysis that would make him seem illogical and uninformed as always.

"From your statements tonight, I presume that you are unaware of the actual situation at St. Luke's." The voice was calm; one pudgy hand lifted briefly in a familiar gesture. How could one hope to defeat such an antagonist? Even in near-collapse he sounded as precise and careful as a professor in an ethics class. "The laymen have positively refused to accept Edgar for another year. A few proved receptive to his ministry, as I had anticipated, but they were all older, and the church is dominated by young adults. Those suburban teen-agers simply find him amusing and out-of-date. They do imitations of him and all that sort of thing." He paused; his brows contracted. "I have finally been compelled to admit that it would not be in his own best interests to return him for another year. He's in over his depth; he's making himself ill; Blanche is writing his sermons almost *in toto* and refuses to face the fact that such a situation cannot continue. So you see, it's not a question of giving Clarence another man's church; the church is vacant."

He lapsed into silence, apparently considering the matter closed. Jack leaned forward.

"Will Edgar know *why* he is being moved?"

"Edgar had an opportunity to face the truth about his limitations when I sent you to offer him a suburban pastorate. But he was too ambitious, or too self-deceived, or too afraid of hurting Blanche. No, he suspects nothing. The laymen have been very kind. He seems to have no inkling that under their very genuine personal affection, they consider him unfit for the job to be done."

"Will he be moved to a church in that bracket?"

The pasty face revealed a sudden, naked pathos.

"It is now obvious that he is out of his class—obvious to everyone but himself, and Blanche. I could never persuade the cabinet to try him in another such church." He smiled faintly. "Once was difficult enough."

So far so good.

"I suppose you know, sir, that Clarence imagines Ed stole St. Luke's from him by conniving with you."

"Ed has mentioned hearing some rumors of Clarence's reaction, but he is much too charitable to believe any minister could entertain such suspicions of a colleague."

Excellent. The man had all the facts; he simply had not let himself think through their implications.

"But have you considered what Edgar may believe about Clarence, and about you, when the appointments are read on Sunday afternoon?

I assume you have not yet had an opportunity to warn him of what's coming. He believed he went to St. Luke's on merit. He thinks he's doing an acceptable job. Now, with only one day's warning, he finds himself snatched up and sent back to some country circuit; he sees Clarence take over St. Luke's, and he discovers that Clarence swapped sides at the last hour of a tough political fight and brought you three other men with him." The mask was beginning to break up. Jack knew that the man was shaken to hear in words the very thoughts he had somehow crowded out of his own awareness. "And if Edgar actually were too good-natured to interpret these facts, Blanche is sure to tell him you sold him out for four votes in an annual conference of almost five hundred members!"

For the first time in his long association with this man, Jack saw the bland, impenetrable shell of self-justification smashed, saw the genuine person emerge naked and perplexed. Even the voice was different.

"But I cannot *make* those laymen take Edgar back! The whole situation is beyond my control. What can I do?"

It was almost as if they were friends again and talking over an interesting problem. Jack pointed to the phone.

"Call Clarence! Tell him you've changed your mind. That way you may still have to move Edgar, but at least he won't imagine you sold him out."

Jack found the situation ironic. For the actual fact was that the man did not need those four votes, yet his haggard face and tormented eyes betrayed that he needed them just the same—even if only in some blind, obscure fashion that no sane man could fathom.

"But, that's unthinkable! I've given Clarence my word."

This was something Jack had overlooked.

"Then your choice is between two evils, isn't it, sir? To break your word would destroy something for which you have been respected for thirty years." Jack tried to rally his weary mind. "But losing this church is going to break Edgar forever. Why add to his bitterness the suspicion that you sold out your oldest and most loyal supporter for four votes in a battle already won?"

"It's not that simple. Clarence is . . . is almost *obsessed* by the idea of paying Edgar back for this imaginary wrong. If he is denied St. Luke's now, no man could say what he might be capable of."

"Then why did you make him such an offer?!" Jack felt new outrage that, just when Motherly had begun turning at last toward courage and self-respect, he should have been tempted with the one bait able to inflame the worst that was in him.

"I felt it was necessary and justifiable. And it never occurred to me that once your group had broken ranks you would still refuse to shake hands and let the church's wounds be healed."

It was the same old pattern: a moral goal, an immoral method reluctantly adopted, an unexpected emergence of still deeper evil, then still more complicated excuses.

Throughout their argument Jack had been increasingly impressed with the older man's obvious exhaustion and also with his iron self-discipline. Jack kept wanting to end the cruel encounter and was dismayed to find that something in his own mind or emotions would not permit it. He heard himself snap:

"You bought yourself a Judas. Now live with him!"

The mask was flung aside now and forgotten. The man pressed his palms over his eyes, ran his trembling fingers down his face, then clasped them between his knees. He spoke slowly and as if to himself alone.

"Through *me* God has built churches, put missionaries in the field, moved literally thousands of entire congregations and communities a step nearer Christ. Despite all the methods idealists delight so to condemn, he has used me more fruitfully than even a man like William Pierce Whitley. With a united delegation behind me at jurisdictional conference this summer, I could almost certainly attain to the episcopacy, and then these same ideas and programs would benefit the world outreach of the entire church." This was the first time Jack had ever heard him refer directly to his ambition to become a bishop. "But now they tell me I do wrong to seek this wider field of service. And why? Because I might cause a *misunderstanding* in the mind of a big, simple-hearted farm boy whose influence will never reach beyond the bounds of a country circuit!"

Jack stared at him coldly and said at last:

"Dr. Worthington, I have fought your views and methods, but at no time have I questioned the sincerity of your claim to be seeking only the ultimate best interests of the church. Edgar was your first defender; in a sense it was he who first set your feet on the road to the episcopacy. He remained faithful almost for a lifetime with no visible reward. And if you can permit him to imagine that you sold him out to the worst bootlicker in the conference to guarantee a security you already possess, to nail down an outcome already as certain as death, if you can do this, sir, I shall be forced to conclude that personal ambition has totally corrupted your sincerity and your humanity!"

The older man stared at him in bland contempt, then shrugged, got up, and walked away. Jack yelled after him:

"And so will your friends!"

He stood staring out the window at the lighted city, hands folded behind him, and shrugged again.

"And so will Patricia!"

This time he did not move. Then he turned slowly, walked back to the chair opposite Jack, and sank down with head bowed, hands clenched between his knees.

"I *do* need those four votes!"

Jack's original outrage was now confused by irony and compassion. To persuade the man that he did not need those few votes was to give him a weapon, but Jack could not help himself.

"Sir, you *must* know that Bill Whitley ended our last chance when he walked out of that caucus tonight. I concede you the victory. It's all over. You've *won*."

"No! I cannot take that chance! No contest is ever won till the last ballot is counted. Who knows what might come from outraging a man in Motherly's state of mind? Or from that crazy trick you played on Whitley? That's the sort of thing that turns whole conferences upside down overnight."

A subtle change came over him. His eyes sought Jack's.

"But there is *one* other possibility . . . one way through which I actually would not need those votes."

"There's no other possibility!" Jack snapped. "Call Clarence and tell him St. Luke's is the one church in the whole conference you could never give him now."

"But it's the one church he insists on! No, that's hopeless. Edgar's salvation lies in your hands."

"In *my* hands!"

"If you would actually concede."

"Sir, I *have!*"

"Then call off your men. Tell them to vote for whomever they please tomorrow. Release them."

The man was obsessed! What was it about the rebel group that still had power to disturb him? Was it simply their continued existence? Their refusal to bow to his sovereign will? Jack slowly and silently shook his head.

"I'll give you Trinity."

"Sir, you couldn't give me Trinity if you wanted to."

"I'll give you Trinity." The round, pale face was quite composed.

Jack felt he would be confessing madness himself to discuss the subject, but he was goaded now by a sudden morbid curiosity to explore the full depths of this fantastic mind and will.

"Sir, do you seriously contend that you could force a green youngster like me on the fourth-largest church in the conference? You couldn't make those wealthy laymen accept Dr. Whitley himself unless they'd asked for him!"

"They'll ask for you."

"They don't even know I exist."

The round blue eyes were confident again; apparently he had no idea why Jack seemed willing to discuss it.

"They know all about you! I've been discussing you with them for over a year." Jack sank back in his chair. It was a fact that great churches sometimes called complete unknowns and were almost indifferent to the ordinary laws of seniority and prestige. . . . "You would have a tremendous field of service for Christ and the church. *From* Trinity you could go to any pulpit in Methodism. Nobody will blame you in the least for conceding. Even those who disagree with you have admired your courage and would rejoice to see you have such an opportunity."

Jack shook his head, almost afraid to speak for fear this mild, round little man would use the words to entangle him further. For the logic was unanswerable. . . .

"Then I take it that you are content simply to go through life being applauded and admired, while accomplishing nothing that will stand when you are gone. Can't you see how empty that sort of victory is? For some ministers spiritual admiration seems sufficient for every need. But I concluded long ago that it's a narcotic, both to him who offers it and him who accepts it, and that it is something a mature and objective person must be able to relinquish.

"Surely this week of annual conference must have demonstrated to you with mathematical certainty which of us has been right during the past four years! You seem not to have realized that to admire a young

Daniel and to wish him every success is one thing. But to climb down silently into the lion's den with him is something entirely different. The less a man feels like a hero himself, the more enthusiastically he eggs you on to do all the things he wishes he could do. Thus far you have reached a peak strength of twenty-two votes out of almost five hundred. Doesn't that indicate to you any fallacy whatever in your generous estimate of human nature?"

He studied Jack for a moment in silence, and the bland pink face looked almost wistful in its entreaty.

"Belovèd, I must confess that I have always looked upon you with mixed emotions. You are the only young man Patricia ever seemed deeply attached to, and I think she may yet feel quite a real affection for you. Everything could still be changed, could be as it once was with all of us. . . . My own conscience is clear. Heaven only knows how hard I have tried to teach you what the church is like, sending you places you had no right to be! Showing you men under pressures that exposed everything in them! Trying to draw you out of your dream world. How often I have thought, 'If only he could rise to the courage *not* to be admired! If only he were daring enough to forget his own integrity and to seize hold of the ugly clay of ordinary humanity and mold it into things that are solid and lasting!'

"It is not yet too late to gain back everything you have lost! You have already gone far beyond all that conscience and courage require. But I challenge you now to go yet one step further: cast in your lot with me again. It would surprise no one if you were tapped by a great church for a great career. And after all, what is your alternative?"

Jack tried to find his way through the closely woven meshes of logic and morality, but could not. He tried to force down the images that kept floating up—images of that glittering congregation at Trinity on a Sunday morning. He wanted to jump up and flee before the images became overwhelming. He shook his head again.

"Your alternative is to do with your own life what Wes Phillips has done with his. Waste it. He has benefited neither God nor man—only his own private sense of integrity. And now you seem determined to seek the same tragic end."

Jack was now gripped by a desire to goad him on to whatever last extremities he might conceive.

"Very true," he said.

"Then why frustrate God's will for your own life, too? Accept Trinity. Do something with your talents!"

Jack shook his head.

"I trust that you are aware you may be choosing this fate not just for yourself, but for nineteen other men and their wives and children."

Shelton must have learned of Burl Avery's signature. . . . With that, and without Motherly's group, the rebels had nineteen men left. This was the most agonizing problem of all. The mild, persistent voice was going to make him yield at last.

"Your group has demonstrated impressive discipline against hopeless odds. But now your ranks are broken, and in tomorrow's balloting your bloc will be indistinguishable from a dozen other odd and accidental groups of votes. So you no longer have anything to gain; you simply destroy yourself and these brave men with you."

Jack nodded dumbly.

"Then for the sake of the church we both love, give up! You are only deepening the wounds and widening the chasms in our Christian fellowship. Give us a unified conference now that the battle is over!"

All true. All impossible to refute.

"Why destroy your own future usefulness? Who will follow you next time if you brand yourself tomorrow morning as a self-seeking martyr? Don't be like Clarence—blind, obsessed!"

Irrefutable. Every word of it. Again he nodded but refused to speak, assenting with his mind but not his will. The soft plump hands were clenched; the persistent voice probed with increasing swiftness for the victory so close at hand.

"Then why punish men with families just because you have none? Release them now and there will be no reprisals. You have my word! Don't deny them the churches where God can use them best, the committee chairmanships, the board jobs, the conference-level opportunities for service and usefulness. They put themselves in your hands because they believed you were a rational being who could face facts. They did not join you to be admired as martyrs or to commit professional suicide but to accomplish something you led them to believe could be accomplished. You yourself now assure me that it cannot be done! How can you explain even to yourself why you feel compelled to drag down with you all these other men and their wives and their children? Has God given you the right to choose martyrdom for others?"

Jack felt hopelessly trapped. He knew he must look ridiculous, slumped in this chair like an obstinate schoolboy. But he only clenched his teeth and stared back in silence.

"Don't make me do these things to men like Adams and Dirkwell—and young Perriman!" He was certainly pulling out all the stops. Suddenly the voice became softer, more deadly:

"And to yourself."

Somehow Jack had known almost from the first word that it would come to this. This was part of the deadly fascination that had urged him on. He straightened and leaned forward, giddy with exhaustion.

"And what will my appointment be, sir?"

Even prepared as he was, even knowing what answer he would receive, the word fell on the air with a chilling shock:

"Foxull."

He slumped back. He knew from the sudden, naked anger in those probing eyes that this was the last weapon and that the other man bitterly resented being forced to use something so ugly, so intimate, so contrary to all traditional practices of the church.

Suddenly something in his own posture recalled a thing from the dim past. A year ago he would have resented the scene's recurrence in any form, for it had never fitted sensibly into that other complex of thoughts he had built up about his father. But now he felt a sudden painful tenderness, a compassionate understanding of that strange man who had also come one day to the end of his own opportunities, to the waste of his talents, the frustration of his dreams . . . that broken man who had grasped at the seeming warmth of a glossy, strengthless love to wrap about his heart and shield its shivering wounds from his own beholding.

But one scene, shining and untarnished, had never fitted those other scenes of tawdriness and shame.

He saw his father again, sitting in the kitchen, the mill's ledgers spread open on the table beside him. And over him towered the vast bulk of Gramps with his bristly white head and fierce black brows. Jack could hear his father's voice sinking lower and lower as he struggled in these same entangling coils, as he mused on how the enemy turned even your own conscience against you and proved that the only right thing was to do wrong.

Deliberately, with an almost impish malice, Jack slumped still further down in the chair and let his hands trail limply on the floor the way his father's had, let his voice sink to a mimicry of his father's as he answered at last:

"I *still* won't do it."

The blue eyes stared fixedly into his for a long moment, as if unable to believe what they saw, then blinked, wavered, and at last the stiffly erect figure sagged. The older man pushed himself up wearily and walked slowly up and down the room several times. His voice was soft, meditative.

"Thirty years ago I stood alone against the world, and Edgar came and stood beside me. Now, he stands between me and the episcopacy. I simply cannot take the chance of enraging Clarence now! And four years from now it will be too late."

Jack raised his head at last and turned about. The superintendent was standing by the window staring out over the pulsing, changing radiance of the city under the night sky—but clearly not seeing it. His fist was clenched in the drapes by his shoulder; the muscles in his cheek stood out in hard knots. Jack felt the same pity tempered by amusement with which he might have watched a sleeper struggle and twist against the seeming terrors of a dream. For the man was obviously tormented by the farfetched possibility that his lack of Motherly's four votes and his inability to destroy an ineffectual handful of rebels could somehow fatally influence the balloting tomorrow.

Did he see, beyond the glittering pulse of the night, images of a dim and buried childhood, even as Jack had seen Gramps and his father? For, with all the light of their learning, Jack realized that he and his enemy were both children of darkness. They were products and victims of buried worlds out of which their adult personalities had only partially emerged, like statues half-chiseled from the shapeless rock that still imprisoned even while it upheld. Was this strange man staring up even now from a child's cot at an aunt who had just kissed her own children goodnight and now turned away, taking the light with her— and his kiss? Or did he see from a separate little table in the kitchen that family table of laughter and fellowship, of children who had a last name, where even a frown or a slap on the wrist would have been treasured as a badge of belonging? Even the voice, curiously precise, reflected the desperate struggle to disentangle facts from the handless grip of the darkness within:

"I do sincerely believe that God has blessed me with unmerited gifts of leadership and administration. I believe it was His hand that guided me through nameless streets in the dead of winter to seek shelter by the chimney of a Methodist parsonage. I believe it was He who arranged that I should grow up in a Methodist institution and learn all its problems with such intimacy. I believe it was He who called me into the ministry of His church, who tempered me through suffering and bereavement, who broadened me through experiences at the grass roots where the bulk of men live and the vast majority of our ministers serve out their days." The hand knotted harder in the drapes; the voice acquired a despairing finality. "I do believe it is His sovereign will that these gifts and graces find their fulfillment at the highest level of the church's life!"

He stood absolutely motionless for a long moment, as if reading back a transcript of his own statement, weighing it, evaluating its progress and conclusion. But when the decision came at last, it was as simple and final as the click of a lock.

He sighed once, let go the drape, glanced at his watch, and turned toward the room.

"It's no use," he said. "I can't do this to Edgar." His tone was so matter-of-fact as to sound almost indifferent. "I'll have to take the chance."

He strode swiftly across to the phone, his voice now clear and pleasant as always, once he had settled on a course of action.

"Operator? Room 1083, please . . . Clarence? Fred Worthington. I'm terribly sorry to trouble you at this hour, but I'm afraid something has come up which we had not anticipated. No, no, please don't bother; I'm still dressed; I'll come right down."

He buttoned his cuffs, then turned toward the mirror, ignoring Jack, and began tying his tie. Jack stared for a moment with pity and with admiration, then walked unsteadily out into the hall and pulled the door shut behind him.

XXXI

The Curtain

JACK walked wearily down the hall to the elevator, but he was suddenly aware that he did not want to be with anyone and, puzzled, he walked down to the offset at the end of the corridor and stood by the window staring down at the lights of the city. A strange, jealous exaltation filled him, wild and pure, and the image of his father floated before his imagination again, sitting by the kitchen table smoking that forbidden third cigar on the night Gramps had tried to persuade him to tamper with the books from Harlowe's Mill. And now he understood for the first time that fierce light in his father's eyes.

Jack realized that what he felt now was the exaltation of having been tested to his depths, of having faced not just the objective ambitions and desires of all men, and the actual fears they face, but also the private horror which lurks in some men as a kind of ultimate abyss they cannot bear to think on. But now, having surmounted that, too, he found himself on a lofty plateau whose attainment yielded a finality and absoluteness which made it different in kind from anything he had experienced before.

It was a reality beyond reason, beyond the explanations and arguments of morality and logic with which his antagonist had attempted to stay his upward climb. It was almost as if he had in him a primeval integrity, an irreducible "ought," which could never be wholly explained or permanently imprisoned in considerations of prudence or justice, but which existed in and for itself. His father had found his way to this lofty plateau and had lingered, treasuring its poignant brevity, knowing instinctively that this was a spot to which he might never find his way again in all the drab mazes of the after-years.

Jack heard a door open, and the sound of voices. It was Patricia, arguing something with her father. At last the voices ceased, but the spell which had enveloped him was broken, and Jack felt an unnerving sense of total exhaustion. The grueling contest was over. He could relax at last. But with this realization came a curious uneasiness. Had he been using this contest in a deliberate effort to prevent relaxation? To stave off any lowering of the bars of will through which something unthinkable might now burst forth? He stepped out from behind the offset, and to his astonishment saw Patricia still standing by the elevator doors. She started at his unexpected appearance.

"Congratulations!" she said. "You made him get up; you excited and upset him; you even maneuvered him into going out again tonight! I hope you're satisfied."

Jack stared at her, too bewildered to reply.

"You know father's had one coronary; you could tell he's on the brink of another—I saw it in your face the instant you caught sight of him. But I never *dreamed* you'd use something so ugly and dangerous."

"Patricia, what *are* you talking about?"

She was pale and trembling; her voice was almost incoherent; she kept knotting her hands in the lapels of her robe. He had never seen her in such a state.

"You're hoping he'll have another, aren't you? You're deliberately prolonging this fight beyond all sense and reason. You know now you're not the stuff big men are made of, that you're a nobody and always will be. But at least you can keep someone else from reaching the top!"

"Pat, surely you can't mean to imply—"

"You're goading him into a collapse, aren't you? Then you can go off to jurisdictional conference this summer, and buzz around in the back rooms and whisper to everyone that father would make a great bishop but, after all, you do happen to know he's had *two* coronaries!"

Jack was so outraged that he shook her.

"That's right," she said when he finally released her, "be violent! Why don't you strike me? You don't care any more about me than you do about . . . about Edgar and Blanche!" She tucked the lapels of her robe in again with shaking fingers. "I finally understood you tonight, Jack Lee, and I can't understand why it took me so long. You're completely wrapped up in yourself, just as father said from the beginning. You don't know or care what anyone else is thinking or suffering. You don't know how to love other people, only how to use them—as you used me, and father, and Wes, and all the men who follow you, and your own mother and father too. Love is what makes things live and grow—the way father loves the church. But everything you touch withers, the way I've withered and deadened in these past five years. But tonight I finally realized what was wrong with you—and with me—and I've finally begun to understand and appreciate Steadman and to recognize that his kind of love for me is real."

She paused, her lips compressed.

"It may interest you to know that Steadman and I are getting married at noon Sunday. He's been asking me, and I've just decided it's what we'll do. Which means in your terms, of course, that your political prestige and your personal standing will suffer."

He extended one hand toward her in protest.

"Patsy! I can't let you do this!"

"Father told me all about you *and* your family connections! But I just wouldn't take it seriously. You nearly killed a boy in a fight once, didn't you? And your mother's father killed a man, didn't he? No wonder your own parents are afraid of you! No wonder we couldn't *drag* your mother to the altar to stand by you when you were ordained. What is it they say in that little place you come from—a Blalock will kill you if you cross him? When I saw what you were doing to father tonight I finally knew what they meant."

He lunged at her clumsily. Something in the way she thrust herself at him, something in the way her voice kept hammering at him about killing was making Jack almost beside himself. He got one hand over her mouth and the other around her waist; she twisted furiously, and his hand brushed across the big, flat button at the waist of her robe. With a hoarse cry he let her go and stumbled backward against the wall, staring at the palm of his hand.

"Jack! What's the matter with you?"

He slowly raised his eyes from his palm, which had nothing in it—nothing at all! She was standing with her fingers pressed flat against her cheeks, her face white as chalk, her eyes wide. She hesitantly extended her hands and advanced on him as if to seize him or hold him up, and he backed away further, his teeth rattling. He felt his heel bump against the wall at the end of the corridor.

The curtain of amnesia was gone now, slashed into tattered streamers, ripped to shreds.

The thing behind it stood waiting.

And she was trying to *make* him look.

He could feel the icy sweat on his face, could hear the quivering hiss of his breath between his chattering teeth.

"Jack, are you ill?" She was beside him now. "Here, I'll open the window."

The stiff, sliding sound of the window seared every nerve in his body. He lunged wildly against her and slammed it down with all his force as she snatched her fingers out of the way.

"*Jack!*"

She was saying something, but he did not hear. He was staring through the mirrored glass down into the darkness and seeing at last, seeing what he had run from, what his amnesia had mercifully erased, seeing and struggling to convince himself that it was not actually there at all . . . that it was surely just the memory of a dream, the recollection of a nightmare that had somehow got all mixed up with wakefulness.

But it had not been a nightmare: It had actually taken place. For he had brought back that red button—!

Slowly, with terrible intensity, as though by his very carefulness he could prevent the dream from bursting through to reality, he slid his left hand into the pocket of his coat. He smiled at Patricia, but the smile did not seem to reassure her. Her eyes widened and her upper lip wrinkled back in an odd expression.

Slowly, with indescribable carefulness, still smiling to reassure her, he pushed his fingertips downward toward the bottom of the pocket till they touched—

The cry was nerve-shattering.

It must have been his own cry, but the voice did not resemble his own at all: it was hoarse, masculine-feminine, so loud it filled all the long corridor and bounced and echoed horrifyingly. He felt his knees giving way; the ceiling began to swim and mist over; beyond her arm and shoulder as she tried to seize him, he saw doors opening along the hall and faces thrusting out, heard voices thronging the corridor again just as they had when everyone came crowding and pushing out to see—

Patricia's white face kept blurring and fading. Then it loomed very close.

"I'll call a doctor!"

He heard his own voice from somewhere, a lifeless mumble, as the mist lowered and darkened and mercifully enveloped him at last:

"It's too . . . late."

XXXII

The Healing Knife

IN HIS dream Jack was running down a gigantic funnel. The sides were painted black, with occasional cracks in the metal which let in thin slivers of yellow light. As the funnel narrowed, it reverberated more loudly with the roaring voices of the creatures pursuing him. Glancing over his shoulder, he could see the rows of white teeth gleaming in the darkness, the pools of green fire that were their eyes. He kept expecting the tunnel about him to open suddenly into spaciousness and sunlight and freedom, but it only grew more constricted with each labored step. The baying was all about him now, and his feet were entangled in a rubbery glue, so that each movement took an eternity. He could feel the pulsation of their hot, fetid breathing, could hear the click and snap of the grinning teeth. His lungs were bursting, his arms weighted by the dark waters. He kicked and struggled upward against the dark delirium of sleep and finally burst through the surface into consciousness and light, panting and sobbing from exhaustion.

He lay for a moment staring at the ceiling. He was in his own bed, in the room he and Wes shared at the Middleton Hotel. Wes was sprawled in the easy chair, the lamp still on, his book on the floor beside him. Someone had removed Jack's watch and placed it on the night table at his head. It was almost two o'clock; outside the sky was dark and starless.

His mind worked foggily backward, and he drew a shuddering breath and flung his arm over his eyes. Everything came back now, stark and photographic in its merciless clarity. He was in Thelma's apartment and she had sunk to the floor at his feet. . . .

She had come to Middleton. She had come to Belfair Church. After all their arguments! After he had been so certain she had gotten the message he kept trying to make plain without actually having to be brutally direct. In January, after that terrible Christmas Eve when Paulo had nearly trapped him in her apartment, he could deny her nothing. She had had her teeth fixed by then, but the left side of her face still had that thickness and her left eye had never completely cleared up. Paulo and Pietro and Bart had beaten her horribly, but somehow her suffering for Jack seemed only to have intensified her love, and the sight of that discolored eye shining with such ecstatic adoration had been almost more than he could bear. In their subsequent meetings, when her appearance had returned nearly to normal, he began trying to communicate to her somehow that the whole thing was impractical, unworkable, unthinkable. Now he realized that nothing he said had even registered.

And so, on Monday morning on the first day of this conference week, she had come to Middleton from New York, and was getting out of a taxi in front of Belfair Methodist Church when Jack recognized her as he stepped off the curb across the intersection. It was surprising that he *did* recognize her: she was wearing a black satin dress with a black hat, white gloves, and black pumps; and when he reached her and bundled her back into the cab, he saw that what he had thought to be a small white purse was a New Testament, and that she was even wearing a crucifix at her throat.

How had he ever gotten her back to New York? He remembered that hideous, trapped feeling as he told the cabbie to take them to Barry's, a small café across town. He remembered the ghastly sensation of smiling and chatting with her, while his mind worked frantically, desperate for some way to get her back on a train for New York. The task actually proved less difficult than he had expected. But it did not dawn on him till later that she had actually not quite believed all her own daydreams till he had smiled and seemed pleased by her arrival. Part of her liveliness and chatter, he realized later, was relief. And her relief was so great that she thought everything he said quite logical and fell in with everything he planned.

He did not need to inquire why she had come any more than he needed to ask what a billboard was advertising. It leaped at you in every detail of her getup, it stuck out in her conversation at every point, from "Gee—my first annual conference!" to the almost hysterically funny, "I wonder where the bishop will send us?" While he was paying the cashier at Barry's after breakfast, she even managed to stand almost touching him while she sucked her toothpick and held her New Testament conspicuously high. It was all mad, hysterical, and unbelievable, and it had happened at the worst of all possible times and places.

There had been no cars at Belfair at that hour, and Jack was unaware that Dirkwell had seen them as she stepped out of her cab. Jack told her that they were much too early for conference, that he had been wanting to buy her something in New York, and that they should spend the day in the city and then come back to Middleton tomorrow, or even on Wednesday, for the opening session.

In New York, as soon as their train got in, he had planned to take her straight to her apartment where they could have it out once and for all. Regardless of his own career, Jack could not allow her to destroy all the other careers now involved with his. That settled the moral issue. Had he acted then as he planned, everything might have happened differently. But instead he waited till they were both so tired. For he kept losing his nerve, and first they window-shopped, and then they bought a bright red jacket she took a fancy to, and then they saw a movie, and then they ate something; and by the time they emerged from the subway entrance before her apartment, it was terribly late.

And then, most fantastic and terrible of all, desire had overwhelmed him, for he had not seen her for almost a month. Or perhaps he allowed it to overwhelm him as yet one more way to postpone telling her. For when the elevator stopped at the twelfth floor and the doors clanged back and they were walking down the hall the few steps to her room, he felt the familiar, sick longing. Inside, he turned from hooking the night-chain and she was in his arms.

He remembered realizing that this was his opportunity to dramatize what words could not get through: he would push her aside, roughly! He would say the words quickly and irrevocably. It would be a kind of surgery: the knife that seemed to be slaying would actually be bringing her ultimate healing and peace. But then she was pulling his head down and kissing him on the lips, and when they parted, she said softly:

"I'll bathe first. Then you."

When he came out after his bath, she was curled up on the bed with his evening paper, reading the funnies. She had on a new gown unlike any she had worn before. It was all white, with an Empire waist and very full skirt that fell into long, Grecian folds at her bare feet when she got up. He remembered thinking what a grotesque combination she was—a buxom Greek goddess with corn-plasters.

"We shouldn't have walked so much," she said. "My feet are killing me. But the funny thing is, I'm not tired a bit. I feel like a million bucks —even with my corns aching! Ain't that funny?" Jack nodded without speaking and sank down on the bed. "Like my gown? I got to thinking: how could I hang out some of those others on the line at a parsonage? Wow!" She studied him a moment. "You look awful tired. I'll tell you what, you rest a while and I'll dance for you."

She snapped on the record player and rummaged among the records. "Know what? I believe it's knowing somebody loves you." She selected a record but did not put it on. "Not just in bed and like that, but knowing they want to marry you and be with you all the time and have their friends meet you. That kind of love." She paused. "Ever since I knew we'd get married, I've felt different—just like I used to when I was a little girl, before Daddy went away. You know—running and jumping and yelling and all excited inside like something wonderful was always just about to happen. Even when Paulo was beating me, I felt that way! I mean it didn't hurt, even when Pietro and Bart came and they all three beat me. It was almost like I liked it, because I knew it was to help you." The brown, puffy-lidded eyes turned on him, almost shyly. "But I can't say things in words, like you can. I'll just dance!"

Jack had acknowledged to himself long ago that she actually was rather stiff and awkward, that her eyes did stare and blink, that her mouth was sulky and inexpressive. But now the inner tensions that generated these outer effects had been dissolved.

Perhaps the barrier of language had also dissolved, and in sudden freedom from the constriction of her limited vocabulary of flat and inelegant words, Thelma found an opportunity to express the subtle shadings, the overpowering glory, the life-giving radiance of her love. Her lips curled upward in a smile of ineffable bliss, her marvelous skin seemed more lucid and dazzling than he had ever seen it, her eyes grew languid and dreamy-lidded, and the thick auburn hair bounced and swirled about her cheeks and shoulders as she danced. Her bare arms flashed softly in the dimness and her whole body seemed lifted and swept about by the music, like a pale autumn leaf swirling on dark waters. She seemed possessed and transfigured by a power not herself.

When the music had ended, she stood motionless in the gloom for several minutes, breathing deeply, apparently still caught up in her own thoughts and feelings. Then she padded across the carpet to the bed. . . .

Afterwards, they dressed and walked down the street to a little snack stand. The apartment seemed stuffy on their return. Jack raised the window by the bed, noticed the light in the corridor window across the angle of the offset, and pulled down the flimsy paper shade. Thelma dropped her red jacket across the chair by the door. Then she noticed that Jack was making no move to undress.

"We better hop in," she said, unbuttoning the top button of her blouse. "We got to get up early."

"Thelma," said Jack, his eyes avoiding hers and his voice sounding hollow and unreal, "I'm going back tonight. Now."

"Now? It's almost twelve o'clock! I don't want to go back at this hour. Let's wait, like we planned."

"We're not going as we planned. I've decided to go back alone."

"But, when do you want me to come?"

Her face was only irritated, not uneasy. He saw that it was going to be even more difficult than he had feared.

"Thelma, let's sit down. We're long overdue for an understanding. We might as well have it tonight and get it over with. Now, it is true that the night Paulo came here I said we might get married sometime—"

As he talked he saw that his words were bouncing harmlessly off the impenetrable armor of her dreams, sliding past the onrushing velocity of her own plans and ideas without leaving a scratch. Jack had begun in shrinking terror of wounding her. Now he began to wonder whether he could make a single mark on the tough glaze of her mind.

He was aware that they were both talking much too loudly, but it seemed necessary to shout now and then to break through her idiotic repetition that he had "promised" and he was a "man of God" and she could not believe a "man of God would ever go back on a promise."

"Yes! Yes, I *am* a man of God!" he finally burst out. "And that's exactly the problem. A man of God cannot marry just because he *wants* to. He has to marry someone with the background and training for his kind of life. Surely you can understand that all I am saying is only for *your* happiness, as well as for the sake of my work! You'd be miserable as a pastor's wife. You know how you hated every minute you lived in Wentworth—small towns, prying eyes, gossipy neighbors. I could never forgive myself if I let you in for something like that, no matter how much I personally might want us to marry. And if you were unhappy, I'd be unhappy too, and you can imagine how difficult it would all be for everyone."

"But a man of God won't just promise a person to marry her and then go back on his word."

The stupid, puffy-lidded, owlish eyes blinked at him uncomprehend-ingly. The sulky mouth was unyielding.

"Of course a man of God would never renege on a promise!" Jack knew that renege was too difficult a word for her and he deliberately passed up the search for a simpler one. "But for the sake of my work, my calling, I am compelled to ask you to release me from that promise. Surely you see we both have a higher duty here than our own personal happiness!"

"I can learn how to be a minister's wife." She nervously buttoned and unbuttoned the top of her blouse and he saw that her stubby fingers trembled slightly, but her voice was firm. "I know I didn't train for it or anything, but that's not my fault. You got me into it. Now you say I've got to just go back like I was. What can I go back to? Rick was all I ever had; and when he was killed in the war, I had to come back here. But I don't have nothing or nobody here. Just three rooms! I don't make friends easy, like some girls, and men don't think I'm good-looking. You do, and Rick did, but not anybody else. They all act like I was too dumb or something, and at school they always teased me and called me ugly names. It never did bother me when Daddy was home because he always said they was just jealous, that's all. But then he went away, and I was always kinda scared inside ever since, and I couldn't think of anything to say, till Rick came along. Then Rick went away and I made up my mind I wasn't going to be a crybaby the rest of my life because I could always remember how he thought I was pretty and everything, and I could think about my wedding and how everybody liked my dress." Her eyes filled with tears, and she rubbed them away, pushing the backs of her bent wrists against her eyes like a small child. "Then . . . you came along. I didn't ask you to. You can't just get a person thinking she can be happy all over again, and then go back on your promise. Nobody could be that mean to a person."

"Thelma, I am *not* being mean! I'm trying to *help* you. Can't you see that? We've had lots of fun; you'll have lots of beautiful and happy things to remember, and someday you'll find someone else. But my con-science won't let me get you involved in a marriage that could only bring unhappiness to us both."

"You always talk about your conscious. But how can a man of God promise a person to make her happy and then not do it?"

Jack had meant to be sensible and detached about it all, but, as al-ways, she dragged him down with her into a whirlpool of muddy emotions. He had hoped he could handle everything cleanly, surgically; but the scalpel turned into a bludgeon before he was aware of it. He jumped up, snatched up a handful of her pop records and thrust them into her face.

"Look! Read these titles! Do you know what this is? Trash, trash, trash! Do you honestly imagine you can play these in a Methodist parsonage?" He slammed them to the floor and ground his heel into them. He grabbed the magazine from the night stand, rattling its pages furiously before her. "Look at this cover! Look—look at the way she's dressed! Read these words!"

Thelma gazed stupidly at the shaking pages, pale but uncomprehending. Jack flung himself into a chair, making a supreme effort to control his temper.

"Thelma," he said in a low voice, "think just a minute: We don't like the same kind of music. We don't read the same kind of magazines or books. We don't enjoy the same movies—no, no, we don't. I sat through them for your sake; but sometimes I was so bored, I could have wept. We don't feel the same way about money. We can't agree about the kind of clothes you wear, or how you keep house, or even what length of time is reasonable for a conversation on the phone! We have no friends in common. We enjoy making love, and you're beautiful and sweet to me, but besides that we have nothing! I confess that plenty of times I have left early not because I had to catch my train, but just because we had nothing to say to each other. I used to go by the public library—or take in a movie that *I* wanted to see."

"I know," said Thelma, avoiding his eyes. "I used to follow you at first, to find out. But you just went to the library."

Jack stared at her. The picture of Thelma following him as he strolled along killing time, after having told her he had to rush for a train, humiliated him intensely. That she should know he had been lying was upsetting enough. But somehow the fact that she had never revealed this, had never made a scene about it, was even more unnerving.

"Well!" he burst out, "then certainly I shouldn't have to tell you what you already know—that we don't like the same things and have no foundation whatever for marriage."

Thelma did not answer. She sat with head bowed, tears running down her pale cheeks, her hands clenched tightly in her lap. Jack felt desperate, stunned by the knowledge that she already knew all the things he had imagined would work a revolution in her thinking. It was terribly late. They were both exhausted. He felt hot and stifled, but refused to take off his coat. To do so would be an admission that he might stay. Finally she got to her feet.

"Maybe we're both just tired out," she said. "You go on back tonight if that's what you want. I'll come tomorrow."

That did it.

Jack had restrained himself all evening from touching on the actual basis of their relationship—their love. He had hoped to settle everything without hurting her there. Now he saw that not a single argument had penetrated her for the simple reason that she believed in their love. Love would find a way!

The words "I'll come tomorrow" shattered the last remnants of his reason and self-control. At the prospect of having to live over again all the nightmarish experiences of this fantastic day he jumped up and seized her violently by the shoulders and thrust his face into hers.

"Have you any idea what you nearly did this morning? Has your stupid, stubborn little brain any faintest notion of how many men's careers and families you endangered? It's not just me you're trying to destroy, it's the church! Can you grasp what my enemies would do with a scandal? With a young widow who turns up at conference at eight o'clock in the morning in a black satin dress!"

The hatred that had smouldered so long, the hatred he had at first not even admitted to himself, suddenly blazed through in the ungovernable fury that he knew burned in his eyes and contorted his features. He shook her frenziedly and flung her back against the wall, his chest heaving, his whole body shaking.

Her face was white, her eyes enormous. At the time he thought it was from terror of physical violence, but later he knew it was from fear of the meaning in his words and appearance. Her voice was small and choked.

"But . . . you acted happy when I came!"

"So help me God, if you come back to that conference again—if you ever in your life come near me again—" He had not meant to say this, but it burst forth, impelled by utter desperation to penetrate at last that dark and stubborn mind, "I refuse to be responsible for what happens to you!"

Now, at last, he saw a change. Now, at last, the message he had been trying to convey so long had got home. She read it plainly in his voice, compressed to a velvet intensity by his hatred. She read it in the violence of his hands, in the naked communication of their eyes. They had always enjoyed a kind of psychic communion about odd and inconsequential things, but their rapport had never previously applied to his true feelings toward her. Now they stood locked in a kind of iron communion, hypnotized, paralyzed by the final clarity that enveloped them both.

Thelma sank very slowly, still pressing herself back hard against the wall as she had when his words and gestures slammed her against it. The material of her blouse and skirt made a sliding sound as she sank in the abrupt silence, and her eyes did not leave his till she had slumped, half-sitting, at his feet. Then she blinked once, and her distended eyes wandered from his face about the room, and finally came to rest on the shattered records about his feet. She reached out with one hand and picked up part of one, then retrieved the other fragment with her other hand, and sat gazing down, trying to fit the two pieces together. Finally she laid the pieces down side by side on the floor between them, her stubby fingers tremulous and uncertain.

Jack felt a kind of awe as he watched her get to her feet, stiffly and clumsily, bracing one palm on the corner of the chair beside her, and then gripping her thigh, as if she were suddenly a feeble old woman. He dared not let himself begin thinking again, now that it was over, and he felt almost afraid to breathe. She stood before him, not lifting her face but turning it away, and she picked up her red jacket from the chair and put it on, still with the same feeble, awkward movements. He started once to reach out a hand to help her, but she moved away very slightly, keeping her back to the wall.

"You don't have to be afraid," she said in an unexpectedly clear, low voice. "I won't bother you no more."

She turned away, still not looking at him, and pulled the hall door shut firmly and softly behind her. After a moment Jack heard the elevator cables hum, the doors clang open, and he sank down trembling on the bed and buried his face in his hands.

He had not wanted it to end this way, but she had compelled him. He had not wanted, and had certainly never planned, that she should ever see his burning hatred. He felt almost too weak to sit up, and he stretched out on the bed, dazed and appalled, but knowing he had done the only thing right and possible. She was terribly hurt now, but she had been terribly hurt when she lost Rick, even to the point of trying to—

Jack turned his head and saw on Thelma's night table among the litter of small objects her bottle of sleeping pills. He sat up, not of his own volition but pulled upright by a sudden convergence of impressions not fully interpreted till that instant. Now they canceled all his thoughts, paralyzed all his emotions with sudden horror, struck through him as though an iron pen had drawn three sharp, swift lines across his heart—all crossing it at a single point: the strange tone in which she had said, "I won't bother you no more"; the realization that he had never heard the elevator go down; the remembrance of a sound—the soft, stiff sound of a window being opened.

Jack landed on his feet beside the bed and, all in the same movement, ripped aside the flimsy paper shade.

Not five feet away he saw Thelma in her bright red jacket, head bowed, shoulders hunched and trembling, sitting on the outer ledge of the corridor window with her legs hanging down into space.

XXXIII

The Ebb of the Tide

Now, reliving in memory those terrible moments, Jack asked himself why he had not done something prompt and practical that would have saved her. He realized, now, that she had not even heard the noise of the shade, so preoccupied had she been with working up her courage, with overcoming her shuddering terror. He could have run swiftly and silently out of the room and down the corridor and seized her in time before she knew he was there.

But how much time had there been? She seemed to hang there for an eternity, but was the whole time actually more than a single instant? He tried to remember how many times the neon sign across the boulevard cast its lurid glow over her face and then withdrew. Once? Twice? He could not remember.

But the most agonizing problem of all was why he had not shouted or spoken. Was it really because he was paralyzed by fear of startling her as she sat so far forward, the whole weight of her body seemingly supported only by her palms on the sooty brickwork, only by her shaking arms? Her very trembling seemed capable of causing her to slip that last inch forward, of making her lose her grip. Was it really because his mind had been stunned by that horrifying vision, as his eyes followed hers down the side of that frightful cliff to the small dark square of the iron grating bordered by its pale curbing? Was it really because his will had been transfixed between two contrary pulls—the desire to lean far out and try to push her back, when he knew quite well she was beyond his reach, and the desire to run for the door and the corridor and seize her?

Or did he hesitate, did he *let* himself be paralyzed by all these things, because somewhere in the darkness of his being there existed—and had existed for months—a single grain of desire that something beyond his own control might remove her from his world forever? And had that single grain, alone and unacknowledged in its hidden darkness, tipped the scales of his will just enough to keep the beam suspended that fatal fraction of a second that might have made the difference?

But would it have made any difference? Would anything have caused it to end differently? These were questions he could not answer, for he could not know afterwards how much time it had all taken, and what his actual motives and intentions had been before the shattering illumination of that moment had brought a drastic re-evaluation of all of life and all of himself.

He found himself in the position of a man whose perspectives on himself and whose interpretations of his own activities had undergone such total transformation that he was unable to remember clearly what he honestly thought of himself before. Did some part of him want her to fall? Or did he only imagine now that he was then capable of that wanting? Did he deliberately allow terror and indecision to paralyze him, or did the judgment of his later self insist on this hostile interpretation because its loathing distorted all vision of things past?

And, overshadowing all, pervading all, was the clear recollection that he had wavered in his conviction that the event was even happening at all. As he stared across the angle between the windows into her downcast face, he felt that he was gazing upon something inconceivable, impossible, in violation of all the laws of being. This was simply not happening! It *could* not be happening. He was witnessing a dream event in the empty, silent world of sleep, and in another instant—as in all his nightmares of the past—the gleaming sphere of sleep would burst and all the inhabitants and emotions of that eerie universe be traceless phantoms.

Her bottom lip was trembling; he could see the tears welling up in her dark eyes; she kept gripping her bottom lip in her teeth and shivering. Jack could feel, as if it were a physical presence, the awesome tug of the void below her feet, like a dark transparent being enveloping her body and will in horrifying tentacles, pulling, pulling, pulling . . . till it seemed utterly impossible that her shaking arms and uncertain palms could longer sustain that fearful weight.

Suddenly she gave a single, almost inaudible sob, and straightened slightly and leaned a little back from the perilous angle, closing her eyes and turning her face away from the pull.

She had lost her nerve.

She was safe.

Jack felt a weakness and trembling replace the suspension of all thought and feeling. He swallowed hard, and blinked, gazing down at the silent street. A single pedestrian was walking rapidly down the sidewalk just below them, not looking up. Suddenly Jack's mind blazed with visions of the whole boulevard jammed with people, just as he had seen them in newspaper accounts of suicides. Police had cordoned off a narrow space below the window. Firemen were frantically raising a ladder. The street swarmed with newsmen, and their flash bulbs burst like blinding suns, and back in Wentworth people were getting up, going out into their yards for the morning paper, seeing his face bracketed with Thelma's under enormous headlines.

Jack glanced up and saw Thelma staring into his face.

How long had she been studying him? He could not now decide. How long did it all take—from the instant he flung up the shade? He did not know. He tried to remember how many steps the pedestrian had taken, the tiny feet blinking in and out under the shoulders and round grayness of the hat. He could not recall. He could only remember her eyes.

They seemed now almost a physical part of him so that when he closed his lids, they appeared as automatically as the sight of his own body when he awoke. And the most terrible part of it all was their hunger, their yearning, their agonized quest.

For she searched his face with an almost studious care, examining each detail as though something she sought might be hidden away in the shape of his mouth, or the line of his jaw or brow. The look of expectancy in her eyes was so sharp as to be painful to behold. Jack stared back, bewildered and unnerved by this strange examination, at first opening his mouth to tell her not to move, that he would come around and help her get safely in, but not speaking after all as her eyes went over his face and finally locked with his own.

For an interminable instant she stared straight into his eyes in the dim light of the street lamps far below, in the flare and shadow of the neon sign, in the faint glow cast by the light in the corridor, by the lamp behind him in her room.

Jack felt it.

He almost heard it.

It was as if a taut strand of thread held close to his ear had snapped. He saw it, as perceptibly as if someone had approached a machine vibrant and humming with warmth and power and had flicked a switch, leaving it in a single instant cold and dark and lifeless. It was the taut, dead snapping of the will to live.

Once, years before, Jack had been walking down a lonely stretch of beach, at the very edge, and suddenly an exceptionally large breaker had swept in toward shore, cresting high and full, then plunging with a soft hiss. Jack had withdrawn a few steps and watched the warm waters swirling toward his feet, obliterating the sand with a glorious, rippling sheen, sparkling and instinct with a myriad iridescent life. Then, as suddenly, the waters were gone. But they did not withdraw. They simply vanished in the dry, white, glistening sand at his feet, draining away and taking with them their own life and that of the sand, and leaving behind a gray waste and deadness.

Now, as Jack watched, he seemed to see that water again, and to see the life ebb from Thelma's eyes, leaving them dead and expressionless. He saw it drain away from her cheeks and lips, so that they ceased trembling, and from her shoulders and arms so that they no longer shook. He thought at first that she had simply bowed her head, but then he realized that her whole body was bending forward as, slowly, and turning slightly away from him, she crossed her forearms over her face, and leaned out into space.

Jack screamed at the top of his lungs as he lunged for her, holding onto one of the radiator pipes by the window and stretching out so far that he nearly fell. The fingers of his left hand grazed the material of her jacket as it fell open, clawed wildly, felt something snap. Then, hanging far out over the window ledge with his right hand still gripping the pipe, his left clenched in space, he watched in wild disbelief.

For she did not fall.

She did not even float down.

She *inched* down with incredible slowness, as though being lowered with painstaking care and slowness on ropes of air! Jack twisted his head to see what was holding her up, felt certain it was all a nightmare, for in his nightmares the law of gravity had no assured effects, and physical objects performed illogically, and time passed either with lightning swiftness or inconceivable slowness. The neon sign, which had blinked so rapidly up till now, had unaccountably slowed to a sustained, methodical alternation of glare and gloom, so that she seemed to lie for a long time on a layer of shadow, then on a layer of light. Jack wanted to cry out his horror and disbelief, and the insane thought kept recurring that if this were actually happening, and were not a dream, and if she actually were inching down the side of the building this way, then the fall could not do her any harm!

When she stopped, this seemed confirmed. For in the last layer of gloom she did not seem to be moving at all, and in the next layer of light he saw her lying diagonally across the iron grating with her head crooked against the angle of the concrete curbing, having come to rest in complete silence—which would have been impossible had she struck the grating with any kind of force. Except that the angle of her head did not seem to fit naturally with the rest of her body.

Jack kept listening for some whisper of sound, horrified by the endless silence, his mind stumbling under the burden of so many impossibilities, but hoping that no sound would come. For this would prove that it actually was only a dream.

But the sound did come.

It came after ages of waiting and silence, and it did not come as a whisper. It struck with physical violence; it shattered and engulfed him like a thunderclap; it smashed the insane concept of nightmare with a single blow—sodden and short, reverberating hollowly through the night with sepulchral finality, like the muffled clang of an iron door in the somber dusk of a tomb.

XXXIV

A Stick for Striking

JACK slept for a while, and at four in the morning he awoke. He glanced at his watch, rolled over, and saw Wes sitting on the edge of the other bed.

"How do you feel, son?"

"Dead." His voice sounded thick and inaudible.

Wes yawned and stretched. Jack realized that the old man had been sleeping in his clothes.

"You've sure been doing a lot of groaning and jumping around. The doc left some pills—"

"Wes," Jack interrupted, waving off the tablets.

"Well?"

The words refused to come out.

But they must! He must tell Wes immediately, get this all straight, decide what to do. . . . Jack struggled to a sitting position.

"Wes . . . I know what happened Monday night. My memory came back."

Wes sank slowly into a chair by the bed.

"Wes, I might as well give it to you straight. I'm not a fair-haired boy who's going to clean up the church. I . . ." Jack swallowed, made his voice go on: "I was having an affair with a woman in New York. I went down Monday to . . . to break off with her." He felt himself beginning to shudder; his voice sank to a whisper. "She killed herself. . . . Before my eyes."

Jack raised his head at last, forcing himself to look into the other man's eyes. To his surprise he saw that they were only watchful, and filled with pity. There was a long silence. Finally Wes said:

"Would it help you, son, to tell somebody about it? I won't ask you anything, if this is all you want to say."

The long, tormenting need to share his burden of guilt and shame overwhelmed him—a need Jack had felt from the beginning, from the moment of his return from that first night in New York nine months ago. He sat in the middle of the bed with his elbows hooked about his knees, not looking at Wes, and poured out the whole story. The old man sat in silence, and when Jack had finished at last his face betrayed neither shock nor condemnation. He got up and walked slowly back and forth several times.

"It's nearly five o'clock," he said. "You get some sleep. I'll be doing some thinking."

Jack awoke a little before eight, while Wes was out for breakfast, and by the time he returned Jack had dressed and was clumsily stuffing his clothes into his grips. The simplest movements seemed burdensome, and nothing seemed to fit. He sank down wearily by the little writing table and tried to eat something from the tray Wes had brought. The coffee helped, but the eggs and toast gagged him.

Wes surveyed the grips.

"You're getting mixed up," he said. "This is only Saturday morning. Did you think it was Sunday afternoon already?"

"I'm getting out." Jack gulped the rest of the coffee.

"You can't leave now! This conference isn't over yet—"

"I'm not leaving the *conference*," Jack said. "I'm leaving the ministry. The church. Everything. For good."

Wes came over and stood before him.

"People have asked me about you this morning who wouldn't have been caught speaking to us yesterday! Anything could happen now. All you've got to do is go down to the church and stand around; let everybody see you haven't quit or got sick or lost your mind. And the worse you look, the better. You can't do this to our men now."

"Look what I've already done to them!" Jack exclaimed. "I feel like I ought to go around and knock on every door of every member of the whole conference and beg forgiveness! Surely you don't think I can go on now the way I've been going."

"You've got no choice. These men have trusted you, believed in you, risked everything for you. And they've won back their own self-respect and integrity through this fight. You can't rush out now and spill a lot of stuff that will destroy everything we've gained so far. One *whisper* of what you've told me would be all over this conference in an hour!"

Jack shoved the food away and put one hand over his eyes.

"Can't you understand how I feel? I can't go out there and put on my white-knight act any longer. I'm . . . I'm a murderer . . . a lecher . . . an egomaniac!"

"Since when?"

"Always! From the beginning. All my life I've been this way, but I just never knew it."

This provoked a long argument, and as Jack tried to put things into words he found that the seeming contradictions and puzzles in his character were gone. Everything was cut from the same cloth, every event and decision and relationship had the same bitter taste of egomania. For now he saw that a stubborn, unyielding conceit ran like a dark thread through all the varied tapestry of his life, binding the whole tormented panorama together, linking the most inconsequential events. He was amazed that he had never even glimpsed this thread before, as he now surveyed his life from its beginnings and tried to explain it to Wes:

His first desire to be a minister had consisted in childish dreams of glory and admiration from lowly blacks in some faraway mission field or from grateful derelicts in the slums. His anguished reaction to Mrs. Catlett's revelations had been trebly painful because of his towering pride. His white-hot certainty that Foxull was intensely interested in him and his family and their ancient follies had been nothing but monumental self-concern. His denunciation of the faculty and student body in that vespers sermon in college, his certainty that such an outburst was the wrath of God and the guarantee of his own prophethood —all this he now viewed as a horrifyingly naked display of wounded, frustrated, rejected egoism. Having been unable to understand or forgive the sins and follies of his parents, being unable to confess his own weakness and mediocrity, he had lashed out wildly at all who shared his own humanity—and at all love and joy. No wonder Christine had told him on the steps of the dormitory that night that hearing his sermon had been like watching someone die.

For that vespers sermon had been the turning point. There, unable to confess or to work with the limited and ineffectual person that he was, he had sought refuge in a shining, professional selfhood. And the little congregation in Norton's Chapel that night had taken his outburst at face value and had proclaimed him a man of God. And the clatter of their tongues and the grip of their hands had riveted the armor into place. And that armor, that self, had thenceforth been his protection against pain and rebuff, his means of attacking all who opposed him, his reason for existence. And its glittering beauty had shielded his eyes forever from the lost, dismayed, uncertain creature trapped inside.

He was astonished now to hear himself telling Wes all about everything in his past with such ease, such absence of pain. For now he realized that the great dynamic of his life, the source of his frenzied, ruthless, driving energy had been simple terror that somewhere, sometime, unexpectedly and unpreventably, he might come face to face with his true self. And then his eyes would behold no demigod, no sublime and heroic greatness making him different in kind from all who had ever gone before him. Rather he would behold only one more limited, blundering, imperfect human being, that same strange amalgam of dust and glory, earth and mystery, arrogance and altruism, sincerity and self-deception which marked the whole family of man. This had been his nemesis, his abyss, his special crucifixion—that he might prove in the end to be only what Mrs. Catlett had said both of his virtue and his sin: "no different than anyone else."

"That was when I started running—and I've been running ever since. I just couldn't face the kind of ordinary, small-town person I was and all the things back home that reminded me of my ordinariness. But as a minister of the Gospel I wasn't ordinary at all. I was somebody at last!"

"Well buck up, boy! It's a great moment in any man's life when he finally realizes he's *like* other people instead of imagining he's different from them. It's a moment that never arrives for most men. Be glad it came for you."

But Jack only turned his eyes away, remembering Thelma, and said: "The price was too high."

Wes, however, refused to accept Jack's over-all interpretation and contested it step by step. He insisted that a man's life takes meaning not only from the secret pride or fear that drives him, but from the conscious, objective goals toward which he strives and the truths and ideals he proclaims.

"After all, most men discover sooner or later that their motives have been mixed, their deepest hearts hidden, and much of life expended on evil and self. The only consolation a man has afterwards is that his blindness was sincere. But if we wait for total purity of purpose before we'll lead or fight, we're condemned to spending life on the sidelines. All a man can do is keep peeling away at his motives, like the layers on an onion, but even the saints never get back permanently to a self of perfect honesty. It's like weeding a garden; it's just something you keep doing. You can root out pride all the days of your life, and as you lie dying it will put up one last shoot.

"What if there was a mixture of evil in your childhood desire to be a minister! Does that make Christ less worthy of disciples? Do you wish now you'd spent all these years in the service of some other master? Would you have better results to show? Or has your new self-understanding made all the things you preached untrue?

"Two and two is still four," Wes grumbled, "even if the teacher only says so for the sadistic delight of making childhood miserable. And the things you said in that vespers sermon were probably true, even if you did say them from a heart full of hatred or frustration as you claim. Who's gonna be left to proclaim truth and right in this world, if not some imperfect human like you or me?"

Furthermore, Wes pointed out, because of the very strength of his false motivations Jack had been able to overcome a little of the enormous inertia of the world.

"Sure, you tackled jobs that nobody in his right mind would have undertaken! Maybe God has to pick up a crooked stick to strike with now and then, if all the nice clean shiny straight ones are too flimsy for the job.

"Sure, you hid in a fake, manufactured personality and enjoyed wearing a special hat and having a special set of reactions ready-made for any situation life could bring. But doesn't every man? Simplicity and naturalness aren't as common as rocks in the road; they're among the most sophisticated and hard-won responses attainable.

"Maybe you *are* nuts; I don't know. But I do know you've shaken up a corrupt conference, and called attention to the problem of power politics in the church, and made the machine offer better candidates this year than ever before. You've inspired at least a handful of men to real courage and self-sacrifice. And it was all worth doing! And I'll bet that in four years of preaching and pastoring you've made this world a little better place to live in—for whatever reasons.

"How can you be so sure you did well on sick calls and funerals *only* because you wanted to be around suffering and death? Or that you chose the ministry again in college *only* because you were afraid of love and sex? An awful lot of men have seen good in you, but pure evil couldn't produce any good at all. And it's sheer presumption for any man to claim he understands someone completely—especially if that someone is himself."

But Jack could not be persuaded. For he saw that, paradoxically, it was his very pride, his desperation to escape the vision of his own ordinariness, that had generated his more than ordinary zeal and courage and yearning for righteousness, his determination to excel even Wes himself.

"All that Belovèd ever had in this conference," said Jack, suddenly averting his eyes, "was political power and political friends. But I wanted more than just to unhorse the boss. I wanted the men to respect me and revere me the way they did you, Wes. I was trying to put you down into second place too."

Jack forced himself to look up. The old man's ice-blue eyes were fixed on him not with resentment but with a lively interest.

"You're so confounded honest," said Wes, "you make everybody uncomfortable."

But Jack doggedly held to his point, remembering how he had been goaded into his attack at the district ministers' meeting partly through recalling Patricia's smiling remark, "After all, my dear, you're not another Wes Phillips!" And there, as everywhere, his falsity of motive, his ultimate self-concern, had blinded him to what was going on in the hearts and minds of his colleagues, and their vote had left him stunned and humiliated. And that night Patricia had revealed her father's actual estimate of Jack, and had returned his ring, and all these sledgehammer blows had loosened every rivet of his armor, had left it within teetering seconds of collapse.

"Because Patricia was part of my armor too. She had beauty and status and connections, and I used her just the way I used everyone else, to prop up my image of myself." Jack paused in astonishment. "And I've never had any idea what the girl was actually like inside—what she really felt or wanted or feared—because I never thought of her except in relation to myself!"

And so he had fled to his last refuge against truth—to Thelma. He had used her shamelessly, ruthlessly, frantically, blind and uncaring as to what this might be doing to her, wanting only the blessed narcotic of her adoration.

"I guess I was literally insane with fear that she'd reject me too," said Jack. "She nearly did once, when I quibbled about buying her a negligee she wanted; and I came within a hair of killing a man, or being killed, trying to raise the money for it. In fact, I guess I was partly mad all the way through. I debated about using a dime I found in a phone booth because it might belong to someone else and that would mean I wasn't morally perfect—and the call I was making was to Thelma! I even lectured her in bed one time about the ethics of sending messages in Christmas cards for three cents!

"But my flight finally came to an end—when Thelma let go of that window ledge. Of course I couldn't think what to do or say while she was sitting there! Because for months I'd been wanting to be rid of her, wanting something to happen to her. Of course I couldn't call out or plead with her! Because in my heart of hearts I was willing for her to die if she'd just do it quietly and let me slip away without involving my good name.

"She was studying me! Searching me for one single trace of interest in *her* pain, *her* need! And seeing only self-concern and indifference . . . not even hatred any more. She couldn't bring herself to jump while she still felt I hated her, because at least that made her feel she mattered to me.

"If something or somebody had saved her, I could probably have squirmed out of facing the truth. I'd done it a dozen times before with other people I'd used and thrown aside, like my own—" his voice almost failed him—"mother . . . and . . . father." His hands were shaking. "But Thelma announced her estimate of me by turning her face away and . . . letting go. . . . And even while she was falling I kept refusing to accept the verdict, but when that . . . that *sound* came up, I knew what I was. I came face to face with myself for the first time: a murderous egomaniac! An inhuman monster incapable of concern for any other creature beyond himself, without even the natural affection the worst of people feel for their own parents! No wonder I blanked out and couldn't remember any of it had ever happened." He stared down dully at his trembling fingers. "I killed Thelma as surely as if I'd pushed her out of that window with my own hands."

"Son, that's not true!" Wes protested. "You said yourself you nearly fell trying to save her."

"Anybody would have grabbed at her then."

Wes tried to persuade him that his hatred of the person he had been was making it impossible for him to form fair estimates of his past intentions or to know the true extent of his responsibility. But Jack clung to the one thing that stood out sharp and clear from this welter of horror and pain: He had finally begun to see himself, and the vision was so shattering that he now had to rethink his entire life and character from the beginning.

"I've got to have time to think!"

"Then take time. But don't make any life-changing decisions in this state of mind. And don't give up the journey just when you're coming out into daylight!"

Jack banged his knee with his fist.

"Wes, can't you see this isn't some sort of theoretical problem with me? It's . . . it's all the things I've *done* to people—to Thelma and Pat and my parents and all these men who've followed me. Using them, throwing them aside, jeopardizing their families and careers, and never really feeling for any of them before. I see now how Belovèd can punish men the way he does. It's not that he's so strong or self-disciplined; it's that he's so tangled up in his own fears and ambitions he doesn't have any feeling for other people's hurts. He's just like I've been—so proud he's terrified of the truth, and so terrified it makes him cruel." Jack smiled faintly. "I wish I could help him find his way out. It's a terrible existence; you can't relax even for a second. . . .

"But now I feel as if I were all naked nerve-endings. I seem to be feeling the hurts I've given everyone throughout my whole life. I keep seeing Thelma on that window-ledge and wondering how a man could be that near someone in such pain and not feel it. . . ."

Jack bowed his face in his hands, shuddering. Wes squeezed his shoulder, and his voice was gentle.

"You're not alone, son. I've been where you are now, and so has every man who's honest. Did you think pride would be lovely to look at when you finally met it face to face? It's not really something manly and exciting and admirable. It's blind and cruel, evasive and cowardly and unbelievably little. It's the primal sin, the natural state of every man, only most men keep their outward lives respectable enough in their own sight so that their system of self-deception never breaks down. They never have to face an inescapable measurement of their own egoism the way you did when that poor girl killed herself before your eyes. The people most of us kill die so gradually that we never recognize ourselves as murderers.

"I wish I could tell you this is the last time you'll ever be horrified or dismayed at what's in your own heart, but you're only at the first stage of a very long pilgrimage. The closer we get to God the more sensitive we become, and as we draw nearer the Light, the things it exposes in the depths of our hearts are often so appalling we feel we must begin all over again."

Somehow, the fact that Wes had apparently experienced some of this same sense of horror and shame was more helpful than anything else he had said. It made Jack feel less monstrous and alone.

Wes stood in silence by the window for a long time. When he turned again to Jack his whole expression and bearing were abruptly changed. His voice was suddenly cold, impersonal, even harsh.

"You've come this far, you might as well learn where the rest of the road goes," he said. "You claim to be sick of yourself, Jack Lee. But self-hatred is just one more form of self-love; the center of all the attention hasn't shifted one inch." Wes stood with his feet spread wide, thumbs hooked in his black vest, his eyes unwavering, and as he talked, Jack kept expecting him to lapse again into his old-time folksiness, deliberately mangling his grammar and hiding his intellectual subtlety in countrified phrases. This swift-spoken surgeon of the spirit was unfamiliar and frightening.

"God forbid that the story you have told me should ever get abroad in the church. If it should, your career would be ended and all of us who trusted in you made ridiculous! And I should be persuaded that your desire for the cleansing and peace of confession had blotted out every consideration except self and its miseries.

"I was about to dismiss your present self-condemnation as merely the screams of wounded spiritual vanity, but then you began talking about the pain you had caused other people. That was the first symptom you'd shown of interest in anyone but yourself. And genuine repentance, you might as well know, involves much more than self-understanding and confession; it involves catching the first glimpses of what our sin has done to other people. For when we truly repent of self we reject it and turn from it and find ourselves interested in someone else. We begin seeing what our world has looked like through other people's eyes, and all our lost opportunities rise up about us and almost crush us under their weight, and all the wounds we've made in other hearts begin to ache in our own.

"Your present grief at the pains of others may be nothing but a subtle pride that even in your sins you were more than merely ordinary. I note that you have not had the courage to confess any ordinary misdoings." Jack winced, but Wes did not pause. "The way out of your misery is plain, if you are actually interested. But possibly you'll prefer to spend the rest of life wallowing in self-hatred and enjoying the extraordinary stature your sins have given you in your own eyes."

There was a long silence.

"I do want some way out," Jack said. "I can't go on being what I am."

"Very well. The path is clear, but it's so ordinary and uninteresting I doubt that you'll be man enough to take it. You have just received an appointment to a church where you know the people better than at any other charge you will ever serve. Granting all the practical and psychological handicaps of serving as pastor in your own home town, at least it's a job to be done. And in your own case, it may be precisely the job you need as the first step in rebuilding your personality from its original starting point. I'm talking about a new inner self, purged, clarified, working from constructive and outgoing motivations. You'll probably be doing all the same things you've been doing for the past four years, but with less friction and tension inside, and with a genuine unity between outward acts and inner spirit.

"Back in your own home town you won't have a single one of the phony assets that a ministerial personality gives. Everybody will know you for what you actually are or have been, and thus you can begin on the solid rock of truth, howevermuch you may have wanted to escape it in the past.

"But there's an even more immediate opportunity for you to demonstrate that your center of interest has shifted. Rightly or wrongly, a group of your colleagues have believed in you, and out at that church this morning are men who've thrown away half a lifetime of labor at your word. Most of them have wives and children. They've risked them too, to give our movement a precarious foothold in this conference. You have become a symbol to them of sacrificial courage and devotion to principle. You cannot possibly let all their sacrifices be thrown away. You cannot let it be thought that the machine has broken your nerve and driven you from the ministry. There's no way back now; you've got to go forward."

The swift voice became even harsher.

"If you are a man at all, if you do find your past self hideous and unacceptable, if the death of that poor girl is not to be utterly meaningless and wasted, if you have been shocked out of total self-interest, then stick with this job till it's done!"

After a long silence he laid one hand on Jack's shoulder, his stern face relaxing.

"Look, son, you're not the first minister who ever went wrong, and you won't be the last. I hold no brief for adultery, but I firmly believe that there's no degradation a man can sink to that God can't twist into an instrument of good if the man will only let him. I'll admit that some of the things you told me were shockers, but I won't stop believing in you till you compel me to.

"I'm asking you in the name of our friendship to put those clothes back in that bureau and get out to the church and let those men believe that you are what they think you are for one more day. Do this, and whatever the outcome, I'll continue to believe in you and to be proud to call myself your friend." Wes straightened, and his wide mouth turned grim. "But if you run off somewhere and hide out with your finger on your own spiritual pulse, I'll be forced to conclude that you once were and still are a murderous egomaniac incapable of genuine interest in any other creature. And I'll be through with you forever!"

He spun on his heel and was gone, slamming the door behind him.

Jack sat for a while staring at the door, then he picked up a batch of clothes from the grip and was staring at them stupidly when the phone rang.

It was Dirkwell. His voice was anxious and uncertain.

"I'm out at the church. They've started a lot of rumors about what happened to you last night. Some of our boys are starting to come unglued. I know it's asking a lot, but if you felt able to come out just for a minute or two—"

Dirkwell paused. For some reason, Jack kept remembering how startled he had been to see Dirkwell so far from his home district that night after the ministers' meeting, and how Dirkwell had said: "Edwina told me if I didn't get over here the fastest way I could, she'd never speak to me again." Jack kept seeing Edwina Dirkwell's face, and Martha Starr's, and Bea Adams', and the faces of all the other parsonage wives who had gone into this thing with their husbands with so much courage and willingness, who had prayed so hard and worked so hard and believed so hard during the past months. For the first time he suddenly seemed to be viewing the whole struggle through their eyes, and in many respects it looked far more frustrating and terrifying than it must have to the men.

"Dirk," he began. "You'll just have to tell the boys . . ." His voice stopped dead. He gripped the instrument tighter to make his hand stop shaking. Finally he drew a deep breath and said in a nearly inaudible voice, "Tell them I said keep their mouths shut and sit tight and I'll be right out."

He put the receiver down, let the handful of clothes fall to the floor, and wearily reached for his hat.

XXXV

The Brothers

JACK walked all the way down the center aisle of Belfair Church alone and took a seat near the front, aware of the sudden whispers that interrupted the sound of the devotional speaker's voice. The journey down the aisle had a dream-world unreality about it, and Jack was so intent on making the entire distance that all the horrors he had anticipated were forgotten. He gazed out across the turning heads and whispering lips. Attendance seemed to be off somewhat this morning, but that was typical of Saturday sessions. After the devotional he rose and made his way back to a vacant seat in the rear of the sanctuary, and the journey against the rising slope of the floor was fearful, but he refused the luxury of holding onto the ends of the pews and deliberately turned his face toward the rows of probing, curious eyes.

Wes stationed Adams on Jack's left and sat down at his right.

"How do you feel?"

"Great!" snapped Jack. "How do I look?"

"Awful. Don't try to talk. As long as we're sitting together, the boys will assume you've got things in hand. I'll handle everything from here on in. Here comes the teller's report."

The bishop was unsealing the report of the tellers on the final ballot of the previous business session the night before. His voice kept swelling and fading as Jack tried to piece together the patches of sound that came through.

"Number of clerical ballots cast . . . Necessary to elect, one hundred and . . . Powers: one hundred and ninety- . . . and . . . is elected . . .

Laye: one hundred fifty-seven . . ." Powers was a machine man and already in. That left two. Laye was a machine man and high enough to go in within a few ballots. Saturday attendance was always off, and the machine as always would have all its men present and voting. "Clerical delegates will write two names. Two names only." The rest of the field had been so scattered that the bishop would probably have to keep them through the lunch hour if he was determined to elect the third and final delegate without holding a Saturday afternoon session. "Number of lay ballots cast . . ."

Well, that settled that.

Jack could feel Wes slump back against the pew. Adams ripped the page of figures off his pad and crumpled it in his fist. It was all over now. Even if the rebels took the final delegate, it would be a meaningless victory, a portent of better luck next time, perhaps, but of no significance at the forthcoming jurisdictional conference.

After what seemed an eternity, Jack saw the ushers starting up the aisle with the ballots. Someone finally thrust one into his outstretched hand; he scrawled on it, folded it; and after another eternity someone else took it out of his hand. Then the tellers were retiring and the bishop was introducing someone. . . .

Jack nudged Wes with his elbow.

"I've got to get out of here . . . think I'm going to faint. They've all seen me now. Tell Dirk to take me back to the hotel."

Lying on his bed at the Middleton at last, after Dirkwell had gone, Jack dozed a while, then lay with his eyes closed, trying to remember how this fearful exhaustion had begun.

How far had he run? Why had he run down the stairs from Thelma's apartment instead of taking the elevator, which was still standing there? He remembered again that horrifying sound coming up from the grating below the window, remembered seeing something disturb the frozen stillness that had enveloped the universe. It was a man. He must have been under one of the trees on the boulevard, and now he suddenly detached himself from the shadows and began running diagonally across the street toward the thing on the grating. His cry, faint and faraway, came drifting up.

Jack could remember stumbling backward from the open window and then for some reason pulling it down. He remembered his own voice making a strange, broken, babbling noise as he staggered into the kitchen looking for something or someone. . . . Had he been expecting to find Thelma? He reeled out again and suddenly realized that his left hand was clenched so tight it was numb. He could not make it unclench and finally had to force it with the thumb and fingers of his right hand to make it relax. The thumb withdrew, the four fingers uncurled, and Jack could feel his eyes bulge from their sockets and a hoarse cry of terror sear his throat as he flung the button away.

It struck the new panel on the door of the bathroom where Paulo had kicked his way out that night. Jack stood with both hands clapped over his mouth, staring at the button—a glossy square of red plastic with a scrap of Thelma's jacket still attached. The tile floor of the bathroom kept rising and falling under it like waves, and the button kept changing its shape, pulsing and glowing like a horrid clot of blood with its mangled veins and arteries trailing along behind it.

Jack snatched up his hat and lunged backward from this horror, but as his hands fumbled at the hall door, he realized he could not possibly leave the button there. It seemed at the time like some sort of evidence he must do away with. He turned, got hold of the button with a kind of grasping revulsion that made him clench at it with fingers that would not close, somehow got it inside his coat pocket, then paused in the middle of the floor.

His letters!

She had shown him a slim packet of them once, all tied up in a lurid satin ribbon. He yanked open the right-hand bottom drawer of the bureau, located the packet under a tangle of underthings, and frantically counted the letters: Eight! All there! He rammed them into his inside coat pocket and snatched open the hall door.

The elevator was standing there with the door still open, just as Thelma had left it after she had pressed the button and then turned away to the window at the end of the corridor. But Jack could not endure the thought of creeping down twelve floors penned up inside that metal box, and he raced past it toward the stairs, plunging down the steps in great, wild leaps, grabbing the rail and letting go, grabbing it again, lunging around the landings, tripping and almost falling, plunging on.

"No, no, no, no non no non no nononono no nonno . . . !"

He was vaguely conscious of voices, shouts, lights, stairwell doors opening, faces with staring eyes, but he raced on. He went past the ground floor, burst out into the basement corridor, and was about to turn back when he remembered the letters. He stuffed them down deep inside a trash container beside the furnace-room door, then ran back up the stairs to the ground floor again. Through the small, square window in the stairwell door he saw a blur of faces streaming past. He stopped, smoothed his hair with shaking fingers, put on his Homburg, waited a moment to get his breath, then stepped out casually into the moving stream.

The doorway of the foyer was jammed. Several people were trying to come in against the tide of those pushing out. On the sidewalk Jack hovered on the rim of the thickening crowd. A policeman suddenly thrust past, elbowing him roughly aside, and at the same instant a young woman inside the circle forced her way out, her face white, sickly, frantic to escape. Jack averted his eyes to keep from seeing what lay on the iron grating, and the crowd surged shut again. Over the strange, hushed murmuring of the bowed heads he saw into the faces of two or three men pressed back against the wall who were evidently standing on the concrete lip about the grating. Their downcast eyes were dark with horror, their lips worked in a pouting revulsion. Jack looked away.

The woman coming out struggled to get past him, but someone was pushing Jack into her, and he asked in a low voice:

"Is she all right?"

The woman's eyes focused on him, and her pale lips suddenly curved upward in a half-smile and her hysterical giggle cut the air.

Her eyes rolled back, her lips sagged down at the corners, and she began to fall, sliding down inside the jam-packed crowd about her. Jack got his hand under one arm, someone grabbed the other, and they forced an opening and the other man was joined by a second. Jack let them take her and turned back, and as he did so a head and face in profile suddenly appeared through a narrow lane of vision. The head was covered with blue-black, greasy curls. The face was ashen under its pitted, swarthy skin. Jack felt a chill break over him.

It was Paulo.

Jack ducked away and heard a man's voice above the murmuring crowd:

"I saw her when she done it, officer! I was cutting across the parkway, and I looked up for some reason, and there she was. Somebody made a grab for her, and for a minute I thought he was gone too. Then I—"

As Jack got clear at last and began walking away, he heard Paulo's voice break in:

"What did he look like? Is he here?"

"Gosh, fella, I'm not even sure it was a man! They were up so high, and it all happened so sudden, and the light—"

The temptation to look back was nearly overwhelming, but Jack maintained a casual stride toward the subway entrance, keeping his face away from the diminishing voices, their buzzing slashed by Paulo's strident cry:

"Hey, Bart! Pietro!"

Why had he decided not to go into the subway? Entrapment. That was it. For all he knew, there might be no train for twenty minutes or more. They would hunt him down like a rabbit in a burrow. If only he had not looked back! But the terror was beyond bearing. He controlled himself all the way down the block. If only someone else had been walking in *his* direction! But the few people on the street were going toward the crowd. He must have stood out unmistakably. And the footstep he thought he heard was clearly that of the man who had passed him going the other way. But at the time he wondered if they had run up swiftly, silently, and were treading on his very heels!

In the shadow of the subway entrance he stepped behind the wall and listened. Unless they had circled around the far side, he might have escaped unnoticed. He took off his hat and leaned out so that only the edge of his temple and eye-socket showed, and looked back.

He saw two figures walking rapidly down the sidewalk, with a third lagging behind, obviously arguing that they were on a false trail. The first stopped so suddenly that the others almost collided with him.

He had seen Jack peering out.

Jack heard his shout, saw the three break into a run, and ducked back, overcome for an instant by a childish yearning to yell at the top of his lungs, to make it a wild brawl in the middle of the intersection. Then the policeman would come, the crowd would rescue him . . . and the reporters would arrive, and the photographers with their flash bulbs. . . .

No. Any way would be better than that. Jack listened for the subway. If it came now, this instant, he could get aboard and be gone before those pounding footsteps had crossed the intersection. But the hollow stair was silent, the pounding feet louder.

He snatched out his billfold, pulled some bills from it, stuck it on the ledge over his head. If they caught him, they could not identify him. If he escaped, he could circle back and pick it up. He ran swiftly across the far lane of the parkway, keeping the shed between him and the staccato footsteps. At the far side, too late, he heard the shuddering roar of the subway.

Jack had only vague notions of the geography of this part of New York. He knew that he was much too tired to try outdistancing his pursuers; his only chance was to lose them in the unlighted jumble of tenements and warehouses, work his way toward the glow of the city beyond, take a taxi, and come back for the rest of his money and his train ticket.

He ducked into the first alley and glanced back through a gap in the crumbling brickwork. They had not yet rounded the subway shed. He raced down the alley to its end, scrambled over a rickety board fence, fell on a pile of rubble and picked himself up. Before him was a vacant lot, cluttered with heaps of dirt or ashes and shadowy hulks of burned-out automobiles. In the distance he saw a single street light, a feeble pinpoint in the watery gloom. The light at the opposite corner was out, and he ran diagonally across the lot toward the darkness.

At the intersection he stopped, breathing hard, and rested a moment, staring back. He thought he saw a movement at the mouth of the alley, and then the sound of a crash came clearly through the silence. The fence must have given under their weight.

Jack knew from an occasional finger of light breaking the darkness that there were people in the buildings that flowed past his pounding feet—except in the warehouses—but he dared not risk his brief lead by stopping to beg for help. They probably would not open to him, and they were not of his kind but of his pursuers'.

As he lost his sense of direction in the crazy angles and intersections of the alleyways, and as the cries sounded first behind him and then ahead of him, and as his strength began to fail more and more, he finally realized that they would corner him sooner or later. But he kept running just the same, from a blind overmastering desperation to stay alive one more block, one more alley, one more minute, one more second, one more step.

He ran until his lungs were bursting and his feet and legs felt as if they were immersed in a monstrous glue. Toward the end he tripped over curbs and garbage cans; he ran into clotheslines whose damp garments snatched at him; he crashed into walls like a blind animal; he half-scrambled, half-fell across rotting fences, and finally he reeled, sobbing, into a narrow alley and sprawled on his hands and knees. He realized that the cries were louder than ever before, and he pulled himself up by a splintered packing crate and stumbled down the alley away from the voices. But it was far too dark in the alley, and even before he caught the new quality in the voices, even before he had dragged his body back and forth twice across the wall's moldering brickwork, he already knew what this intenser darkness meant.

He was in a blind alley.

He fell face downward on the damp coldness, his vision ablaze with circles of green fire, his heart hammering so he could scarcely hear. At last he rolled over on his back to get the weight off his agonized chest, to draw another breath before they came. He felt unmanageably stiff and inflexible, and crazy images of a fox hunt floated through his world of suffocating darkness and flashing fire. He had heard once that a fox sometimes ran from hounds till its legs were stiff as wood. He felt wooden all over, numb and dead with fatigue, except for the pain in his chest.

He was gradually aware that the agony was subsiding, that he was able to breathe again instead of gasping out choked little sobs. The green fires burned out. He could see a little. He rolled his head sideways on the bricks, wondering why the feet had stopped. Then he saw the figures at the mouth of the alley, against the watery gloom of the street. There seemed to be two . . . then one . . . then two again. They merged and wavered, as if he were looking through walls of dark water. He finally decided there were two and that they were waiting for the third to come up.

Jack had read of men who reviewed their entire lives during the last few seconds before death, but he had no thoughts, saw no great truths, reviewed none of his past. His entire mind, in all its complexity and depth, narrowed and shallowed to a single icy drop of terror, a simple pinpoint of purest will to live. He saw, as his eyes grew more accustomed to the deeper darkness of the alley, some garbage cans by the wall, and he crawled toward them and gathered himself up into a tight ball, digging his elbows into his abdomen and groin, and feeling an idiotic desire to make the flesh of his face and neck and the bones of his skull shrink inward, be less visible when the third figure arrived and the three began to come forward into the darkness.

The garbage cans had been made by cutting the tops out of oil drums, and now Jack hooked his fingers over the rusty lip, peering over the masses of cans and paper and food scraps, flinching at the rustle of cockroaches. Something warm and heavy, like a hand, came to rest on his shoulder and he gave a strangled, involuntary cry and knew that it was a huge rat—ponderous, loathsome, puzzled, sniffing about his neck and shoulder. He wanted to spring up and shake the horror off, but at last the creature crawled to the top of his shoulder, its warm furry side brushing his neck, gathered itself, and jumped to the top of the can as Jack squeezed his head sideways against the wall.

Then the two figures became three.

He knew now he would die, and with that certainty the frozen drop of terror thawed, cracked, and trickled forth into the multiplicity of thought. He had no means of identification on him. He had lost his hat somewhere, but it bore no identification even if they found it. So at least they would not know whom they had killed.

The three figures were spaced apart, were advancing very slowly, and he saw something glitter as one of them took the last step that carried him beyond the dimness from the street. Jack shivered, as though the silvery glitter had touched a nerve in his stomach.

He lifted his head to keep from seeing it again, and against a less intense darkness of sky overhead, he saw something: it was the framework of a fire escape, and his straining eyes followed it down and saw that it ended at a considerable height above the alley—twelve feet? Fifteen feet? It was between him and the advancing figures. . . . If only he could delay them momentarily . . .

Jack picked up a bottle from the rubbish beside one of the cans and stood up slowly and silently. It was slippery and he was aware of a smell of olive oil among the stenches. He lobbed the bottle high over the heads of the wavering figures; it vanished in the gloom, and an instant later he heard its explosive burst in the street. The figures froze, then merged. One withdrew, and Jack knew that he had run back to the entrance while the others waited.

Jack lifted the loose cans and bottles off the top of the first drum, laid them silently on the bricks. Then, with fearful concentration he tilted the drum, got his right hand under the bottom, lifted it up, and tiptoed forward through the darkness toward the motionless figures. He noiselessly set the can down under the fire escape and went back for a second. He had intended to place this atop the first, but saw at once that, since they were all the same diameter, he would never be able to climb up on his perch without having it fall. He ran back for another, leaving the first two side by side, careless now of the whisper and scuffle of his shoes. The third figure had returned.

In his frantic haste Jack forgot to take the loose stuff off the top of the third drum and when he lifted it, a bottle toppled out and smashed. The advancing figures became motionless.

Jack ran forward and upended the third drum with a violent crash atop the first, and clambered up, using the second as a stairstep, certain that the whole teetering arrangement would collapse at any instant. The lowest rung of the fire escape was inches above his fingertips. He crouched and jumped, and the bar slapped his palms violently and he clutched it, waiting for the sickening give that would tell him the whole structure was swinging against its counterweight and lowering him to the ground again. But, as he had hoped, its pivots were locked from rust and long disuse, and with a last desperate burst of effort he chinned himself up, grabbed the next rung, then the next, and finally hooked one leg through.

The rolling thunder of the oil drums boomed out amidst the cacophony of running footsteps, shouts, and a clatter of cans and bottles. Jack clung to the rusty irons, panting, and he realized as he gazed down that they did not know where he had vanished, and were coursing back and forth, heads down, whirling and half-trotting among the rolling drums and the litter, like dogs driven wild by the sudden disappearance of their prey.

He cautiously began to climb, but his feet would not obey properly; they stumbled and kept falling short. He heard a cry and glanced down through the grating at the first landing, but could make out nothing in the darkness. Curses and shouts mingled, and then Paulo's voice ripped through the night:

"Let him go! There's no way down! We've got him!"

A stream of unintelligible curses rang out, mixed with laughter. At the second landing he rested and listened to them dragging the drums back and stacking them up, but apparently not in haste.

On the fourth landing Jack rested again. It seemed senseless to continue the flight. He heard a booming clatter below; their first attempt to get someone up must have failed. He climbed the last two flights to the roof. All the windows he had passed were boarded shut, and when he reached the roof, he walked to the far edge and looked down. No other fire escape. He circled about. Nothing. The roof was flat, bordered by a stone lip perhaps six inches high, and had a tar-paper roof covered with fine gravel. There was a murky half-light on the roof and across the next alley he could see another warehouse exactly like this, and far beyond it the radiance of the city.

The only object on the roof was a piece of loose brick by a gap in the coping where the ancient masonry had crumbled away. He used it to smash a hole in the skylight near the hasp. The wire in the glass gave way sooner than he had expected, and the brick got away from him. He heard a metallic clangor, but it had taken far too long to strike. The floor was obviously a long way down, and he might land on steel rods or machinery. . . . He got his hand in, undid the hasp, and turned the heavy glass coop back on its hinges. Then he hung by his fingers and kicked in all directions without touching anything. Afterwards he lay on his back for a while beside the opening, gasping and covered with sweat. He wished he had not let the brick get away; it would have been better than nothing against the knives.

Far below he heard another clattering boom, followed by furious curses. Apparently the brothers were as exhausted as he. He walked slowly about his rooftop prison a second time, and came to a stop facing the warehouse on the opposite side of the building from the fire escape. It was the same height as Jack's building; it had a flat graveled roof and a skylight, and Jack suddenly realized that it probably had a fire escape on the far side. If only it were a few feet nearer he could jump across. . . . In the uncertain light he tried to measure the distance with his eye. Probably about eighteen feet . . . maybe twenty. He could use the gap for his take-off point. In college he had once done nineteen feet eleven inches in the broad jump. But then he had been ten years younger, and in perfect condition, and wearing spiked shoes, and taking off from a cinder path. He had not done it on a tar-paper roof, in a state of near collapse, with a stone ledge to clear at the far end, and a penalty of instant death.

He gazed down and suddenly seemed to be watching Thelma fall again, and he sat down and began unlacing his shoes. It would be only right and just if he fell too, and at least he would cheat the brothers out of doing the job their way.

And there was always a chance in a thousand he might make it. . . .

He took off his shoes, tied them up in his coat, and lobbed the bundle across to the other roof. Behind him a hoarse cry came echoing up. They had got the first man on. Jack turned his back to the other building, put his heel against the stone coping, and paced off his run, counting in a whisper. Then he laid his handkerchief down to mark his starting point, and stood by the skylight breathing long, deep, rhythmic breaths.

He knew that he ought to pray, but he could not fix his mind on anything except that darkness between the two warehouses, and the sound Thelma's body had made. He kept remembering how his feet had refused to function as he tried to climb the fire escape, how they seemed to misjudge each rung, falling a little short. Then he heard a metallic thumping. The brothers were on their way up.

Jack withdrew a few paces from the handkerchief, took several small, mincing steps and then began his run, not allowing his mind to function, deliberately suspending all thought except the single thought of keeping his stride smooth and regular. The count ran out before he reached the gap; he saw that he could not use it as his springboard without breaking his stride; and he jumped from a spot about two feet before the coping, jumped with utter desperation, knowing that the fact the count had run out meant that his feet had been unable to respond, had fallen a little short at each step from the big, full, running stride he needed. He felt certain that he was jumping to his death, and in the air he felt for a fleeting instant a wild sensation of total freedom, as if he had broken every tie, had found release from fear and shame and guilt, from past and future.

Then his sock feet struck the pebbly gravel with a searing flash so ecstatic and so incredible that for an instant his nerves and mind seemed incapable of any reaction to the agonizing pain except a near-hysterical joy. He sprawled briefly, struggled erect, hobbled across to his coat and shoes and then to the fire escape on the far side. As he half-stumbled, half-fell down below the level of the coping, he heard the three voices burst out onto the other rooftop. He hung on, clutching his bundle to his stomach, grinning hugely with clenched teeth and laughing silently a wild, voiceless, hysterical laugh as he heard Paulo calling down taunts and obscene promises into the open skylight of the empty warehouse.

And they had never seen his face!

He crept silently to the first landing below the roof, peeled off the bloody shreds that remained of his socks, and started to fling them away. Then he hesitated, rolled them into soggy balls, and stuffed them in his pocket. He would not leave a single clue except the plain white handkerchief! He had bought it only a few days before; it would not even bear a laundry mark! Let them spend the rest of the night ransacking the empty warehouse, cursing and blaming each other!

When he tried to put his shoes on, the pain was more than he could bear, so he sat resting for a while, hanging his feet over the landing. Then he forced himself to put the shoes on, leaving the laces untied, and stood up and struggled into his coat.

In the distance, far away yet no longer impossibly far, stood the dazzling radiance he had been pursuing. He could see the shining spires and clean, illumined canyons, the jeweled throughways diminishing into the distance like graduated gems, the broad streets where policemen stood at corners, the lighted windows of homes where people answered knocks at the door. Raising his head, he saw above the city a glowing vault of clouds reflecting the luster below, and here and there, in a passage between the clouds, cold and serene and infinitely distant, the light of a star.

Jack dozed off again. He was awakened by the noises of the traffic on the street before the Middleton Hotel and lay awhile gazing out the window at the steeple of Belfair Methodist Church on the horizon, standing up sharp and clean against the afternoon sky. One-twenty. The bishop must have kept the conference in session through lunch to elect that last remaining delegate. Just then Jack heard the sound of laughter and voices in the hall; the door burst open; and people spilled into the room—Haycox, Bradley, Starr, Adams, Perriman, Wes, Avery, Dirkwell, and the rest—the whole crew. They smiled and shoved one another, crowding about the bed.

"How did it go?" Jack sat up and stared about the ring of grinning faces. "You look like we took the last two delegates."

"The last *one*," Dirkwell corrected.

"Well, I can't see that that's anything to get all steamed up about. Who was it?"

Dan Starr nudged Dirkwell.

"You tell him, Dirk. You're his oldest friend."

Dirkwell pursed his lips, his freckled face contracted into frowns of unaccustomed dignity, and he intoned solemnly:

"It gives me great honor to present the reform ticket's gift to the forthcoming jurisdictional conference of the Methodist Church," he turned grandly, sweeping his arm in a vast arc, "the Very Reverend Wesley A. Phillips!"

A chorus of yells went up. Jack gazed up at Wes in amazement and delight. The old man grinned cockily, his shapeless hat perched at an angle over his white thatch, his frayed cigar sticking up rakishly from one corner of his wide mouth.

"Has anyone," he asked disdainfully, "got a match?"

Nobody had. Finally, in disgust, Wes handed a paper of matches to Dan Starr, who held the flame for him with exaggerated deference while Wes blew the smoke in his face.

"But . . . but who put him on the slate?" asked Jack.

Dirkwell again assumed his pontifical tone.

"The peeeepul! Laye went in on the first ballot; then with the whole conference split twenty ways, somebody wrote Wes Phillips on a ballot, and on the very next he was up to twenty-seven. Then he jumped to sixty-one, and just kept going!"

"Sort of a consolation prize," said Bradley. "People wanted some way to let the machine know they were aware of us, and that they admired our guts for sticking till the last ballot was counted."

"It was a symbol, all right," said Adams. "I believe a lot of ministers in this conference suddenly realized Wes would be retiring next year, and they wanted to give him a sort of farewell present, as a symbolic gesture of respect and affection."

"Whaddya mean, symbolic!" Wes snorted. "I was elected on the basis of my vast experience in public life!"

"How did Belovèd take it?" asked Jack.

"Well, sir," said Dirkwell, "in a way it was really his biggest hour. I had to hand it to him for sheer guts and self-control. He got up and walked clear across the sanctuary and shook Wes by the hand. You'd have thought we'd just elected his dearest friend."

Jack nodded.

"He'll probably be meticulously fair in the appointments, to show everyone he can take a setback with good grace, and that he's the kind of stuff bishops are made of."

"He may not punish the rest of us," said Haycox, "but I've got a feeling he'll find some way to make Jack pay for not knowing when he was licked."

"No doubt," said Jack drily, "but getting Wes elected to something after all these years almost makes the whole thing worth while."

"The whole thing *was* worth while," said Dan Starr, "even if we hadn't taken a single delegate."

The smiling faces sobered. In the sudden silence they all nodded, glancing about at each other and at Jack.

"And it will be worth while," said Bradley, "even if we stay a minority the rest of our lives. I'm different, and my ministry is going to be different, because of what we've got right here. And I believe the church will be different."

"Maybe in this world," said Adams thoughtfully, "men who own their own souls will always be a minority. But they guard the conscience of the rest. They're the leaven, the salt that preserves the meat from rotting altogether."

He glanced about him, and Jack saw the same silent affirmation on every face, in every eye.

"And so," said Dirkwell, suddenly pushing forward toward the head of the bed, "we've got a little memento for the guy who started the ball rolling. He probably won't get much of a church when the bishop reads out the appointments tomorrow afternoon, but he's the one who stayed in there pitching when all the rest of us were ready to fold up and quit. And wherever he goes, the hearts of all brave men go with him."

He took out a small package done up in gift wrapping and thrust it into Jack's hands.

"That's quite a speech, Dirk," Jack said, tearing open the paper. "If my next church pays no salary, you boys can pass the hat again and—"

Suddenly his voice got out of control. Inside the small velvet box was a wrist watch, and on its back were engraved the words: "To Jack from the Rebels. June 8–12, 1960." His old watch was lying on the bureau. He wound the new one slowly and carefully, taking a long time about it.

"Has anybody got the time?" he asked at last.

"One thirty-four," said Perriman.

Jack set the watch, hesitated, then slipped it on his wrist. Nobody smiled or spoke. Jack's eyes moved about the close-packed circle of faces, remembering why he had been so willing to gamble with their careers and families, why he had risked everything himself to win this very moment.

"Boys," he said, "Wes Phillips is really the one who—"

His voice stopped. The unashamed respect and affection were too much. For now the tributes he had craved so long evoked no answering self-respect. Now the attainment of admiration and leadership had a taste of ashes. He wanted to take the watch off, to beg their forgiveness for his maniacal drive to power that would have dragged them all down in its quest for a crown of martyrdom. He saw that they had at last set him up where he had so blindly longed to be—*above* Wes. For Wes, with a lifetime of fidelity, with sincerity of purpose and with a courage born of genuine concern for the church, had failed to establish an opposition to the machine. And Jack, with an unbreakable self-confidence founded on murderous pride and a courage born of terror, had succeeded.

His eyes met the old man's and he detected an almost imperceptible shake of the head.

"Now, boy," Wes rumbled, "don't start telling us you feel unworthy of this great honor, because we'd all know you were lying. Let these poor men have their hero; there ain't many left in the world as it is. Anyway, the watch is engraved and the jeweler won't take it back."

Everybody laughed a little too heartily.

"Know something?" said Dirkwell. "We haven't even had lunch yet! I'm starving!"

Then they were crowding about and shaking Jack's hand, and at last they were gone. Wes stood with his back to the door, studying Jack.

"Besides," he said, "we got it at a discount."

XXXVI

With This Ring

JACK breakfasted alone in the Coffee Shop of the Middleton Hotel on the final day of the conference, although now he no longer felt that overwhelming shame and dread at facing his colleagues. The horror and the devastating remorse over Thelma's death still weighed him down like a physical presence, but beyond this he felt a strange empti-ness, a release from the incredible vigor and the blind terrors that had dominated him so long. He felt a detached curiosity to see what life and people might look like in his new condition, and he gazed about him almost as if he were a visitor from another planet.

As he walked the last two blocks from his parked car to Belfair Church the world of nature suddenly broke in upon him with startling unexpectedness, sharp and crystalline, as if dark, distorting lenses had fallen from his eyes. Every leaf of every tree, every wisp of cloud, every blade of grass seemed to have a fierce independent existence of its own, where previously all had somehow felt real only in relation to himself.

As he neared the church, he caught sight of Fred Hummaker, the lay delegate from Foxull, and for the first time Jack felt no need or desire to avoid him. For now Hummaker, like the tree and the grass, suddenly emerged into separate existence, apart from Jack, almost as if he had burst forth from a thick concealing shrubbery that was somehow part of Jack himself. Jack looked him over with curiosity and surprise, and found himself wondering for the first time why Fred Hummaker came to conference every year. Could it be to fill the emptiness of his life since he retired from the barber shop? To get away from a house that was too big now and too silent since his children had married and Mrs. Hummaker had died?

The wizened little face went blank for an instant, then burst into a radiant beaming when Jack smiled.

"Well, howdy, Parson!" the familiar twangy voice rang out.

Jack had not meant to reveal his appointment, but he found himself doing so, knowing it would give importance to Hummaker's hitherto empty role as delegate from the Foxull church.

"Parson is right, Mr. Hummaker!" Jack shook the outstretched hand, then held onto it: "Now, don't spread this around, because it's confidential till the bishop reads the appointments this afternoon, but—" Jack lowered his voice—"I've got the word about your next pastor."

"Who's it gonna be?"

"Me."

Hummaker's jaw sagged; he straightened and flung back his head; he pumped Jack's hand violently. They stood and talked till time for the morning devotional, when Jack said:

"I've got a lot of things to finish up at Wentworth this week. Tell everybody I'll be at the Foxull church at eleven next Sunday morning."

Jack left him beaming with mystery and importance. The first confrontation had hardly been painful at all! But he knew it would be a different matter to face the entire community in a body at the Foxull Methodist Church.

"Going to the wedding, Jaaaaack?"

Jack recognized Emma Schell's cutting voice as he walked across the courtyard from the sanctuary to the chapel after the bishop's Sunday morning sermon. It was the same voice with which she had greeted him four years ago at another annual conference, when Dr. Worthington had given Jack her husband's church. He waited and chatted with her a moment by the chapel door, but now that cutting voice could not scratch the surface of what he knew he had been, and the unconcealed triumph of her smile seemed to relate only to a self he had known long ago.

He found a seat in the rear, on the aisle. He was aware of alert eyes seeking out his face from time to time, but it made little difference. He could not possibly have communicated to anyone—not even to Patricia herself—what this wedding meant now.

For it was all so exactly as he himself had dreamed and planned—yet all so empty of the meanings and emotions with which his imagination had invested it: the lovely Gothic chapel crowded with the most important people of the conference; the white candelabra and the flowers; the organ music and the vocal, all done with such brilliance; the fact that the bishop himself was officiating; the presence of the newsmen and photographers. His own dream precisely! Yet when he saw Steadman's face as he turned at the altar and looked toward the rear door of the chapel, Jack knew how desperately juvenile, snobbish, and unreal that dream had been. For Steadman clearly had no need of such props; the quiet security and rightness of his love were unmistakable, and he was aware of nothing but Patricia.

A mist of white lace from her gown brushed Jack's shoulder as she moved down the narrow aisle on her father's arm, and he saw her profile, its clean chiseled planes softened by her veil and by something else —by a radiant serenity, a kind of vibrant peacefulness quite unlike her ordinary cool self-possession. The bishop's voice arose:

"Dearly belovèd, we are gathered here . . ."

Jack knew what Emma Schell was thinking, and what most of his friends and foes were thinking: that after breaking up in September, he and Patricia had met again night before last and had had some kind of stormy wrangle, so stormy that he had momentarily cracked up; and Patricia, in a fit of pique, had decided to marry Steadman; and Steadman was so unimaginative he had been quite happy to win her on these terms. And everyone would be astonished to discover, as the years came and went, that the marriage seemed undeniably happy!

"Steadman, wilt thou have this woman to be thy wedded wife . . ."

For this union had been inevitable from the beginning, and only Jack's total preoccupation with himself had prevented his foreseeing it: Steadman had been a constant visitor in the Worthington home for years. He sincerely revered her father, as Patricia had expected Jack to do. The two of them wanted the same things from life and were of one mind as to the right way to go about getting them. And they were both sensible, effective people who together would accomplish something constructive and practical in the life of the church. Thus they could marry safely on one day's notice, while Jack and Patricia could not have done so after an engagement of four years.

"Patricia, wilt thou have this man to be thy wedded husband . . ."

And a love founded on respect and understanding would carry them safely through the intricacies of the wedding night, for Steadman was not a neurotic coward whose sole thought was that he might blunder or seem inexpert. His calm gray eyes were fixed on Patricia's face, and already Jack could read the totality of her response to that selfless concern for her own fears and needs and insecurities. For Steadman loved her with a love that brought life and not as an object, a thing he could use.

"I, Steadman, take thee, Patricia . . ."

But none of Jack's relationships to this woman had been a conscious or deliberate plot. He had used her without knowing that he was doing so, and his own sincere self-deception had deceived and confused Patricia herself almost to the end. The sight of her bowed head and the lines of her veil falling into crisp angles at her shoulders brought back sudden painful images of Thelma and Rick. . . .

And now he heard Patricia's silvery counterpoint:

"I, Patricia, take thee, Steadman . . ."

Whatever Jack's memory touched on, all had the same bitter taste of maniacal egoism clothed in a pretended concern for others. Patricia had recognized the flavor in time, and saved herself. Thelma had recognized it too late. Jack shivered and forced his attention back to the ceremony and to Steadman's voice:

"With this ring . . . I thee wed . . ."

He remembered how Patricia's fingers had trembled that night as she placed the ring on the sofa cushion between them, and he wondered now whether it had been he who had wanted that very thing to happen. Was it his own hidden fear and lack of love that had prolonged their engagement so unbearably, and not Patricia's caution and insecurity? For the first time he realized that their engagement must have been as painful and demanding to her as to him, and that he had preferred inflicting this frustration upon her rather than face the possibility of his own ineptness in love. For he saw now that it was only his own pride and cowardice that had made him so terrified of being less than perfect, that had made him so certain Patricia would be cool and unresponsive and even amused, that had caused him to find someone like Thelma irresistible.

For his very first meeting with Thelma had shaken to pieces all his fear-based purity and imagined self-control. And he had found the torrents of his pent-up passion suddenly threatening to burst every barrier, and himself totally demoralized by the conviction that in the eyes of this uncritically adoring woman a man could do no wrong.

The appalling vision of his unconscious brutality and sadism suddenly cast its light over all his ministry. Of course he had said precisely the wrong things to Thelma in her terrible weeks after Rick's death! He had wanted to bring pain. Of course he had been his most poised, efficient self in sickrooms and at funerals! And even in college he had turned as inevitably toward pain, death, and bereavement as other ministerial students turned toward joy and life. He had honestly imagined himself filled with a Christlike compassion, while in reality his wounded self-love and his bitter shame could find happiness only in the presence of people more miserable than himself.

But Patricia's voice was confident and happy at last as she gazed at Steadman and repeated:

"In token and pledge . . . of the vow between us made . . . with this ring . . . I thee wed . . ."

It was probably true, as Wes insisted, that the worst motives could occasionally bring good results. But how blundering and inefficient had been Jack's self-deceived, neurotic love that concealed virulent hatred and insatiable vengefulness under its smiling compassion. How many times had it found a way to wound and destroy. And with what grinding friction had it endlessly attempted to carry out its double-minded intentions. But the most disturbing sensation of all came from the new, sudden, piercing glimpses he kept having of all these people. He found himself plagued by the grotesque image of a soldier who suddenly discovers that the object he has been using for bayonet practice is a living person.

Steadman and Patricia had been kneeling, and now they rose, and he lifted her veil and kissed her, and then they were coming up the aisle toward Jack. He had never seen Patricia so beautiful. The hint of a chill reserve, the poise that had always seemed a little too perfect—these were suffused now by a glowing warmth that subtly transmuted the familiar proud tilt of the small golden head and all the movements of her body as with swift steps she drew nearer, till he could even hear the rustle of her gown, like a soft whispered response to the pealing of the music.

The clear blue eyes crossed his fleetingly as she passed, but they conveyed no message other than the deep indwelling joy they conveyed to everyone. And Jack knew that now he could never convey to her any part of his devastating new self-knowledge or even any hint of the bitterness of his regret at the pain and waste he had brought her. His only comfort, as Wes had anticipated, was that to all his own monstrous falsity and egoism he had been sincerely blind.

He slipped out by a side door, not following the crowd, and walked down the flagstone path beside the chapel alone. The sun was warm, and from the open windows he could still hear the organ and the gay voices and laughter.

Patricia had found real love at last, but perhaps the love she and Jack had known had not been utterly wasted. For all young love probably had a wild, destructive streak in it and was, like theirs, a tormented entanglement of young hearts impatient to recognize the one true bloom of glory while groping in the half-light of a dawning self-understanding.

Jack sat by himself in the crowded sanctuary of Belfair that final afternoon, during the reading of the appointments, and as the bishop's voice called off the districts and churches, Jack was pleased to note that the machine had been careful not to seem punitive. There was a slight stir when Jack's name was read out for Foxull, but few of the delegates realized that it was his own home town. And suddenly the list was finished, the conference was over, and they were all standing and singing:

> *God be with you till we meet again!*
> *By his counsels guide, uphold you,*
> *With his sheep securely fold you;*
> *God be with you till we meet again!*

A young man in front of Jack took this opportunity to slip out ahead of the crowd, and Jack saw that he had been standing by Pastor Elwood. Jack went to stand beside the old man, putting his arm about his shoulders and lifting his voice alongside Pastor Elwood's feeble one:

> *God be with you till we meet again!*
> *'Neath his wings securely hide you,*
> *Daily manna still provide you;*
> *God be with you till we meet again!*

At the close of the hymn the old man gripped Jack's hand and they parted wordlessly. Jack sought refuge in the tower room from the turmoil of questions and farewells, not wanting to have to explain to the rebels the meaning of his appointment. Wes found him there later, and they stood chatting for a while, gazing down through the open window at the crowd below—mostly ministers and their wives, with a scattering of children—moving down the broad steps and across the lawn to the parking lot.

Jack's eyes followed the glittering stream of cars down the wide boulevard from the mushrooming suburb around Belfair Church and into the gray haze which, even on this clear Sunday afternoon, clung about the sprawling factories and railyards and slums of the city. Above the city's farther horizon a jetliner inched across the sky, its vapor trails leaving a thin silver scar.

"Off we go again!" said Wes, removing the frayed cigar from his mouth and spitting a shred of tobacco on the floor. "To heal a sin-sick world!"

"And there," said Jack, "goes the man!"

They watched Dr. Worthington's roly-poly figure in its rumpled summer suit. He was hatless, and from above they saw the round pink head fringed by wisps of white hair as it turned this way and that while he moved erratically from group to group, squeezing an elbow here, putting an arm about a shoulder there, cracking some sort of joke that left one circle laughing. Except for the battered briefcase in one pudgy fist, he looked for all the world like another country parson preparing to ride off to a year of small church suppers and rural revivals, of badly heated churches on cold winter mornings, and perhaps of too much fishing in the lazy heat of summer when all his flock were well and the hospital beds empty and fuel bills and finances not quite so pressing.

He pivoted suddenly and hustled across to the curb to hold a car door for the wife of one of the retired men, saw her safely inside, and then strode away at last toward the parking lot.

"Who knows," said Jack. "The next time we see him we may be saying, 'Bishop Worthington.' I wonder if he'll make it. . . ."

"He will," said Wes, choosing his words with slow deliberation, "if the very human art of politics can elevate a man to the highest office in the church today."

XXXVII

Oley

JACK returned to Wentworth on Monday and by Thursday he had packed his things, shipping the bulk of them to Foxull by rail, and was on his way home.

He spent Thursday and Friday nights at Dirkwell's parsonage, which was half a day's driving out of his way. He knew this was mere procrastination, but was powerless to help himself. By Saturday afternoon he had reached Otha City, scarcely thirty minutes' drive from Foxull. Wes had urged him to go on home and get it over with, but again his nerve failed, and he decided to put up that night at the Otha City Hotel.

Walking past a clothing store, he caught sight of himself reflected in the glass of the show window, paused, studied the reflection, and went in. The store, like all those in Otha City, had a very limited selection of goods, and a month ago he would not have bought a pocket handkerchief in such a place. But now for the first time he suddenly realized that a flaw in the tailoring of his suit would have been an advertisement of his own unacknowledged imperfection; a speck of dust on his gleaming shoes would have been a reminder of his own dusty ordinariness.

He laid his dark Homburg on the counter, and let the clerk help him select a summer straw. It was delightful to be content to look and dress like the man next to you. As Jack walked out, the clerk called after him:

"Hey! You left your Homburg!"

"I know," said Jack.

At nine the next morning he was on the road, and as the familiar landscapes slipped away, he found his thoughts fragmented by present and past, by the farewell party his congregation had given him in Wentworth Wednesday night . . . by bits of his long arguments with Wes . . . by recollections of his mother and father.

He had kept all thoughts of Foxull out of his awareness for so many years now, except for the occasional remembrances brought back by the chitchat in Christine's letters, that he was surprised to find his images of the town and its people so sharp. He caught occasional glimpses of the railway, and kept thinking of Mrs. Catlett buying a ticket at the Foxull station and swaggering across the cinder platform carrying in her gaudy handbag his father's lifetime's savings. How much did it take to put someone in business as a beauty operator? If only Chris had not waited till the day of his college graduation to tell him all this! But no . . . she could not have told him before. . . .

He had imagined that the journey home would be endless, so vast was the continent of experiences that lay between him and the past, but the new highway swept him down the little valley with frightening swiftness, and suddenly he had topped the rise by the railway embankment. He slowed, unconsciously expecting to see something ugly and distasteful, and was startled to behold again the long, graceful curve of the railway like a giant sickle narrowing to a point where the village nestled, smokeless and peaceful in the clear sunlight of a Sunday morning in June.

To his right he glimpsed the shadowy crescent of the culvert where he had slept beneath the tracks that rainy night ten years ago, and he seemed to see again an awkward, adolescent boy, half-mad with pain and shame as he stumbled up the tracks to the crossing and surveyed the little village, certain that every lighted window was ablaze with interest in his affairs! Yet the events that had so obsessed his imagination had occurred seventeen years before that terrible night!

Jack was startled to gaze at the approaching village and feel none of the anguish he had expected. Even its location and appearance had a sudden beauty and simplicity hitherto blotted from his memory. The highway passed behind a hill and came out near the cemetery half a mile above the town, and he pulled off onto the lane by the gate, and turned to look at Foxull. He studied the church, the school, the mill, the railway station, and finally, with a reluctance whose origins he could not quite admit to himself, Jack let his eyes wander down Main Street and up the slopes to the Bannisters' and then to the rambling white frame house next door.

At first he did not recognize it, as if something strange and frightening had been set down beside Dr. Bannister's familiar house. For it leaped at him with a shocking, ugly nakedness, its white weatherboarding too harshly white, its outlines too cruelly sharp.

Then he remembered.

Then he knew why he had put off this instant as long as possible. For where once the entire house had been set in a framework of formal, meticulously groomed and unchanging loveliness, it now stood out stark and pitiless, the ground bare of any vestige of a lifetime of painstaking labor and love.

His father had sold the boxwoods.

Jack turned away, but in his mind's eye he could see the inside of the house, also stripped and scarred by his calculated extravagance, by all those checks he had written in college and seminary, by his desire to make his parents pay and pay and pay for the wounds given his fantastic pride by the sins of their youth. He could see the dining room, stripped of the mahogany suite they had labored so many years to call their own. He saw the living room, bare of the piano that had been his mother's joy and consolation. He could even see the dusty interior of the garage, stripped of the ancient automobile in which they had gone out for rides on Sunday afternoons. . . .

And Christine had told him all this on the day of his graduation from college and he had only smirked!

He stood for a time with head bowed, hands gripping the rusty iron pickets of the fence. Then he passed through the creaky gate and wandered among the mounds, stopping here and there to read the newer headstones. He found Gramps's grave, and beside its headstone was that of Grandmother Blalock, who had died almost ten years before her husband. Jack wondered what kind of person she had been, and what her death had meant to Gramps. Gazing at the old man's name, Jack seemed to hear again that profane, bellowing voice which knew only shouts and threats or words that were ugly and suggestive, which had never consciously employed a single phrase of beauty except once, quoting Grandmother Blalock about Jack's mother:

"Mil's like a young birch—the harder you bend her down and rub her nose in the dirt, the straighter and prettier she stands up again."

Jack remembered his mother's unwearying patience as she lifted her father and turned and bathed and changed him week after week, month after month. He remembered how that mute, stricken giant had struggled so desperately to communicate with his daughter at the end, and how Jack had fathomed his message that afternoon:

"He wants to say he's sorry."

It was probably the first time in Gramps's life. What had finally cracked the iron of his pride? The fact that Jack's mother had refused to turn away from him as the others did, but had taken his pain into her own body and had gone down into his awful prison with him. She had broken her own health when Gramps's health broke, and that stubborn heart no battering ram of rage could dent, no hail of arrowed words could wound, had opened its impenetrable gates at last—to the whisper of suffering love. And then fate had denied him even his own voice in which to say he was sorry, and at Jack's words he could only make that harsh, grating noise that expressed nothing yet expressed everything.

Sorry for what? For so much more than Jack had been able to imagine then, or since.

Shocked and startled, he turned his eyes toward the hollow beyond the railway crossing and saw again the faded hulk of the rooming house where Mrs. Catlett had lived. For the first time he found himself able to remember with detachment and calm reason her virulent portraits of his mother and Gramps. And for the first time it occurred to him to question her accuracy!

Now the actual situation which that vain, rejected creature had painted with such malignant distortion floated up into clear focus:

Mrs. Catlett had always loved Jack's father, from her childhood, and then one day Mildred Blalock appeared on the schoolground—as slim and elfin and quick as Vivian was big and slow and dark. What was it Mrs. Bannister had said? "The prettiest girl Foxull ever saw!" And his father *had* loved her, and *had* wanted to marry her, and Gramps in his domineering obstinacy had forbidden it, and had probably threatened and beaten his daughter, and had stalled off two young people desperately in love just as in his pastorate Jack had known young people to be stalled, till unyielding parents had strained youthful self-control beyond the breaking point. And then, having himself provoked the necessity that so crucified his pride, Gramps had denied all his own guilt by pretending he had to force them into the tawdry shame of a midnight wedding.

But Vivian Catlett's wounded vanity could never believe that they had wanted to marry and would have married regardless, and perhaps to that extent her frenzied accusations had contained a leaven of sincerity.

And now the pity that had never touched his heart before suddenly leavened his own memories of this woman he had hated to the point of madness. For he, too, had been incredibly vain and arrogant; he, too, had shrunk back in terror from the wounds of life; he, too, had built a shell about himself, expressed even in his walk and posture and choice of clothes. And now he saw her suddenly with an unfamiliar pity, based on kinship, as she swaggered down Main Street in her spectacularly sexy clothes, a hard, sophisticated woman wrapped around the heart of a bewildered child. For that child had one day seen the only love of her life snatched suddenly from her by a willowy, light-footed girl who raced away with dazzling grace and swiftness, just as Christine had been startled that afternoon when Jack's mother chased her down among the autumn leaves and took the bobbin from her. He could see Christine again, red-faced, her brown hair full of dust and leaves, her voice gasping and incredulous:

"Gosh! She's like lightning! Who'da thought your mother could out-run *me?*"

But Mrs. Catlett had not laughed and picked herself up and gone on. She had remained startled and disbelieving all her days, and had sought the answer to this bewildering mystery in a handsome army officer whose astonishing good looks and glittering uniform perhaps persuaded her for a while that none of this was true. But he too had been snatched from her, by an even more unfathomable mystery, and shipped home in a box she was advised not to open.

And so she had taken advantage of a man whose wife had been ill, a man whose defenses had been broken down by frustrations of mind and career, and had tried to steal back the thing she had lost in her youth. And then one day, when this tawdry adventure had left her shaken and hopeless and addicted to drink, along came a youthful reincarnation of the man she had loved who stared at her, stripped of all merciful disguises, and dealt the last, most cruel wound of all:

"You're ugly and old."

Where was she now? Had she yielded up her shell and her self-deception and vanity at last, as Jack had been compelled to under the sledgehammer blows of actuality? Or was she still struggling, still unfreed, as she reassured her heart by ministering daily to the vanity of other women? Jack found himself to his surprise wishing that she too might find the life-giving release he had found. It seemed unbelievable that so complex and heartbreaking a world as Mrs. Catlett's had stood before him for ten years a mystery, and that the darkness had not lain in that world itself—whose walls were flimsiest glass!—but in his own unseeing eyes, his own unfeeling heart.

As Jack turned toward the gate, he saw someone climbing the long hill toward the cemetery. When the figure drew nearer he recognized Oley Larsen, and it seemed ironically appropriate that Oley should be the first person Jack saw on his return to Foxull. For Oley had been almost the last person he saw, except for his mother and Christine, the morning he left.

Jack's earliest memories of Oley were of the Foxull schoolground, and of a clumsy, silent figure towering over the other children—too strong to be attacked physically, but too slow of mind to know whose words had brought such screams of laughter or which expressionless face had conceived the latest, most bewildering prank. He hovered always at the edge of the schoolyard, alone, by the south gate, which was always described in Foxull after that year simply as "Oley's gate." He often stood with one huge hand resting on the gate, and Jack had assumed that he did this because he wanted to flee, but now the strange thought occurred to him that perhaps Oley had received some sort of reassurance from the feel of the wire and metal. For they were the first things his hands touched each afternoon before his feet touched the path that led to the road that led to a gentle, bowed little woman who would put her thin arms about his great shoulders and kiss away that day's mysterious cruelty.

After a year his mother withdrew him, and Oley never came near the schoolground again, not even to ball games or carnivals.

Mrs. Larsen had married late; Oley was her only child, and she lavished her whole affection on that one clouded mind and heart. She was painfully timid, never spoke an unnecessary word, and went out only to shop once a week, on which occasions she was always accompanied by Oley, like a huge friendly brown dog with clumsy feet and a perpetual grin. Christine had written Jack that since Mrs. Larsen's death of a heart attack the past winter, "Oley has simply been lost. He still goes to the cemetery every day, rain or shine."

Oley was now a hulking giant of a man in his early thirties, and as he drew near Jack saw again the familiar lank brown hair hanging down his forehead and the sudden, meaningless grin. He had stopped Jack in the road that last morning, when Jack was trying to slip back home unnoticed after sleeping in the culvert, and Jack had yanked himself away from the other man's grip so violently that he fell sprawling at Oley's feet. And for ten years now he had winced at the memory of that grotesque incident, and the sight of Oley grinning down at him had burned itself into his tormented imagination as an ineffaceable symbol of the whole town's supposed concern with himself and his parents and their past.

Now Jack felt appalled by this evidence of his own irrationality, and by his blindness to the cause of Oley's obvious excitement that morning. For Oley had known that people were searching for Jack, and to his immense delight and astonishment, he, Oley Larsen, had found him! It was very possibly the one occasion in his life when Oley could have enjoyed a sense of having accomplished something difficult and important before the whole village, but Jack had only yanked himself away in a fury.

He recalled now with dismay his frenzied certainty that Christine had deliberately brought up the name of Oley's father at the railway station that morning to test him, to taunt him with the role of the justice of the peace in his parents' wedding. Jack had always pictured it as performed in the Larsens' kitchen, with the Larsens in their bathrobes, and Gramps with his gun, and Oley—the crowning touch of indignity—grinning through the sleazy curtains from the bedroom.

For now he realized that, had the child even been awake, he could not possibly have grasped the meaning of that scene. Yet Jack had dreaded Oley Larsen above everyone else in Foxull, certain that he had seen and understood and remembered, and that if Jack ever returned, Oley would blurt out before everyone some unforgettable, crucifying idiot's joke about it all! He had been certain that the circle of his own universe overlapped exactly the circle of Oley Larsen's, enclosing all the same events and emotions in precisely the same arrangement and intensity.

And now he knew that those two circles had never even touched! With this certainty came an awareness that he himself knew nothing of what lay within the closed circle of that other mind. For to Jack, Oley had been only a threat—as he must have been also to the fat, pompous justice of the peace. To children he was a gleeful curiosity; to the town drunk a saving sense of superiority; even to passing strangers he was probably a cause for secret pride and thankfulness. But to whom had Oley ever been a person in his own right, with meanings and values of his own?

Oley passed him, grinning but obviously not recognizing him, and went to stand by his mother's grave.

Jack thought of the mature and highly educated minds he had seen stumble and falter at the brink of this last and most unfathomable mystery of all. What then did it mean to one who had stumbled all his days over simple, everyday things? An adult mind could scarcely endure the sight of love and warmth and understanding turned suddenly to earth; what then of a childlike, undeveloped mind to whom that earth had been the only love, the only warmth, the only understanding? Was this fixed grin really only an evidence of senseless bad taste, forgivable but still upsetting, or was it not even a smile at all but a distress signal from some far gulf of bewildered loneliness, some immensity of depth and danger from which the one fixed star had unaccountably vanished?

Jack approached the other man, possessed by an almost maternal compassion to enter that isolated world—but how? Who could enter such worlds? It could not be anyone to whom this strange being was of importance only as he related to things important and meaningful to another. It would have to be someone other than a professional church-man, for already Jack had become aware of fitting Oley into the grooved, uncreative thought-patterns of the promoter of an institution: Oley could not support the church in any way, through his presence or his prayers or his gifts or his service, but—like many of the aged and the dy-ing and the chronically ill—he was related to someone who *could!* But this sort of secondhand importance gave one no direct access into the person himself, no single glimmer of insight into *him.*

Jack studied the grinning face, noting that the eyes were utterly un-smiling . . . were hungry and . . . and puzzled. He felt a sudden baffled impatience to be rid of the old thought-patterns, the calculating, subtly selfish acuteness of mind which can fit even the most irrelevant fragment of life into the framework of one's own self-interest. If only he could attain somehow to a total simplicity and spontaneity of reac-tion to this other being, could respond with utter candor and childlikeness—devoid of pride and fear, of past and future—would he not enter that closed circle as Oley's mother had, through the unbarred door of love?

For love had sustained Mrs. Larsen through the immense heartbreak and labor of life, a labor compounded of her husband's financial irresponsibility, and the piecework she did at home for a clothing store, and the endless vigilance over her strong, clumsy son whom some people wanted sent away. No one had guessed how heavy the burden had been till the day Oley found her thin, birdlike form crumpled over her sewing machine.

Jack stood, hat in hand, and studied Oley across the width of the narrow grassy mound: Oley kept cocking his head slightly, sweeping his big hand along the length of the grave and indicating the headstone. Did he want Jack to read it? Jack knelt down and called out the name and the dates, touching each symbol with his forefinger as he spoke it and glancing at Oley for some clue. Then he read the bit of Scripture in the same way:

For so He giveth His beloved sleep.

Sleep! His mother—or someone—had told Oley that death was like going to sleep. Jack tapped the word again, then cocked his own head over and let it rest briefly on his folded hands, palms together. The grin vanished. So it *had* been a signal! Oley cocked his head again, making an odd, crooning sound deep in his throat, probably an imitation of his mother's singing him to sleep. Jack felt a sudden sense of awe and wonder at having made this first step into the world of Oley Larsen —whom he had seen all his life, yet never seen at all.

He took out his Testament and Psalms, found Psalm 127, and pointed out the same words, touching each in turn, and at the word "sleep" Oley nodded over and over. Was he indicating his understanding that the words on the stone were no ordinary words, but words of Scripture? Jack turned the Testament over several times, showing him the black leather cover and the gold edging. But the different appearance of any particular book would not be apparent to Oley. No . . . it was something else that delighted him—something obvious, near at hand, uncomplicated. Jack gazed at him, baffled. They were standing side by side now, and suddenly the grin flashed on again, and Oley seized Jack's forearm and squeezed it in a bruising grip, not letting go. Once Jack would have been frightened, for Oley was immensely strong; but he endured the grip without wincing, sure that this was no irresponsible portent of violence but some kind of message. Studying the long face and the brown eyes and the wide mouth, Jack saw that this time Oley was not grinning but smiling, not signaling but expressing some vast unexpected delight. But what? If he were Oley, why would this encounter—

Communication!

Oley was ecstatic that someone had broken through his terrifying isolation; that he had communicated a thought to another being, and that being had understood! It was not the meaning of the word "sleep," but the fact that he had *shared* the meaning. The frightening grip was Oley's attempt to say, "We have a bond—we are in touch with each other!" Jack cocked his head slightly, gripped Oley's forearm with his free hand, and nodded. The artless bliss shining in the brown eyes at this second evidence of communication was almost too painful to look upon.

Two tiny steps inside that vast dark circle!

Jack wanted desperately to take a third before they parted, but what could it be? To fail would be unthinkable now, would cast Oley back into his isolation perhaps even more terrified than before.

He would read some Scripture and pray. The sight of the Testament, the sound of a ministerial tone different from the tones in which other people spoke, might convey something. . . . Possibly Oley's mother had told him about Heaven, certain that there at least, if not in this world, her child would find playmates and companionship and a place of peace and belonging.

Jack opened his Testament to the fourteenth chapter of John and read in a slow, clear voice:

"In my Father's house are many mansions: if it were not so, I would have told you. I go to prepare a place for you. And if I go and prepare a place for you, I will come again, and receive you unto myself; that where I am, there ye may be also."

Then, on an impulse, he turned to First Corinthians:

"For now we see through a glass, darkly; but then face to face: now I know in part; but then shall I know even as also I am known."

Jack bowed his head. The grass in the shade of the big elm looked still damp. . . . But would Oley even realize this *was* a prayer unless Jack knelt? He would kneel on one knee, as he did on the rostrum in church. No . . . Oley never went to church. A car hummed slowly past behind them. Would not people think it ridiculous to see the new pastor kneeling on both knees before Oley Larsen in the cemetery? Jack glanced up and saw Oley's brown eyes fixed on him with patient confidence, certain that some further astonishing act of communication was to come. Well . . . Wes had said pride would spring right up again, that one could only hope to keep on weeding the garden.

Jack knelt on both knees in the damp grass. Oley went at once and knelt the same way on the other side of the mound. Jack placed his palms together, fingertips pointing up. Oley did the same, bowing his head and saying one word in an unexpectedly fitting tone:

"Now!"

Jack was startled, both by the voice he had so rarely heard and by the tone of command, so apt but so unlikely. He drew a breath to begin, but hesitated. He *must* not blunder now. If it were not a command, what could it be? Another car hummed past, but Jack was only half-aware of how they must look, nor did it matter to him now. He must make that third step! He tried to still his mind, to think with Oley, not about him. But why would someone kneel, put his hands together, bow his head, and say—

Jack found his voice at the same instant he found the answer; he abandoned any thought of assuming a ministerial tone. He spoke with the measured singsong of childhood:

> *Now I lay me down to sleep;*
> *I pray thee, Lord, my soul to keep;*
> *If I should die before I wake,*
> *I pray thee, Lord, my soul to take.*

He opened his eyes and stole a glance at Oley's face. Oley's lashes still rested on his cheeks; the huge hands were pressed neatly together; the bowed face was relaxed and seemed pensive, suffused by a childlike simplicity and trust.

As Jack gazed, he was overwhelmed by a strange new love and pity, and by an immense, peaceful joy unlike any he had ever tasted. For it seemed not properly his own; it belonged to Oley, and Jack was only sharing it. He was in no haste to rise, despite the hum of the passing cars, and was amused to realize that two Sundays ago it would have taken more courage than he possessed to kneel here in this undignified, childlike way with Oley Larsen. But now it took no courage at all! He had simply been pulled out of himself by an immense compassion. He recalled the legend that St. Francis had known the language of birds and animals, and now it seemed not impossible. For Francis had had no possessions, no ambitions, no fears, no attachments of any kind to his own world to stay his perfect entry into the world of others. But, more than mere negative detachment, Francis had been utterly possessed by that One who died to self that He might live in all men.

As Jack rose from his knees, a verse of Scripture floated up into memory:

"We know that we have passed from death unto life, because we love the brethren."

XXXVIII

A Music at Dawning

JACK parked his car and walked up the street to the church. It was ten-thirty; the Sunday school classes were in session, and the sidewalk was deserted except for the janitor, Mr. Douglas, who was putting up something on the bulletin board. He was one of Jack's father's old cronies and greeted Jack with obvious delight. He had just put up in big white metal letters at the top of the bulletin board:

J. WINTERS LEE
MINISTER

Jack put one hand on his shoulder and said:

"Now where on earth did you get that name?"

"It was in the yearbook once. After all, you're not just anybody now. You're the minister!"

Jack shook his head, opened the glass door, removed the first two lines, and, after a moment's thought, took some letters from Douglas' box and put up:

J. W. "JACKIE" LEE
MINISTER

Douglas tried to protest as Jack firmly closed the glass.

"It ain't dignified!" said Douglas, grinning.

"But it's me," said Jack, as the janitor walked away.

"Welcome home!" said a voice behind him.

Jack turned.

It was Christine.

Her eyes were not on him, but on the bulletin board. Jack glanced at it again, and remembered the last time they had met as friends. They had talked on the steps of her dormitory after his vespers sermon and she had said:

"Be Jackie Lee from Foxull again, please!"

He had been outraged, beside himself at that simple plea, but now he understood it simply and clearly.

The familiar green eyes met his, clear and pleasant and watchful, as if trying to determine how much more the bulletin board might imply than she had guessed. It occurred to him that his mental image of Christine down through the long years of their strange correspondence had remained unchanging: he always pictured the writer as a shy, abrupt, unpredictable college girl who did not know how to dress properly and was not particularly interested, who insisted on subscribing to her home-town paper and reading it to the girls in the dorm, and whose appearance and personality were always for him inextricably confused by a background of memories too painful to think on.

Now Christine suddenly stood before him as someone separate from that painful, distorting background. He saw the same familiar alert green eyes, but now they no longer seemed alert to probe or harm; the same mischievous pucker at the corner of her mouth, but now not mischievous with suggestion or malice. The thick brown hair, once so indifferently groomed, was arranged in an unfamiliar way that was extremely becoming, and her entire dress and grooming were those of a woman of mature and cultivated taste. She had always worn scuffed and unattractive shoes, and Jack now stared down at her slim ankles and neat pumps with absorbed interest.

"Really!" said Christine, laughing, "I don't know when I've had a new minister look me over so thoroughly!"

He jerked his head up, reddening.

"I . . ." He hesitated and then said slowly, "It's good to be back." He saw that the simplicity of the statement did not deceive her, for her smile vanished and he knew that she too was remembering that night at the steps of her dormitory following his sermon and how, beginning to cry, she had said:

"You've gone away."

And all through the years of his absence from his home and his parents and from himself, she had tried to keep open his contacts, however flimsy and indirect, with those who loved him. He had imagined himself the great lover of humanity and had dismissed Christine's affection for Foxull as childish and sentimental, but now he saw that hers had been the genuine love, the selfless outgoing concern that healed wounds and planted the seeds of forgiveness, and kept dignity and self-respect alive in two people whom he had crucified by his iron unforgivingness.

As they talked he saw that the green eyes were understanding now, not blazing with anger and incredulity the way they had been the day of his graduation from college, or the time they had wrangled over the expense of his joining a fraternity. For the first time he realized why Christine had never felt any need of external props to her self-respect, like a sorority pin: her interests were all in other people. She accepted them for what they were in themselves, simply and artlessly, and entered at once into the universe of their dreams and disappointments and moved about among their heart's familiar furniture not as a stranger but as one of the family. So she had made herself a daughter to his parents when their only child rejected them. She had shared with them those bits of himself she could wrest from him, refusing to accept as final—or to let them accept—the face he had turned toward them.

Under the too casual flow of their small talk, Jack now caught a new and bewildering glimpse of Christine, a double glimpse that revealed in the same instant how he must have appeared to her and how she had most deeply seemed to him.

His fantastic pride and sensitivity had made him certain that Christine could never love him while knowing all about his shameful origin. And since leaving home he had unconsciously been aware that he was turning to her a face still more unlovable—snobbish, ungrateful, merciless, punishing beyond all need or limit, and hiding all the while in an armor of pious self-righteousness. And the wounded conviction that she could never love such a person had made him refuse to confess even to his inmost heart how desperately he longed for that love and how poignant was his own long-standing, inescapable love for Christine.

Jack remembered something Wes had said the previous Sunday:

"Now you can love where your own heart leads you."

And this was where his heart had been leading all these years, but he had rejected that leading as he had rejected everything else connected with home and past. But now it occurred to him that perhaps Christine had returned to this little village to work for her father simply because she was waiting, as he had been waiting, for the fulfillment of the promise of that September afternoon so long ago when he had stood with the tips of his fingers resting on the inside of her wrist and had lightly touched his lips to hers. Could it be that, even as she had somehow looked beyond the worst in so many people, she might someday be able to look beyond that malignant self which had possessed him for so many years, might remember and see again the original person?

The lovely, mature, controlled face before him gave no clue.

"Your mother will probably be here this morning," she was saying. The words broke over him out of a kind of fog. "But your father hasn't come to church for several years. He . . . works every Sunday at the office."

"I'll go up after the service," Jack said. He hesitated, then asked, "Do you think . . ." His voice died, but she understood the unfinished question. She nodded.

"But it will take time. You'll have to feel your way. He's very . . . withdrawn."

He wanted to ask about his mother, but people were coming up out of the Sunday school rooms in the basement now, and getting out of cars at the church steps, and he and Christine were surrounded. They crowded about, shaking his hand, smiling from faces suddenly lined and nodding heads suddenly gray. They called him "Jack" or "Mr. Lee" and protested, laughing, about the name on the bulletin board. They were astonished at his accurate knowledge of all their doings, and over their heads he saw Christine's eyes—knowing and mischievous —as people kept exclaiming:

"We thought you'd forgotten us!"

He kept glancing down the street, expecting to see his mother getting out of the family car, till he remembered that they had sold the car and that she would be walking . . . if she came.

Miss Martin, his high school English teacher, pressed through the group toward him. He had always associated her in memory with his disastrous reference to the Lee family coat of arms in high school chapel, but as she squeezed his hand tightly in her neat, gloved one he suddenly saw a brilliant, shy, sensitive young woman getting off the train in Foxull twenty years before, a plain girl—too plain and perhaps too brilliant to attract any young man in this sleepy little town. He saw the emptiness of her years filled by the substituted warmth of poetry and art; he saw the succession of Foxull youngsters who sat through her classes unmoved by all the things that moved her most.

Christine had understood Miss Martin, and had sent her clippings about Jack from college. But he, using the skills she had transmitted to him with her patient fidelity and imagination, using them in each day's conversation or bit of correspondence or sermon preparation, had not once in all those years written her the briefest note of gratitude!

As he talked and answered questions, Jack was astonished that he had dreaded this encounter so long, that he had imagined they would all despise him, would say things with double meanings, would only pretend friendship and interest. Looking into their faces, listening to their words, Jack realized that they were proud of his long schooling— but also a little distrustful of it; that they loved him and wanted him to succeed—but they also wanted him to admit that his father was a bookkeeper at Harlowe's Mill and that his mother was a Blalock. He was aware that no one mentioned his parents, but no one had an opportunity to say more than a word or two before someone else pushed forward. And then Douglas was ringing the bell the second time to remind them of the worship hour, and they finally let him go.

As he moved down the aisle, Jack was surprised to find the sanctuary so small! Somehow he had expected the ceiling to be immensely high, the neat little stained glass windows enormously tall, the aisle practically endless, and all the people taller and bigger than they were. When he sat down in the middle chair behind the pulpit, a chair that had always seemed so enormous to him in childhood, he saw Fred Hummaker beaming up from a front pew. Christine was also sitting near the front with her mother and Alex, and a girl Jack decided must be Alex's wife. Dr. Bannister was probably out on a call, as always.

As the service moved along, Jack studied the congregation. He saw the Blalocks all sitting together, the men heavier and grayer than he had remembered them, and all very self-conscious, just as they had been at Gramps's funeral. The Blalock men never went to church except on special occasions such as the present one, when apparently the entire town had turned out.

Always, when he had sat in the pulpit before a congregation in the past, Jack had felt an oppressive weight, a weight he had first become aware of in this very church, the first Sunday he had announced his entrance into the ministry. But now the ministry no longer seemed a load he must lift alone, but an adventure he and his congregation were entering together, exhorting and heartening each other from a common fund of understanding and forgiveness.

He remembered how his parents had invited Pastor Elwood to lunch that day so long ago. Jack could see the noncommittal expression on his father's face when the pastor spoke out against dancing. And now, above the sound of the hymn, Jack heard again the tinny music of the radio rousing him from sleep, and saw a little boy peeping through the crack of the living room door while his mother's trim ankles and flashing feet described intricate patterns on the floor, and his father puffed and gasped. But she had been grave and queenly as she presided at the table that day, passing things to the minister with her deft, graceful hands and even carving the roast with such skillful precision because Jack's father said he "always butchered it."

It was all a way of saying to the minister, "We believe in you and what you're trying to do." And now Jack found himself suddenly relaxed and unweighted in the knowledge of this comradeship, secure in the realization that he was not different or better than his congregation. What he had imagined to be the burden of responsibility in a high calling had actually been only the burden of his own pride and sensitivity. But now he felt burdened in an entirely different way—by a sympathy and a compassionate yearning to share with others the possibility of release and rest.

He was standing, singing the final verse of the hymn, which had been one of his mother's favorites. He could see the familiar living room again and himself curled on the sofa watching the delightful mystery of her flying fingers on the keyboard of the old upright piano— fingers so slender and tapering, yet so astonishingly swift and powerful, so unerringly accurate as each found precisely the right key at the precise split-second.

Jack was vaguely aware of confronting the congregation as he began his sermon. He had re-written it a dozen times during the past week, and in his dread of this occasion had memorized the entire manuscript. Now he found his voice rolling out the paragraphs mechanically, automatically, while his thoughts kept wandering and his eyes kept returning to the second pew from the rear on the right side, where his mother always sat. They had scarcely left room for her. . . . Christine had said she would probably come, but perhaps it would be better this way. Possibly she did not want to upset him on his first Sunday. He would go up to the house after the service, before he went to the mill office. . . .

Once, long ago, he had taken his mother's lunch to the mill when she forgot it, and had stood for a long time watching her at work as she passed the endless widths of material across a kind of lighted screen, making an occasional mark along the edge or with prompt and tireless fingers correcting some tiny defect. That had been almost fifteen years ago. She had rarely missed a day in the mill, except for illness. . . .

Jack kept thinking of Mrs. Catlett's gaudy purse bearing away from Foxull all those years of painstaking, faultless labor . . . of how shocking the house had looked with the boxwoods dug up and sold, leaving only wounded earth. . . . His mother should have quit the mill years ago. . . .

But Jack had never allowed her to quit.

From that first day when he had sent Christine from the railway station to the mill office to get that hundred dollars from his father, he had used a deliberate extravagance to make them both atone to him for the sins of their youth, had cultivated a taste for expensive clothes, had flung money away, knowing without quite letting himself know, how many squares of cloth it must have taken to pay for that new suit, how many hours on outside accounting jobs it must have taken his father to cover that last check.

He shifted uneasily as he remembered Christine's trembling voice that day of his college commencement when he had refused to see his father and mother.

"Of course you don't want to see her, because then you'd see what you're doing to her! It's not just that your extravagance makes her keep working when she's sick. Dad says that by all the laws of medicine your mother should get well. But he says something is undermining her resistance to illness. Well, I know what it is: it's your hatred and unforgivingness!"

And in truth his extravagance in college and seminary had long before ceased to be a method for making them atone, if it had ever really been. It had become mere vengefulness—remorseless, unforgiving, cold as ice, impenetrable as stone. Atonement had a different sort of flavor. . . . He could hear again his mother defending her decision to nurse Gramps:

"It's not a burden, Bruce. It's an opportunity."

"For what?"

"To make it all up to him. To atone."

And then his father's voice, a voice Jack had never heard him use before:

"I *have* atoned!"

Now Jack understood that voice, grasped its full bitterness: For his father had been saying, "I have been made to seem cowardly and dishonorable; I have been made to appear one who was compelled to do what he had begged and wanted to do from the beginning, and would have done regardless. I have been a man of honor who must endure the stigma of dishonor at the hands of the very one who provoked him to dishonorable deeds!"

For the first time Jack realized that his father had never regretted the marriage itself, as Mrs. Catlett insisted, only the unfairness of the setting Gramps had given it. The loneliness, the waste of talent, the isolation that sealed off a brilliant mind from the companionship of similar minds, might have come anyway, as they came to so many. But to be publicly branded as only doing right under compulsion—that had indeed been a fearful atonement for the sins of his youth. Perhaps then, or certainly when he had drawn everything from the bank and sent it down to Mrs. Catlett, he should have been permitted to write across the ledger of his life, "Paid in Full."

For it was clear that Foxull had forgiven, and would long ago have forgotten, but Jack had kept his mother and father nailed to the cross of the past with the daily hammer blow of an empty mailbox, the public embarrassment of a child who never came home at Thanksgiving, or Christmas, or Easter, or even in times of illness or bereavement. He had proclaimed that for him no repentance and no sacrifice would ever be enough to heal the wound in his pride.

He had almost finished his sermon when out of the corner of his eye he was aware that they were helping old Mrs. Garrett in through the side door to her familiar place on the front pew by the wall. She was painfully shy about her infirmities and he remembered how Pastor Elwood never embarrassed her by glancing that way. He tactfully kept his eyes on the congregation before him, folding up his sermon notes and pushing them aside.

"In closing," he said, "let me say a personal word to all those who have been so kind to me and to my parents down through the years. My mother and father have deserved your love and appreciation, if I have not."

Before he knew it, he heard himself confessing that he had looked forward to this day with mixed emotions, and found himself trying to communicate, at least to the older folk, a little of what he felt.

"Sometimes a young man must journey far out of himself before he is able to see himself, must leave his own home town in order to appreciate and understand it. Good is there, but he cannot see it because he himself is evil; love and loyalty and patient heroism are there, but he cannot confess them because of his hatreds and fears. And this is often why he can't go home again, because every street and house, every lined face and whitened head and cemetery stone cry out to him that he is hopelessly and forever in debt—in debt to a vast multitude whom he can never repay: to family, to neighbors, to teachers and counselors, to ministers and helpers and friends.

"And in that terrible hour when he finally comes face to face with his own ingratitude and cruelty, and when he feels the vast weight of the world's unconcern, he finds his empty heart responding once again to the warmth and friendships of his youth. And he turns toward home the feet that have wandered so far, content at last to be forgiven without his deserving and to be loved because he is understood—not as he had first wanted to be loved, as someone good or great or different, but simply as he is, with all his sins and follies on him."

Then they were all standing and singing the final hymn, and he was pronouncing the benediction. It was past twelve, but it seemed odd that nobody lingered to chat, the way they always did in Foxull. Of course, he had greeted almost everyone before the service, but he had the strange impression that they were deliberately not lingering, for some reason understood by everyone. . . .

Throughout the close of his sermon some kind of error had kept trying to intrude upon his attention, a sense of something not correct. Now, as he closed the big pulpit Bible and put away his notes, he glanced again toward the rear of the rapidly emptying sanctuary. Somehow he half-expected to see his mother coming down toward him with her light, firm step.

And then the error came into focus. He could see again the page of the letter, and Christine's bold, flowing script: "I meant to write last month that old Mrs. Garrett died—"

But he had just *seen* them helping Mrs. Garrett through the side door of the church!

Then who . . . ?

A chill swept over him.

He was aware of the sudden silence and of the organist walking up the empty aisle. Only Christine remained, sitting alone and carefully pulling on her white gloves, not looking at him. Christine and . . .

Slowly, cautiously, he ran his eyes along the edge of the carpet toward the front pew on his left, the one by the door and out of his normal line of vision. He did not raise his eyes, but carefully kept them fixed on the carpet till they came to rest on a pair of shoes. They were an old woman's shoes. He had seen dozens like them in his calls on arthritics. Behind them, under the pew, lay a walking stick. The shoes were wide and flat, and they had been split at the ball with a razor or knife, to make them still wider, and the ankles were swollen like the feet, so that they bulged down over the tops of the shoes.

Cautiously, fearfully, Jack lifted his eyes to the hands. They were arthritic too, with the lumpy knuckles and the stiff, unbending fingers twisted sideways like the straw of a worn-out broom. They were fumbling now with the folded church bulletin, trying to tuck it into a purse, and one forefinger scratched at the clasp of the purse with a slow, painful motion and then abruptly ceased.

Jack knew before he raised his eyes what he would see, for even as he felt the shock of those dreadful feet and fearsome hands, he realized that he had known all the time they would be like this. Christine's letters had never told such things directly, after an initial outburst from Jack. But she had told the whole story just the same—between the lines, by innocent phrases, through other things. But he had refused to admit that he saw anything between the lines, had pushed the yearly accumulations of knowledge out of mind, and had preferred to keep thinking of a slender young birch, unscarred, unbowed, unaged by all the storms of life.

He lifted his eyes from the thick, twisted body and the stooped shoulders.

It was his mother.

And gazing at last into her eyes, he knew what it was that had wrung from Gramps that harsh, terrible cry. He knew why he had refused to admit this terrifying portrait into consciousness. For he had known somewhere, somehow, from that day he had left her standing so stricken and yet so proud, that this incredible woman would win him back at last. And suddenly he saw his mother as one whom Christ had redeemed and who in turn might now redeem him, and the words of the communion service, "This is my body, which is broken for you," seemed to hang in the air before her. For here was a sort of earthly counterpart of that divine love which had led Christ to his cross.

What could he do now to atone to her—and to his father? He knew that it would take months, perhaps years, to bridge the terrible chasm between himself and his father, to discover some means of communicating again, to reweave even partially the delicate fabric of trust and understanding which he had slashed and disfigured with such violence, such relentlessness, through so many years.

And he knew too that this shattering vision of his mother would go with him to his grave, along with all the other irreparable consequences of his pride and fear. And it was all part of what his mother had said to him of sin so many years ago, that even the forgiveness of God Himself cannot disentangle the knotted skeins of earthly consequences, and that when we meet these we shall know them as our own. She had said it with bravery and sadness, and now he realized that she had known then that some portion of her son's life would be the most terrible part of her own consequences.

He came down from the pulpit and approached her, slowly and almost fearfully, and stood hesitantly before her as she sat gazing up into his face.

Her eyes were bright with tears, but they were bright also with a deep and radiant happiness. And with that strange clairvoyance which now seemed to give him immediate entrance into others' worlds, he knew that her greatest anguish through the years of his absence had not been her loneliness or humiliation or illness or the daily agony of her work. It had been the knowledge that her son was living his life in flight and pain. And now, beholding him healed, she had found happiness again, and the harvest of her tears was past.

He tried to speak, but his power of speech seemed to have died, and only a terrible little sound emerged, like a croak. He tried again, and this time two words came out:

"Mother, how—"

The "how" was barely audible, but he saw that the familiar eyes understood his whole question and the whole enormous awful message for which he could not now choke out a single understandable word

. . . the familiar eyes in their unfamiliar setting of lines he had never imagined, of hair that should have been a soft, flowing gold instead of this drab and brittle gray. The eyes said clearly that they understood the sentence he had tried to say:

"How can you look at me now with eyes of love?"

He sank down timidly on the seat beside her, not daring to touch her, or even extend his hands toward her, but sitting with his fingers twisted together on his knees. He wanted to weep, but he could not, just as he often could not in childhood on some occasion when the hugeness and pain and mystery of life were beyond believing. He wanted to kneel at her feet and ask her forgiveness, but he could not, for the enormity of his sin would have made such an act seem presumptuous, as if he imagined the things he had done could be atoned for by a moment's penitence or apology.

And so he could only sit in a paralyzed silence, with his unfinished question hanging in the air between them. And suddenly she moved one of those frightening hands, and he tried not to tremble as it approached him and she laid it across his own, and the gentle impact of its stiff, unfamiliar uselessness quite broke his heart.

But the voice that came with it was not clumsy or uneven. The voice was the same, warm and serene and almost surprised, as when in his childhood she had gently reproved him for overlooking something too obvious to be missed.

For all she said was:

"You're my son."

And then Christine had sunk down beside his mother, opposite him, and when he gazed into her eyes he saw his clue, his sign that Christine had never stopped believing that this very hour would come to him at last. Her face was still, her eyes wide and shining with tears, and her lips slightly parted, just as they had been that instant so long ago when he had kissed her and they had stood motionless, caught up in a darkness and a silence, as of a myriad of nesting birds about to rise and fill the dawn with music.

But now the pristine glory was tarnished, and the light of that once pure dawn was clouded by shadows from the dark night of his long and terrible pilgrimage. For in the presence of real love, all the joys he had mistaken for love seemed tawdry and unglorious, all the ecstasies he had reveled in seemed a degrading animality.

And between him and all the rest of life stood his new awareness of the pains he had caused in other hearts, stood visions whose somber and unfading colors would tinge every future bliss, every accomplishment, every deed that he might do by way of atonement. Visions of his mother . . . his father . . . Patricia . . . and, most terrible of all, of Thelma. Her face rose before him again, desperate, tormented, anguished in its yearning for some hint of simple humanity or life-giving love.

And these very gifts he now possessed at last and held securely, but not in joy or pride. He held them in a sober humility as things priceless and never to be surrendered, purchased for him at an irrevocable cost by all who had loved him best.